PRAISE FOR THE NOVELS
OF TESS GERRITSEN

The Mephisto Club

"Readers can't be blamed for suddenly finding themselves fifty pages into this book and it's midnight—Gerritsen is that good at what she does."
—*The Tampa Tribune*

"Will keep readers feverishly turning pages."
—*Newsday*

"Suspenseful . . . a haunting mystery."
—*Chicago Sun-Times*

Vanish

"Spellbinding . . . There's no denying the power of Gerritsen's storytelling. *Vanish* is a perfect example of the bestselling thriller: action-packed, entertaining and compulsively readable."
—*Chicago Sun-Times*

"Gives women readers a plucky heroine to root for."
—*The Washington Post Book World*

"A tense, taut thriller that grabs readers from the get-go and never lets up."
—*Booklist*

"Vivid . . . authentic."
—*Publishers Weekly*

"Distinctive and edgy."
—*Library Journal*

Body Double

"Richly suspenseful and provocative, Gerritsen's latest leaves the reader breathless."
—*The Philadelphia Inquirer*

"A complicated and involving mystery with lots of surprises and thrills."
—*San Jose Mercury News*

"Gerritsen does a masterful job of ratcheting up the suspense."
—*Bangor Daily News*

"An electric series of startling twists, the revelation of ghoulishly practical motives and a nail-biting finale make this Gerritsen's best to date."
—*Publishers Weekly* (starred review)

THE
MEPHISTO
CLUB

A Novel

TESS
GERRITSEN

BALLANTINE BOOKS • NEW YORK

2007 Ballantine Books Mass Market Edition
Copyright © 2006 by Tess Gerritsen

Excerpt from *The Bone Garden* copyright © 2008 by Tess Gerritsen

Published in the United States by Ballantine Books, an imprint of The Random House Publishing Group, a division of Random House, Inc., New York.

BALLANTINE and colophon are registered trademarks of Random House, Inc.

Originally published in hardcover in the United States by Ballantine Books, an imprint of The Random House Publishing Group, a division of Random House, Inc., in 2006.

This book contains an excerpt from the forthcoming book *The Bone Garden* by Tess Gerritsen. This excerpt has been set for this edition only and may not reflect the final content of the forthcoming edition.

ISBN 978-0-345-47700-2

Cover design: Carl D. Galian
Cover illustration: Ron Koeberer / Getty Images

Printed in the United States of America

www.ballantinebooks.com

OPM   9   8   7   6   5   4   3   2   1

To Neil and Mary

ACKNOWLEDGMENTS

Every book is a challenge to write, a seemingly impossible mountain to climb. No matter how difficult the writing may be, I have the comfort of knowing that wonderful colleagues and friends stand by me. Many thanks to my incomparable agent, Meg Ruley, and the team at Jane Rotrosen Agency. Your guidance has been the star I've steered by. Thanks also to my amazing editor, Linda Marrow, who can make any writer shine, to Gina Centrello, for her enthusiasm through the years, and to Gilly Hailparn for all her kind attention. And across the pond, Selina Walker at Transworld has been my unflagging cheerleader.

Finally, I must thank the one person who's been with me the longest. My husband Jacob knows just how difficult it is to be married to a writer. Yet he's still here.

"And destroy all the spirits of the reprobate, and the children of the Watchers, because they have wronged mankind."

—*The Book of Enoch* X:15,
ancient Jewish text, 2nd century B.C.

ONE

THEY LOOKED like the perfect family.

This was what the boy thought as he stood beside his father's open grave, as he listened to the hired minister read platitudes from the Bible. Only a small group had gathered on that warm and buggy June day to mourn the passing of Montague Saul, no more than a dozen people, many of whom the boy had just met. For the past six months, he had been away at boarding school, and today he was seeing some of these people for the very first time. Most of them did not interest him in the least.

But his uncle's family—they interested him very much. They were worth studying.

Dr. Peter Saul looked very much like his dead brother Montague, slender and cerebral in owlish glasses, brown hair thinning toward inevitable baldness. His wife, Amy, had a round, sweet face, and she kept darting anxious looks at her fifteen-year-old nephew, as though aching to wrap her arms around him and smother him with a hug. Their son, Teddy, was ten years old, all skinny arms and legs. A little clone of Peter Saul, right down to the same owlish glasses.

Finally, there was the daughter, Lily. Sixteen years old.

Tendrils of her hair had come loose from the ponytail and now clung to her face in the heat. She looked uncomfortable in her black dress, and she kept shifting coltishly back and forth, as though preparing to bolt. As though she'd rather be anywhere than in this cemetery, waving away buzzing insects.

They look so normal, so average, the boy thought. *So different from me.* Then Lily's gaze suddenly met his, and he felt a tremor of surprise. Of mutual recognition. In that instant, he could almost feel her gaze penetrating the darkest fissures of his brain, examining all the secret places that no one else had ever seen. That he'd never allowed them to see.

Disquieted, he looked away. Focused, instead, on the other people standing around the grave: His father's housekeeper. The attorney. The two next-door neighbors. Mere acquaintances who were here out of a sense of propriety, not affection. They knew Montague Saul only as the quiet scholar who'd recently returned from Cyprus, who spent his days fussing over books and maps and little pieces of pottery. They did not really know the man. Just as they did not really know his son.

At last the service ended, and the gathering moved toward the boy, like an amoeba preparing to engulf him in sympathy, to tell him how sorry they were that he'd lost his father. And so soon after moving to the United States.

"At least you have family here to help you," said the minister.

Family? Yes, I suppose these people are my family, the boy thought, as little Teddy shyly approached, urged forward by his mother.

"You're going to be my brother now," said Teddy.

"Am I?"

"Mom has your room all ready for you. It's right next to mine."

"But I'm staying here. In my father's house."

Bewildered, Teddy looked at his mother. "Isn't he coming home with us?"

Amy Saul quickly said, "You really can't live all by yourself, dear. You're only fifteen. Maybe you'll like it so much in Purity, you'll want to stay with us."

"My school's in Connecticut."

"Yes, but the school year's over now. In September, if you want to return to your boarding school, of course you can. But for the summer, you'll come home with us."

"I won't be alone here. My mother will come for me."

There was a long silence. Amy and Peter looked at each other, and the boy could guess what they were thinking. *His mother abandoned him ages ago.*

"She *is* coming for me," he insisted.

Uncle Peter said, gently, "We'll talk about it later, son."

In the night, the boy laid awake in his bed, in his father's town house, listening to the voices of his aunt and uncle murmuring downstairs in the study. The same study where Montague Saul had labored these past months to translate his fragile little scraps of papyrus. The same study where, five days ago, he'd had a stroke and collapsed at his desk. Those people should not be in there, among his father's precious things. They were invaders in his house.

"He's still just a boy, Peter. He needs a family."

"We can't exactly drag him back to Purity if he doesn't want to come with us."

"When you're only fifteen, you have no choice in the matter. Adults have to make the decisions."

The boy rose from bed and slipped out of his room. He crept halfway down the stairs to listen in on the conversation.

"And really, how many adults has he known? Your brother didn't exactly qualify. He was so wrapped up in his old mummy linens, he probably never noticed there was a child underfoot."

"That's not fair, Amy. My brother was a good man."

"Good, but clueless. I can't imagine what kind of woman would dream of having a child with him. And then she leaves the boy behind for Monty to raise? I don't understand any woman who'd do that."

"Monty didn't do such a bad job raising him. The boy's getting top marks in school."

"That's your measurement for what makes a good father? The fact that the boy gets top marks?"

"He's also a poised young man. Look how well he held up at the service."

"He's numb, Peter. Did you see a single emotion on his face today?"

"Monty was like that, too."

"Cold-blooded, you mean?"

"No, intellectual. Logical."

"But underneath it all, you *know* that boy has got to be hurting. It makes me want to cry, how much he needs his mother right now. How he keeps insisting she'll come back for him, when we know she won't."

"We don't know that."

"We've never even met the woman! Monty just writes us from Cairo one day, to tell us he has a brand-new son. For all we know, he plucked him up from the reeds, like baby Moses."

The boy heard the floor creak above him, and he glanced toward the top of the stairs. He was startled to see his cousin Lily staring down at him over the banister. She was watching him, studying him, as if he were some exotic creature she'd never before encountered and she was trying to decide if he was dangerous.

"Oh!" said Aunt Amy. "You're up!"

His aunt and uncle had just come out of the study, and they were standing at the bottom of the stairs, looking up at him. Looking a little dismayed, too, at the possibility that he had overheard their entire conversation.

"Are you feeling all right, dear?" said Amy.

"Yes, Auntie."

"It's so late. Maybe you should go back to bed now?"

But he didn't move. He paused on the stairs for a moment, wondering what it would be like to live with these people. What he might learn from them. It would make the summer interesting, until his mother came for him.

He said, "Aunt Amy, I've made up my mind."

"About what?"

"About my summer, and where I'd like to spend it."

She instantly assumed the worst. "Please don't be too hasty! We have a really nice house, right on the lake, and you'd have your own room. At least come for a visit before you decide."

"But I've decided to come stay with you."

His aunt paused, temporarily stunned. Then her face lit up in a smile, and she hurried up the steps to give him a hug. She smelled like Dove soap and Breck shampoo. So average, so ordinary. Then a grinning Uncle Peter gave him an affectionate clap on the shoulder, his way of welcoming a new son. Their happiness was like a web of spun sugar, drawing him into their universe, where all was love and light and laughter.

"The kids will be so glad you're coming back with us!" said Amy.

He glanced toward the top of the stairs, but Lily was no longer there. She had slipped away, unnoticed. *I will have to keep my eye on her,* he thought. *Because already, she's keeping her eye on me.*

"You're part of our family now," said Amy.

As they walked up the stairs together, she was already telling him her plans for the summer. All the places they'd take him, all the special meals they'd cook for him when they got back home. She sounded happy, even giddy, like a mother with her brand-new baby.

Amy Saul had no idea what they were about to bring home with them.

TWO

TWELVE YEARS LATER.

Perhaps this was a mistake.

Dr. Maura Isles paused outside the doors of Our Lady of Divine Light, uncertain whether she should enter. The parishioners had already filed in, and she stood alone in the night as snow whispered down onto her uncovered head. Through the closed church doors she heard the organist begin playing "Adeste Fidelis," and she knew that by now everyone would be seated. If she was going to join them, this was the time to step inside.

She hesitated, because she did not truly belong among the believers inside that church. But the music called to her, as did the promise of warmth and the solace of familiar rituals. Out here, on the dark street, she stood alone. Alone on Christmas Eve.

She walked up the steps, into the building.

Even at this late hour, the pews were filled with families and sleepy children who'd been roused from their beds for midnight Mass. Maura's tardy arrival attracted several glances, and as the strains of "Adeste Fidelis" faded, she quickly slipped into the first empty seat she could find, near the back. Almost immediately, she had to rise to her feet again, to stand with the rest of the congregation as the entrance song began. Father Daniel Brophy approached the altar and made the sign of the cross.

"The grace and peace of God our Father and the Lord Jesus Christ be with you," he said.

"And also with you," Maura murmured along with the congregation. Even after all these years away from the church, the responses flowed naturally from her lips, ingrained there by all the Sundays of her childhood. "Lord have mercy. Christ have mercy. Lord have mercy."

Although Daniel was unaware of her presence, Maura was focused only on him. On the dark hair, the graceful gestures, the rich baritone voice. Tonight she could watch him without shame, without embarrassment. Tonight it was safe to stare.

"Bring us eternal joy in the kingdom of Heaven, where he lives and reigns with you and the Holy Spirit, one God forever and ever."

Settling back onto the bench, Maura heard muffled coughs and the whimpers of tired children. Candles flickered on the altar in a celebration of light and hope on this winter's night.

Daniel began to read. "And the angel said unto them, 'Fear not, for behold, I bring you good tidings of great joy which shall be to all people . . .'"

Saint Luke, thought Maura, recognizing the passage. Luke, the physician.

"'. . . and this shall be a sign unto you: Ye shall find the babe wrapped in . . .'" He paused, his gaze suddenly pausing on Maura. And she thought: *Is it such a surprise to see me here tonight, Daniel?*

He cleared his throat, looked down at his notes, and continued reading. " 'Ye shall find the babe wrapped in swaddling clothes, lying in a manger.' "

Although he now knew she was seated among his flock, his gaze did not again meet hers. Not during the singing of "Cantate Domino" and "Dies Sanctificatus," not during the offertory or the liturgy of the Eucharist. As others around her rose to their feet and filed forward to receive Communion, Maura remained in her seat. If you did not believe, it was hypocrisy to partake of the Host, to sip the wine.

Then what am I doing here?

Yet she remained through the concluding rites, through the blessing and the dismissal.

"Go in the peace of Christ."

"Thanks be to God," the parishioners responded.

The Mass now ended, people began to file out of the church, buttoning coats, pulling on gloves as they shuffled to the exit. Maura, too, stood up and was just stepping into the aisle when she glimpsed Daniel trying to catch her attention, imploring her, silently, not to leave. She sat back down, conscious of the curious gazes of people as they filed past her pew. She knew what they saw, or what they imagined they saw: a lone woman, hungry for a priest's words of comfort on Christmas Eve.

Or did they see more?

She did not return their looks. As the church emptied, she stared straight ahead, stoically focused on the altar. Thinking: *It's late, and I should go home.*

I don't know what good can possibly come of staying.

"Hello, Maura."

She looked up and met Daniel's gaze. The church was not yet empty. The organist was still packing up her sheet music, and several choir members were still pulling on their coats, yet at that moment Daniel's attention was so centered on Maura, she might have been the only other person in the room.

"It's been a long time since you visited," he said.

"I suppose it has been."

"Not since August, wasn't it?"

So you've been keeping track, too.

He slid onto the bench beside her. "I'm surprised to see you here."

"It's Christmas Eve, after all."

"But you don't believe."

"I still enjoy the rituals. The songs."

"That's the only reason you came? To sing a few hymns? Chant a few *Amens* and *Thanks be to Gods*?"

"I wanted to hear some music. Be around other people."

"Don't tell me you're all alone tonight."

She gave a shrug, a laugh. "You know me, Daniel. I'm not exactly a party animal."

"I just thought . . . I mean, I assumed . . ."

"What?"

"That you'd be with someone. Especially tonight."

I am. I'm with you.

They both fell silent as the organist came walking

up the aisle, carrying her tote bag of music. "Good night, Father Brophy."

"Good night, Mrs. Easton. Thank you for the lovely performance."

"It was a pleasure." The organist cast a final, probing glance at Maura, then continued toward the exit. They heard the door swing shut, and they were finally alone.

"So why has it been so long?" he asked.

"Well, you know the death business. It never lets up. One of our pathologists had to go into the hospital for back surgery a few weeks ago, and we've had to cover for him. It's been busy, that's all."

"You can always pick up the phone and call."

"Yes, I know." He could, too, but he never did. Daniel Brophy would never step one foot over the line, and perhaps that was a good thing—she was struggling with enough temptation for them both.

"So how have you been?" she asked.

"You know about Father Roy's stroke last month? I've stepped in as police chaplain."

"Detective Rizzoli told me."

"I was at that Dorchester crime scene a few weeks ago. The police officer who was shot. I saw you there."

"I didn't see you. You should have said hello."

"Well, you were busy. Totally focused as usual." He smiled. "You can look so fierce, Maura. Did you know that?"

She gave a laugh. "Maybe that's my problem."

"Problem?"

"I scare men away."

"You haven't scared me."

How could I? She thought. *Your heart isn't available for breaking.* Deliberately she glanced at her watch and rose to her feet. "It's so late, and I've already taken up too much of your time."

"It's not as if I have any pressing business," he said as he walked with her toward the exit.

"You have a whole flock of souls to look after. And it *is* Christmas Eve."

"You'll notice I have nowhere else to go tonight, either."

She paused and turned to face him. They stood alone in the church, breathing in the scents of candle wax and incense, familiar smells that brought back a childhood of other Christmases, other Masses. The days when stepping into a church provoked none of the turmoil she was now feeling. "Good night, Daniel," she said, turning toward the door.

"Will it be another four months until I see you again?" he called out after her.

"I don't know."

"I've missed our talks, Maura."

Again she hesitated, her hand poised to push open the door. "I've missed them, too. Maybe that's why we shouldn't have them anymore."

"We haven't done anything to be ashamed of."

"Not yet," she said softly, her gaze not on him, but on the heavy carved door, which stood between her and escape.

"Maura, let's not leave it like this between us. There's no reason we can't maintain some sort of—" He stopped.

Her cell phone was ringing.

She fished it out of her purse. At this hour, a ring-ing phone could not mean anything good. As she answered the call, she felt Daniel's eyes on her, felt her own jittery reaction to his gaze.

"Dr. Isles," she said, her voice unnaturally cool.

"Merry Christmas," said Detective Jane Rizzoli. "I'm kind of surprised you're not at home right now. I tried calling there first."

"I came to midnight Mass."

"Geez, it's already one A.M. Isn't it over yet?"

"Yes, Jane. It's over, and I'm about to leave," said Maura, in a tone of voice that cut off any more queries. "What have you got for me?" she asked. Because she already knew that this call was not a simple hello, but a summons.

"Address is two-ten Prescott Street, East Boston. A private residence. Frost and I got here about a half hour ago."

"Details?"

"We're looking at one vic, a young woman."

"Homicide?"

"Oh, yeah."

"You sound pretty sure of yourself."

"You'll see when you get here."

She disconnected and found Daniel still watching her. But the moment for taking risks, for saying things they both might come to regret, had passed. Death had intervened.

"You have to go to work?"

"I'm covering tonight." She slipped the phone back into her purse. "Since I don't have any family in town, I volunteered."

"On this of all nights?"

"The fact that it's Christmas doesn't make much difference to me."

She buttoned up her coat collar and walked out of the building, into the night. He followed her outside, and as she tramped through freshly fallen snow to her car, he stood watching her from the steps, his white vestments flapping in the wind. Glancing back, she saw him raise his hand in a good-bye wave.

He was still waving as she drove away.

THREE

THE BLUE LIGHTS of three cruisers pulsed through a filigree of falling snow, announcing to all who approached: Something has happened here, something terrible. Maura felt her front bumper scrape against ice as she squeezed her Lexus up next to the snowbank, to make room for other vehicles to pass. At this hour, on Christmas Eve, the only vehicles likely to turn up on the narrow street would be, like hers, members of Death's entourage. She took a moment to steel herself against the exhausting hours to come, her tired eyes mesmerized by all the flashing lights. Her limbs felt numb; her circulation turned to sludge. *Wake up,* she thought. *It's time to go to work.*

She stepped out of the car and the sudden blast of cold air blew the sleep from her brain. She walked through freshly fallen powder that whispered away like white feathers before her boots. Although it was one-thirty, lights were burning in several of the modest homes along the street, and through a window decorated with holiday stencils of flying reindeer and candy canes, she saw the silhouette of a curious neighbor peering out from his warm house, at a night that was no longer silent or holy.

"Hey, Dr. Isles?" called out a patrolman, an older cop whom she vaguely recognized. Clearly he knew exactly who she was. They all knew who she was. "How'd you get so lucky tonight, huh?"

"I could ask the same of you, Officer."

"Guess we both drew the short straws." He gave a laugh. "Merry goddamn Christmas."

"Is Detective Rizzoli inside?"

"Yeah, she and Frost have been videotaping." He pointed toward a residence where all the lights were shining, a boxy little house crammed into a row of tired older homes. "By now, they're probably ready for you."

The sound of violent retching made her glance toward the street, where a blond woman stood doubled over, clutching at her long coat to avoid soiling the hem as she threw up in the snowbank.

The patrolman gave a snort. Muttered to Maura, "That one's gonna make a *fine* homicide detective. She came striding onto the scene right outta *Cagney and Lacey*. Ordered us all around. Yeah, a real tough one. Then she goes in the house, gets one look, and next thing you know, she's out here puking in the snow." He laughed.

"I haven't seen her before. She's from Homicide?"

"I hear she just transferred over from Narcotics and Vice. The commissioner's bright idea to bring in more girls." He shook his head. "She's not gonna last long. That's my prediction."

The woman detective wiped her mouth and moved

unsteadily toward the porch steps, where she sank down.

"Hey. *Detective!*" called out the patrolman. "You might wanna move away from the crime scene? If you're gonna puke again, at least do it where they're not collecting evidence."

A younger cop, standing nearby, snickered.

The blond detective jerked back to her feet, and in bright strobe flashes the cruiser lights illuminated her mortified face. "I think I'll go sit in my car for a minute," she murmured.

"Yeah. You do that, ma'am."

Maura watched the detective retreat to the shelter of her vehicle. What horrors was she about to face inside that house?

"Doc," called out Detective Barry Frost. He had just emerged from the house and was standing on the porch, hunched in a Windbreaker. His blond hair stood up in tufts, as though he had just rolled out of bed. Though his face had always been sallow, the yellow glow cast by the porch light made him look sicklier than usual.

"I gather it's pretty bad in there," she said.

"Not the kind of thing you want to see on Christmas. Thought I'd better come out here and get some air."

She paused at the bottom of the steps, noting the jumble of footprints that had been left on the snow-dusted porch. "Okay to walk in this way?"

"Yeah. Those prints are all Boston PD."

"What about footwear evidence?"

"We didn't find much out here."

"What, did he fly in the window?"

"It looks like he swept up after himself. You can still see some of the whisk marks."

She frowned. "This perp pays attention to detail."

"Wait till you see what's inside."

She walked up the steps and pulled on shoe covers and gloves. Close up, Frost looked even worse, his face gaunt and drained of all color. But he took a breath and offered gamely: "I can walk you in."

"No, you take your time out here. Rizzoli can show me around."

He nodded, but he wasn't looking at her; he was staring off at the street with the fierce concentration of a man trying to hold on to his dinner. She left him to his battle and reached for the doorknob. Already she was braced for the worst. Only moments ago, she had arrived exhausted, trying to shake herself awake; now she could feel tension sizzling like static through her nerves.

She stepped into the house. Paused there, her pulse throbbing, and gazed at an utterly unalarming scene. The foyer had a scuffed oak floor. Through the doorway she could see into the living room, which was furnished with cheap mismatches: a sagging futon couch, a beanbag chair, a bookcase cobbled together from particleboard planks and concrete blocks. Nothing so far that screamed *crime scene*. The horror was yet to come; she knew it was waiting in this house, because she had seen its reflection in Barry Frost's eyes and in the ashen face of the woman detective.

She walked through the living room into the dining room, where she saw four chairs around a pine table. But it was not the furniture she focused on; it was the place settings that had been laid out on the table, as though for a family meal. Dinner for four.

One of the plates had a linen napkin draped over it, the fabric spattered with blood.

Gingerly she reached for the napkin. Lifting it up by the corner, she took one look at what lay underneath it, on the plate. Instantly she dropped the napkin and stumbled backward, gasping.

"I see you found the left hand," a voice said.

Maura spun around. "You scared the shit out of me."

"You want some seriously scary shit?" said Detective Jane Rizzoli. "Just follow me." She turned and led Maura up a hallway. Like Frost, Jane looked as if she had just rolled out of bed. Her slacks were wrinkled, her dark hair a wiry tangle. Unlike Frost, she moved fearlessly, her paper-covered shoes whishing across the floor. Of all the detectives who regularly showed up in the autopsy room, Jane was the one most likely to push right up to the table, to lean in for a closer look, and she betrayed no hesitation now as she moved along the hall. It was Maura who lagged behind, her gaze drawn downward to the drips of blood on the floor.

"Stay along this side," said Jane. "We've got some indistinct footprints here, going in both directions. Some kind of athletic shoe. They're pretty much dry now, but I don't want to smear anything."

"Who called in the report?"

"It was a nine-one-one call. Came in just after midnight."

"From where?"

"This residence."

Maura frowned. "The victim? Did she try to get help?"

"No voice on the line. Someone just dialed the emergency operator and left the phone off the hook. First cruiser got here ten minutes after the call. Patrolman found the door unlocked, came into the bedroom, and freaked out." Jane paused at a doorway and glanced over her shoulder at Maura. A warning look. "Here's where it gets hairy."

The severed hand was bad enough.

Jane moved aside to let Maura gaze into the bedroom. She did not see the victim; all she saw was the blood. The average human body contains perhaps five liters of it. The same volume of red paint, splashed around a small room, could splatter every surface. What her stunned eyes encountered, as she stared through the doorway, were just such extravagant splatters, like bright streamers flung by boisterous hands across white walls, across furniture and linen.

"Arterial," said Rizzoli.

Maura could only nod, silent, as her gaze followed the arcs of spray, reading the horror story written in red on these walls. As a fourth-year medical student serving a clerkship rotation in the ER, she had once watched a gunshot victim exsanguinate on the trauma table. With the blood pressure crashing, the surgery resident in desperation had performed an emergency laparotomy, hoping to control the internal bleeding. He'd sliced open the belly, releasing a fountain of arterial blood that gushed out of the torn aorta, splashing doctors' gowns and faces. In the final frantic seconds, as they'd suctioned and packed in sterile towels, all Maura could focus on was that blood. Its brilliant gloss, its meaty smell. She'd reached into the open abdomen to grab a retractor, and the warmth that had soaked through the sleeves of her gown had felt as soothing as a bath. That day, in the operating room, Maura had seen the alarming spurt that even a weak arterial pressure can generate.

Now, as she gazed at the walls of the bedroom, it was once again the blood that held her focus, that recorded the story of the victim's final seconds. *When the first cut was made, the victim's heart was still beating, still generating a blood pressure.* There, above the bed, was where the first machine-gun splatter hit, arcing high onto the wall. After a few vigorous pulses, the arcs began to decay. The body would try to compensate for the falling pressure, the arteries clamping down, the pulse quickening. But with every heartbeat, it would drain itself, accelerating its own demise. When at last the pressure faded and the heart stopped, there would be no more spurts, just a quiet trickle as the last blood seeped out. This was the death Maura saw recorded on these walls, and on this bed.

Then her gaze halted, riveted on something she had almost missed among all the splatters. Something that made the hairs on the back of her neck suddenly stand up. On one wall, drawn in blood, were three upside-down crosses. And beneath that, a series of cryptic symbols:

╫
jvp)))q

"What does that mean?" said Maura softly.

"We have no idea. We've been trying to figure it out."

Maura could not tear her gaze from the writing. She swallowed. "What the hell are we dealing with here?"

"Wait till you see what comes next." Jane circled around to the other side of the bed and pointed to the floor. "The victim's right here. Most of her, anyway."

Only as Maura rounded the bed did the woman come into view. She was lying unclothed and on her back. Exsanguination had drained the skin to the color of alabaster, and Maura suddenly remembered her visit to a room in the British Museum, where dozens of fragmented Roman statues were on display. The wear of centuries had chipped at the marble, cracking off heads, breaking off arms, until they were little more than anonymous torsos. That's what she saw now, staring down at the body. *A broken Venus. With no head.*

"It looks like he killed her there, on the bed," said Jane. "That would explain the splatters on that particular wall and all the blood on the mattress. Then he pulled her onto the floor, maybe because he needed a firm surface to finish cutting." Jane took a breath and turned away, as though she had suddenly reached her limit, and could not look at the corpse any longer.

"You said the first cruiser took ten minutes to respond to that nine-one-one call," said Maura.

"That's right."

"What was done here—these amputations, the removal of the head—that would have taken longer than ten minutes."

"We realize that. I don't think it was the victim who made that call."

The creak of a footstep made them both turn, and they saw Barry Frost standing in the doorway, looking less than eager to enter the room.

"Crime Scene Unit's here," he said.

"Tell them to come on in." Jane paused. "You don't look so hot."

"I think I'm doing pretty good. Considering."

"How's Kassovitz? She finished puking? We could use some help in here."

Frost shook his head. "She's still sitting in her car. I don't think her stomach's ready for this one. I'll go get CSU."

"Tell her to grow a spine, for God's sake!" Jane called after him as he walked out of the room. "I hate it when a woman lets me down. Gives us all a bad name."

Maura's gaze returned to the torso on the floor. "Have you found—"

"The rest of her?" said Jane. "Yeah. You've already

seen the left hand. The right arm's sitting in the bathtub. And now I guess it's time to show you the
kitchen."

"What's in there?"

"More surprises." Jane started across the room,
toward the hallway.

Turning to follow her, Maura caught a sudden
glimpse of herself in the bedroom mirror. Her reflection stared back at her with tired eyes, the black hair
limp from melted snow. But it was not the image of
her own face that made her freeze. "Jane," she whispered. "Look at this."

"What?"

"In the mirror. The symbols." Maura turned and
stared at the writing on the wall. "Do you see it? It's
a reverse image! Those aren't symbols, those are letters, meant to be read in the mirror."

Jane looked at the wall, then at the mirror. "That's
a word?"

"Yes. It spells out *Peccavi*."

Jane shook her head. "Even in reverse, it doesn't
mean a thing to me."

"It's Latin, Jane."

"For what?"

"*I have sinned.*"

For a moment, the two women stared at each
other. Then Jane gave a sudden laugh. "Well, that's a
doozy of a confession for you. You think a few *Hail
Marys* will erase this particular sin?"

"Maybe this word doesn't refer to the killer.
Maybe it's all about the victim." She looked at Jane.
"*I have sinned.*"

"Punishment," said Jane. "Vengeance."

"It's a possible motive. She did something to anger the killer. She sinned against him. And this is his payback."

Jane took a deep breath. "Let's go into the kitchen." She led Maura down the hallway. At the kitchen doorway she stopped and looked at Maura, who had halted on the threshold, too stunned by what she saw to say a word.

On the tiled floor, a large red circle had been drawn in what looked like red chalk. Spaced around its circumference were five black puddles of wax that had melted and congealed. *Candles,* thought Maura. In the center of that circle, positioned so that the eyes were staring at them, was a woman's severed head.

A circle. Five black candles. *It's a ritual offering.*

"So now I'm supposed to go home to my little girl," said Jane. "In the morning, we'll all sit around the tree and open presents and pretend there's peace on earth. But I'll be thinking of . . . that thing . . . staring back at me. Merry frigging Christmas."

Maura swallowed. "Do we know who she is?"

"Well, I haven't dragged in her friends and neighbors to make a positive ID. *Hey, you recognize that head on the kitchen floor?* But based on her driver's license photo, I'd say this is Lori-Ann Tucker. Twenty-eight years old. Brown hair, brown eyes." Abruptly, Jane laughed. "Put all the body parts together, and that's about what you'd get."

"What do you know about her?"

"We found a paycheck stub in her purse. She works over at the Science Museum. We don't know in what capacity, but judging by the house, the

furniture"—Jane glanced toward the dining room—
"she's not making a ton of money."

They heard voices, and the creak of footsteps as
CSU moved into the house. Jane at once straightened
to greet them with some semblance of her usual
aplomb. The unshrinking Detective Rizzoli that
everyone knew.

"Hey, guys," she said as Frost and two male criminalists gingerly stepped into the kitchen. "We got
ourselves a fun one."

"Jesus," one of the criminalists murmured.
"Where's the rest of the victim?"

"In several rooms. You might want to start with—"
She stopped, her body suddenly snapping straight.

The phone on the kitchen counter was ringing.

Frost was standing closest to it. "What do you
think?" he asked, glancing at Rizzoli.

"Answer it."

Gingerly Frost picked up the receiver in his gloved
hand. "Hello? Hello?" After a moment he set it
down again. "They hung up."

"What's Caller ID say?"

Frost pressed the call history button. "It's a
Boston number."

Jane took out her cell phone and looked at the
number on the display. "I'll try calling it back," she
said, and dialed. Stood listening as it rang. "No answer."

"Let me see if that number's called here before,"
said Frost. He cycled back through the history, re-
viewing every call that had come in or gone out on
the line. "Okay, here's that call to nine-one-one.
Twelve-ten A.M."

"Our perp, announcing his handiwork."

"There's another call, just before that one. A Cambridge number." He looked up. "It was at twelve-oh-five."

"Did our perp make *two* calls from this phone?"

"If it was our perp."

Jane stared at the phone. "Let's think about this. He's standing here in the kitchen. He's just killed her and cut her up. Sliced off her hand, her arm. Sets her head right here, on the floor. Why call someone? Does he want to brag about it? And who's he gonna call?"

"Find out," said Maura.

Jane once again used her cell phone, this time to call the Cambridge number. "It's ringing. Okay, I'm getting an answering machine." She paused, and her gaze suddenly whipped to Maura. "You're not going to believe who this number belongs to."

"Who?"

Jane hung up and dialed the number again. Handed Maura the cell phone.

Maura heard it ring four times. Then the answering machine picked up and a recording played. The voice was instantly, chillingly familiar.

You've reached Dr. Joyce P. O'Donnell. I do want to hear from you, so please leave a message, and I'll return your call.

Maura disconnected and met Jane's equally stunned gaze. "Why would the killer call Joyce O'Donnell?"

"You're kidding," said Frost. "It's *her* number?"

"Who is she?" one of the criminalists asked.

Jane looked at him. "Joyce O'Donnell," she said, "is a vampire."

FOUR

This was not where Jane wanted to be on Christmas morning.

She and Frost sat in her parked Subaru on Brattle Street, gazing at the large white colonial residence. The last time Jane had visited this house, it had been summer, and the front garden had been impeccably groomed. Seeing it now, in a different season, she was once again impressed by how tasteful every detail was, from the slate-gray trim to the handsome wreath on the front door. The wrought-iron gate was decorated with pine boughs and red ribbon, and through the front window she could see the tree, glittering with ornaments. That was a surprise. Even bloodsuckers celebrated Christmas.

"If you don't want to do this," said Frost, "I can talk to her."

"You think I can't handle this?"

"I think this has gotta be hard for you."

"What'll be hard is keeping my hands off her throat."

"You see? That's what I mean. Your attitude's going to get in the way. You two have a history, and that colors everything. You can't be neutral."

"No one could be neutral, knowing who she is. What she does."

"Rizzoli, she just does what she's paid to do."

"So do whores." Except whores don't hurt anyone, thought Jane, staring at Joyce O'Donnell's house. A house paid for with the blood of murder victims. Whores don't waltz into courtrooms in sleek St. John suits and take the witness stand in defense of butchers.

"All I'm saying is, try to keep your cool, okay?" said Frost. "We don't have to like her. But we can't afford to piss her off."

"You think that's my plan?"

"Look at you. Your claws are already out."

"Purely in self-defense." Jane shoved open the car door. "Because I know this bitch is going to try to sink hers in me." She stepped out, sinking calf-deep into snow, but she scarcely felt the cold seeping through her socks; her deepest chill was not physical. Her focus was on the house, on the encounter to come, with a woman who knew Jane's secret fears only too well. Who also knew how to exploit those fears.

Frost swung open the gate, and they walked up the shoveled path. The flagstones were icy, and Jane was trying so hard not to slip that by the time she reached the porch steps, she already felt off balance and unsure of her footing. Not the best way to face Joyce O'Donnell. Nor did it help that when the front door opened, O'Donnell was looking her usual elegant self, blond hair cut in a sleek bob, her pink button-down shirt and khaki slacks perfectly tailored to her athletic frame. Jane, in her tired black pantsuit, with her trouser cuffs damp from melted snow, felt like the supplicant at the manor house door. *Exactly how she wants me to feel.*

O'Donnell gave a cool nod. "Detectives." She did not immediately step aside, a pause intended to demonstrate that here, on her own territory, she was in command.

"May we come in?" Jane finally asked. Knowing that, of course, they would be allowed in. That the game had already begun.

O'Donnell waved them into the house. "This isn't how I care to spend Christmas day," she said.

"It's not exactly how we want to spend it either," Jane countered. "And I'm sure it's not what the victim wanted."

"As I told you, the recording's already been erased," said O'Donnell, leading the way into her living room. "You can listen to it, but there's nothing to hear."

Not much had changed since the last time Jane had visited this house. She saw the same abstract paintings on the walls, the same richly hued Oriental carpets. The only new feature was the Christmas tree. The trees of Jane's childhood had been decorated with haphazard taste, the branches hung with the mismatched assortment of ornaments hardy enough to have survived earlier Rizzoli Christmases. And there'd been tinsel—lots and lots of it. *Vegas trees,* Jane used to call them.

But on this tree, there was not a single strand of tinsel. No Vegas in this house. Instead, the branches were hung with crystal prisms and silver teardrops, reflecting wintry sunshine on the walls, like dancing chips of light. *Even her damn Christmas tree makes me feel inadequate.*

O'Donnell crossed to her answering machine. "This is all I have now," she said, and pressed Play. The digital voice announced: "You have no new messages." She looked at the detectives. "I'm afraid the recording you asked about is gone. As soon as I got home last night, I played all my messages. Erased them as I went. By the time I got to your message, about preserving the recording, it was too late."

"How many messages were there?" asked Jane.

"Four. Yours was the last."

"The call we're interested in would have come in around twelve-ten."

"Yes, and the number's still there, in the electronic log." O'Donnell pressed a button, cycling back to the 12:10 call. "But whoever called at that time didn't say anything." She looked at Jane. "There was no message at all."

"What did you hear?"

"I told you. There was nothing."

"Extraneous noises? TV, traffic?"

"Not even heavy breathing. Just a few seconds of silence, and then the hang-up click. That's why I immediately erased it. There was nothing to hear."

"Is the caller's number familiar to you?" asked Frost.

"Should it be?"

"That's what we're asking you," Jane said, the bite in her voice unmistakable.

O'Donnell's gaze met hers and Jane saw, in those eyes, a flash of disdain. *As though I'm not even worth her attention.* "No, I didn't recognize the phone number," said O'Donnell.

"Do you know the name Lori-Ann Tucker?"

"No. Who's that?"

"She was murdered last night, in her own home. That call was made from her telephone."

O'Donnell paused and said, reasonably, "It could have been a wrong number."

"I don't think so, Dr. O'Donnell. I think the call was meant to reach *you.*"

"Why call me and then say nothing? It's more likely that she heard the recording on my answering machine, realized she'd made a mistake, and simply hung up."

"I don't believe it was the victim who called you."

Again, O'Donnell paused, this time longer. "I see," she said. She moved to an armchair and sat down, but not because she was shaken. She looked perfectly unruffled sitting in that chair, an empress holding court. "You think it was the killer who called me."

"You don't sound at all worried by that possibility."

"I don't know enough yet to be worried. I don't know anything about this case. So why don't you tell me more?" She gestured to the couch, an invitation for her visitors to sit down. It was the first hint of hospitality that she'd offered.

Because now we have something interesting to offer her, thought Jane. *She's caught a whiff of blood. It's exactly what this woman craves.*

The couch was a pristine white, and Frost paused before settling onto it, as though afraid to smudge the fabric. But Jane didn't give it a second glance. She sat down in her snow-dampened slacks, her focus on O'Donnell.

"The victim was a twenty-eight-year-old woman," said Jane. "She was killed last night, around midnight."

"Suspects?"

"We've made no arrests."

"So you have no idea who the killer is."

"I'm only saying that we've made no arrests. What we're doing is following leads."

"And I'm one of them."

"Someone called you from the victim's home. It could well have been the perp."

"And why would he—assuming it's a he—want to talk to me?"

Jane leaned forward. "We both know why, Doctor. It's what you do for a living. You probably have a nice little fan club out there, all the killers who consider you their friend. You're famous, you know, among the murderer set. You're the lady shrink who talks to monsters."

"I try to understand them, that's all. Study them."

"You defend them."

"I'm a neuropsychiatrist. I'm far more qualified to testify in court than most expert witnesses. Not every killer belongs in prison. Some of them are seriously damaged people."

"Yeah, I know your theory. Bonk a kid on the head, screw up his frontal lobes, and he's absolved of all responsibility for anything he does from then on. He can kill a woman, chop her up into pieces, and you'll still defend him in court."

"Is that what happened to this victim?" O'Donnell's face had taken on a disturbing alertness, her eyes bright and feral. "Was she dismembered?"

"Why do you ask?"

"I'd just like to know."

"Professional curiosity?"

O'Donnell sat back in her chair. "Detective Rizzoli, I've interviewed a lot of killers. Over the years, I've compiled extensive statistics on motives, methods, patterns. So yes, it is professional curiosity." She paused. "Dismemberment is not that unusual. Especially if it's to aid in disposal of the victim."

"That wasn't the reason for it in this case."

"You know that?"

"It's pretty clear."

"Did he purposefully display the body parts? Was it staged?"

"Why? You happen to have any sicko pals who're into that kind of thing? Any names you want to share with us? They write to you, don't they? Your name's out there. The doctor who loves to hear all the details."

"If they write me, it's usually anonymous. They don't tell me their names."

"But you do get letters," said Frost.

"I hear from people."

"Killers."

"Or fabricators. Whether they tell the truth or not is impossible for me to determine."

"You think some of them are just sharing their fantasies?"

"And they'll probably never act on them. They

just need a way to express unacceptable urges. We all have them. The mildest-mannered man occasionally daydreams about things he'd like to do to women. Things so twisted he doesn't dare tell anyone. I bet that even you entertain a few inappropriate thoughts, Detective Frost." She kept her gaze on him, a look that was meant to make him uncomfortable. Frost, to his credit, did not even flush.

"Has anyone written you about fantasies of dismemberment?" he asked.

"Not lately."

"But someone has?"

"As I said, dismemberment is not unusual."

"As a fantasy or a real act?"

"Both."

Jane said, "Who's been writing you about their fantasies, Dr. O'Donnell?"

The woman met Jane's gaze. "That correspondence is confidential. That's why they feel safe telling me their secrets, their desires, their daydreams."

"Do these people ever call you?"

"Rarely."

"And you talk to them?"

"I don't avoid them."

"Do you keep a list of these callers?"

"Hardly a list. I can't remember the last time it happened."

"It happened last night."

"Well, I wasn't here to answer it."

"You weren't here at two A.M., either," said Frost. "We called then, and got your machine."

"Where were you last night?" Jane asked.

O'Donnell shrugged. "Out."

"At two A.M., on Christmas Eve?"

"I was with friends."

"What time did you get home?"

"Probably around two-thirty."

"They must be very good friends. You mind telling us their names?"

"Yes, I do."

"Why?"

"Why don't I want my privacy violated? Do I actually have to answer that question?"

"This is a homicide investigation. A woman was slaughtered last night. It was one of the most brutal crime scenes I've ever walked into."

"And you want my alibi."

"I'm just curious why you won't tell us."

"Am I a suspect? Or are you just trying to show me who's in charge?"

"You're not a suspect. At the moment."

"Then I'm under no obligation to even talk to you." Abruptly, O'Donnell rose to her feet and started toward the door. "I'll walk you out, now."

Frost, too, started to get up, then saw that Jane wasn't budging, and he sank back down again.

Jane said, "If you gave one damn about the victim, if you saw what he did to Lori-Ann Tucker—"

O'Donnell turned to face her. "Why don't you tell me? What, exactly, *was* done to her?"

"You want the details, do you?"

"It's my field of study. I need to know the details." She moved toward Jane. "It helps me understand."

Or it turns you on. That's why you suddenly look interested. Even eager.

"You said she was dismembered," said O'Donnell. "Was the head removed?"

"Rizzoli," said Frost, a cautionary note in his voice.

But Jane did not need to reveal a thing; O'Donnell had already drawn her own conclusions. "The head is such a powerful symbol. So personal. So individual." O'Donnell stepped closer, moving in like a predator. "Did he take it with him, as a trophy? A reminder of his kill?"

"Tell us where you were last night."

"Or did he leave the head at the scene? Someplace where it would elicit maximum shock? Someplace it would be impossible to miss? A kitchen counter, perhaps? Or a prominent place on the floor?"

"Who were you with?"

"It's a potent message, displaying a head, a face. It's the killer's way of telling you he's in complete control. He's showing you how powerless you are, Detective. And how powerful he is."

"*Who were you with?*" The instant the words were out, Jane knew they were a mistake. She'd allowed O'Donnell to goad her, and she had lost her temper. The ultimate sign of weakness.

"My friendships are private," O'Donnell said, and added, with a quiet smile, "Except for the one you already know about. Our mutual acquaintance. He keeps asking about you, you know. Always wants to know what you're up to." She did not have to say his name. They both knew she was talking about Warren Hoyt.

Don't react, thought Jane. *Don't let her see how deeply she's dug her claws into me.* But she could feel her own face snap taut and saw Frost glance at her with concern. The scars that Hoyt had left on Jane's hands were only the most obvious wounds; there were far deeper ones. Even now, over two years later, she flinched at the mention of his name.

"He's a fan of yours, Detective," said O'Donnell. "Even though he'll never walk again because of you, he bears you absolutely no grudge."

"I couldn't care less what he thinks."

"I went to see him last week. He showed me his collection of news clippings. His *Janie file,* as he calls it. When you were trapped in that hospital siege, over the summer, he kept the TV on all night. Watched every second of it." O'Donnell paused. "He told me you had a baby girl."

Jane's back went rigid. *Don't let her do this to you. Don't let her dig those claws in deeper.*

"I believe your daughter's name is Regina, isn't it?"

Jane rose to her feet, and though she was shorter than O'Donnell, something in Jane's eyes made the other woman abruptly step back. "We'll be calling on you again," said Jane.

"Call me all you want," said O'Donnell. "I have nothing else to tell you."

"She's lying," said Jane.

She yanked open the car door and slid in behind the wheel. There she sat, staring at a scene that was Christmas card–pretty, the sun glistening on icicles, the snow-frosted houses decked in tasteful wreaths and holly. No garish Santas and reindeer on this street, no rooftop extravaganzas like the ones in Revere, where she had grown up. She thought of Johnny Silva's house, just down the street from her parents', and of the long lines of rubberneckers from miles around who'd detour onto their street, just to gape at the eye-popping light show that the Silvas put up in their front yard every December. There you'd find Santa and the three wise men and the manger with Mary and Jesus and a menagerie of so many animals it would've sunk Noah's ark. All lit up like a carnival. You could have powered a small African nation with the electricity the Silvas burned through every Christmas.

But here on Brattle Street, there were no such gaudy spectacles, only understated elegance. No Johnny Silvas lived here. She'd rather have that moron Johnny for a neighbor than the woman who lived in this house.

"She knows more about this case than she's telling us."

"How do you draw that conclusion?" asked Frost.

"Instinct."

"I thought you didn't believe in instinct. That's what you always tell me. That it's nothing better than a lucky guess."

"But I know this woman. I know what makes her tick." She looked at Frost, whose winter pallor seemed even more pronounced in the weak sunshine. "She got more than a hang-up call from the killer last night."

"You're guessing."

"Why did she erase it?"

"Why wouldn't she? If the caller left no message?"

"That's her story."

"Oh man. She got to you." He shook his head. "I knew she would."

"She didn't get close."

"Yeah? When she started talking about Regina, that didn't light your fuse? She's a shrink. She knows just how to manipulate you. You shouldn't even be dealing with her."

"Who should? You? That weenie Kassovitz?"

"Someone who doesn't have a history with her. Someone she can't touch." He gave Jane a probing look that made her want to turn away. They had been partners for two years now, and even though they were not the closest of friends, they understood each other in a way that mere friends or even lovers seldom did, because they had shared the same horrors, fought the same battles. Frost, better than anyone, even better than her husband, Gabriel, knew her history with Joyce O'Donnell.

And with the killer known as the Surgeon.

"She still scares you, doesn't she?" he asked quietly.

"All she does is piss me off."

"Because she knows what *does* scare you. And she never stops reminding you of him, never forgets to bring up his name."

"Like I'm the least bit afraid of a guy who can't even wiggle his toes? Who can't pee unless some nurse shoves a tube up his dick? Oh yeah, I'm real scared of Warren Hoyt."

"You still having the nightmares?"

His question stopped her cold. She couldn't lie to him; he'd see it. So she said nothing at all, but just looked straight ahead, at that perfect street with its perfect houses.

"I'd be having them," he said, "if it'd happened to me."

But it didn't, she thought. *I'm the one who felt Hoyt's blade at my throat, who bears the scars from his scalpel. I'm the one he still thinks about, fantasizes about.* Though he could never again hurt her, just knowing that she was the object of his desires made her skin crawl.

"Why are we talking about him?" she said. "This is about O'Donnell."

"You can't separate the two."

"I'm not the one who keeps bringing up his name. Let's stick to the subject, okay? Joyce P. O'Donnell, and why the killer chose to call her."

"We can't be sure it *was* the perp who called her."

"Talking to O'Donnell is every pervert's idea of great phone sex. They can tell her their sickest fantasies, and she'd lap it up and beg for more, all the while taking notes. That's why he'd call her. He'd want to crow about his accomplishment. He'd want a willing ear, and she's the obvious person to call. Dr. Murder." With an angry twist of the key, she started the car. Cold air blasted from the heating vents. "That's why he called her. To brag. To bask in her attention."

"Why would she lie about it?"

"Why wouldn't she tell us where she was last night? It makes you wonder who she was with. Whether that call wasn't an invitation."

Frost frowned at her. "Are you saying what I think you're saying?"

"Sometime before midnight, our perp does his slice-and-dice on Lori-Ann Tucker. Then he makes a phone call to O'Donnell. She claims she wasn't home—that her answering machine picked up. But what if she *was* at home at the time? What if they actually spoke to each other?"

"We called her house at two A.M. She wasn't answering then."

"Because she was no longer at home. She said she was out with *friends*." Jane looked at him. "What if it was just *one* friend? One bright, shiny new friend."

"Come on. You really think she'd protect this perp?"

"I wouldn't put anything past her." Jane let out the brake and pulled away from the curb. "Anything."

FIVE

"THIS IS no way to spend Christmas day," said Angela Rizzoli, glancing up from the stove at her daughter. Four pots simmered on the burners, lids clattering, as steam curled in a wispy wreath around Angela's sweat-dampened hair. She lifted a pot lid and slid a plateful of homemade gnocchi into the boiling water. They plopped in, their splash announcing that dinner was now imminent. Jane gazed around the kitchen at endless platters of food. Angela Rizzoli's worst fear was that someone, someday, would leave her house hungry.

Today was not that day.

On the countertop was a roasted leg of lamb, fragrant with oregano and garlic, and a pan of sizzling potatoes browned with rosemary. Jane saw ciabatta bread and a salad of sliced tomatoes and mozzarella. A green bean salad was the lone contribution that Jane and Gabriel had brought to the feast. On the stove, the simmering pots released yet other aromas, and in the boiling water, tender gnocchi bobbed and swirled.

"What can I do in here, Mom?" asked Jane.

"Nothing. You worked today. You sit there."

"You want me to grate the cheese?"

"No, no. You must be tired. Gabriel says you were up all night." Angela gave the pot a quick stir with a wooden spoon. "I don't see why you had to work today, too. It's unreasonable."

"It's what I gotta do."

"But it's Christmas."

"Tell it to the bad guys." Jane pulled the grater from the drawer and began scraping a block of Parmesan cheese across the blades. She could not just sit still in this kitchen. "How come Mike and Frankie aren't helping in here, anyway? You must've been cooking all morning."

"Oh, you know your brothers."

"Yeah." She snorted. *Unfortunately.*

In the other room, football was blaring from the TV, as usual. Men's shouts joined the roar of stadium crowds, all cheering some guy with a tight butt and a pigskin ball.

Angela bustled over to inspect the green bean salad. "Oh, this looks good! What's in the dressing?"

"I don't know. Gabriel made it."

"You're so lucky, Janie. You got a man who cooks."

"You starve Dad a few days, he'll know how to cook, too."

"No, he wouldn't. He'd just waste away at the dining table, waiting for dinner to float in all by itself." Angela lifted up the pot of boiling water and turned it upside down, dumping the cooked gnocchi into a colander. As the steam cleared, Jane saw Angela's sweating face, framed by tendrils of hair. Outside, the wind sliced across ice-glazed streets, but here in her mother's kitchen, heat flushed their faces and steamed the windows.

"Here's Mommy," said Gabriel, walking into the kitchen with a wide-awake Regina in his arms. "Look who's up from her nap already."

"She didn't sleep long," said Jane.

"With that football game going on?" He laughed. "Our daughter is definitely a Patriots fan. You should have heard her howl when the Dolphins scored."

"Let me hold her." Jane opened her arms and hugged a squirming Regina against her chest. *Only four months old,* she thought, *and already my baby is trying to wriggle away from me.* Ferocious little Regina had come into the world with fists swinging, her face purple from screaming. *Are you so impatient to grow up?* Jane wondered as she rocked her daughter. *Won't you stay a baby for a while and let me hold you, enjoy you, before the passing years send you walking out our door?*

Regina grabbed Jane's hair and gave it a painful yank. Wincing, Jane pried away tenacious fingers and stared down at her daughter's hand. And she thought, suddenly, of another hand, cold and lifeless. Someone else's daughter, now lying in pieces in the morgue. *Here it is, Christmas. Of all days, I should not have to think of dead women.* But as she kissed Regina's silky hair, as she inhaled the scent of soap and baby shampoo, she could not shut out the memory of another kitchen and of what had stared up at her from the tiled floor.

"Hey, Ma, it's halftime. When're we gonna eat?"

Jane looked up as her older brother, Frankie, lumbered into the room. The last time Jane had seen him was a year ago, when he'd flown home from California for Christmas. Since then, his shoulders had bulked up even more. Every year, Frankie seemed to grow bigger, and his arms were now so thick with muscle that they could not hang straight, but swung in simian arcs. *All those hours in the weight room,* she thought, *and where has it gotten him? Bigger, but definitely no smarter.* She shot an appreciative glance at Gabriel, who was opening a bottle of Chianti. Taller and leaner than Frankie, he was built like a racehorse, not a draft horse. *When you have a brain,* she thought, *who needs monster muscles?*

"Dinner's in ten minutes," said Angela.

"That means it'll run into the third quarter," said Frankie.

"Why don't you guys just turn off the TV?" said Jane. "It's Christmas dinner."

"Yeah, and we'd all be eating a lot earlier if you'd shown up on time."

"Frankie," snapped Angela. "Your sister worked all night. And look, she's in here helping. So don't you go picking on her!"

There was sudden silence in the kitchen as both brother and sister stared at Angela in surprise. *Did Mom actually take my side, for once?*

"Well. This is some great Christmas," said Frankie, and he walked out of the kitchen.

Angela slid the colander of drained gnocchi into a serving bowl and ladled on steaming veal sauce. "No appreciation for what women do," she muttered.

Jane laughed. "You just noticed?"

"Like we don't deserve some respect?" Angela reached for a chef's knife and attacked a bunch of parsley, mincing it with machine-gun raps. "I blame myself. Should have taught him better. But really, it's your father's fault. He sets the example. No appreciation for me whatsoever."

Jane glanced at Gabriel, who chose just that moment to conveniently escape the room. "Uh . . . Mom? Did Dad do something to tick you off?"

Angela looked over her shoulder at Jane, her knife blade poised over the mangled parsley. "You don't want to know."

"Yes I do."

"I'm not going to go there, Janie. Oh, no. I believe every father deserves his child's respect, no matter *what* he does."

"So he did do something."

"I told you, I'm not going to go there." Angela scooped up the minced parsley and flung it onto the bowl of gnocchi. Then she stomped to the doorway and yelled, over the sound of the TV: "Dinner! *Sit.*"

Despite Angela's command, it was a few minutes before Frank Rizzoli and his two sons could tear themselves away from the TV. The halftime show had begun, and leggy girls in sequins strutted across the stage. The three Rizzoli men sat with eyes transfixed on the screen. Only Gabriel rose to help Jane and Angela shuttle platters of food into the dining room. Though he didn't say a word, Jane could read the look he gave her.

Since when did Christmas dinner turn into a war zone?

Angela slammed the bowl of roast potatoes on the table, walked into the living room, and snatched up the remote. With one click, she shut off the TV.

Frankie groaned. "Aw, Mom. They got Jessica Simpson coming on in ten . . ." He saw Angela's face and instantly shut up.

Mike was the first to jump up from the couch. Without a word, he scooted obediently into the dining room, followed at a more sullen pace by his brother Frankie and Frank senior.

The table was magnificently set. Candles flickered in crystal holders. Angela had laid out her blue and gold china and linen napkins and the new wineglasses she'd just bought over at the Dansk outlet. When Angela sat down and surveyed the feast, it was not with pride but with a look of sour dissatisfaction.

"This looks wonderful, Mrs. Rizzoli," said Gabriel.

"Why, *thank* you. I know *you* appreciate how much work goes into a meal like this. Since *you* know how to cook."

"Well, I didn't really have a choice, living on my own for so many years." He reached under the table and squeezed Jane's hand. "I'm lucky I found a girl who can cook." *When she gets around to it* was what he should have added.

"I taught Janie everything I know."

"Ma, can you pass the lamb?" called Frankie.

"*Excuse* me?"

"The lamb."

"What happened to *please*? I'm not passing it until you say the word."

Jane's father sighed. "Geez Louise, Angie. It's Christmas. Can we just feed the boy?"

"I've been feeding this boy for thirty-six years. He's not going to starve just because I ask for a little courtesy."

"Um . . . Mom?" ventured Mike. "Could you, uh, please pass the potatoes?" Meekly, he added again, "Please?"

"Yes, Mikey." Angela handed him the bowl.

For a moment no one spoke. The only sounds were jaws chewing and silverware sawing against china. Jane glanced at her father, seated at one end of the table, and then at her mother, seated at the other end. There was no eye contact between them. They might have been dining in different rooms, so distant were they from each other. Jane did not often take the time to study her parents, but tonight she felt compelled to, and what she saw depressed her. When did they get so old? When did Mom's eyes start to droop, and Dad's hair recede to such thin wisps?

When did they start hating each other?

"So Janie, tell us what kept you so busy last night," said her dad, his gaze on his daughter, studiously avoiding even a glance at Angela.

"Um, no one really wants to hear about it, Dad."

"I do," said Frankie.

"It's Christmas. I think maybe—"

"Who got whacked?"

She glanced across the table at her older brother. "A young woman. It wasn't pretty."

"Doesn't bother me any to talk about it," Frankie said, shoving a chunk of pink lamb into his mouth.

Frankie the Master Sergeant, challenging her to gross him out.

"This one *would* bother you. It sure as hell bothers me."

"Was she good-looking?"

"What's that got to do with it?"

"Just wondering."

"It's an idiotic question."

"Why? If she's good-looking, it helps you understand the guy's motive."

"To *kill* her? Jesus, Frankie."

"Jane," said her dad. "It's Christmas."

"Well, Janie has a point," snapped Angela.

Frank looked at his wife in astonishment. "Your daughter cusses at the dinner table, and you're getting on *my* back?"

"You think that only pretty women are worth killing?"

"Ma, I didn't say that," said Frankie.

"He didn't say that," said his father.

"But it's what you think. Both of you. Only good-looking women are worth the attention. Love 'em or kill 'em, it's only interesting if they're *pretty*."

"Oh, please."

"Please what, Frank? You know it's true. Look at *you*."

Jane and her brothers all frowned at their father.

"Look at him why, Ma?" asked Mike.

"Angela," said Frank, "it's Christmas."

"I *know* it's Christmas!" Angela jumped to her feet and gave a sob. "I *know*." She walked out of the room, into the kitchen.

Jane looked at her father. "What's going on?"

Frank shrugged. "Women that age. Change of life."

"This isn't just change of life. I'm going to go see what's bothering her." Jane rose from her chair and followed her mother into the kitchen.

"Mom?"

Angela did not seem to hear her. She was standing with her back turned, whipping cream in a stainless steel bowl. The beater clattered, sending flecks of white spraying across the countertop.

"Mom, are you okay?"

"Gotta get the dessert started. I completely forgot about whipping the cream."

"What's the matter?"

"I should have had this ready before we sat down. You know your brother Frankie gets impatient if he has to wait too long for the next course. If we make him sit there for more than five minutes, next thing you know, he'll turn on that TV again." Angela reached for the sugar and sprinkled a spoonful of it into the bowl as the beater churned up the cream. "At least Mikey tries his best to be nice. Even when all he sees are bad examples. Every which way he looks, just bad examples."

"Look, I *know* something's wrong."

Angela shut off the beater and, with shoulders slumped, she stared at the cream, now whipped up so thick it was almost butter. "It's not your problem, Janie."

"If it's yours, it's mine."

Her mother turned and looked at her. "Marriage is harder than you think."

"What did Dad do?"

Angela untied her apron and tossed it on the counter. "Can you serve the shortcake for me? I've got a headache. I'm going upstairs to lie down."

"Mom, let's talk about this."

"I'm not going to say anything else. I'm not that kind of mother. I'd never force my kids to choose sides." Angela walked out of the kitchen and thumped upstairs to her bedroom.

Bewildered, Jane went back into the dining room. Frankie was too busy sawing into his second helping of lamb even to look up. But Mike had an anxious look on his face. Frankie might be thick as a plank, but Mike clearly understood that something was seriously wrong tonight. She looked at her father, who was emptying the bottle of Chianti into his glass.

"Dad? You want to tell me what this is all about?"

Her father took a gulp of wine. "No."

"She's really upset."

"And that's between her and me, okay?" He stood up and gave Frankie a clap on the shoulder. "C'mon. I think we can still catch the third quarter."

"This was the most screwed-up Christmas we've ever had," said Jane as they drove home. Regina had fallen asleep in her car seat, and for the first time all evening Jane and Gabriel could have a conversation without distractions. "It's not usually this way. I mean, we have our squabbles and all, but my mom usually wrangles us all together in the end." She glanced at her husband, whose face was unreadable in the shadowy car. "I'm sorry."

"For what?"

"You had no idea you were marrying into a nuthouse. Now you're probably wondering what you got yourself into."

"Yep. I'd say it's time to trade in the wife."

"Well, you're thinking that a *little,* aren't you?"

"Jane, don't be ridiculous."

"Hell, there are times when *I'd* like to run away from my family."

"But I definitely don't want to run away from you." He turned his gaze back to the road, where windblown snow swirled past their headlights. For a moment they drove without speaking. Then he said, "You know, I never heard my parents argue. Not once, in all the years I was growing up."

"Go ahead, rub it in. I know my family's a bunch of loudmouths."

"You come from a family that makes its feelings known, that's all. They slam doors and they yell and they laugh like hyenas."

"Oh, this is getting better and better."

"I wish I'd grown up in a family like that."

"Right." She laughed.

"My parents didn't yell, Jane, and they didn't slam doors. They didn't laugh much, either. No, Colonel Dean's family was far too disciplined to ever stoop to anything as common as emotions. I don't remember him ever saying, 'I love you,' to either me or to my mother. I had to learn to say it. And I'm still learning." He looked at her. "You taught me how."

She touched his thigh. Her cool impenetrable guy. There were still a few things left to teach him.

"So never apologize for them," he said. "They're the ones who made you."

"Sometimes I wonder about that. I look at Frankie

and I think, please God, let me be the baby they found on the doorstep."

He laughed. "It was pretty tense tonight. What *was* the story there, anyway?"

"I don't know." She sank back against the seat. "But sooner or later, we'll hear all about it."

SIX

JANE SLIPPED paper booties over her shoes, donned a surgical gown, and looped the ties behind her waist. Gazing through the glass partition into the autopsy lab, she thought: *I really don't want to go in there*. But already Frost was in the room, gowned and masked, with just enough of his face visible for Jane to see his grimace. Maura's assistant, Yoshima, pulled x-rays out of an envelope and mounted them on the viewing box. Maura's back obstructed Jane's view of the table, hiding what she had little wish to confront. Just an hour ago, she had been sitting at her kitchen table, Regina cooing on her lap as Gabriel had cooked breakfast. Now the scrambled eggs churned in her stomach and she wanted to yank off this gown and walk back out of the building, into the purifying snow.

Instead she pushed through the door, into the autopsy room.

Maura glanced over her shoulder, and her face betrayed no qualms about the procedure to follow. She was merely a professional like any other, about to do her job. Though they both dealt in death, Maura was on far more intimate terms with it, far more comfortable staring into its face.

"We were just about to start," said Maura.

"I got hung up in traffic. The roads are a mess out there this morning." Jane tied on her mask as she moved toward the foot of the table. She avoided looking at the remains but focused, instead, on the x-ray viewing box.

Yoshima flipped the switch and the light flickered on, glowing behind two rows of films. Skull x-rays. But these were unlike any skull films Jane had seen before. Where the cervical spine should be, she saw only a few vertebrae, and then . . . nothing. Just the ragged shadow of soft tissue where the neck had been severed. She pictured Yoshima positioning that head for the films. Had it rolled around like a beach ball as he'd set it on the film cassette, as he'd angled the collimator? She turned away from the light box.

And found herself staring at the table. At the remains, displayed in anatomical position. The torso was on its back, the severed parts laid out approximately where they should be. A jigsaw puzzle in flesh and bone, the pieces waiting for reassembly. Though she did not want to look at it, there it was: the head, which had tilted onto its left ear, as though the victim was turning to look sideways.

"I need to approximate this wound," said Maura. "Can you help me hold it in position?" A pause. "Jane?"

Startled, Jane met Maura's gaze. "What?"

"Yoshima's going to take photos, and I need to get a look through the magnifier." Maura grasped the cranium in her gloved hands and rotated the head, trying to match the wound edges. "Here, just hold it in this position. Pull on some gloves and come around to this end."

Jane glanced at Frost. *Better you than me,* his eyes said. She moved to the head of the table. There she paused to snap on gloves, then reached down to cradle the head. Found herself gazing into the victim's eyes, the corneas dull as wax. A day and a half in a refrigerator had chilled the flesh, and as she cupped the face, she thought of the butcher counter in her local supermarket, with its icy chickens wrapped in plastic. We are all, in the end, merely meat.

Maura bent over the wound, studying it through the magnifier. "There seems to be a single sweep across the anterior. Very sharp blade. The only notching I see is quite a ways back, under the ears. Minimal bread-knife repetition."

"A bread knife's not exactly sharp," said Frost, his voice sounding very far away. Jane looked up and saw that he had retreated from the table and was standing halfway to the sink, his hand covering his mask.

"By bread-knifing, I'm not referring to the blade," said Maura. "It's a cutting pattern. Repeated slices going deeper, in the same plane. What we see here is one very deep initial slice, cutting right through the thyroid cartilage, down to the spinal column. Then a quick disarticulation, between the second and third cervical vertebrae. It could have taken less than a minute to complete this decapitation."

Yoshima moved in with the digital camera, taking photos of the approximated wound. Frontal view, lateral. Horror from every angle.

"Okay, Jane," said Maura. "Let's take a look at the incision plane." Maura grasped the head and turned it upside down. "Hold it there for me."

Jane caught a glimpse of severed flesh and the open windpipe, and she abruptly averted her gaze, blindly holding the head in place.

Again, Maura moved in with the magnifier to examine the cut surface. "I see striations on the thyroid cartilage. I think the blade was serrated. Get some shots of this."

Once again, the shutter clicked as Yoshima leaned in for more photos. *My hands will be in these shots,* thought Jane, *this moment preserved for the evidence files. Her head, my hands.*

"You said . . . you said that was arterial spray on the wall," said Frost.

Maura nodded. "In the bedroom."

"She was alive."

"Yes."

"And this—decapitation—took only seconds?"

"With a sharp knife, a skillful hand, a killer could certainly do it in that time. Only the vertebral column might slow him down."

"Then she knew, didn't she? She must have felt it."

"I highly doubt that."

"If someone cuts off your head, you'd be conscious for at least a few seconds. That's what I heard on *The Art Bell Show.* Some doctor was on the radio with him, talking about what it's like to be guillotined. That you're probably still conscious as your head drops into the bucket. You can actually feel yourself falling into it."

"That may be true, but—"

"The doctor said that Mary, Queen of Scots was still trying to speak, even after they cut off her head. Her lips kept moving."

"Jesus, Frost," said Jane. "Like I need to be creeped out even more?"

"It's possible, isn't it? That this victim felt her head come off?"

"It's highly unlikely," said Maura. "And I'm not saying that just to ease your mind." She turned the head sideways on the table. "Feel the cranium. Right here."

Frost stared at her in horror. "No, that's okay. I don't need to."

"Come on. Pull on a glove and run your fingers over the temporal bone. There's a scalp laceration. I didn't see it until we washed away the blood. Palpate the skull here and tell me what you feel."

It was clearly the last thing Frost wanted to do, but he pulled on a glove and tentatively placed his fingers on the cranium. "There's a, uh, dip in the bone."

"A depressed skull fracture. You can see it on x-ray." Maura crossed to the light box and pointed to the skull table. "On the lateral film, you see fractures fanning out from that impact point. They radiate like a spiderweb across the temporal bone. In fact, that's exactly what we call this type of fracture. A mosaic or spiderweb pattern. It's in a particularly critical location, because the middle meningeal artery runs right under here. If you rupture that, the patient bleeds into the cranial cavity. When we open the skull, we'll see if that's what happened." She looked at Frost. "This was a significant blow to the head. I think the victim was unconscious when the cutting began."

"But still alive."

"Yes. She was definitely still alive."

"You don't *know* that she was unconscious."

"There are no defense wounds on her limbs. No physical evidence that she fought back. You don't just let someone cut your throat without a struggle. I think she was stunned by that blow. I don't think she felt the blade." Maura paused and added, quietly, "At least, I hope not." She moved to the corpse's right side, grasped the amputated arm, and lifted the incised end to the magnifier. "We have more tool markings here on the cartilage surface, where he disarticulated the elbow joint," she said. "It looks like the same blade was used here. Very sharp, serrated edge." She opposed the unattached arm to the elbow, as though assembling a mannequin, and eyed the match. There was no expression of horror on her face, only concentration. She might be studying widgets or ball bearings, not incised flesh. Not the limb of a woman who'd once lifted that arm to brush back her hair, to wave, to dance. How did Maura do it? How did she walk into this building every morning, knowing what waited for her? Day after day, picking up the scalpel, dissecting the tragedy of lives cut short? *I deal with those tragedies, too. But I don't have to saw open skulls or thrust my hands into chests.*

Maura circled to the corpse's left side. Without hesitation, she picked up the severed hand. Chilled and drained of blood, it looked like wax, not flesh, like a movie propmaster's idea of what a real hand would look like. Maura swung the magnifier over it and inspected the raw, cut surface. For a moment she said nothing, but a frown was now etched on her forehead.

She set down the hand and lifted the left arm to examine the wrist stump. Her frown deepened. Again she picked up the hand and opposed the two wounds, trying to match the incised surfaces, hand to wrist, waxy skin to waxy skin.

Abruptly she set down the body parts and looked at Yoshima. "Could you put up the wrist and hand films?"

"You're done with all these skull x-rays?"

"I'll get back to those later. Right now I want to see the left hand and wrist."

Yoshima removed the first set of x-rays and mounted a fresh set. Against the backlight of the viewing box, hand and finger bones glowed, the columns of phalanges like slender stalks of bamboo. Maura stripped off her gloves and approached the light box, her gaze riveted on the images. She said nothing; it was her silence that told Jane that something was very wrong.

Maura turned and looked at her. "Have you searched the victim's entire house?"

"Yes, of course."

"The *whole* house? Every closet, every drawer?"

"There wasn't a lot there. She'd moved in just a few months before."

"And the refrigerator? The freezer?"

"CSU went through it. Why?"

"Come look at this x-ray."

Jane pulled off her soiled gloves and crossed to the light box to scan the films. She saw nothing there to account for Maura's sudden tone of urgency, nothing that did not correspond with what she saw lying on the table. "What am I supposed to look at?"

"You see this view of the hand? These little bones here are called the carpals. They make up the base of the hand, before the finger bones branch off." Maura took Jane's hand to demonstrate, turning it palm side up, revealing the scar that would forever remind Jane of what another killer had done to her. A record of violence, marked in her flesh by Warren Hoyt. But Maura made no comment on the scar; instead she pointed to the meaty base of Jane's palm, near the wrist.

"The carpal bones are here. On the x-ray, they look like eight little stones. They're just small chunks of bone, held together by ligaments and muscles and connective tissue. These give our hands flexibility, allow us to do a whole range of amazing tasks, from sculpting to playing the piano."

"Okay. So?"

"This one here, in this proximal row"—Maura pointed to the x-ray, to a bone near the wrist—"it's called the scaphoid. You'll notice there's a joint space beneath it, and then on this film, there's a distinct chip of another bone. It's part of the styloid process. When he cut off this hand, he also took off a fragment of the arm bone."

"I'm still not getting the significance."

"Now look at the x-ray of the arm stump." Maura pointed to a different film. "You see the distal end of the two forearm bones. The thinner bone is the ulna—the funny bone. And the thick one, on the thumb side, is the radius. Here's that styloid process I was talking about earlier. You see what I'm getting at?"

Jane frowned. "It's intact. On this arm x-ray, that bone is all here."

"That's right. Not only is it intact, there's even a chunk of the next bone still attached to it. A chip from the scaphoid."

In that chilly room, Jane's face suddenly felt numb. "Oh man," she said softly. "This is starting to sound bad."

"It is bad."

Jane turned and crossed back to the table. She stared down at the severed hand, lying beside what she had believed—what they had all believed—was the arm it had once been attached to.

"The cut surfaces don't match," said Maura. "Neither do the x-rays."

Frost said, "You're telling us this hand doesn't belong to her?"

"We'll need DNA analysis to confirm it. But I think the evidence is right here, on the light box." She turned and looked at Jane. "There's another victim that you haven't found yet. And we have her left hand."

SEVEN

JULY 15, WEDNESDAY. Phase of the moon: New.

These are the rituals of the Saul family.

At one P.M., Uncle Peter comes home from his half day at the clinic. He changes into jeans and a T-shirt and heads for his vegetable garden, where a jungle of tomato plants and cucumber vines weigh down their string trellises.

At two P.M., little Teddy comes up the hill from the lake, carrying his fishing pole. But no catch. I have not yet seen him bring home a single fish.

At two-fifteen, Lily's two girlfriends walk up the hill, carrying bathing suits and beach towels. The taller one—I think her name is Sarah—also brings a radio. Its strange and thumping music now disturbs the otherwise silent afternoon. Their towels spread out on the lawn, the three girls bask in the sun like drowsy felines. Their skin gleams with suntan lotion. Lily sits up and reaches for her bottle of water. As she lifts it to her lips, she suddenly goes still, her gaze on my window. She sees me watching her.

It is not the first time.

Slowly she sets down the water bottle and says something to her two friends. The other girls now sit up and look in my direction. For a moment they stare at me, as I am staring at them. Sarah shuts off the radio. They all rise to their feet, shake out their towels, and come into the house.

A moment later, Lily knocks on my door. She doesn't wait for an answer but walks uninvited into my room.

"Why do you watch us?" she says.

"I was just looking out the window."

"You're looking at us."

"Because you happen to be there."

Her gaze falls on my desk. Lying open there is the book my mother gave me when I turned ten years old. Popularly known as the Egyptian Book of the Dead, it is a collection of ancient coffin texts. All the spells and incantations one needs to navigate the afterlife. She moves closer to the book, but hesitates to touch it, as though the pages might burn her fingers.

"Are you interested in death rituals?" I ask.

"It's just superstition."

"How do you know unless you've tried them?"

"You can actually read these hieroglyphs?"

"My mother taught me. But those are just minor spells. Not the really powerful ones."

"And what can a powerful spell do?" She looks at me, her gaze so direct and unflinching that I wonder if she is more than she seems. If I've underestimated her.

"The most powerful spells," I tell her, "can bring the dead back to life."

"You mean, like in The Mummy?" She laughs.

I hear more giggles behind me and turn to see her two friends standing in the doorway. They've been eavesdropping, and they look at me with disdain. I am clearly the weirdest boy they have ever met. They have no idea how different I really am.

Lily closes the Book of the Dead. "Let's go swimming, girls," she says, and walks out of the room, trailing the sweet scent of her suntan lotion.

Through my window, I watch them head down the hill, toward the lake. The house is now quiet.

I go into Lily's room. From her hairbrush, I pull off long brown strands of hair and slip them into my pocket. I uncap the lotions and creams on her dresser and sniff them; each scent brings with it the flash of a memory: Lily at the breakfast table. Lily sitting beside me in the car. I open her drawers, her closet, and touch her clothes. Clothes that any American teenager might wear. She's just a girl after all, nothing more. But she needs watching.

It's what I do best.

EIGHT

Lily Saul bolted awake, straight from a deep sleep, and lay gasping among twisted bedsheets. The amber light of late afternoon glowed through the crack between the partially closed wooden shutters. In the gloom above her bed, a fly buzzed, circling in anticipation of a taste of her damp flesh. Her fear. She sat up on the thin mattress, shoved back tangled hair, and massaged her head as her heartbeat gradually slowed. Sweat trickled from her armpits, soaking into her T-shirt. She had managed to sleep through the worst heat of the afternoon, but the room still felt suffocating, the air thick enough to smother her. I can't keep living this way forever, she thought, or I'll go insane.

Maybe I'm already insane.

She rose from the bed and crossed to the window. Even the ceramic tiles beneath her feet radiated heat. Throwing open the shutters, she gazed across the tiny piazza, at buildings baking like stone ovens in the sun. A golden haze leafed domes and rooftops in umber. The summer heat had driven the sensible locals of Siena indoors; only the tourists would be out now, wandering wide-eyed through narrow alleys, huffing and sweating their way up the steep incline to the basilica or posing for photographs on the Piazza del Campo, their shoe soles melting and tacky on the scorching brickwork: all the usual tourist things that she herself had done when she'd first arrived in Siena, before she'd settled into the rhythms of the natives, before the heat of August had closed in on this medieval city.

Below her window, on the piazzetta, not a soul moved. But as she was turning away, she spied a twitch of motion in the shadow of a doorway. She went very still, her gaze fixed on the spot. *I can't see him. Can he see me?* Then the inhabitant sheltering in that doorway emerged from its hiding place, trotted across the piazzetta, and vanished.

Only a dog.

With a laugh, she turned from the window. Not every shadow hid a monster. *But some did. Some shadows follow you, threaten you, wherever you go.*

In her tiny bathroom she splashed lukewarm water on her face, pulled back her dark hair in a ponytail. She did not waste time with makeup; over the past year, she had shed any habits that slowed her down. She lived out of one small suitcase plus a backpack, owned only two pairs of shoes, her sandals and sneakers. Jeans and T-shirts and sweaters took her from the heat of summer to the sleet of winter. When you got right down to it, survival was all a matter of layering, whether it was with clothes or emotional defenses. Keep out the elements, ward off attachments.

Stay safe.

She grabbed her backpack and stepped out of the room into the gloomy hallway. There she paused, as she always did, and inserted a torn bit of cardboard matchstick into the lower jamb as she closed the door and locked it. Not that the ancient lock would keep anyone out. Like the building, it was probably centuries old.

Bracing herself for the heat, she walked outside, into the piazzetta. She paused, scanning the deserted space. It was still too early for most locals to be out and about, but in another hour or so, they would stir from their meal-induced naps and start back to their shops, their offices. Lily still had some time to herself before Giorgio expected her back at work. It was a chance to walk and clear away the cobwebs, to visit her favorite haunts in her favorite city. She had been in Siena only three months, and already she could feel the town slipping away from her. Soon she'd have to leave it, as she'd left every other place she'd loved.

I have stayed here too long already.

She walked through the piazzetta and headed up the narrow alley leading to Via di Fontebranda. Her route took her toward the town's ancient fountain house, past buildings that once housed medieval craftsmen and later slaughterhouses. The Fontebranda was a Siena landmark once celebrated by Dante, and its waters were still clear, still inviting, even after the passage of centuries. She had walked here once beneath the full moon. According to legend, that was when werewolves came to bathe in the waters, just before transforming back to their human forms. That night, she'd glimpsed no werewolves, only drunken tourists. Perhaps they were one and the same.

Moving up the hill now, her sturdy sandals slapping against griddle-hot stones, she walked past the Sanctuary and House of Saint Catherine, the patron saint of Siena, who had survived for long periods on no other food but the Blessed Sacrament. Saint Catherine had experienced vivid visions of Hell and Purgatory and Heaven, and had lusted for the glory and divine agony of martyrdom. After a long and uncomfortable illness, all she'd managed was a disappointingly ordinary death. As Lily labored up the hill, she thought: *I have seen visions of Hell, too. But I want no part of martyrdom. I want to live. I'll do anything to live.*

By the time she climbed to the Basilica di San Domenico, her T-shirt was soaked with sweat. She stood panting at the top of the hill, gazing down upon the city, its tiled roofs blurred to soft focus in the summery haze. It was a view that made her heart ache, because she knew she would have to leave it. Already she'd lingered in Siena longer than she should have, and she could now feel the evil catching up to her, could almost smell its faint, foul odor wafting in on the wind. All around her, doughy-thighed tourists swarmed the hilltop, but she stood in silent isolation, a ghost among the living. *Already dead,* she thought. *For me, this is borrowed time.*

"Excuse me, Miss? Do you speak English?"

Startled, Lily turned to see a middle-aged man and woman wearing matching U Penn T-shirts and baggy shorts. The man was clutching a complicated-looking camera.

"Do you want me to take your picture?" Lily asked.

"That'd be great! Thanks."

Lily took the camera. "Is there a trick to this one?"

"No, just press the button."

The couple linked arms and posed with the view of Siena stretching like a medieval tapestry behind them. Their souvenir of a strenuous climb on a hot day.

"You're American, aren't you?" said the woman as Lily handed back the camera. "So where are you from?" It was merely a friendly question, something countless tourists asked each other, a way to connect with fellow travelers far from home. Instantly it put Lily on guard. *Their curiosity is almost certainly innocent. But I don't know these people. I can't be certain.*

"Oregon," she lied.

"Really? Our son lives there! Which city?"

"Portland."

"Now, isn't it a small world? He lives on Northwest Irving Street. Is that anywhere near you?"

"No." Already Lily was backing away, retreating from these overbearing people who would probably next insist that she join them for coffee, and ask her ever more questions, probing for details she had no intention of sharing. "Have a nice visit!"

"Say, would you like to—"

"I have to meet someone." She gave a wave and fled. The doors of the basilica loomed ahead, offering sanctuary. She stepped inside, into cool silence, and breathed a sigh of relief. The church was nearly empty; only a few tourists wandered the vast space, and their voices were blessedly hushed. She walked toward the Gothic arch, where the sun glowed through stained glass in chips of jeweled light, past the tombs of Sienese nobles that lined both walls. Turning into a chapel niche, she stopped before the gilded marble altar and stared at the tabernacle containing the preserved head of Saint Catherine of Siena. Her mortal remains had been divided and distributed as holy relics, her body in Rome, her foot in Venice. Had she known this would be her fate? That her head would be wrenched from her decaying torso, her mummified face displayed to countless sweaty tourists and chattering schoolchildren?

The saint's leathery eye sockets gazed back from behind glass. *This is what death looks like. But you already know, don't you, Lily Saul?*

Shivering, Lily left the chapel niche and hurried through the echoing church, back toward the exit. Outside again, she was almost grateful for the heat. But not for the tourists. So many strangers with cameras. Any one of them might be furtively snapping her photo.

She left the basilica and started back downhill, through the Piazza Salimbeni, past the Palazzo Tolomei. The tangle of narrow streets easily befuddled tourists, but Lily knew the way through the maze, and she walked quickly, purposefully, toward her destination. She was late now, because she'd lingered too long on the hill, and Giorgio would surely scold her. Not that the prospect offered any sort of terror, for Giorgio's grumblings never resulted in consequences of any significance.

So when she arrived at work fifteen minutes late, she did not feel even a hint of trepidation. The little bell tinkled on the door, announcing her entrance as she stepped into the shop, and she inhaled the familiar scents of dusty books and camphor and cigarette smoke. Giorgio and his son, Paolo, were hunched over a desk near the back of the shop, both of them wearing magnifying loupes around their heads. When Paolo looked up, one enormous eye stared like a cyclops at Lily.

"You must see this!" he called out to her in Italian. "It just arrived. Sent by a collector from Israel."

They were so excited, they hadn't even noticed she was late. She set her backpack down behind her desk and squeezed her way past the antique table and the oak monastery bench. Past the Roman sarcophagus, which now served ignominiously as a temporary container for file storage. She stepped over an open crate that had spilled wooden packing shavings onto the floor, and frowned at the object on Giorgio's desk. It was a block of carved marble, perhaps part of an edifice. She noticed the patina on two adjoining surfaces, a soft gleam left by centuries of exposure to wind and rain and sun. It was a cornerstone.

Young Paolo pulled off his loupe, and his dark hair stood up. Grinning at her with those earlike tufts of hair, he looked like one of the legendary Sienese werewolves, albeit a perfectly harmless and utterly charming one. Like his father, Paolo possessed not a single ounce of cruelty, and were it not for the fact that she would inevitably be forced to break his heart, Lily would happily have taken him as a lover.

"I think you will like this piece," he said, and offered her his magnifier. "It is just the sort of thing you're always interested in."

She bent over the cornerstone and studied the manlike figure carved there. It was standing upright, with a skirt around its waist and decorative bracelets and anklets. But the head was not human. She slid the magnifier over her head and leaned in closer. As the details came alive through the lens, she felt a sudden chill. She saw jutting canine teeth and fingers tipped with claws. And horns.

She straightened, her throat dry, her voice oddly distant. "You said the collector is from Israel?"

Giorgio nodded and took off his loupe, revealing an older, plumper version of Paolo. The same dark eyes, but webbed with laugh lines. "This man is new to us. So we're not sure of the provenance. Whether to trust him."

"How did he happen to send us this piece?"

Giorgio shrugged. "It arrived in the crate today. That's all I know."

"He wants you to sell it for him?"

"He asked only for an appraisal. What do you think?"

She rubbed a finger across the patina. Felt the chill again, seeping from the stone to her flesh. "Where does he say it comes from?"

Giorgio reached for a bundle of papers. "He says he acquired it eight years ago, in Tehran. I think it must be smuggled." He gave another shrug, a wink. "But what do we know, eh?"

"Persian," she murmured. "This is Ahriman."

"What is Ahriman?" asked Paolo.

"Not a what, a who. In ancient Persia, Ahriman is

a demon. The spirit of destruction." She set the magnifier on the desk and took a deep breath. "He's their personification of evil."

Giorgio gave a laugh and rubbed his hands in glee. "You see, Paolo? I told you she'd know. Devils, demons, she knows them all. Every time, she has the answer."

"Why?" Paolo looked at her. "I never understood why you're so interested in evil things."

How could she answer that question? How could she tell him that she'd once looked the Beast in the eye, and It had looked right back at her? Had seen her? *It's been pursuing me ever since.*

"So it is authentic?" asked Giorgio. "This cornerstone?"

"Yes, I believe it is."

"Then I should write him at once, eh? Our new friend in Tel Aviv. Tell him he has sent it to the right dealer, one who understands its value." With great care, he set the stone back into its packing crate. "For something this special, we will certainly find a buyer."

Who would want that monstrosity in their home? Lily thought. *Who'd want to have evil staring at you from your own wall?*

"Ah, I almost forgot," said Giorgio. "Did you know you have an admirer?"

Lily frowned at him. "What?"

"A man, he came to the shop at lunchtime. He asked if an American woman worked for me."

She went very still. "What did you tell him?"

Paolo said, "I stopped Father from saying anything. We could get into trouble, since you have no permit."

"But now I've been thinking about it some more," said Giorgio. "And I think maybe the man's just sweet on you. And that's why he inquired." Giorgio winked.

She swallowed. "Did he say his name?"

Giorgio gave his son a playful slap on the arm. "You see?" he scolded. "You move too slowly, boy. Now another man will come and swoop her away from us."

"What was his name?" Lily asked again, her voice sharper. But neither father nor son seemed to register the change in her demeanor. They were too busy teasing each other.

"He didn't leave one," said Giorgio. "I think he wants to play the incognito game, eh? Make you guess."

"Was he a young man? What did he look like?"

"Oh. So you're interested."

"Was there anything"—she paused—"unusual about him?"

"What do you mean, unusual?"

Not human was what she wanted to say.

"He had very blue eyes," offered Paolo brightly. "Strange eyes. Bright, like an angel's."

Quite the opposite of an angel.

She turned and immediately crossed to the window, where she peered out through dusty glass at passersby. *He's here,* she thought. *He's found me in Siena.*

"He'll come back, *cara mia.* Just be patient," said Giorgio.

And when he does, I can't be here.

She snatched up her backpack. "I'm sorry," she said. "I'm not feeling well."

"What's the matter?"

"I think I shouldn't have eaten that fish last night. It's not agreeing with me. I need to go home."

"Paolo will walk you there."

"No! No." She yanked open the door, setting off a violent jangle of the bell. "I'll be fine." She fled the shop and did not glance back, for fear that Paolo would try to run after her, would insist on playing the gentleman and escort. She couldn't afford to let him slow her down. Haste was everything now.

She took a circuitous route back to her flat, avoiding crowded piazzas and major streets. Instead she cut through tiny alleys, scrambled up narrow steps between medieval walls, steadily circling toward the Fontebranda neighborhood. It would take her only five minutes to pack. She had learned to be mobile, to move at an instant's notice, and all she had to do was toss her clothes and toilet case into the suitcase and grab the stash of Euros from its hiding place behind the dresser. These past three months, Giorgio had paid her under the table in cash, knowing full well that she had no work permit. She'd collected a nice nest egg to tide her over between jobs, enough to last her till she settled into a new town. She should grab the cash and suitcase and just go. Straight to the bus station.

No. No, on second thought, that's where he'd expect her to go. A taxi would be better. Costly, yes, but if she used it only to get out of town, maybe as far as San Gimignano, she could catch a train to Florence. There, among the teeming crowds, she could disappear.

She did not enter her building through the piazzetta; instead, she approached through the shadowy side street, past rubbish cans and locked bicycles, and climbed the back stairs. Music was blaring in one of the other flats, spilling out an open doorway into the hall. It was that sullen teenager next door. Tito and his damn radio. She caught a glimpse of the boy, slouched like a zombie on the couch. She continued past his flat, toward hers. She was just taking out her keys when she spotted the torn matchstick and froze.

It was no longer wedged in the doorjamb; it had fallen to the floor.

Her heart pounded as she backed away. As she retreated past Tito's doorway, the boy looked up from the couch and waved. Of all the inconvenient times for him to start being friendly. *Don't say a word to me,* she silently pleaded. *Don't you dare say a word.*

"You're not at work today?" he called out in Italian.

She turned and ran down the stairs. Almost tripped over the bicycles as she fled into the alley. *I'm too fucking late,* she thought as she hurtled around the corner and scrambled up a short flight of steps. Ducking into an overgrown garden, she crouched behind a crumbling wall and froze there, scarcely daring to breathe. Five minutes, ten. She heard no footsteps, no sounds of pursuit.

Maybe the matchstick fell by itself. Maybe I can still get my suitcase. My money.

Risking a glance over the wall, she stared up the alley. No one.

Do I chance it? Do I dare?

She slipped into the alley again. Made her way down a series of narrow streets until she reached the outskirts of the piazzetta. But she did not step into the open; instead she edged toward the corner of a building and peered up at the window of her own flat. The wooden shutters were open, as she'd left them. Through the gathering twilight, she saw something move in that window. A silhouette, just for a second, framed by the shutters.

She jerked back behind the building. Shit. *Shit.*

She unzipped her backpack and rifled through her wallet. Forty-eight Euros. Enough for a few meals and a bus ticket. Maybe enough for a cab ride to San Gimignano, but not much more. She had an ATM card, but she dared not use it except in large cities, where she could easily slip straight into a crowd. The last time she'd used it was in Florence, on a Saturday night, when the streets were thronged.

Not here, she thought. *Not in Siena.*

She left the piazzetta and headed deep into the back alleys of the Fontebranda. Here was the neighborhood she knew best; here she could elude anyone. She found her way to a tiny coffee bar that she'd discovered weeks ago, frequented only by locals. Inside, it was gloomy as a cave and thick with cigarette smoke. She settled at a corner table, ordered a cheese and tomato sandwich and an espresso. Then, as the evening passed, another espresso. And another. Tonight, she would not be sleeping. She could walk to Florence. It was only—what, twenty, twenty-five miles? She'd slept in the fields before. She'd stolen peaches, plucked grapes in the dark. She could do it again.

She devoured her sandwich, swept every last crumb into her mouth. No telling when she'd eat again. By the time she stepped out of the coffee bar, night had fallen and she could move through dark streets with little fear of being recognized. There was one other option. It was risky, but it would save her from a twenty-five-mile hike.

And Giorgio would do it for her. He would drive her to Florence.

She walked and walked, giving the busy Campo a wide berth, sticking to the side streets. By the time she reached Giorgio's residence, her calves were aching, her feet sore from the uneven cobblestones. She paused in the cover of darkness, gazing at the window. Giorgio's wife had died years ago, and father and son now shared the flat. The lights were on inside, but she saw no movement on the first floor.

She was not foolhardy enough to knock at the front door. Instead she circled around to the small garden in back, let herself in through the gate, and brushed past fragrant thyme and lavender to knock at the kitchen door.

No one answered.

She strained to hear if the TV was on, thinking that perhaps they couldn't hear her, but she heard only the muted sounds of traffic from the street.

She tried the knob; the door swung open.

One look was all it took. One glimpse of blood, of

splayed arms and ruined faces. Of Giorgio and Paolo, tangled together in a last embrace.

She backed away, hand clapped to her mouth, her vision blurred in a wash of tears. *My fault. This is all my fault. They were killed because of me.*

Stumbling backward through lavender, she collided with the wooden gate. The jolt snapped her back to her senses.

Go. Run.

She scrambled out of the garden, not bothering to latch the gate behind her, and fled down the street, her sandals slapping against the cobblestones.

She did not slow her pace until she reached the outskirts of Siena.

NINE

"ARE WE absolutely certain there *is* a second victim?" asked Lieutenant Marquette. "We don't have DNA confirmation yet."

"But we do have two different blood types," said Jane. "The amputated hand belonged to someone with O positive blood. Lori-Ann Tucker is A positive. So Dr. Isles was absolutely correct."

There was a long silence in the conference room.

Dr. Zucker said softly, "This is getting very interesting."

Jane looked across the table at him. Forensic psychologist Dr. Lawrence Zucker's intent stare had always made her uncomfortable. He looked at her now as though she were the sole focus of his curiosity, and she could almost feel his gaze tunneling into her brain. They had worked together during the Surgeon investigation two and a half years ago, and Zucker knew just how haunted she'd been in the aftermath. He knew about her nightmares, her panic attacks. He'd seen the way she used to rub incessantly at the scars on her palms, as though to massage away the memories. Since then, the nightmares of Warren Hoyt had faded. But when Zucker looked at her this way, she felt exposed, because he knew just how vulnerable she'd once been. And she resented him for it.

She broke off her gaze and focused instead on the other two detectives, Barry Frost and Eve Kassovitz. Adding Kassovitz to the team had been a mistake. The woman's very public barfing into the snowbank was now common knowledge in the unit, and Jane could have predicted the practical jokes that followed. The day after Christmas, a giant plastic bucket, labeled with Kassovitz's name, had mysteriously appeared on the unit's reception desk. The woman should have just laughed it off, or maybe gotten pissed about it. Instead she looked as beaten down as a clubbed seal, and she sat slumped in her chair, too demoralized to say much. No way was Kassovitz going to survive this boys' club if she didn't learn to punch back.

"So we have a killer who not only dismembers his victims," said Zucker, "but he also transfers body parts between his crime scenes. Do you have a photo of the hand?"

"We have lots of photos," said Jane. She passed the autopsy file to Zucker. "By its appearance, we're pretty sure the hand is a female's."

The images were gruesome enough to turn anyone's stomach, but Zucker's face betrayed no shock, no disgust, as he flipped through them. Only keen curiosity. Or was that eagerness she saw in his eyes? Did he enjoy the view of atrocities visited on a young woman's body?

He paused over the photo of the hand. "No nail polish, but the fingers definitely look manicured.

Yes, I agree it looks like a woman's." He glanced at Jane, his pale eyes peering at her over wire-rim glasses. "What do you have back on these fingerprints?"

"The owner of that hand has no criminal record. No military service. Nothing in NCIC."

"She's not in any database?"

"Not her fingerprints, anyway."

"And this hand isn't medical waste? A hospital amputation, maybe?"

Frost said, "I checked with every medical center in the greater Boston area. In the past two weeks, there've been two hand amps, one at Mass Gen, another at Pilgrim Hospital. Both were the result of trauma. The first was a chain saw accident. The second was a dog attack. In both cases, the hands were so badly mangled they couldn't be reattached. And the first case was a man's."

"This hand was not dug up out of hospital waste," said Jane. "And it wasn't mangled. It was sliced off with a very sharp, serrated blade. Also, it wasn't done with any particular surgical skill. The tip of the radius was sheared off, with no apparent attempt at controlling blood loss. No tied-off vessels, no dissection of skin layers. Just a clean cut."

"Do we have any missing persons it might match?"

"Not in Massachusetts," said Frost. "We're widening the net. Any white female. She can't have gone missing too long ago, since the hand looks pretty fresh."

"It could have been frozen," said Marquette.

"No," said Jane. "There's no cellular damage under the microscope. That's what Dr. Isles said. When you freeze tissue, the expansion of water ruptures cells, and she didn't find that. The hand may have been refrigerated, or packed in ice water, like they do to transport harvested organs. But it wasn't frozen. So we think the owner of that hand was probably killed no more than a few days ago."

"If she was killed," said Zucker.

They all stared at him. The terrible implication of his words made them all pause.

"You think she could still be *alive*?" said Frost.

"Amputations in and of themselves aren't fatal."

"Oh, man," said Frost. "Cut off her hand without killing her . . ."

Zucker flipped through the rest of the autopsy photos, pausing over each one with the concentration of a jeweler peering through his loupe. At last he set them down. "There are two possible reasons why a killer would cut up a body. The first is purely practical. He needs to dispose of it. These are killers who are self-aware and goal-directed. They understand the need to dispose of forensic evidence and hide their crimes."

"Organized killers," said Frost.

"If dismemberment is followed by the scattering or concealment of body parts, that would imply planning. A cognitive killer."

"These parts weren't in any way concealed," said Jane. "They were left around the house, in places where he knew they'd be found." She handed another stack of photos to Zucker. "Those are from the crime scene."

He opened the folder and paused, staring at the

first image. "This gets even more interesting," he murmured.

He looks at a severed hand on a dinner plate, and that's the word that comes to mind?

"Who set the table?" He looked up at her. "Who laid out the dishes, the silverware, the wineglasses?"

"We believe the perp did."

"Why?"

"Who the hell knows why?"

"I mean, why do you assume *he* was the one who did it?"

"Because there was a smear of blood under one of the plates, where he handled it."

"Fingerprints?"

"Unfortunately, no. He wore gloves."

"Evidence of advance planning. Forethought." Zucker directed his gaze, once again, at the photo. "This is a setting for four. Is that significant?"

"Your guess is as good as ours. There were eight plates in the cabinet, so he could have put down more. But he chose to use only four."

Lieutenant Marquette asked, "What do you think we're dealing with here, Dr. Zucker?"

The psychologist didn't answer. He paged slowly through the photos, pausing at the image of the severed arm in the bathtub. Then he flipped to the photo of the kitchen, and he stopped. There was a very long silence as he stared at the melted candles, at the circle drawn on the floor. At what sat at the center of that circle.

"It looked like some kind of a weird ritual setup to us," said Frost. "The chalk circle, the burned candles."

"This certainly appears ritualistic." Zucker looked up, and the glitter in his eyes made a chill wash up the back of Jane's neck. "Did the perp draw this circle?"

Jane hesitated, startled by his question. "You mean—as opposed to the victim?"

"I'm not making any assumptions here. I hope you don't either. What makes you so certain the victim didn't draw this circle? That she didn't start off as a willing participant in the ritual?"

Jane felt like laughing. *Yeah, I'd volunteer to get my head cut off, too.* She said, "It had to be the killer who drew that circle and lit those candles. Because we found no pieces of chalk in the house. After he used it to draw on that kitchen floor, he took it with him."

Zucker leaned back in his chair, thinking. "So this killer dismembers, but doesn't conceal the body parts. He doesn't disfigure the face. He leaves little in the way of forensic evidence, indicating an awareness of law enforcement. Yet he hands us—so to speak—the biggest clue of all: the body part of another victim." He paused. "Was there semen left behind?"

"None was detected in the victim's body."

"And the crime scene?"

"CSU went all over that house with UV. The CrimeScope picked up hairs too numerous to count, but no semen."

"Again, characteristic of cognitive behavior. He leaves no evidence of sexual activity. If he is indeed a sexual killer, then he's controlled enough to wait until it's safe to enjoy his release."

"And if he's not a sexual killer?" asked Marquette.

"Then I'm not entirely sure what all of this represents," said Zucker. "But the dismemberment, the display of body parts. The candles, the chalk circle." He looked around the table. "I'm sure we're all thinking the same thing. Satanic rituals."

"It was Christmas Eve," added Marquette. "The holiest of nights."

"And our killer isn't there to honor the Prince of Peace," said Zucker. "No, he's trying to summon the Prince of Darkness."

"There's one other photo you should look at," said Jane, pointing to the stack of images that Zucker hadn't yet seen. "There was some writing, left on the wall. Drawn in the victim's blood."

Zucker found the photo. "Three upside-down crosses," he said. "These could well have satanic meanings. But what are these symbols beneath the crosses?"

"It's a word."

"I don't see it."

"It's a reverse image. You can read it if you hold it up to a mirror."

Zucker's eyebrow lifted. "You do know, don't you, the significance of mirror writing?"

"No. What's the significance?"

"When the Devil makes a deal to buy your soul, the pact is drawn up and signed in mirror writing." He frowned at the word. "So what does it say?"

"*Peccavi.* It's Latin. It means: 'I have sinned.' "

"A confession?" suggested Marquette.

"Or a boast," said Zucker. "Announcing to Satan,

'I've done your bidding, Master.' " He gazed at all the photos laid out on the table. "I would love to get this killer into an interview room. There's so much symbolism here. Why did he arrange the body parts in just this way? What's the meaning of the hand on the plate? The four place settings on the dining table?"

"The Four Horsemen of the Apocalypse," Detective Kassovitz said softly. It was one of the few times she'd spoken during the meeting.

"Why do you suggest that?" asked Zucker.

"We're talking about Satan. About sin." Kassovitz cleared her throat, seemed to gain her voice as she sat straighter. "These are biblical themes."

"The four place settings could also mean he has three invisible friends who are joining him for a midnight snack," said Jane.

"You don't buy into the biblical theme?" said Zucker.

"I know it *looks* like Satanism," said Jane. "I mean, we've got it all here—the circle and the candles. The mirror writing, the upside-down crosses. It's like we're *supposed* to come to that conclusion."

"You think it was merely staged this way?"

"Maybe to hide the real reason Lori-Ann Tucker was killed."

"What motives would there be? Did she have romantic problems?"

"She's divorced, but her ex-husband lives in New Mexico. They apparently had an amicable parting. She moved to Boston only three months ago. There seem to be no boyfriends."

"She had a job?"

Eve Kassovitz said, "I interviewed her supervisor over at the Science Museum. Lori-Ann worked in the gift shop. No one knew of any conflicts or any problems."

Zucker asked, "Are we absolutely sure about that?" He directed his question at Jane, not Kassovitz, a snub that made Kassovitz flush. It was yet another blow to her already battered self-esteem.

"Detective Kassovitz just told you what we know," said Jane, backing up her teammate.

"Okay," said Zucker. "Then why was this woman killed? Why stage it to *look* like Satanism, if it really isn't?"

"To make it interesting. To draw attention."

Zucker laughed. "As if it wouldn't already draw our attention?"

"Not ours. The attention of someone who's much more important to this perp."

"You're talking about Dr. O'Donnell, aren't you?"

"We know the killer called O'Donnell, but she claims she wasn't home."

"You don't believe her?"

"We can't confirm it, since she erased any phone message. She said it was a hang-up call."

"What makes you think that's not the truth?"

"You know who she is, don't you?"

He regarded her for a moment. "I know you two have had conflicts. That her friendship with Warren Hoyt bothers you."

"This isn't about me and O'Donnell—"

"But it is. She maintains a friendship with the man who almost killed you, the man whose most deeply held fantasy is to complete that job."

Jane leaned forward, every muscle suddenly taut. "Don't go there, Dr. Zucker," she said quietly.

He stared at her, and something he saw in her eyes made him slowly lean back in retreat. "You consider O'Donnell a suspect?" he said.

"I don't trust her. She's a gunslinger for the bad guys. Pay her enough to testify, and she'll walk into court and defend just about any killer. She'll claim he's neurologically damaged and not responsible for his actions. That he belongs in a hospital, not a jail."

Marquette added, "She's not popular with law enforcement, Dr. Zucker. Anywhere."

"Look, even if we *loved* her," said Jane, "we're still left with unanswered questions. Why did the killer call her from the crime scene? Why wasn't she at home? Why won't she tell us where she was?"

"Because she knows you're already hostile."

She has no idea how hostile I can get.

"Detective Rizzoli, are you implying that Dr. O'Donnell had something to do with this crime?"

"No. But she's not above exploiting it. Feeding off it. Whether she meant to or not, she inspired it."

"How?"

"You know how a pet cat will sometimes kill a mouse and bring it home to its master as sort of an offering? A token of affection?"

"You think our killer is trying to impress O'Donnell."

"That's why he called her. That's why he set up this elaborate death scene, to pique her interest. Then, to make sure his work gets noticed, he calls nine-one-one. And a few hours later, while we're standing in the kitchen, he calls the victim's house from a pay phone, just to make sure we're there. This perp is reeling us all in. Law enforcement. And O'Donnell."

Marquette said, "Does she realize how much danger she could be in? Being the focus of a killer's attention?"

"She didn't seem too impressed."

"What does it take to scare that woman?"

"Maybe when he sends her that little token of affection. The equivalent of a dead mouse." Jane paused. "Let's not forget. Lori-Ann Tucker's hand is still missing."

TEN

JANE COULD NOT STOP thinking about that hand as she stood in her kitchen, slicing cold chicken for a late-night snack. She carried it to the table, where her usually impeccably groomed husband was sitting with his sleeves rolled up, baby drool on his collar. Was there anything sexier than a man patiently burping his daughter? Regina gave a lusty belch and Gabriel laughed. What a sweet and perfect moment this was. All of them together and safe and healthy.

Then she looked down at the sliced chicken and she thought of what had rested on another dinner plate, on another woman's dining table. She pushed the plate aside.

We are just meat. Like chicken. Like beef.

"I thought you were hungry," said Gabriel.

"I guess I changed my mind. It suddenly doesn't look so appetizing."

"It's the case, isn't it?"

"I wish I could stop thinking about it."

"I saw the files you brought home tonight. Couldn't help looking through them. I'd be preoccupied, too."

Jane shook her head. "You're supposed to be on

vacation. What are you doing, checking out autopsy photos?"

"They were lying right there on the counter." He set Regina in her infant carrier. "You want to talk about it? Bounce it off me, if you'd like. If you think it'll help."

She glanced at Regina, who was watching them with alert eyes, and suddenly she gave a laugh. "Geez, when she's old enough to understand, this is gonna be *really* appropriate family conversation. *So, honey, how many headless corpses have you seen today?*"

"She can't understand us. So talk to me."

Jane got up and went to the refrigerator, took out a bottle of Adam's Ale, and popped off the top.

"Jane?"

"You really want to hear the details?"

"I want to know what's bothering you so much."

"You saw the photos. You know what's bothering me." She sat down again and took a gulp of beer. "Sometimes," she said quietly, looking down at the sweating bottle, "I think it's crazy to have children. You love them, raise them. Then you watch them walk into a world where they just get hurt. Where they meet up with people like . . ." *Like Warren Hoyt* was what she was thinking, but she didn't say his name; she almost never said his name. It was as if saying it aloud was to summon the Devil himself.

The sudden buzz of the intercom made her snap straight. She looked up at the wall clock. "It's ten-thirty."

"Let me see who it is." Gabriel walked into the

living room and pressed the intercom button. "Yes?"

An unexpected voice responded over the speaker. "It's me," said Jane's mother.

"Come on up, Mrs. Rizzoli," said Gabriel, and buzzed her in. He shot a surprised look at Jane.

"It's so late. What's she doing here?"

"I'm almost afraid to ask."

They heard Angela's footsteps on the stairs, slower and more ponderous than usual, accompanied by an intermittent thumping, as though she were hauling something behind her. Only when she reached the second-floor landing did they see what it was.

A suitcase.

"Mom?" said Jane, but even as she said it, she could not quite believe that this woman with the wild hair and even wilder eyes was her mother. Angela's coat was unbuttoned, the flap of her collar was turned under, and her slacks were soaked to the knees, as though she'd trudged through a snowbank to reach their building. She gripped the suitcase with both hands and looked ready to fling it at someone. Anyone.

She looked dangerous.

"I need to stay with you tonight," said Angela.

"What?"

"Well, can I come in or not?"

"Of course, Mom."

"Here, let me get that for you, Mrs. Rizzoli," Gabriel said, taking the suitcase.

"You see?" said Angela, pointing to Gabriel.

"*That's* how a man's supposed to behave! He sees that a woman needs help, and he steps right up to the plate. That's what a *gentleman's* supposed to do."

"Mom, what happened?"

"What happened? What *happened*? I don't know where to begin!"

Regina gave a wail of protest at being ignored for too long.

At once, Angela scurried into the kitchen and lifted her granddaughter from the infant seat. "Oh baby, poor little girl! You have no idea what you're in for when you grow up." She sat down at the table and rocked the baby, hugging her so tightly that Regina squirmed, trying to free herself from this suffocating madwoman.

"Okay, Mom," sighed Jane. "What did Dad do?"

"You won't hear it from me."

"Then who am I going to hear it from?"

"I won't poison my children against their father. It's not right for parents to bad-mouth each other."

"I'm not a kid anymore. I need to know what's going on."

But Angela did not offer an explanation. She continued to rock back and forth, hugging the baby. Regina looked more and more desperate to escape.

"Um . . . how long do you think you'll be with us, Mom?"

"I don't know."

Jane looked up at Gabriel, who'd been wise enough so far to stay out of the conversation. She saw the same flash of panic in his eyes.

"I might need to find a new place to live," said Angela. "My own apartment."

"Wait, Mom. You're not saying you're *never* going back."

"That's exactly what I'm saying. I'm going to make a new life, Janie." She looked at her daughter, her chin jutting up in defiance. "Other women do it. They leave their husbands and they do just fine. We don't need them. We can survive all by ourselves."

"Mom, you don't have a job."

"What do you think I've been doing for the past thirty-seven years? Cooking and cleaning for *that man*? You think he ever appreciated it? Just comes home and gulps down what I put in front of him. Doesn't taste the care that goes into it. You know how many people have told me I should open up a restaurant?"

Actually, thought Jane, *it'd be a great restaurant.* But she wasn't about to say anything to encourage this insanity.

"So don't ever say to me, *You don't have a job.* My job was to take care of that man, and I've got nothing to show for it. I might as well do the same work and get paid." She hugged Regina with renewed vigor and the baby let out a squawk of protest. "I'll stay with you only a little while. I'll sleep in the baby's room. On the floor is perfectly okay with me. And I'll watch her when you two go to work. It takes a village, you know."

"All right, Mom." Jane sighed and crossed to the telephone. "If you won't tell me what's going on, maybe Dad will."

"What are you doing?"

"Calling him. I bet he's all ready to apologize." *I bet he's hungry and wants his personal chef back.* She picked up the receiver and dialed.

"Don't even bother," said Angela.

The phone rang once, twice.

"I'm telling you, he won't answer. He's not even there."

"Well, where is he?" asked Jane.

"He's at *her* house."

Jane froze as the phone in her parents' home rang and rang unanswered. Slowly she hung up and turned to face her mother. "Whose house?"

"Hers. The slut's."

"Jesus, Ma."

"Jesus has nothing to do with it." Angela took in a sudden gulp of air and her throat clamped down on a sob. She rocked forward, Regina clutched to her chest.

"Dad's seeing another woman?"

Wordlessly, Angela nodded. Lifted her hand up to wipe her face.

"Who? Who's he seeing?" Jane sat down to look her mother in the eye. "Mom, who is she?"

"At work . . ." Angela whispered.

"But he works with a bunch of old guys."

"She's new. She—she's"—Angela's voice suddenly broke—"*younger.*"

The phone rang.

Angela's head shot up. "I won't talk to him. You tell him that."

Jane glanced at the number on the digital readout, but she didn't recognize it. Maybe it was her dad calling. Maybe he was calling from *her* phone. The slut's.

"Detective Rizzoli," she snapped.

A pause, then, "Having a rough night, are you?"

And getting worse, she thought, recognizing the voice of Detective Darren Crowe.

"What's up?" she asked.

"Bad things. We're up on Beacon Hill. You and Frost will want to get over here. I hate being the one to tell you about this, but—"

"Isn't this your night?"

"This one belongs to all of us, Rizzoli." Crowe sounded grimmer than she'd ever heard him, without a trace of his usual sarcasm. He said, quietly, "It's one of ours."

One of ours. A cop.

"Who is it?" she asked.

"It's Eve Kassovitz."

Jane couldn't speak. She stood with her fingers growing numb around the telephone, thinking, *I saw her only a few hours ago.*

"Rizzoli?"

She cleared her throat. "Give me the address."

When she hung up, she found that Gabriel had taken Regina into the other room, and Angela was now sitting with shoulders slumped, her arms sadly empty. "I'm sorry, Mom," said Jane. "I have to go out."

Angela gave a demoralized shrug. "Of course. You go."

"We'll talk when I get back." She bent to kiss her mom's cheek and saw up close Angela's sagging skin, her drooping eyes. *When did my mother get so old?*

She buckled on her weapon and pulled her coat out of the closet. As she buttoned up, she heard Gabriel say, "This is pretty bad timing."

She turned to look at him. *What happens when I get old, like my mom? Will you leave me for a younger woman, too?* "I could be gone awhile," she said. "Don't wait up."

ELEVEN

Maura stepped out of her Lexus and her boots crunched on rime-glazed pavement, cracking through ice as brittle as glass. Snow that had melted during the warmer daylight hours had been flash-frozen again in the brutally cold wind that had kicked up at nightfall, and in the multiple flashes from cruiser lights, every surface gleamed, slick and dangerous. She saw a cop skate his way along the sidewalk, arms windmilling for balance, and saw the CSU van skid sideways as it braked, barely kissing the rear bumper of a parked cruiser.

"Watch your step there, Doc," a patrolman called out from across the street. "Already had one officer go down on the ice tonight. Think he mighta broke his wrist."

"Someone should salt this road."

"Yeah." He gave a grunt. "*Someone* should. Since the city sure ain't keeping up with the job tonight."

"Where's Detective Crowe?"

The cop waved a gloved hand toward the row of elegant town homes. "Number forty-one. It's a few houses up the street. I can walk you there."

"No, I'm fine. Thank you." She paused as another

cruiser rounded the corner and skidded up against the curb. She counted at least eight parked cruisers already clogging the narrow street.

"We're going to need room for the morgue van to get through," she said. "Do all these patrol cars really need to be here?"

"Yeah, they do," the cop said. The tone of his voice made her turn to look at him. Lit by the strobe flashes of rack lights, his face was carved in bleak shadows. "We all need to be here. We owe it to her."

Maura thought about the death scene on Christmas Eve, when Eve Kassovitz had stood doubled over in the street, retching into a snowbank. She remembered, too, how the patrol officers had snickered about the barfing girl detective. Now that detective was dead, and the snickers were silent, replaced by the grim respect due every police officer who has fallen.

The cop's breath came out in an angry rush. "Her boyfriend, he's one, too."

"Another police officer?"

"Yeah. Help us get this perp, Doc."

She nodded. "We will." She started up the sidewalk, aware, suddenly, of all the eyes that must be watching her progress, all the officers who had surely taken note of her arrival. They knew her car; they all knew who she was. She saw nods of recognition among the shadowy figures who stood huddled together, their breaths steaming, like smokers gathered for a furtive round of cigarettes. They knew the grim purpose of her visit, just as they knew that any one of them might someday be the unfortunate object of her attention.

The wind suddenly kicked up a cloud of snow, and she squinted, lowering her head against the sting. When she raised it again she found herself staring at someone she had not expected to see here. Across the street stood Father Daniel Brophy, talking softly to a young police officer who had sagged backward against a Boston PD cruiser, as though too weak to stand on his own feet. Brophy put his arm around the other man's shoulder to comfort him, and the officer collapsed against him, sobbing, as Brophy wrapped both arms around him. Other cops stood nearby in awkward silence, boots shuffling, their gazes to the ground, clearly uncomfortable with this display of raw grief. Although Maura could not hear the words Brophy murmured, she saw the young cop nod, heard him force out a tear-choked response.

I could never do what Daniel does, she thought. It was far easier to cut dead flesh and drill through bone than to confront the pain of the living. Suddenly Daniel's head lifted and he noticed her. For a moment they just stared at each other. Then she turned and continued toward the town house, where a streamer of crime-scene tape fluttered from the porch's cast-iron railing. He had his job and she had hers. It was time to focus. But even as she kept her gaze on the sidewalk ahead, her mind was on Daniel. Whether he would still be there when she finished her task here. And if he was, what happened next? Should she invite him out for a cup of coffee? Would that make her seem too forward, too needy? Should she simply say good night and go her own way, as always?

What do I want to happen?

She reached the building and paused on the sidewalk, gazing up at the handsome three-story residence. Inside, every light was blazing. Brick steps led up to a massive front door, where a brass knocker gleamed in the glow of decorative gaslight lanterns. Despite the season, there were no holiday decorations on this porch. This was the only front door on the street without a wreath. Through the large bow windows, she saw the flicker of a fire burning in the hearth, but no twinkle of Christmas tree lights.

"Dr. Isles?"

She heard the squeal of metal hinges and glanced at the detective who had just pushed open the wrought-iron gate at the side of the house. Roland Tripp was one of the older cops in the homicide unit and tonight he was definitely showing his age. He stood beneath the gaslight lamp and the glow yellowed his skin, emphasizing his baggy eyes and drooping lids. Despite the bulky down jacket, he looked chilled, and he spoke with a clenched jaw, as though trying to suppress chattering teeth.

"The victim's back here," he said, holding open the gate to let her in.

Maura walked through, and the gate clanged shut behind them. He led the way into a narrow side yard, their path lit by the jerky beam of his flashlight. The walkway had been shoveled since the last storm, and the bricks had only a light dusting of windblown snow. Tripp halted, his flashlight aimed at the low mound of snow at the edge of the walkway. At the splash of red.

"This is what got the butler worried. He saw this blood."

"There's a butler here?"

"Oh, yeah. We're talking that kind of money."

"What does he do? The owner of this house?"

"He says he's a retired history professor. Taught at Boston College."

"I had no idea history professors did this well."

"You should take a look inside. This ain't no professor's house. This guy's got other money." Tripp aimed his flashlight at a side door. "Butler came out this exit here, carrying a bag of garbage. Started toward those trash cans when he noticed the gate was open. That's when he first got an inkling that something wasn't right. So he comes back, up this side yard, looking around. Spots the blood and knows that something *really* isn't right. And notices more blood streaking along these bricks, toward the back of the house."

Maura stared at the ground. "The victim was dragged along this walkway."

"I'll show you." Detective Tripp continued toward the rear of the town house, into a small courtyard. His flashlight swept across ice-glazed flagstones and flower beds, now covered with a winter protection of pine boughs. At the center of the courtyard was a white gazebo. In the summertime, it would no doubt be a delightful spot to linger, a shady place to sit and sip coffee and breathe in the scents of the garden.

But the current occupant of that gazebo was not breathing at all.

Maura took off her wool gloves and pulled on latex ones instead. They were no protection against the chill wind that pierced straight to her flesh. Crouching down, she pulled back the plastic sheet that had been draped over the crumpled form.

Detective Eve Kassovitz lay flat on her back, arms at her sides, her blond hair matted with blood. She was dressed in dark clothes—wool pants, a pea coat, and black boots. The coat was unbuttoned, and the sweater halfway pulled up to reveal bare skin smeared with blood. She was wearing a holster, and the weapon was still buckled in place. But it was the corpse's face that Maura stared at, and what she saw made her draw back in horror. The woman's eyelids had been sliced away, her eyes left wide open in an eternal stare. Trickles of blood had dried on both temples, like red tears.

"I saw her just six days ago," said Maura. "At another death scene." She looked up at Tripp. His face was hidden in shadow, and all she saw was that hulking silhouette looming above her. "The one over in East Boston."

He nodded. "Eve joined the unit just a few weeks ago. Came over from Narcotics and Vice."

"Does she live in this neighborhood?"

"No, ma'am. Her apartment's down in Mattapan."

"Then what's she doing here on Beacon Hill?"

"Even her boyfriend doesn't know. But we have some theories."

Maura thought of the young cop she'd just seen sobbing in Daniel's arms. "Her boyfriend is that police officer? The one with Father Brophy?"

"Ben's taking it pretty hard. Goddamn awful way to find out about it, too. Out on patrol when he heard the chatter on the radio."

"And he has no idea what she's doing in this neighborhood? Dressed in black, and packing a weapon?"

Tripp hesitated, just long enough for Maura to notice.

"Detective Tripp?" she said.

He sighed. "We gave her kind of a hard time. You know, about what happened on Christmas Eve. Maybe the teasing got a little out of hand."

"This is about her getting sick at the crime scene?"

"Yeah. I know it's juvenile. It's just something we do to each other in the unit. We kid around, insult each other. But Eve, I'm afraid she took it pretty personally."

"That still doesn't explain what she's doing on Beacon Hill."

"Ben says that after all the teasing, she was pretty fixed on proving herself. We think she was up here working the case. If so, she didn't bother to tell anyone else on her team."

Maura looked down at Eve Kassovitz's face. At the staring eyes. With gloved hands, she pulled aside strands of blood-stiffened hair to reveal a scalp laceration, but she could palpate no fractures. The blow that had ripped that flap of scalp did not seem serious enough to have caused death. She focused next on the torso. Gently she lifted the sweater, uncovering the rib cage, and stared at the bloodstained bra. The stab wound penetrated the skin just beneath the sternum. Already, the blood had dried, a frozen crust of it obscuring the margins of the wound.

"What time was she found?"

"Around ten P.M. Butler came out earlier, around six P.M., to bring out a trash bag, and didn't see her then."

"He took out the trash twice tonight?"

"There was a dinner party for five people inside the house. Lotta cooking, lotta garbage."

"So we're looking at a time of death between six and ten P.M."

"That's right."

"And the last time Detective Kassovitz was seen alive by her boyfriend?"

"About three this afternoon. Just before he headed to his shift."

"So he has an alibi."

"Airtight. Partner was with him all evening." Tripp paused. "You need to take a body temp or something? 'Cause we already got the ambient temperature if you need it. It's twelve degrees."

Maura eyed the corpse's heavy clothes. "I'm not going to take a rectal temp here. I don't want to undress her in the dark. Your witness has already narrowed down the time of death. Assuming he's correct about the times."

Tripp gave a grunt. "Probably down to the split second. You should meet this butler guy, Jeremy. I now know the meaning of anal retentive."

A light slashed the darkness. She glanced up to see a silhouette approaching, flashlight beam sweeping the courtyard.

"Hey, Doc," said Jane. "Didn't know you were already here."

"I just arrived." Maura rose to her feet. In the gloom, she could not see Jane's face, only the voluminous halo of her hair. "I didn't expect to see you here. Crowe was the one who called me."

"He called me, too."

"Where is he?"

"He's inside, interviewing the home owner."

Tripp gave a snort. "Of course he is. It's warm in there. I'm the one who has to freeze his butt out here."

"Geez, Tripp," said Jane. "Sounds like you love Crowe as much as I do."

"Oh yeah, such a lovable guy. No wonder his old partner took early retirement." He huffed out a breath, and the steam spiraled up into darkness. "I think we should rotate Crowe around the unit. Spread the pain a little. We can each take turns putting up with Pretty Boy."

"Believe me, I've already put up with him more than I should have to," said Jane. She focused on Eve Kassovitz, and her voice softened. "He was an asshole to her. That was Crowe's idea, wasn't it? The puke bucket on the desk?"

"Yeah," Tripp admitted. "But we're all responsible, in a way. Maybe she wouldn't be here if . . ." He sighed. "You're right. We were all assholes."

"You said she came here working the case," said Maura. "Was there a lead?"

"O'Donnell," said Jane. "She was one of the dinner guests tonight."

"Kassovitz was tailing her?"

"We briefly discussed surveillance. It was just a consideration. She never told me she was going to act on it."

"O'Donnell was here, in this house?"

"She's still inside, being interviewed." Jane's gaze was back on the body. "I'd say O'Donnell's devoted fan has just left her another offering."

"You think this is the same perp."

"I know it is."

"There's mutilation of the eyes here, but no dismemberment. No ritualistic symbols like in East Boston."

Jane glanced at Tripp. "You didn't show her?"

"I was about to."

"Show me what?" asked Maura.

Jane raised her flashlight and shone it on the back door of the residence. What Maura saw sent a chill coiling up her spine. On the door were three upside-down crosses. And drawn beneath it, in red chalk, was a single staring eye.

"I'd say that's our boy's work," said Jane.

"It could be a copycat. A number of people saw those symbols in Lori-Ann Tucker's bedroom. And cops talk."

"If you still need convincing . . ." Jane aimed her flashlight at the bottom of the door. On the single granite step, leading into the house, was a small cloth-covered bundle. "We unwrapped it just enough to look inside," said Jane. "I think we've found Lori-Ann Tucker's left hand."

A sudden gust of wind swept the courtyard, kicking up a mist of snow that stung Maura's eyes, flash-froze her cheeks. Dead leaves rattled across the patio, and the gazebo creaked and shuddered above them.

"Have you considered the possibility," said Maura softly, "that this murder tonight has nothing to do with Joyce O'Donnell?"

"Of course it does. Kassovitz tails O'Donnell here. The killer sees her, chooses her as his next victim. It still gets back to O'Donnell."

"Or he could have seen Kassovitz on Christmas Eve. She was there at the crime scene. He could have been watching Lori-Ann Tucker's house."

"You mean, enjoying all the action?" said Tripp.

"Yes. Enjoying the fact that all the excitement, all the cops, were because of *him*. Because of what he'd just done. What a sense of power."

"So he follows *Kassovitz* here," said Tripp, "because she caught his eye that night? Man, that puts a different spin on this."

Jane looked at Maura. "It means he could've been watching any one of us. He'd know all our faces now."

Maura bent down and pulled the sheet back over the body. Her hands were numb and clumsy as she stripped off the latex gloves and pulled on her wool ones. "I'm freezing. I can't do anything else out here. We should just move her to the morgue. And I need to defrost my hands."

"Have you already called for pickup?"

"They're on their way. If you don't mind, I think I'll wait for them in my car. I want to get out of this wind."

"I think we should *all* get out of this wind," said Tripp.

They walked back along the side yard and stepped through the iron gate into the liverish glow of the gas lamp. Across the street, silhouetted in strobe by cruiser rack lights, was a huddle of cops. Daniel stood among them, taller than the other men, hands buried in the pockets of his overcoat.

"You can come inside with us and wait," said Jane.

"No," said Maura, her gaze on Daniel. "I'll just sit in my car."

Jane was silent for a moment. She'd noticed Daniel, too, and she could probably guess why Maura was lingering outside.

"If you're looking to get warm, Doc," said Jane, "you're not going to find it out here. But I guess that's your choice." She clapped Tripp on the shoulder. "Come on. Let's go back inside. See how Pretty Boy's doing." They walked up the steps, into the house.

Maura paused on the sidewalk, her gaze on Daniel. He did not seem to notice that she was there. It was awkward with all those cops standing around him. But what was there to be embarrassed about, really? She was here to do her job, and so was he. It's the most natural thing in the world for two acquaintances to greet each other.

She crossed the street, toward the circle of cops. Only then did Daniel see her. So did the other men, and they all fell silent as she approached. Though she dealt with police officers every day, saw them at every crime scene, she had never felt entirely comfortable with them, or they with her. That mutual discomfort was never more obvious than at this moment, when she felt their gazes on her. She could guess what they thought of her. The chilly Dr. Isles, never a barrel of laughs. Or maybe they were intimidated; maybe it was the MD behind her name that set her apart, made her unapproachable.

Or maybe it's just me. Maybe they are afraid of me.

"The morgue van should be here any minute," she said, opening the conversation on pure business. "If you could make room for it on the street."

"Sure thing, Doc," one of the cops said, and coughed.

Another silence followed, the cops looking off in other directions, everywhere but at her, their feet shuffling on cold pavement.

"Well, thank you," she said. "I'll be waiting in my car." She didn't cast a glance at Daniel, but simply turned and walked away.

"Maura?"

She glanced back at the sound of his voice, and saw that the cops were still watching. *There's always an audience,* she thought. *Daniel and I are never alone.*

"What do you know so far?" he asked.

She hesitated, aware of all the eyes. "Not much more than anyone else, at this point."

"Can we talk about it? It might help me comfort Officer Lyall if I knew more about what happened."

"It's awkward. I'm not sure . . ."

"You don't have to tell me anything you don't feel comfortable revealing."

She hesitated. "Let's sit in my car. It's right down the street."

They walked together, hands thrust in pockets,

heads bent against icy gusts. She thought of Eve Kassovitz, lying alone in the courtyard, her corpse already chilled, her blood freezing in her veins. On this night, in this wind, no one wanted to keep company with the dead. They reached her car and slid inside. She turned on the engine to run the heater, but the air that puffed through the vents offered no warmth.

"Officer Lyall was her boyfriend?" she asked.

"He's devastated. I don't think I was able to offer much comfort."

"I couldn't do your job, Daniel. I'm not good at dealing with grief."

"But you do deal with it. You have to."

"Not on the level you do, when it's still so raw, so fresh. I'm the one they expect all the answers from, not the one they call in to give comfort." She looked at him. In the gloom of her car he was just a silhouette. "The last Boston PD chaplain lasted only two years. I'm sure the stress contributed to his stroke."

"Father Roy *was* sixty-five, you know."

"And he looked eighty the last time I saw him."

"Well, taking night calls isn't easy," he admitted, his breath steaming the window. "It's not easy for cops, either. Or doctors or firemen. But it's not all bad," he added with a soft laugh, "since going to death scenes is the only time I ever get to see you."

Although she could not read his eyes, she felt his gaze on her face and was grateful for the darkness.

"You used to visit me," he said. "Why did you stop?"

"I came for midnight Mass, didn't I?"

He gave a weary laugh. "Everyone shows up at Christmas. Even the ones who don't believe."

"But I *was* there. I wasn't avoiding you."

"Have you been, Maura? Avoiding me?"

She said nothing. For a moment they regarded each other in the gloom of her car. The air blowing from the vent had barely warmed and her fingers were still numb, but she could feel heat rise to her cheeks.

"I know what's going on," he said quietly.

"You have no idea."

"I'm just as human as you are, Maura."

Suddenly she laughed. It was a bitter sound. "Well, *this* is a cliché. The priest and the woman parishioner."

"Don't reduce it to that."

"But it is a cliché. It's probably happened a thousand times before. Priests and bored housewives. Priests and lonely widows. Is it the first time for you, Daniel? Because it sure as hell is the first time for me." Suddenly ashamed that she had turned her anger on him, she looked away. What had he done, really, except offer her his friendship, his attention? *I am the architect of my own unhappiness.*

"If it makes you feel any better," he said quietly, "you're not the only one who's miserable."

She sat perfectly still as air hissed from the vents. She kept her gaze focused straight ahead, on the windshield now fogged with condensation, but all her other senses were painfully focused on him. Even if she were blind and deaf, she'd still know he was there, so attuned was she to every aspect of his presence. Attuned, as well, to her own pounding heart, to the sizzling of her nerves. She'd felt a perverse thrill from his declaration of unhappiness. At least she was not the only one suffering, not the only one who lay sleepless at night. In affairs of the heart, misery yearns for company.

There was a loud rapping on her window. Startled, she turned to see a ghostly silhouette peering in through the fogged glass. She lowered her window and stared into the face of a Boston PD cop.

"Dr. Isles? The morgue van just arrived."

"Thank you. I'll be right there." Her window hummed shut again, leaving the glass streaked with watery lines. She shut off the car engine and looked at Daniel. "We have a choice," she said. "We can both be miserable. Or we can move on with our lives. I'm choosing to move on." She stepped out of the car and closed the door. She took one breath of air so cold it seemed to sear her throat. But it also swept any last indecision from her brain, leaving it clearer and focused with laser intensity on what she had to do next. She left her car and did not look back. Once again, she headed up the sidewalk, moving from pool to pool of light as she passed beneath streetlamps. Daniel was behind her now; ahead waited a dead woman. And all these cops, standing around. What were they waiting for? Answers that she might not be able to give them?

She pulled her coat tighter, as though to ward off their stares, thinking of Christmas Eve and another death scene. Of Eve Kassovitz, who'd lingered on the street that night, emptying her stomach into the snowbank. Had Kassovitz experienced even a flicker of a premonition that she would be the next object of Maura's attention?

The cops all gathered in silence near the house as

the morgue team wheeled Eve Kassovitz along the side yard. When the stretcher bearing the shrouded corpse emerged through the iron gate, they stood with heads bared in the frigid wind, a solemn blue line honoring one of their own. Even after the stretcher had disappeared into the vehicle and the doors had swung shut, they did not break ranks. Only when the taillights winked away into the darkness did the hats go back on, and they began to drift back to their cruisers.

Maura, too, was about to walk to her car when the front door of the residence opened. She looked up as warm light spilled out and saw the silhouette of a man standing there, looking at her.

"Excuse me. Are you Dr. Isles?" he asked.

"Yes?"

"Mr. Sansone would like to invite you to step inside the house. It's a great deal warmer in here, and I've just made a fresh pot of coffee."

She hesitated at the foot of the steps, looking up at the warm glow that framed the manservant. He stood very straight, watching her with an eerie stillness that made her think of a life-size statue she'd once seen in a gag store, a papier-mâché butler holding a tray of fake drinks. She glanced down the street toward her car. Daniel had already left, and she had nothing to look forward to but a lonely drive home and an empty house.

"Thank you," she said, and started up the steps. "I could use a cup of coffee."

TWELVE

SHE STEPPED into the warmth of the front parlor. Her face was still numb from the bite of the wind. Only as she stood before the fireplace, waiting for the butler to notify Mr. Sansone, did sensation slowly creep back into her cheeks; she felt the pleasant sting of reawakened nerves, of flushing skin. She could hear the murmur of conversation in another room—Detective Crowe's voice, pointed with questioning, answered by a softer response, barely audible. A woman's. In the fireplace, sparks popped and smoke puffed up, and she realized these were real logs burning, that it was not the fake gas fireplace she'd assumed it was. The medieval oil painting that hung above the hearth might well be authentic as well. It was a portrait of a man wearing robes of wine-red velvet, with a gold crucifix around his neck. Though he was not young, and his dark hair was woven with silver, his eyes burned with a youthful fire. In that room's flickering light, those eyes seemed piercingly alive.

She shivered and turned away, strangely intimidated by the stare of a man almost certainly long dead. The room had other curiosities, other treasures to examine. She saw chairs upholstered in striped silk, a Chinese vase that gleamed with the patina of centuries, a rosewood butler's table that held a cigar box and a crystal decanter of brandy. The carpet she stood on bore a well-worn path down its center, evidence of its age and the countless shoes that had trod across it, but the relatively untouched perimeter revealed the unmistakable quality of thick wool and the craftsmanship of the weaver. She looked down at her feet, at a tapestry of intricate vines twining across burgundy to frame a unicorn reclining beneath a bower of trees. Suddenly she felt guilty that she was standing on such a masterpiece. She stepped off it, onto the wood floor, and closer to the hearth.

Once again, she was facing the portrait over the mantelpiece. Once again, her gaze lifted to the priest's piercing eyes, eyes that seemed to stare straight back at her.

"It's been in my family for generations. It's amazing, isn't it, how vivid the colors still are? Even after four centuries."

Maura turned to face the man who had just stepped into the room. He had entered so quietly, it was as though he had simply materialized behind her, and she was too taken by surprise to know quite what to say. He was dressed in a dark turtleneck, which made his silver hair all the more striking. Yet his face looked no older than fifty. Had they merely passed each other on the street, she would have stared at him because his features were so arresting and so hauntingly familiar. She saw a high forehead, an aristocratic bearing. His dark eyes caught the flicker of firelight, so that they seemed lit from within. He had referred to the portrait as an heirloom, and she saw at once the familial resemblance between the portrait and the living man. The eyes were the same.

He held out his hand. "Hello, Dr. Isles. I'm Anthony Sansone." His gaze was focused with such intensity on her face that she wondered if they had met before.

No. I certainly would have remembered a man this attractive.

"I'm glad to finally make your acquaintance," he said, shaking her hand. "After everything I've heard about you."

"From whom?"

"Dr. O'Donnell."

Maura felt her hand go cold in his grasp, and she pulled away. "I can't imagine why I'd be a subject of conversation."

"She had only good things to say about you. Believe me."

"That's a surprise."

"Why?"

"Because I can't say the same thing about her," she said.

He gave a knowing nod. "She can be off-putting. Until you get the chance to know her. Value her insights."

The door swung open so quietly, Maura did not hear it. Only the gentle clink of chinaware alerted her to the fact that the butler had stepped into the room, carrying a tray with cups and a coffeepot. He set them on an end table, regarded Sansone with a questioning look, then withdrew from the room. Not a single word had passed between them; the only communication had been that look, and the returning nod—all the vocabulary needed between two men who obviously knew each other well enough to dispense with unnecessary words.

Sansone gestured for her to sit down, and Maura sank into an Empire armchair upholstered in striped silk.

"I apologize for confining you to the front parlor," he said. "But Boston PD seems to have commandeered the other rooms while they conduct their interviews." He poured coffee and handed her a cup. "I take it you've examined the victim?"

"I saw her."

"What did you think?"

"You know I can't comment."

He leaned back in his chair, looking perfectly at ease against blue and gold brocade. "I'm not talking about the body itself," he said. "I perfectly understand why you can't discuss your medical findings. I was referring to the scene itself. The gestalt of the crime."

"You should ask the lead investigator, Detective Rizzoli."

"I'm more interested in your impressions."

"I'm a physician. Not a detective."

"But I'm guessing you have a special insight into what happened in my garden tonight." He leaned forward, coal-dark eyes riveted on hers. "You saw the symbols drawn on my back door?"

"I can't talk about—"

"Dr. Isles, you won't be giving away anything. I

saw the body. So did Dr. O'Donnell. When Jeremy found the woman, he came straight into the house to tell us."

"And then you and O'Donnell tramped outside like tourists to have a look?"

"We're the furthest thing from tourists."

"Did you stop to think about the footprints you might have destroyed? The trace evidence you've contaminated?"

"We understood exactly what we were doing. We had to see the crime scene."

"Had to?"

"This house isn't just my residence. It's also a meeting place for colleagues from around the world. The fact that violence has struck so close alarms us."

"It would alarm anyone to find a dead body in their garden. But most people wouldn't troop outside with their dinner guest to look at it."

"We needed to know if it was merely an act of random violence."

"As opposed to what?"

"A warning, meant specifically for us." He set down his coffee cup and focused his attention so completely on her that she felt pinned to the silk-upholstered chair. "You did see the chalk symbols on the door? The eye. The three upside-down crosses?"

"Yes."

"I understand there was another slaying, on Christmas Eve. Another woman. Another crime scene with reverse crosses drawn on the bedroom wall."

She didn't need to confirm it; this man had surely

read the answer in her face. She could almost feel his gaze probing deep, and seeing too much.

"We might as well talk about it," he said. "I already know the pertinent details."

"How do you know? Who told you?"

"People I trust."

She gave a disbelieving laugh. "Dr. O'Donnell being one of them?"

"Whether you like her or not, she is an authority in her field. Look at her body of work on serial murderers. She understands these creatures."

"Some would say she identifies with them."

"On some level, you'd have to. She's willing to crawl inside their heads. Examine every crevice."

The way Maura herself had felt examined by Sansone's gaze only moments ago.

"It takes a monster to know one," said Maura.

"You really believe that?"

"About Joyce O'Donnell, yes. I do believe that."

He leaned even closer, and his voice dropped to an intimate murmur. "Could your dislike of Joyce be merely personal?"

"Personal?"

"Because she knows so much about you? About your family?"

Maura stared back, stunned into silence.

"She told us about Amalthea," he said.

"She had no right to."

"Your mother's incarceration is a matter of public record. We all know what Amalthea did."

"This is my private life—"

"Yes, and she's one of your personal demons. I understand that."

"Why the hell is this of any interest to you?"

"Because *you're* of interest. You've looked evil in the eye. You've seen it in your own mother's face. You know it's there, in your bloodline. That's what fascinates me, Dr. Isles—that you come from such violent stock, yet here you are, working on the side of the angels."

"I work on the side of science and reason, Mr. Sansone. Angels aren't involved."

"All right, so you don't believe in angels. But do you believe in their counterparts?"

"Do you mean *demons*?" She gave a laugh. "Of course not."

He regarded her for a moment with a look of vague disappointment. "Since your religion seems to be science and reason, as you put it, how does science explain what happened in my garden tonight? What happened to that woman on Christmas Eve?"

"You're asking me to explain evil."

"Yes."

"I can't. Neither can science. It just *is*."

He nodded. "That's exactly right. It just is, and it's always been with us. A real entity, living among us, stalking us. Waiting for its chance to feed. Most people aren't aware of it, and they don't recognize it, even when it brushes up against them, when it passes them on the street." His voice had dropped to a whisper. In the momentary hush, she heard the crackle of flames in the hearth, the murmur of voices in the other room. "But *you* do," he said. "You've seen it with your own eyes."

"I've only seen what every homicide cop has seen."

"I'm not talking about everyday crimes. Spouses killing spouses, drug dealers shooting the competition. I'm talking about what you saw in your mother's eyes. The gleam. The spark. Not divine, but something unholy."

A draft moaned down the flue, scattering ashes against the fire screen. The flames shuddered, quailing before an invisible intruder. The room suddenly felt cold, as though all heat, all light, had just been sucked from it.

"I understand perfectly," he said, "why you wouldn't want to talk about Amalthea. It's a terrible bloodline to inherit."

"She has nothing to do with who I am," Maura said. "She didn't raise me. I didn't even know she existed until a few months ago."

"Yet you're sensitive about the subject."

She met his gaze. "I really don't care."

"I find it strange that you don't care."

"We don't inherit our parents' sins. Or their virtues."

"Some legacies are too powerful to ignore." He pointed to the painting over the hearth. "Sixteen generations separate me from that man. Yet I'll never escape his legacy. I'll never be washed clean of the things he did."

Maura stared at the portrait. Once again, she was struck by the resemblance between the living man sitting beside her and the face on the canvas. "You said that painting was an heirloom."

"Not one that I was happy to inherit."

"Who was he?"

"Monsignore Antonino Sansone. This portrait

was painted in Venice in 1561. At the height of his power. Or, you might also say, at the depth of his depravity."

"Antonino Sansone? Your name?"

"I'm his direct descendent."

She frowned at the painting. "But he—"

"He was a priest. That's what you're about to say, isn't it?"

"Yes."

"It would take all night to tell you his story. Another time, maybe. Let's just say that Antonino was not a godly man. He did things to other human beings that would make you question the very meaning of—" He paused. "He's not an ancestor I'm proud of."

"Yet you have his portrait hanging in your house."

"As a reminder."

"Of what?"

"Look at him, Dr. Isles. He looks like me, don't you think?"

"Eerily so."

"In fact, we could be brothers. That's why he's hanging there. To remind me that evil has a human face, maybe even a pleasant face. You could walk past that man, see him smile back at you, and you'd never imagine what he's thinking about you. You can study a face all you want, but you never really know what lies beneath the mask." He leaned toward her, his hair reflecting firelight like a silvery helmet. "They look just like us, Dr. Isles," he said softly.

"They? You make it sound like a separate species."

"Maybe they are. Throwbacks to an ancient era. All I know is, they are not like us. And the only way to identify them is to track what they do. Follow the bloody trail, listen for the screams. Search for what most police departments are too overwhelmed to notice: the patterns. We look beyond the background noise of everyday crimes, of routine bloodshed, to see the hot spots. We watch for the footprints of monsters."

"Who do you mean by *we*?"

"The people who were here tonight."

"Your dinner guests."

"We share a belief that evil isn't just a concept. It's real, and it has a physical presence. It has a *face*." He paused. "At some time in our lives, we've each seen it in the flesh."

Maura's eyebrow lifted. "Satan?"

"Whatever name you want to use." He shrugged. "There've been so many names, dating back to the ancients. Lucifer, Abigor, Samael, Mastema. Every culture has its name for evil. My friends and I have each personally brushed up against it. We've seen its power, and I'll admit it, Dr. Isles. We're scared." His gaze met hers. "Tonight, more than ever."

"You think this killing in your garden—"

"It has to do with us. With what we do here."

"Which is?"

"We monitor the work of monsters. Around the country, around the world."

"A club of armchair detectives? That's what it sounds like to me." Her gaze moved back to the portrait of Antonino Sansone, which was no doubt worth a fortune. Just a glance around this drawing room told her that this man had money to burn. And the time to waste on eccentric interests.

"Why was that woman killed in my garden, Dr. Isles?" he said. "Why choose my house, on this particular evening?"

"You think it's all about you and your club?"

"You saw the chalk drawings on my door. And the drawings at the Christmas Eve slaying."

"And I have no idea what any of them mean."

"The upside-down crosses are common satanic symbols. But what interests me is the chalk circle in Lori-Ann Tucker's house. The one drawn on her kitchen floor."

There was no point denying the facts; this man already knew the details. "So what does the circle mean?"

"It could be a ring of protection. Another symbol taken from satanic rituals. By drawing that circle, Lori-Ann may have been trying to shield herself. She may have been trying to control the very forces she was calling from the darkness."

"Wait. You think the *victim* drew it, to ward off the devil?" Her tone of voice left no doubt what she thought of his theory: *utter nonsense*.

"If she did draw it, then she had no idea who—or what—she was summoning."

The fire suddenly fluttered, flames reaching up in a bright claw. Maura turned as the inner door swung open and Dr. Joyce O'Donnell emerged. She paused, clearly surprised to see Maura. Then her attention shifted to Sansone.

"Lucky me. After two hours of questions, Boston's

finest finally decided to let me go home. You throw a hell of a dinner party, Anthony. This is one evening you'll never be able to top."

"Let's hope I never do," said Sansone. "Let me get your coat." He rose and pushed open a wooden panel, exposing a hidden closet. He held up O'Donnell's fur-trimmed coat and she slipped her arms into the sleeves with feline grace, her blond hair brushing across his hands. Maura saw familiarity in that momentary contact, a comfortable dance between two people who knew each other well.

Perhaps very well.

As she buttoned, O'Donnell's gaze settled on Maura. "It's been a while, Dr. Isles," she said. "How is your mother?"

She always goes straight for the jugular. Don't let her see she's drawn blood.

"I have no idea," said Maura.

"You haven't been back to see her?"

"No. But you probably already know that."

"Oh, I finished my interviews with Amalthea over a month ago. I haven't seen her since." Slowly, O'Donnell pulled woolen gloves over long, elegant fingers. "She was doing well when I last saw her, in case you're interested."

"I'm not."

"They have her working in the prison library now. She's turned into quite the bookworm. Reads every psychology textbook she can get her hands on." O'Donnell paused to give her glove a last tug. "If she'd ever had the chance to go to college, she could have been a star."

Instead, my mother chose a different path. Predator. Butcher. No matter how hard Maura worked to distance herself, no matter how deeply she buried any thoughts of Amalthea, she could not look at her own reflection without seeing her mother's eyes, her mother's jaw. The monster peering back from the mirror.

"Her case history will take up a whole chapter in my next book," said O'Donnell. "If you're ever willing to sit down and talk with me, it would contribute a great deal to her history."

"I have absolutely nothing to add."

O'Donnell simply smiled, clearly expecting the snub. "Always worth asking," she said, and looked at Sansone. A gaze that lingered, as though she had something more to say, but could not say it in Maura's presence. "Good night, Anthony."

"Shall I have Jeremy follow you home, just to be sure?"

"Absolutely not." She flashed him a smile that struck Maura as distinctly flirtatious. "I can take care of myself."

"These are different circumstances, Joyce."

"Afraid?"

"We'd be crazy if we weren't."

She flung her scarf around her neck, a theatrical flourish to emphasize that she, for one, was not going to let something as trivial as fear slow her down. "I'll call you tomorrow."

He opened the door, letting in a whoosh of frigid air, a flurry of snowflakes that scattered like glitter across the antique carpet. "Stay safe," he said. He waited in the doorway, watching as O'Donnell walked to her car. Only after she drove away did he close the door. Once again, he faced Maura.

"So you and your friends think you're on the side of the angels," said Maura.

"I believe we are."

"Whose side is *she* on?"

"I know there's no love lost between her and law enforcement. It's her job as a defense witness to be at odds with the prosecution. But I've known Joyce for three years now. I know where she stands."

"Can you really be sure?" Maura picked up her coat, which she'd left draped over a settee. He did not attempt to help her on with it; perhaps he sensed that she, unlike O'Donnell, was not in the mood to be indulged. As she buttoned her coat, she felt she was being watched by two sets of eyes. The portrait of Antonino Sansone was watching her as well, his gaze piercing the mist of four centuries, and she could not help a glance in the portrait's direction, at the man whose actions, so many generations ago, could still make his namesake shudder.

"You say you've looked evil in the eye," she said, turning back to her host.

"We both have."

"Then you should know by now," she said, "that it wears a pretty damn good disguise."

She stepped out of the house and breathed in air that sparkled with frozen mist. The sidewalk stretched before her like a dark river; streetlamps cast pale islands of light. A lone Boston PD cruiser was parked across the street, engine idling, and she saw the silhouette of a patrolman sitting in the driver's seat. She raised her hand in a wave.

He waved back.

No reason to be nervous, she thought, as she started walking. *My car's just down the street, and a cop's nearby.* So was Sansone. She glanced back and saw that he was still standing on his front steps, watching her. Nevertheless she pulled out her car keys, kept her thumb poised on the panic button. Even as she moved down the sidewalk, she scanned shadows, searching for even a flicker of movement. Only after she'd climbed into her car and locked it did she feel the tension ease from her shoulders.

Time to go home. Time for a stiff drink.

When she walked into her house, she found two new messages on her answering machine. She went into the kitchen first, to pour herself a glass of brandy, came back into the living room, sipping her drink, and pressed Play. At the sound of the first caller's voice, she went very still.

"It's Daniel. I don't care how late it is when you hear this. Just call me, please. I hate to think that you and I—" A pause. "We need to talk, Maura. Call me."

She did not move. Just stood clutching her brandy, her fingers numb around the glass as the second message played.

"Dr. Isles, it's Anthony Sansone. I just wanted to make sure you got home safely. Give me a call and let me know, will you?"

The machine went silent. She took a breath, reached for the phone, and dialed.

"Sansone residence. This is Jeremy."

"It's Dr. Isles. Could you—"

"Hello, Dr. Isles. Let me get him for you."

"Just let him know that I'm home."

"I know that he'd like very much to talk to you himself."

"There's no need to disturb him. Good night."

"Good night, Doctor."

She hung up and hovered over the receiver, poised to make the second call.

A sharp thump on her porch made her back snap straight. She went to the front door and flipped on the porch light. Outside, the wind swirled snow fine as dust. On the porch, a fallen icicle lay in glistening shards, like a broken dagger. She turned off the light but lingered at the window and watched as a municipal truck rumbled past, scattering sand across the icy road.

She returned to the couch and stared at the phone as she drank the last of her brandy.

We need to talk, Maura. Call me.

She set down the glass, turned off the lamp, and went to bed.

THIRTEEN

JULY 22. Phase of the moon: First Quarter.

Aunt Amy stands at the stove stirring a pot of stew, her face as contented as a cow's. On this overcast day, with dark clouds gathering in the western sky, she seems oblivious to the rumble of thunder. In my aunt's world, every day is a sunny one. She sees no evil, fears no evil. She is like the livestock fattening on clover on the farm down the road, the cattle that know nothing of the slaughterhouse. She cannot see beyond the glow of her own happiness, to the precipice just beyond her feet.

She is nothing like my mother.

Aunt Amy turns from the stove and says, "Dinner's almost ready."

"I'll set the table," I offer, and she flashes me a grateful smile. It takes so little to please her. As I set the plates and napkins on the table and lay the forks tines-down, in the French way, I feel her loving gaze. She sees only a quiet and agreeable boy; she's blind to who I really am.

Only my mother knows. My mother can trace our bloodline all the way back to the Hyksos, who ruled Egypt from the north, in the age when the God of

War was sacred. "The blood of ancient hunters runs in your veins," my mother said. "But it's best never to speak of it, because people will not understand."

I say little as we sit down to dinner. The family chatters enough to fill any silence. They talk about what Teddy did at the lake today, what Lily heard while at Lori-Ann's house. What a nice crop of tomatoes they'll be harvesting in August.

When we have finished eating, Uncle Peter says, "Who wants to go into town for ice cream?"

I am the only one who chooses to stay home.

I watch from the front door as their car drives away. As soon as it vanishes down the hill, I climb the stairs and walk into my aunt and uncle's bedroom. I've been waiting for the chance to explore it. The room smells like lemon furniture polish. The bed is neatly made, but there are minor touches of disorder—my uncle's jeans draped over a chair, a few magazines on the nightstand—to confirm that real people live in this room.

In their bathroom, I open the medicine cabinet and find, along with the usual headache pills and cold capsules, a two-year-old prescription, made out to Dr. Peter Saul:

"Valium, 5 mg. Take one tablet three times a day as needed for back spasms."

There are at least a dozen pills still left in the bottle.

I return to the bedroom. I open dresser drawers and discover that my aunt's bra size is 36B, that her underwear is cotton, and that my uncle wears medium jockey shorts. In a bottom drawer, I also find a key. It's too small for a door. I think I know what it opens.

Downstairs, in my uncle's study, I fit the key into a lock, and the cabinet door swings open. On the shelf inside is his handgun. It's an old one that he inherited from his father, which is the only reason he has not gotten rid of it. He never takes it out; I think he is a little afraid of it.

I lock the cabinet and return the key to its drawer.

An hour later, I hear their car pulling into the driveway, and I go downstairs to greet them as they come back into the house.

Aunt Amy smiles when she sees me. "I'm so sorry you didn't come with us. Were you terribly bored?"

FOURTEEN

THE SQUEAL of the truck's air brakes startled Lily Saul awake. She raised her head, groaning at the ache in her neck, and blinked with sleepy eyes at the passing countryside. Dawn was just breaking and the morning mist was a haze of gold over sloping vineyards and dew-laden orchards. She hoped that poor Paolo and Giorgio had passed on to a place this beautiful; if anyone deserved Heaven, they did.

But I will not be seeing them there. This will be my only chance at Heaven. Here, now. A moment of peace, infinitely sweet because I know it won't last.

"You're awake at last," the driver said in Italian, dark eyes appraising her. Last night, when he had stopped at the side of the road just outside Florence to offer her a ride, she had not gotten a good look at him. Now, with the morning light slanting into the truck's cab, she saw coarse features, a jutting brow, and a day's dark stubble on his jaw. Oh, she could read that look he gave her. *Will we or won't we, Signorina?* American girls were easy. Give them a lift, offer them a place to stay, and they'll sleep with you.

When Hell freezes over, thought Lily. Not that she *hadn't* slept with a stranger or two. Or three, when desperate measures were called for. But those men had not been without their charms, and they had offered what she'd sorely needed at the time—not shelter, but the comfort of a man's arms. The chance to enjoy the brief but lovely delusion that someone could protect her.

"If you need a place to stay," the driver said, "I have an apartment, in the city."

"Thank you, but no."

"You have some place to go?"

"I have . . . friends. They've offered to let me stay."

"Where is their address in Rome? I will drop you off."

He knew she was lying. He was testing her.

"Really," he said. "It is no trouble."

"Just leave me at the train station. They live near there."

Again, his gaze raked across her face. She did not like his eyes. She saw meanness there, like the gleam of a coiled snake that could, at any instant, strike.

Suddenly he gave a shrug, a grin, as if it didn't matter to him in the least.

"You have been to Rome before?"

"Yes."

"Your Italian is very good."

But not good enough, she thought. *I open my mouth and they know I'm foreign.*

"How long will you stay in the city?"

"I don't know." *Until it's no longer safe. Until I can plan my next move.*

"If you ever need help, you can call me." He

pulled a business card from his shirt pocket and handed it to her. "The number for my mobile."

"I'll give you a call sometime," she said, dropping the card inside her backpack. Let him hang on to his fantasy. He'd give her less trouble when she left.

At Rome's Stazione Termine, she climbed out of the truck and gave him a good-bye wave. She could feel his gaze as she crossed the street toward the train station. She didn't glance back, but walked straight into the building. There, behind windows, she turned to watch his truck. Saw it just sitting there, waiting. *Go on,* she thought. *Get the hell away from me.*

Behind the truck, a taxicab blared its horn; only then did the truck move on.

She emerged from the station and wandered into Piazza della Repubblica where she paused, dazed by the crowds, by the heat and noise and gas fumes. Just before leaving Florence, she had chanced a stop at an ATM and withdrawn three hundred Euros, so she was feeling flush now. If she was careful, she could make the cash last for two weeks. Live on bread and cheese and coffee, check into rock-bottom tourist hotels. This was the neighborhood to find cheap accommodations. And with the swarms of foreign tourists moving in and out of the train station, she would easily blend in.

But she had to be cautious.

Pausing outside a sundries store, she considered how she could most easily alter her appearance. A dye job? No. In the land of dark-haired beauties, it was best to stay a brunette. A change of clothes, perhaps. Stop looking so American. Ditch the jeans for a cheap dress. She wandered into a dusty shop and emerged a half hour later wearing a blue cotton frock.

In a fit of extravagance, she next treated herself to a heaping plate of spaghetti Bolognese, her first hot meal in two days. It was a mediocre sauce, and the noodles were soggy and overcooked, but she devoured it all, sopping up every particle of meat with the stale bread. Then, her belly full, the heat weighing down on her shoulders, she trudged sleepily in search of a hotel. She found one on a dirty side street. Dogs had left their stinking souvenirs near the front entrance. Laundry flapped from windows, and a trash can, buzzing with flies, overflowed with garbage and broken glass.

Perfect.

The room she checked into looked over a shadowy interior courtyard. As she unbuttoned her dress, she stood gazing down at a scrawny cat pouncing on something too small for Lily to make out. A piece of string? A doomed mouse?

Stripped down to her underwear, she collapsed onto the lumpy bed and listened to the rattle of window air conditioners in the courtyard, to the honking horns and roaring buses of the Eternal City. A city of four million is a good place to hide for a while, she thought. No one will easily find me here.

Not even the Devil.

FIFTEEN

EDWINA FELWAY'S HOUSE was in the suburb of Newton. It sat at the edge of the snow-covered Braeburn Country Club, overlooking the east branch of Cheesecake Brook, which was now a gleaming ribbon of ice. Although it was certainly not the largest house on this road of grand residences, its charming eccentricities distinguished it from its more stately neighbors. Thick vines of wisteria had clambered up its stone walls and clung there like arthritic fingers, waiting for spring to warm their knobby joints and coax forth blooms. Framed by one of the gables, a large ocular of stained glass peered like a multicolored eye. Beneath the peaked slate roof, icicles sparkled like jagged teeth. In the front yard, sculptures reared ice-encrusted heads, as though emerging from snowbound hibernation: A winged fairy, still flash-frozen in mid-flight. A dragon, its fiery breath temporarily extinguished. A willowy maiden, the flower wreath on her head transformed by winter to a crown of snowdrops.

"What do you think?" asked Jane as she stared out the car window at the house. "Two million? Two and a half?"

"This neighborhood, right on the golf course? I'm guessing more like four," said Barry Frost.

"For that weird old house?"

"I don't think it's all that old."

"Well, someone went to a lot of trouble to make it look old."

"Atmospheric. That's what I'd call it."

"Right. Home of the Seven Dwarfs." Jane turned the car into the driveway and parked beside a van. As they stepped out, onto well-sanded cobblestones, Jane noticed the handicapped placard on the van's dashboard. Peering through the rear window, she saw a wheelchair lift.

"Hello, there! Are you the detectives?" a booming voice called out. The woman who stood on the porch waving at them was obviously able-bodied.

"Mrs. Felway?" said Jane.

"Yes. And you must be Detective Rizzoli."

"And my partner, Detective Frost."

"Watch those cobblestones, they're slippery. I try to keep the driveway sanded for visitors, but really, there's no substitute for sensible shoes." *Sensible* was a word that clearly applied to Edwina Felway's wardrobe, Jane noted, as she climbed the steps to shake the woman's hand. Edwina wore a baggy tweed jacket and wool trousers and rubber Wellingtons, the outfit of an English countrywoman, a role she certainly seemed to fulfill, from her accent right down to her green garden boots. Although she had to be sixty, she stood straight and sturdy as a tree, her handsome face ruddy in the cold, her shoulders as broad as a man's. The gray hair, cut in a neat pageboy, was pinned back with tortoiseshell barrettes, fully exposing a face with prominent cheek-bones and direct blue eyes. She had no need for makeup; she was striking enough without it.

"I've put the kettle on," said Edwina, ushering them into the house. "In case you'd like some tea." She shut the door, pulled off her boots, and shoved her stocking feet into worn slippers. From upstairs came the excited barking of dogs. Big dogs, by the sound of them. "Oh, I've shut them up in the bed room. They're not all that disciplined around strangers. And they're quite intimidating."

"Do you want us to take off our shoes?" asked Frost.

"Heavens, forget it. The dogs are in and out all the time anyway, tracking in sand. I can't worry about the floor. Here, let me take your coats."

As Jane pulled off her jacket, she could not help staring upward at the ceiling that arched overhead. The open rafters were like the beams of a medieval hall. The stained-glass ocular that she had noticed outside beamed in a circle of candy-colored light. Everywhere she looked, on every wall, she saw odd-ities. A niche with a wooden Madonna, decorated in gold leaf and multicolored glass. A Russian Ortho-dox triptych painted in jewel tones. Carved animal statues and Tibetan prayer shawls, and a row of me-dieval oaken pews. Against one wall was a Native American totem pole that thrust all the way to the two-story ceiling.

"Wow," said Frost. "You've got a really interest-ing place here, ma'am."

"My husband was an anthropologist. And a col-lector, until we ran out of space to put it all." She pointed at the eagle's head that glared down from the totem pole. "That thing was his favorite. There's even more of this stuff in storage. It's probably worth a fortune, but I've gotten attached to every hideous piece and I can't bring myself to let any of it go."

"And your husband is—"

"Dead." She said it without hesitation. Just a fact of life. "He was quite a bit older than me. I've been a widow for years now. But we had a good fifteen years together." She hung up their coats, and Jane caught a glimpse into the cluttered closet, saw an ebony walking stick topped by a human skull. *That monstrosity,* she thought, *I would've tossed out a long time ago.*

Edwina shut the closet door and looked at them. "I'm sure you detectives have your hands full with this investigation. So we thought we'd make things easier for you."

"Easier?" asked Jane.

The rising squeal of a teakettle made Edwina glance toward the hallway. "Let's go sit in the kitchen," she said, and led the way up the hall, her worn slippers whisking across the tired oak floor. "Anthony warned us you'd have a lot of questions, so we wrote out a complete timeline for you. Everything we remember from last evening."

"Mr. Sansone discussed this with you?"

"He called last night, to tell me everything that happened after I left."

"I'm sorry he did. It would have been better if you hadn't talked to him about it."

Edwina paused in the hallway. "Why? So we can

approach this like blind men? If we want to be help-ful to the police, we need to be sure of our facts."

"I'd rather have independent statements from our witnesses."

"Every member of our group is *quite* independent, believe me. We each maintain our own opinions. Anthony wouldn't want it any other way. It's why we work so well together."

The scream of the teakettle abruptly cut off, and Edwina glanced toward the kitchen. "Oh, I guess he got it."

He? Who else was in the house?

Edwina scurried into the kitchen and said, "Here, let me do it."

"It's fine, Winnie, I've already filled the pot. You wanted Irish breakfast tea, right?"

The man sat in a wheelchair, his back turned to the visitors. Here was the owner of the van in the driveway. He pivoted his chair around to greet them, and Jane saw a thatch of limp brown hair and eye-glasses with thick tortoiseshell frames. The gray eyes that met her gaze were focused and curious. He looked young enough to be Edwina's son—no older than his mid-twenties. But he sounded American, and there was no family resemblance between the robustly healthy Edwina and this pale young man.

"Let me introduce you," said Edwina. "This is Detective Frost and Detective Rizzoli. And this is Oliver Stark."

Jane frowned at the young man. "You were one of the dinner guests last night. At Sansone's house."

"Yes." Oliver paused, reading her face. "Is that a problem?"

"We had hoped to talk to you separately."

"They're not happy we've already discussed the case amongst ourselves," Edwina told him.

"Didn't I predict they'd say that, Winnie?"

"But it's so much more efficient this way, nailing down the details together. It saves everyone time." Edwina crossed to the kitchen table and gathered up a huge mountain of newspapers, everything from the *Bangkok Post* to *The Irish Times*. She moved them to a countertop, then pulled out two chairs. "Come, everyone, sit down. I'll go up and get the file."

"File?" asked Jane.

"Of course we've already started a file. Anthony thought you'd want copies." She strode out of the kitchen and they heard her thump solidly up the stairs.

"Like a mighty redwood, isn't she?" said Oliver. "I never knew they grew them that big in England." He wheeled his chair to the kitchen table and waved at them to join him. "I know it goes against everything you police believe in. Independent questioning of witnesses and all that. But this really is more efficient. Plus, we had a conference call with Gottfried this morning, so you're getting three witness statements at once."

"That would be Gottfried Baum?" asked Jane. "The fourth dinner guest?"

"Yes. He had to catch a flight back to Brussels last night, which is why he and Edwina left dinner early. We called him a few hours ago to compare notes. All our memories are pretty much in agreement." He gave Jane a wan smile. "It may be one of the *only* times in history that we're all in agreement about something."

Jane sighed. "You know, Mr. Stark—"

"No one calls me that. I'm Ollie."

Jane sat down so that her gaze was level with his. He met her look with one of mild amusement, and it irritated her. It said: *I'm smart and I know it. Certainly smarter than some policewoman.* It also irritated her that he was probably right; he *looked* like the stereotypical boy genius that you always dreaded sitting next to in math class. The kid who handed in his algebra exam while everyone else was still struggling with problem number one.

"We're not trying to mess up your usual protocol," said Oliver. "We just want to be helpful. And we can be, if we work together."

Upstairs, the dogs were barking, claws tapping back and forth across the floor as Edwina shushed them, and a door thudded shut.

"You can help us by just answering our questions," said Jane.

"I think you misunderstand."

"What am I not getting?"

"How useful we can be to you. Our group."

"Right. Mr. Sansone told me about your little crime-fighting club."

"It's a society, not a club."

"What's the difference?" asked Frost.

Oliver looked at him. "Gravity, Detective. We have members around the world. And we're not amateurs."

"Are you a law enforcement professional, Ollie?" asked Jane.

"Actually, I'm a mathematician. But my real interest is symbology."

"Excuse me?"

"I interpret symbols. Their origins and their meanings, both apparent and hidden."

"Uh-huh. And Mrs. Felway?"

"She's an anthropologist. She just joined us. Came highly recommended from our London branch."

"And Mr. Sansone? He's certainly not law enforcement."

"He might as well be."

"He told us he's a retired academic. A Boston College history professor. That doesn't sound like a cop to me."

Oliver laughed. "Anthony *would* underplay himself. That's just like him."

Edwina came back into the kitchen, carrying a file folder. "Just like whom, Ollie?"

"We're talking about Anthony. The police think he's just a retired college professor."

"And that's just the way he likes it." Edwina sat down. "It doesn't help to advertise."

"What are we supposed to know about him, anyway?" asked Frost.

"Well, you know he's quite wealthy," said Edwina.

"That was pretty obvious."

"I mean, *seriously* wealthy. That house on Beacon Hill, it's nothing compared to his estate in Florence."

"Or his house in London," said Oliver.

"And we're supposed to be impressed by that?" said Jane.

Edwina's response was a cool stare. "Money alone seldom makes a man impressive. It's what he does with it." She placed the file folder on the table in front of Jane. "For you, Detective."

Jane opened the folder to the first page. It was a neatly typed chronology of last night's events, as recalled by three of the dinner guests, Edwina and Oliver and the mysterious Gottfried Baum.

(All times are approximate)
6:00: Edwina and Gottfried arrive.
6:15: Oliver Stark arrives.
6:20: Joyce O'Donnell arrives.
6:40: First course served by Jeremy . . .

The entire menu was listed. Consommé followed by salmon aspic and a salad of baby lettuces. Beef tournedos with crisp potato cakes. A tasting of port to accompany slivers of Reblochon cheese. And finally, with coffee, a Sacher torte and thick cream.

At nine-thirty, Edwina and Gottfried departed together for Logan Airport, where Edwina dropped Gottfried off for his flight to Brussels.

At nine forty-five Oliver left Beacon Hill and drove straight home.

"And that's what we remember of the timeline," said Edwina. "We tried to be as accurate as possible."

Right down to the consommé, thought Jane, scanning the chronology. There was nothing particularly helpful here; it repeated the same information that Sansone and his butler had already provided, but with the additional culinary details. The overall picture was the same: A winter's night. Four guests arrive on Beacon Hill within twenty minutes of one another. They and their host share an elegant supper and sip wine while they discuss the crimes of the day, never realizing that, just outside, in the frigid garden behind their building, a woman was being murdered.

Some crime-fighting club. These amateurs are less than useless.

The next page in the folder was a sheet of stationery with only a single letter printed at the top: "M," in a gothic font. And beneath it, the handwritten note: "Oliver, your analysis? A.S." Anthony Sansone? Jane flipped to the next page and stared at a photograph that she immediately recognized: the symbols that had been drawn on Sansone's garden door.

"This is from the crime scene last night," said Jane. "How did you get this?"

"Anthony sent it over this morning. It's one of the photos he took last night."

"This isn't meant for public distribution," said Jane. "It's evidence."

"Very interesting evidence," said Oliver. "You know the significance, don't you? Of those symbols?"

"They're satanic."

"Oh, that's the automatic answer. You see weird symbols at a crime scene and you just assume it's the work of some nasty satanic cult. Everyone's favorite villains."

Frost said, "Do you think this is something else?"

"I'm not saying this *couldn't* be a cult. Satanists do use the reverse cross as a symbol of the Antichrist. And that slaying on Christmas Eve, the one with the decapitation, there was that circle drawn on the floor around the victim's head. And the burned candles. That certainly calls to mind a satanic ritual."

"How do you know about all this?"

Oliver glanced at Edwina. "They really think we're clueless, don't they?"

"It doesn't matter how we learned the details," said Edwina. "The fact is, we do know about the case."

"Then what do you think about this symbol?" asked Frost, pointing to the photograph. "The one that looks like an eye? Is that satanic as well?"

"It depends," said Oliver. "First, let's consider what you saw at the Christmas Eve death scene. There was a red chalk circle where he'd placed the victim's severed head. And there were five candles burned at the perimeter."

"Meaning?"

"Well, circles in and of themselves are quite primitive symbols, and they are universal. They can mean all sorts of things. The sun, the moon. Protection. Eternity. Rebirth, the cycle of life. And yes, it's also used by satanic cults to represent the female sexual organ. We don't really know what it meant to the person who drew it that night."

"But it could have a satanic meaning," said Frost.

"Of course. And the five candles may represent the five points of a pentagram. Now, let's look at what was drawn last night, on Anthony's garden door." He pointed to the photograph. "What do you see?"

"An eye."

"Tell me more about this eye."

"It's got, like, a teardrop. And an eyelash sticking out below it."

Oliver took a pen from his shirt pocket and flipped the sheet of stationery to its blank side. "Let me draw it more clearly, so you'll see exactly what the different elements are in this symbol." On the sheet of paper, he reproduced the drawing:

"It still looks like an eye," said Frost.

"Yes, but all these features—the eyelash, the teardrop—that makes it a very specific eye. This symbol is called Udjat. Experts on satanic cults will tell you this is a symbol for Lucifer's all-seeing eye. The teardrop is because he mourns for those souls outside his influence. Some conspiracy theorists claim it's the same eye printed on U.S. currency."

"You mean on the top of the pyramid?"

"Right. Their so-called proof that the world's finances are run by worshippers of Satan."

"So we're back to satanic symbols," said Jane.

"That's one interpretation."

"What others are there?"

"This is also a symbol used by the ancient fraternity of Freemasons. In which case it has quite a benign meaning. For them, it symbolizes enlightenment, illumination."

"The seeking of knowledge," said Edwina. "It's about learning the secrets of their craft."

Jane said, "You're saying this murder was done by a Freemason?"

"Good grief, no!" said Oliver. "That's not at all what I'm saying. The poor Freemasons have been the target of so many malicious accusations, I'm not even going to repeat them. I'm just giving you a quick history lesson. This is my field, you know, the interpretation of symbols. I'm trying to explain that this symbol, Udjat, is quite an old one. It's been used throughout history for various purposes. For some people, its meaning is sacred. For others, it's terrifying, a symbol of evil. But its original meaning, in the time of ancient Egypt, was quite a bit less threatening. And rather practical."

"What did it mean then?"

"It represented the eye of Horus, the sun god. Horus is usually depicted in paintings or sculptures as a falcon's head on a man's body. He was personified on earth by the Pharaoh."

Jane sighed. "So it could be a satanic symbol, or a symbol for illumination. Or the eye of some Egyptian god with a bird's head."

"There's yet another possibility."

"I thought you'd say that."

Oliver picked up the pen again and drew another variation of the eye. "This symbol," he said, "came into use in Egypt around 1200 B.C. It's found in hieratic script."

"Is that still the eye of Horus?" asked Frost.

"Yes, but notice how the eye is now made up of separate sections. The iris is represented by this circle, between two halves of the sclera. Then there's the teardrop and the curling lash, as you called it. It looks like just a stylized version of Udjat, but it actually had a very practical use, as a mathematical symbol. Each part of the eye represents a fraction." He wrote numbers on the sketch now:

"These fractions arise by dividing subsequent numbers in half. The entire eye represents the whole number, one. The left half of the sclera represents the fraction one half. The eyelash is one thirty-second.

"Are we getting around to some kind of point here?" asked Jane.

"Of course."

"And that would be?"

"That maybe there's a specific *message* in this eye. In the first death scene, the severed head was enclosed by a circle. In the second scene, there's a drawing of Udjat on the door. What if they're connected, those two symbols? What if one symbol was supposed to be the *key* to interpreting the other?"

"A mathematical key, you mean?"

"Yes. And the circle, at the first killing, represented an element of Udjat."

Jane frowned at Oliver's sketches, at the numbers he had jotted in the various sections of the all-seeing eye. "You're saying that the circle at the first killing is really supposed to be the iris."

"Yes. And it has a value."

"You mean it represents a number? A fraction."

She looked up at Oliver and saw that he was leaning toward her, a flush of excitement in his cheeks.

"Exactly," he said. "And that fraction would be?"

"One fourth," she said.

"Right." He smiled. *"Right."*

"One fourth of what?" asked Frost.

"Oh, that we don't know yet. It could mean a quarter moon. Or one of the four seasons."

"Or it could mean he's completed only a quarter of his task," said Edwina.

"Yes," said Oliver. "Maybe he's telling us there are more kills to come. That he's planning a total of four."

Jane looked at Frost. "There were four place settings at the dining table."

In the pause that followed, the ringing of Jane's cell phone sounded startlingly loud. She recognized the number for the crime-scene lab and answered it at once.

"Rizzoli."

"Hi, Detective. It's Erin in Trace Evidence. You know that red circle that was drawn on the kitchen floor?"

"Yeah. We're talking about it right now."

"I've compared that pigment with the symbols from the Beacon Hill crime scene. The drawings on the door. The pigments do match."

"So our perp used the same red chalk at both scenes."

"Well, that's why I'm calling. It's not red chalk."

"What is it?"

"It's something a lot more interesting."

SIXTEEN

THE CRIME LAB was in the south wing of Boston PD's Schroeder Plaza, right down the hallway from the homicide unit offices. The walk took Jane and Frost past windows that looked out over the tired and broken neighborhood of Roxbury. Today, under a cloak of snow, all was purified and white; even the sky had been cleansed, the air crystalline. But that sparkling view of skyline drew only a glance from Jane; her focus was on Room S269, the trace evidence lab.

Criminalist Erin Volchko was waiting for them. As soon as Jane and Frost walked into the room, she swiveled around from the microscope that she'd been hunched over and swept up a file that was sitting on the countertop. "You two owe me a stiff drink," she said, "after all the work I put into this one."

"You always say that," said Frost.

"This time I mean it. Out of all the trace evidence that came in from that first scene, I thought this would be the one we'd have the least trouble with. Instead, I had to chase all over the place to find out what that circle was drawn with."

"And it's not plain old chalk," said Jane.

"Nope." Erin handed her the folder. "Take a look."

Jane opened the file. On top was a photographic sheet with a series of images. Red blobs on a blurred background.

"I started with high-magnification light microscopy," said Erin. "About 600X to 1000X. Those blobs you see there are pigment particles, collected from the red circle drawn on the kitchen floor."

"So what does this mean?"

"A few things. You can see there are varying degrees of color. The particles aren't uniform. The refractive index also varied, from 2.5 to 3.01, and many of those particles are birefringent."

"Meaning?"

"Those are anhydrous iron oxide particles. A quite common substance found around the world. It's what gives clay its distinctive hues. It's used in artists' pigments to produce the colors red, yellow, and brown."

"That doesn't sound like anything special."

"That's what I thought, until I dug deeper into the subject. I assumed it came from a piece of chalk or a pastel crayon, so I ran comparisons against samples we obtained from two local artists' supply stores."

"Any matches?"

"None. The difference was immediately apparent under the microscope. First, the red pigment granules in the pastel crayons showed far less variability in color and refractive index. That's because most anhydrous iron oxide used in pigments today is synthetic—manufactured, not mined from the earth. They commonly use a compound called Mars Red, a mixture of iron and aluminum oxides."

"So these pigment granules here, in this photo, aren't synthetic?"

"No, this is naturally occurring anhydrous iron oxide. It's also called hematite, derived from the Greek word for blood. Because it's sometimes red."

"Do they use the natural stuff in art supplies?"

"We did find a few specialty chalks and pastel crayons that use natural hematite as a pigment. But chalks contain calcium carbonate. And manufactured pastel crayons usually use a natural glue to bind the pigment. Some kind of starch, like methyl cellulose or gum tragacanth. It's all mixed together into a paste, which is then extruded through a mold to make crayons. We found no traces of gum tragacanth or any binding starch in the crime-scene samples. Nor did we find enough calcium carbonate to indicate that this came from colored chalk."

"Then we're not dealing with something you'd find at an art supply store."

"Not locally."

"So where *did* this red stuff come from?"

"Well, let's talk about this red stuff first. What it is, exactly."

"You called it hematite."

"Right. Anhydrous iron oxide. But when it's found in tinted clay, it has another name as well: ocher."

Frost said, "Isn't that, like, what American Indians used to paint their faces?"

"Ocher has been used by mankind for at least

three hundred thousand years. It's even been found in Neanderthal graves. Red ocher in particular seems to have been universally valued in death ceremonies, probably because of its similarity to blood. It's found in Stone Age cave paintings and on walls in Pompeii. It was used by the ancients to color their bodies as decoration or war paint. And it was used in magical rituals."

"Including satanic ceremonies?"

"It's the color of blood. Whatever your religion, that color has symbolic power." Erin paused. "This killer makes quite unusual choices."

"I think we already know that," said Jane.

"What I mean is, he's in touch with history. He doesn't use common chalk for his ritual drawings. Instead he uses the same primitive pigment that was used in the Paleolithic era. And he didn't just dig it up in his own backyard."

"But you said that red ocher is found in common clay," said Frost. "So maybe he did dig it up."

"Not if his backyard is anywhere around here." Erin nodded at the file folder Jane was holding. "Check out the chemical analysis. What we found on gas chromatography and Raman spectroscopy."

Jane flipped to the next page and saw a computer printout. A graph with multiple spikes. "You want to interpret this for us?"

"Sure. First, the Raman spectroscopy."

"Never heard of it."

"It's an archaeologist's technique for analysis of historic artifacts. It uses the light spectrum of a substance to determine its properties. The big advantage for archaeologists is that it doesn't destroy the artifact itself. You can analyze the pigments on everything from mummy wrappings to the Shroud of Turin and not damage the article in any way. I asked Dr. Ian MacAvoy, from the Harvard archaeology department, to analyze the Raman spectra results, and he confirmed that the sample contains iron oxide plus clay plus silica."

"That's red ocher?"

"Yes. Red ocher."

"But you already knew that."

"Still, it was nice to have him confirm it. Then Dr. MacAvoy offered to help me track down its source. Where in the world this particular red ocher came from."

"You can actually do that?"

"The technique's still in its research stages. It probably wouldn't hold up in court as evidence. But he was curious enough to run a comparison against a library of ocher profiles he's compiled from around the world. He determines the concentrations of eleven other elements in the samples, such as magnesium, titanium, and thorium. The theory is, a particular geographic source will have a distinctive trace element profile. It's like looking at soil samples from a car tire and knowing that it has the lead-zinc profile of a mining district in Missouri. In this case, with this ocher, we're checking the sample against eleven separate variables."

"Those other trace elements."

"Right. And archaeologists have compiled a library of ocher sources."

"Why?"

"Because it helps determine the provenance of an

artifact. For instance, where did the pigment on the Shroud of Turin come from? Was it France or Israel? The answer may establish the shroud's origins. Or an ancient cave painting—where did the artist get his ocher? If it came from a thousand miles away, it tells you that either he's traveled that distance himself, or that there was some form of prehistoric trade. That's why the ocher source library is so valuable. It gives us a window into the lives of the ancients."

"What do we know about our pigment sample?" asked Frost.

"Well." Erin smiled. "First, it has rather a large proportion of manganese dioxide—fifteen percent, giving it a deeper, richer tone. It's the same proportion found in red ochers that were used in medieval Italy."

"It's Italian?"

"No. The Venetians imported it from elsewhere. When Dr. MacAvoy compared the entire elemental profile, he found that it matched one location in particular, a place where they're still mining red ocher even today. The island of Cyprus."

Jane said, "I need to see a world map."

Erin pointed to the file. "It just so happens that I pulled one off the Internet."

Jane flipped to the page. "Okay, I see. It's in the Mediterranean, just south of Turkey."

"It seems to me that red chalk would've been a lot easier to use," said Frost.

"And far cheaper. Your killer chose an unusual pigment, from an obscure source. Maybe he has ties to Cyprus."

"Or he could just be playing games with us," said Frost. "Drawing weird symbols. Using weird pigments. It's like he wants to screw around with our heads."

Jane was still studying the map. She thought of the symbol drawn on the door in Anthony Sansone's garden. Udjat, the all-seeing eye. She looked at Frost. "Egypt is directly south of Cyprus."

"You're thinking of the eye of Horus?"

"What's that?" Erin asked.

"That symbol left at the Beacon Hill crime scene," said Jane. "Horus is the Egyptian sun god."

"Is that a satanic symbol?"

"We don't know what it means to this perp," said Frost. "Everyone's got a theory. He's a Satanist. He's a history buff. Or it could just be plain old-fashioned insanity."

Erin nodded. "Like Son of Sam. I remember the police wasted a lot of time wondering who the mysterious Sam was. It turned out to be nothing more than the killer's auditory hallucination. A talking dog."

Jane closed the folder. "You know, I kind of hope our perp is crazy, too."

"Why?" asked Erin.

"Because I'm a lot more scared of the alternative. That this killer is perfectly sane."

Jane and Frost sat in the car as the engine warmed and the defroster melted the fog from the windshield. If only it was so easy to clear the mist cloaking the killer. She couldn't form a picture of him; she couldn't begin to imagine what he looked like. A mystic? An artist? An historian? *All I do know is that he's a butcher.*

Frost shifted into gear, and they pulled into traffic, which was moving far more slowly than usual, on roads slick with ice. Under clear skies, the temperature was dropping, and tonight the cold would be the bitterest so far this winter. It was a night to stay home and eat a hearty stew, a night, she hoped, when evil would stay off the streets.

Frost drove east on Columbus Avenue, then headed toward Beacon Hill, where they planned to take another look at the crime scene. The car at last had warmed, and she dreaded stepping out again, into that wind, into Sansone's courtyard, still stained with frozen blood.

She noticed they were approaching Massachusetts Avenue and she said, suddenly, "Could you turn right?"

"Aren't we going to Sansone's place?"

"Just turn here."

"If you say so." He made a right.

"Keep going. Toward Albany Street."

"We going to the M.E.'s?"

"No."

"So where we headed?"

"It's right down here. Another few blocks." She watched the addresses go by, and said, "Stop. Right here." She stared across the street.

Frost pulled over to the curb and frowned at her. "Kinko's?"

"My dad works there." She glanced at her watch. "And it's just about noon."

"What are we doing?"

"Waiting."

"Aw geez, Rizzoli. This isn't about your mom, is it?"

"It's screwing up my whole life right now."

"Your parents are having a tiff. It happens."

"Wait till your mother moves in with *you*. See how Alice likes it."

"I'm sure this'll blow over and your mom'll go home."

"Not if there's another woman involved." She sat up straight. "There he is."

Frank Rizzoli stepped out the front door of Kinko's and zipped up his jacket. He glanced at the sky, gave a visible shiver, and exhaled a breath that swirled white in the cold.

"Looks like he's going on his lunch break," said Frost. "What's the big deal?"

"That," said Jane softly. "*That's* the big deal."

A woman had just stepped out the door as well, a big-haired blond wearing a black leather jacket over skintight blue jeans. Frank grinned and slipped his arm around her waist. They began to walk down the street, away from Jane and Frost, arms wrapped around each other.

"What the fuck," said Jane. "It's true."

"You know, I think we should probably just move on."

"Look at them. *Look* at them!"

Frost started the engine. "I could really use some lunch. How about we go to—"

Jane shoved open the door and stepped out.

"Aw, Rizzoli! Come on."

She darted across the street and stalked up the

sidewalk, right behind her father. "Hey," she yelled. *"Hey!"*

Frank halted, his arm dropping from around the woman's waist. He turned to stare, slack-jawed, as his daughter approached. The blond had not yet released her grip and she continued to cling to Frank, even as he made futile attempts to extricate himself. From a distance, the woman had looked like a real eye-catcher, but as Jane drew closer she saw, fanning out from the woman's eyes, deep creases that even thick makeup couldn't conceal, and she caught a whiff of cigarette smoke. *This* was the piece of ass Frank had traded up to, a bimbo with big hair? This human equivalent of a golden retriever?

"Janie," said Frank. "This isn't the time to—"

"When *is* the time?"

"I'll call you, okay? We'll talk about it tonight."

"Frankie honey, what's going on?" the blond asked.

Don't you call him Frankie! Jane glared at the woman. "And what's *your* name?"

The woman's chin jutted up. "Who wants to know?"

"Just answer the fucking question."

"Yeah, make me!" The blond looked at Frank. "Who the hell is this?"

Frank lifted a hand to his head and gave a moan, as though in pain. "Oh, man."

"Boston PD," said Jane. She pulled out her ID and thrust it in the woman's face. "Now tell me your name."

The blond didn't even look at the ID; her startled gaze was on Jane. "Sandie," she murmured.

"Sandie what?"

"Huffington."

"ID," ordered Jane.

"Janie," said her dad. "That's enough."

Sandie obediently pulled out her wallet to show her driver's license. "What did we do wrong?" She shot a suspicious look at Frank. "What'd *you* do?"

"This is all bullshit," he said.

"And when's the bullshit going to end, huh?" Jane shot back at him. "When are you going to grow up?"

"This is none of your beeswax."

"Oh no? She's sitting in my apartment right now, probably crying her eyes out. All because you can't keep your goddamn pants zipped."

"She?" said Sandie. "Who're we talking about?"

"Thirty-seven years of marriage, and you dump her for boom-boom here?"

"You don't understand," said Frank.

"Oh, I understand just fine."

"You have no idea what it's like. Just a damn worker bee, that's all I am. Some drone to put food on the table. I'm sixty-one years old, and what do I got to show for it? You don't think I deserve a little fun, for once in my life?"

"You think Mom's having any fun?"

"That's *her* problem."

"It's mine, too."

"Well, I take no responsibility for *that*."

"Hey," said Sandie. "This is your daughter?" She looked at Jane. "You said you were a cop."

Frank sighed. "She *is* a cop."

"You're breaking her heart, you know that?" said Jane. "Do you even care?"

"What about *my* heart?" Sandie cut in.

Jane ignored the bimbo and kept her gaze on Frank. "I don't even know who you are anymore, Dad. I used to respect you. Now look at you! Pathetic, just pathetic. This blondie shakes her ass and you're like some idiot dog, sniffing at it. Oh yeah, Dad, hump away."

Frank shoved a finger at her. "That's enough outta *you*!"

"You think boom-boom here is gonna take care of you when you're sick, huh? You think she'll stand by you? Hell, does she even know how to cook?"

"How dare you," said Sandie. "You used your badge to scare me."

"Mom'll take you back, Dad. I know she will. Go talk to her."

"There's a law against what you did," said Sandie. "There's gotta be! It's police harassment!"

"I'll show you what police harassment is," Jane shot back. "You just keep pushing me."

"What're you gonna do, arrest me?" Sandie leaned into her, eyes narrowed to slits of mascara. "Go ahead." The woman shoved her finger against Jane's chest and gave a hard shove. "I dare you."

What happened next was purely reflexive. Jane didn't even stop to think, but simply reacted. With one sweep of her hand, she grasped Sandie's wrist, twisted her around. Through the rushing of her own blood, she heard Sandie screaming obscenities. Heard her dad yell, "Stop it! For God's sake, stop!"

But she was operating on automatic now, all nerves firing on full thrust as she shoved Sandie to her knees, the way she'd handle any perp. But this time there was rage fueling her, making her twist harder than she had to, making her want to hurt this woman. Humiliate her.

"Rizzoli! Jesus, Rizzoli, that's *enough*!"

The sound of Frost's voice finally penetrated the pounding of her own pulse. Abruptly she released Sandie and stepped back, breathing hard. She stared down at the woman who knelt whimpering on the sidewalk. Frank dropped to his knees beside Sandie and helped her to her feet.

"What the hell're you gonna do now?" Frank looked up at his daughter. "Arrest her?"

"You saw it. She shoved me."

"She was upset."

"*She* made the first contact."

"Rizzoli," Frost said quietly. "Let's just drop it, okay?"

"I *could* arrest her," said Jane. "Damn it, I *could*."

"Yeah, okay," said Frost. "You could. But do you really want to?"

She heaved out a breath. "I got better things to do," she muttered. Then she turned and walked back to the car. By the time she climbed in, her dad and the blond had already vanished around the corner.

Frost slid in beside her and pulled his door shut. "That," he said, "was not a cool thing to do."

"Just drive."

"You went in looking for a fight."

"Did you see her? My dad's going out with a friggin' bimbo!"

"All the more reason why you need to stay a hundred miles away from her. You two were gonna kill each other."

Jane sighed and dropped her head in her hand. "What do I tell my mom?"

"Nothing." Frost started the car and pulled away from the curb. "Their marriage is not your business."

"I'm gonna have to go home and look at her face. See all the hurt there. That *makes* it my business."

"Then be a good daughter. Give her a shoulder to cry on," he said. "Because she's gonna need one."

What do I tell my mom?

Jane pulled into a parking space outside her apartment and sat for a moment, dreading what came next. Maybe she shouldn't tell her what happened today. Angela already knew about Dad and Miss Golden Retriever. Why rub her face in it? Why humiliate her even more?

Because if I were Mom, I'd want to be told. I wouldn't want my daughter keeping secrets from me, no matter how painful they were.

Jane stepped out of the car, debating what to say, knowing that, no matter what she decided, this was going to be a miserable evening, and that little she could do or say would ease her mother's pain. Be a good daughter, Frost had said; give her a shoulder to cry on. Okay, that much she could manage.

She climbed the stairs to the second floor, her feet

feeling heavier with every step as she silently cursed Miss Sandie Huffington, who had screwed up all their lives. *Oh, I've got my eye on you. You so much as jaywalk, Bimbo, and I'm gonna be right there. Outstanding parking tickets? Bad news for you. Mom can't hit back, but I sure as hell can.* She thrust her key into her apartment door and paused, frowning at the sound of her mother's voice inside. The sound of her laughter.

Mom?

Pushing open the door, she inhaled the scent of cinnamon and vanilla. Heard a different laugh now, startlingly familiar. A man's. She walked into the kitchen and stared at retired detective Vince Korsak, who sat at the table with a cup of coffee. In front of him was a huge plate of sugar cookies.

"Hey," he said, lifting his coffee cup in greeting. Baby Regina, sitting right beside him in her infant carrier, lifted her tiny hand, too, as though in imitation.

"Um . . . what are you doing here?"

"Janie!" scolded Angela, setting a pan of freshly baked cookies on the stovetop to cool. "What a thing to say to Vince."

Vince? She's calling him Vince?

"He called to invite you and Gabriel to a party," said Angela.

"And you, too, Mrs. Rizzoli," Korsak said, winking at Angela. "The more chicks that come, the better!"

Angela flushed, and it wasn't from the oven's heat.

"And I bet he smelled the cookies over the phone," said Jane.

"I just happened to be here baking. I told him that if he came right over, I'd whip up an extra batch for him."

"No way I'd pass up an offer like that," laughed Korsak. "Hey, pretty nice having your mom here, huh?"

Jane eyed the crumbs all over his wrinkled shirt. "I see you're off your diet."

"And I see you're in a good mood." He took a sloppy gulp of coffee and swiped a fat hand across his mouth. "I hear you caught yourself a freakin' weird one." He paused, glanced at Angela. "Pardon my French, Mrs. Rizzoli."

"Oh, say whatever you want," said Angela. "I want you to feel right at home."

Please don't encourage him.

"Some kinda satanic cult," he said.

"You heard that?"

"Retirement didn't make me deaf."

Or dumb. As much as he might irritate her with his crude jokes and appalling hygiene, Korsak was one of the sharpest investigators she knew. Although retired since his heart attack last year, he had never really left the badge behind. On a weekend night, she could still find him hanging out at JP Doyle's, a favorite Boston PD watering hole, catching up on the latest war stories. Retired or not, Vince Korsak would die a cop.

"What else did you hear?" asked Jane, sitting down at the table.

"That your perp's an artist. Leaves cute little drawings behind. And he likes to"—Korsak paused and glanced at Angela, who was sliding cookies off the pan—"slice and dice. Am I warm?"

"A little too warm."

Angela lifted off the last of the cookies and sealed them in a ziplock bag. With a flourish, she placed them in front of Korsak. This was not the Angela whom Jane had expected to come home to. Her mother was actually *bustling* around the kitchen now, gathering pans and bowls, splashing soapsuds as she washed up in the sink. She didn't look miserable or abandoned or depressed; she looked ten years younger. *Is this what happens when your husband walks out on you?*

"Tell Jane more about your party," said Angela, refilling Korsak's coffee cup.

"Oh yeah." He took a noisy slurp. "See, I signed my divorce papers last week. Almost a year of wrangling over money, and it's finally over. I figured it was time to celebrate my new status as a free man. I got my apartment all decorated. Nice leather couch, big-screen TV. I'm gonna buy a few cases, get some friends together, and we're all gonna par-*tee*!"

He'd turned into a fifty-five-year-old teenager with a potbelly and a comb-over. Could he get any more pathetic?

"So you're coming, right?" he asked Jane. "Second Saturday in January."

"Let me check the date with Gabriel."

"If he can't make it, you can always come stag. Just be sure to bring your older sister here." He gave Angela a wink, and she giggled.

This was getting more painful by the minute. Jane was almost relieved to hear the muffled ringing of her cell phone. She went into the living room, where she'd left her purse, and dug out her phone.

"Rizzoli," she said.

Lieutenant Marquette did not waste time with pleasantries. "You need to be more respectful of Anthony Sansone," he said.

In the kitchen, she could hear Korsak laughing, and the sound suddenly irritated her. *If you're going to flirt with my mom, for God's sake, take it somewhere else.*

"I hear you've been giving him and his friends a hard time," said Marquette.

"Maybe you could define what you mean by *hard time?*"

"You questioned him for nearly two hours. Grilled his butler, his dinner guests. Then you went back to see him again this afternoon. You're making him feel as if he's the one under investigation."

"Well, gee, I'm sorry if I hurt his feelings. We're just doing what we always do."

"Rizzoli, try to keep in mind the man is not a suspect."

"I haven't reached that conclusion yet. O'Donnell was in his house. Eve Kassovitz was killed in his garden. And when his butler finds the body, what does Sansone do? He takes photos. Passes them around to his friends. You wanna know the truth? These people are not normal. Certainly Sansone isn't."

"He's not a suspect."

"I haven't eliminated him."

"You can trust me on this. Leave him alone."

She paused. "You want to tell me more, Lieutenant?" she asked quietly. "What do I not know about Anthony Sansone?"

"He's not a man we want to alienate."

"Do you know him?"

"Not personally. I'm just conveying the word from above. We've been told to treat him with respect."

She hung up. Moving to the window, she stared out at an afternoon sky that was no longer blue. More snow was probably on the way. She thought: *One minute you think you can see forever, and then the clouds move in and obscure everything.*

She reached for her cell phone again and began to dial.

SEVENTEEN

MAURA WATCHED through the viewing window as Yoshima, wearing a lead apron, positioned the collimator over the abdomen. Some people walk into work on Monday mornings dreading nothing worse awaiting them than a stack of fresh paperwork or message slips. On this Monday morning, what had awaited Maura was the woman who lay on that table, her body now stripped bare. Maura saw Yoshima reemerge from behind the lead shield to retrieve the film cassette for processing. He glanced up and gave a nod.

Maura pushed through the door, back into the autopsy lab.

The night she had crouched shivering in Anthony Sansone's garden, she had seen this body only under the glow of flashlight beams. Today, Detective Eve Kassovitz lay fully bared to view, harsh lights washing out every shadow. The blood had been rinsed away, revealing raw, pink injuries. A scalp laceration. A stab wound on the chest, beneath the sternum. And the lidless eyes, the corneas now clouded from exposure. That was what Maura could not help staring at: those mutilated eyes.

The whish of the door announced Jane's arrival. "You haven't started yet?" Jane asked.

"No. Is anyone else joining us?"

"It's just me today." Jane paused in the midst of tying on her gown, her gaze suddenly fixed on the table. On the face of her dead colleague. "I should have stood up for her," she said quietly. "When those jerks in the unit started in with the stupid jokes, I should have put a stop to it right there."

"They're the ones who should feel guilty, Jane. Not you."

"But I've been there myself. I know how it feels." Jane kept looking down at the exposed corneas. "They won't be able to pretty up these eyes for the funeral."

"It will have to be a closed coffin."

"The eye of Horus," Jane said softly.

"What?"

"That drawing on Sansone's door. It's an ancient symbol, dating back to the Egyptians. It's called Udjat, the all-seeing eye."

"Who told you about that?"

"One of Sansone's dinner guests." She looked at Maura. "These people—Sansone and his friends—they're weird. The more I find out about them, the more they creep me out. Especially *him*."

Yoshima came out of the processing room, carrying a sheaf of freshly developed films. They gave a musical twang as he clipped them to the light box.

Maura reached for the ruler and measured the scalp laceration, jotting its dimensions on a clipboard. "He called me that night, you know," she said, without looking up. "To make sure I got home safely."

"*Sansone* did?"

Maura glanced up. "Do you consider him a suspect?"

"Think about this: After they found the body, do you know what Sansone did? Before he even called the police? He got out his camera and snapped some photos. Had his butler deliver them to his friends the next morning. Tell me that isn't weird."

"But do you consider him a suspect?"

After a pause, Jane admitted, "No. And if I did, it would present problems."

"What do you mean?"

"Gabriel tried to do a little digging for me. He called around to find out more about the guy. All he did was ask a few questions, and suddenly doors slammed shut. The FBI, Interpol, no one wanted to talk about Sansone. Obviously he has friends in high places who are ready to protect him."

Maura thought of the house on Beacon Hill. The butler, the antiques. "His wealth could have something to do with it."

"It's all inherited. He sure didn't make his fortune teaching medieval history at Boston College."

"How wealthy are we talking about?"

"That house on Beacon Hill? It's his equivalent of slumming. He's also got homes in London and Paris, plus a family estate in Italy. The guy's an eligible bachelor, he's loaded, and he's good-looking. But he never turns up on the society pages. No charity balls, no black-tie fundraisers. He's like a total recluse."

"He didn't strike me as the kind of man you'd find on the party circuit."

"What else did you think about him?"

"We didn't have that long a conversation."

"But you did have one that night."

"It was freezing outside, and he invited me in for coffee."

"Didn't that seem a little weird?"

"What?"

"That he made a special effort to invite you in?"

"I appreciated the gesture. And for the record, it was the butler who came out to get me."

"You, specifically? He knew who you were?"

Maura hesitated. "Yes."

"What did he want from you, Doc?"

Maura had moved on to the torso, and she now measured the stab wound on the chest and jotted the dimensions on her clipboard. The questions were getting too pointed, and she didn't like the implications: that she'd let herself be used by Anthony Sansone. "I didn't reveal anything vital about the case, Jane. If that's what you're asking."

"But you did talk about it?"

"About a number of things. And yes, he wanted to know what I thought. It's not surprising, since the body was found in his garden. Understandably, he's curious. And maybe a little eccentric." She met Jane's gaze and found it uncomfortably probing. She dropped her attention back to the corpse, to wounds that did not disturb her nearly as much as Jane's questions.

"Eccentric? That's the only word you can think of?"

She thought of the way Sansone had studied her that night, how his eyes had reflected the firelight, and other words came to mind. *Intelligent. Attractive. Intimidating.*

"You don't think he's just a little bit creepy?" asked Jane. "Because I sure do."

"Why?"

"You saw his house. It's like stepping into a time warp. And you never saw the other rooms, with all those portraits staring from the walls. It's like walking into Dracula's castle."

"He's a history professor."

"Was. He's not teaching anymore."

"Those are probably heirlooms, and priceless. Clearly he appreciates his family legacy."

"Oh yeah, the family legacy. That's where he got lucky. He's a fourth-generation trust-funder."

"Yet he pursued a successful academic career. You have to give him some credit for that. He didn't just turn into an idle playboy."

"Here's the interesting twist. The family trust fund was established back in 1905, by his great-grandfather. Guess what the name of that trust fund is?"

"I have no idea."

"It's called the Mephisto Foundation."

Maura glanced up, startled. "Mephisto?" she murmured.

"You gotta wonder," said Jane, "with a name like that, what kind of family legacy are we talking about?"

Yoshima asked, "What's the significance of that name? Mephisto?"

"I looked it up," said Jane. "It's short for Mephistopheles. Doc here probably knows who he was."

"The name comes from the legend of Dr. Faustus," said Maura.

"Who?" asked Yoshima.

"Dr. Faustus was a magician," said Maura. "He drew secret symbols to summon the Devil. An evil spirit named Mephistopheles appeared and offered him a deal."

"What kind of deal?"

"In exchange for the full knowledge of magic, Dr. Faustus sold his soul to the Devil."

"So Mephisto is . . ."

"A servant of Satan."

A voice suddenly spoke over the intercom. "Dr. Isles," said Maura's secretary, Louise. "You have an outside call on line one. It's a Mr. Sansone. Do you want to pick up, or shall I take a message?"

Speak of the Devil.

Maura met Jane's gaze and saw Jane give a quick nod.

"I'll take the call," said Maura. Stripping off her gloves, she crossed to the wall phone and picked up the receiver. "Mr. Sansone?"

"I hope I'm not interrupting you," he said.

She looked at the body on the table. *Eve Kassovitz won't mind,* she thought. *There is no one as patient as the dead.* "I have a minute to talk."

"This Saturday, I'm hosting a supper here at my home. I'd love to have you join us."

Maura paused, acutely aware that Jane was watching her. "I'll need to think about it," she said.

"I'm sure you're wondering what this is all about."

"Actually, I am."

"I promise not to pick your brain about the investigation."

"I can't talk about it anyway. You do know that."

"Understood. That's not why I'm inviting you."

"Then why?" A blunt, inelegant question, but she had to ask it.

"We share common interests. Common concerns."

"I'm not sure I understand what you mean."

"Join us on Saturday, around seven. We can talk about it then."

"Let me check my schedule first. I'll let you know." She hung up.

"What was that all about?" asked Jane.

"He just invited me to dinner."

"He wants something from you."

"Not a thing, he claims." Maura crossed to the cabinet for a fresh pair of gloves. Although her hands were steady as she pulled them on, she could feel her face flushing, her pulse throbbing in her fingertips.

"You believe that?"

"Of course not. That's why I'm not going."

Jane said quietly, "Maybe you should."

Maura turned to look at her. "You can't be serious."

"I'd like to know more about the Mephisto Foundation. Who they are, what they do at their secret little meetings. I may not be able to get the information any other way."

"So you want me to do it for you?"

"All I'm saying is, I don't think it's necessarily a bad idea if you go. As long as you're careful."

Maura crossed to the table. Staring down at Eve Kassovitz, she thought: *This woman was a cop and she was armed. Yet even she wasn't careful enough.* Maura picked up the knife and began to cut.

Her blade traced a Y on the torso, two incisions slicing from both shoulders to meet lower than usual beneath the sternum. To preserve the stab wound. Even before the ribs were cut, before the chest was opened, she knew what she would find inside the thorax. She could see it in the chest films now hanging on the light box: the globular outline of the heart, far larger than it should be in a healthy young woman. Lifting off the shield of breastbone and ribs, she peered into the chest and slid her hand beneath the swollen sac that contained the heart.

It felt like a bag filled with blood.

"Pericardial tamponade," she said, and looked up at Jane. "She bled into the sac that surrounds her heart. Since it's a confined space, the sac becomes so taut, the heart can't pump. Or the stab itself may have caused a fatal arrhythmia. Either way, this was a quick and efficient kill. But he had to know where to aim the blade."

"He knew what he was doing."

"Or he got lucky." She pointed to the wound. "You can see the blade pierced just below the xiphoid process. Anywhere above that, the heart's pretty well protected by the sternum and ribs. But if you enter here, where this wound is located, and aim the blade at just the right angle . . ."

"You'll hit the heart?"

"It's not difficult. I did it as an intern, on my ER rotation. With a needle, of course."

"On a dead person, I hope."

"No, she was alive. But we couldn't hear her heartbeat, her blood pressure was crashing, and the chest x-ray showed a globular heart. I had to do something."

"So you *stabbed* her?"

"With a cardiac needle. Removed enough blood from the sac to keep her alive until she could make it to surgery."

"It's like that spy novel, *Eye of the Needle,*" said Yoshima. "The killer stabs his victims straight in the heart, and they die so fast, there's hardly any blood. It makes a pretty clean kill."

"Thank you for that useful tip," said Jane.

"Actually, Yoshima raises a good point," said Maura. "Our perp chose a quick method to kill Eve Kassovitz. But with Lori-Ann Tucker, he took his time removing the hand, the arm, the head. And then he drew the symbols. With this victim, he didn't waste a lot of time. Which makes me think Eve was killed for a more practical reason. Maybe she surprised him, and he simply had to get rid of her, on the spot. So he did it the fastest way he could. A blow to the head. And then a quick stab to the heart."

"He took the time to draw those symbols on the door."

"How do we know he didn't draw them first? To go with the bundle he'd just delivered on the doorstep?"

"You mean the hand."

Maura nodded. "His offering."

Her blade was back at work, cutting, resecting. Out came lungs, which she dropped into a steel basin, where they formed a spongy mass. A glance at the pink surface, a few slices into each of the lobes, told her these had been the healthy lungs of a non-smoker, designed to serve their owner well into old age. Maura moved on to the peritoneal cavity, gloved hands reaching into the abdomen to resect stomach and pancreas and liver. Eve Kassovitz's belly had been enviably flat, the reward no doubt of many hours laboring at sit-ups and stomach crunches. How easily all that effort was reduced by a scalpel to incised muscle and gaping skin. The basin slowly filled with organs, loops of small intestine glistening like tangled eels, liver and spleen settling into a bloody mound. Everything healthy, so healthy. She sliced into the retroperitoneum, removed velvety smooth kidneys, sliced off tiny chunks, which she dropped into a specimen jar. They sank into formalin, trailing swirls of blood.

Straightening, she looked at Yoshima. "Can you put up the skull films now? Let's see what we have."

He pulled down the torso x-rays and began mounting a new set, which she had not yet examined. Films of the head now glowed on the viewing box. She focused on the table of bone just beneath the scalp laceration, searching the outline of the cranium for some telltale fracture line or depression that she'd been unable to palpate, but she saw none. Even without a fracture, the blow could still have been enough to stun the victim into submission, to bring her down long enough for the killer to yank open her jacket and lift her sweater.

To thrust the blade into her heart.

At first, the skull was what held Maura's focus. Then she moved on to a lateral view and focused on the neck, her gaze stopping on the hyoid bone. Posterior to it was a cone-shaped opacity unlike anything she had seen before. Frowning, she moved closer to the light box and stood staring at the anomaly. On the frontal view, it was almost hidden against the greater density of the cervical vertebrae. But on the lateral view it was clearly visible, and it was not part of the skeletal structure.

"What on earth is this?" she murmured.

Jane moved beside her. "What're you looking at?"

"This thing here. It's not bone. It's not a normal part of the neck."

"Is that something in her throat?"

Maura turned back to the table and said to Yoshima, "Could you get the laryngoscope for me?"

Standing at the head of the table, Maura tilted up the chin. She had first used a laryngoscope as a fourth-year medical student, when she'd tried to insert an endotracheal tube into a man who was not breathing. The circumstances were frantic, the patient in cardiac arrest. Her supervising resident allowed Maura only one attempt at the intubation. "You get ten seconds," he'd said, "and if you can't, then I take over." She'd slipped in the laryngoscope and peered into the throat, looking for the vocal cords, but all she could see was tongue and mucosa. As the seconds ticked by, as a nurse pumped on the chest and the Code Blue team watched, Maura had struggled with the instrument, knowing that with every second the patient was deprived of oxygen, more brain cells could die. The resident finally took the instrument from her hands and nudged her aside to do the job himself. It had been a humiliating demonstration of her incompetence.

The dead do not require such speedy intervention. Now, as she slid the laryngoscope blade into the mouth, there was no squealing heart monitor, no Code Blue team staring at her, no life hanging in the balance. Eve Kassovitz was a patient subject as Maura tilted the blade, lifting the tongue out of the way. She bent down and peered into the throat. The neck was long and slender, and on her first try, Maura easily spotted the vocal cords, like pale pink straps flanking the airway. Trapped between them was an object that glistened back at her.

"Forceps," she said, holding out her hand. Yoshima placed the instrument in her palm.

"You see it?" asked Jane.

"Yes."

Maura snagged the object and gently withdrew it from the throat. She dropped it onto a specimen tray, and it clattered against stainless steel.

"Is that what I think it is?" said Jane.

Maura turned over the specimen, and it gleamed like a pearl under the bright lights.

A seashell.

EIGHTEEN

THE AFTERNOON LIGHT had darkened to a somber gray by the time Jane drove onto the Harvard University campus and parked her car behind Conant Hall. The lot was nearly empty, and as she stepped out into a bitter wind, she glanced at old brick buildings that looked deserted, at fine feathers of snow swirling across frozen pavement, and she realized that by the time she finished her task here, it would be dark.

Eve Kassovitz was a cop, too. Yet she never saw death coming.

Jane buttoned up her coat collar and started toward the University Museum buildings. In a few days, when students returned from winter break, the campus would come alive again. But on this cold afternoon, Jane walked alone, eyes narrowed against the wind's bite. She reached the side entrance to the museum and found the door locked. No surprise; it was a Sunday afternoon. She circled around to the front, trudging a shoveled path between banks of dirty snow. At the Oxford Street entrance she paused to stare up at the massive brick building. The words above the doorway read, MUSEUM OF COM-PARATIVE ZOOLOGY.

She climbed the granite stairs and stepped into the building, and into a different era. Wood floors creaked beneath her feet. She smelled the dust of many decades and the heat of ancient radiators, and saw row after row of wooden display cabinets.

But no people. The entrance hall was deserted.

She walked deeper into the building, past glass-enclosed specimen cases, and paused to stare at a collection of insects mounted on pins. She saw monstrous black beetles with pincers poised to nip tender skin, and winged roaches, carapaces gleaming. With a shudder she walked on, past butterflies bright as jewels, past a cabinet with birds' eggs that would never hatch, and mounted finches that would never again sing.

The creak of a footstep told her she was not alone.

She turned and stared up the narrow aisle between two tall cabinets. Backlit by the wintry light glowing through the window, the man was just a bent and faceless silhouette shuffling toward her. Only as he moved closer, emerging at last from his dusty hiding place, did she see the creased face, the wire-rim spectacles. Distorted blue eyes peered at her through thick lenses.

"You wouldn't be that woman from the police, would you?" he asked.

"Dr. Von Schiller? I'm Detective Rizzoli."

"I knew you had to be. No one else would wander in this late in the day. The door's normally locked by now, so you're getting a bit of a private tour here." He gave a wink, as though this special treat should stay a secret between them. A rare chance to ogle dead bugs and stuffed birds without the hordes pressing in. "Well, did you bring it?" he asked.

"I've got it right here." She removed the evidence bag from her pocket, and his eyes lit up at the sight of the contents, visible through the clear plastic.

"Come, on, then! Let's go up to my office where I can get a good look at it under my magnifier. My eyes aren't so good anymore. I hate the fluorescent lamp up there, but I do need it for something like this."

She followed him toward the stairwell, matching her pace to his agonizingly slow shuffle. Could this guy still be teaching? He seemed far too old to even make it up the stairs. But Von Schiller was the name recommended to her when she'd called the comparative zoology department, and there was no mistaking the gleam of excitement in his eyes when he'd spotted what she had brought in her pocket. He could not wait to get his hands on it.

"Do you know much about seashells, Detective?" Von Schiller asked as he slowly climbed the stairs, his gnarled hand grasping the carved banister.

"Only what I've learned from eating clams."

"You mean you've never collected them?" He glanced back. "Did you know Robert Louis Stevenson once said, 'It is perhaps a more fortunate destiny to have a taste for collecting shells than to be born a millionaire'?"

"Did he, now?" *I think I'd rather be a millionaire.*

"It's a passion I've had since I was a child. My parents would take us every year to the Amalfi Coast. My bedroom was filled with so many boxes of shells

I could barely turn around. I still have them all, you know. Including a lovely specimen of *Epitonium celesti*. Rather rare. I bought it when I was twelve, and paid quite a dear price for it. But I've always thought that spending money on shells is an investment. The most exquisite art of Mother Nature."

"Did you get a look at the photos I e-mailed you?"

"Oh, yes. I forwarded the photo to Stefano Rufini, an old friend of mine. Consults for a company called Medshells. They locate rare specimens from around the world and sell them to wealthy collectors. He and I agree about your shell's probable origins."

"So what is this shell?"

Von Schiller glanced back at her with a smile. "You think I'd give you a final answer without actually examining it?"

"You seem to know already."

"I've narrowed it down, that's all I can tell you." He resumed climbing the stairs. "Its class is Gastropoda," he said. Climbed another step. "Order: Caenogastropoda." Another step, another chant. "Superfamily: Buccinacea."

"Excuse me. What does all that mean?"

"It means that your little seashell is, first of all, a gastropod, which translates to *stomach foot*. It's the same general class of mollusk as a land snail or a limpet. They're univalves, with a muscular foot."

"That's the name of this shell?"

"No, that's just the phylogenetic class. There are at least fifty thousand different varieties of gastropods around the world, and not all of them are ocean dwellers. The common land slug, for instance, is a gastropod, even though it has no shell." He reached the top of the stairs and led the way through a hall with yet more display cases containing a silent menagerie of creatures, their glassy eyes staring back at Jane in disapproval. So vivid was her impression of being watched that she paused and glanced back at the deserted gallery, at cabinet after cabinet of mounted specimens.

Nobody here but us murdered animals.

She turned to follow Von Schiller.

He had vanished.

For a moment she stood alone in that vast gallery, hearing only the thump of her own heartbeat, feeling the hostile gazes of those countless creatures trapped behind glass. "Dr. Von Schiller?" she called, and her voice seemed to echo through hall after hall.

His head popped out from behind a cabinet. "Well, aren't you coming?" he asked. "My office is right here."

Office was too grand a word for the space he occupied. A door with the plaque—DR. HENRY VON SCHILLER, PROFESSOR EMERITUS—led to a windowless nook scarcely larger than a broom closet. Crammed inside were a desk, two chairs, and little else. He flipped on the wall switch and squinted in the harsh fluorescent glare.

"Let's see it, then," he said, and eagerly snatched the ziplock bag that she held out to him. "You say you found this at a crime scene?"

She hesitated, then said, merely, yes. *Rammed down the throat of a dead woman* was what she didn't say.

"Why do you think it's significant?"

"I'm hoping you can tell me."

"May I handle it?"

"If you really need to."

He opened the bag and, with arthritic fingers, he removed the seashell. "Oh yes," he murmured as he squeezed behind his desk and settled into a creaking chair. He turned on a gooseneck lamp and pulled out a magnifying glass and a ruler. "Yes, it's what I thought. Looks like about, oh, twenty-one millimeters long. Not a particularly nice specimen. These striations aren't all that pretty, and it's got a few chips here, you see? Could be an old shell that's been tumbled around in some hobbyist's collection box." He looked up, blue eyes watery behind spectacles. *"Pisania maculosa."*

"Is that its name?"

"Yes."

"Are you sure?"

He set down the magnifying lens with a thud and stood up. "You don't trust me?" he snapped. "Come on, then."

"I'm not saying I don't trust—"

"Of course that's what you're saying." Von Schiller scuttled out of his office, moving with a speed she had not known he was capable of. Annoyed and in a hurry to defend himself, he shuffled through gallery after gallery, leading Jane deep into a gloomy maze of specimen cabinets, past the stares of countless dead eyes, and down a row of display cases tucked into the farthest corner of the building. Clearly, this was not a well-visited section of the museum. Typed display labels were yellowed with age, and dust filmed the glass cases. Von Schiller squeezed down a narrow corridor between cabinets, pulled open a drawer, and took out a specimen box.

"Here," he said, opening the box. He took out a handful of shells and placed them, one by one, on top of a glass case. "*Pisania maculosa*. And here's another, and another. And here's *yours*." He looked at her with the indignation of an insulted academic. "Well?"

Jane scanned the array of seashells, all of them with the same graceful curves, the same spiraling striations. "They do look alike."

"Of course they do! They're the same species! I know what I'm talking about. This *is* my field, Detective."

And what a really useful field it is, she thought as she took out her notebook. "What's the species name again?"

"Here, give that to me." He snatched away her notebook and she watched him write down the name, scowling as he did it. This was not a nice old guy. No wonder they hid him away in a broom closet.

He handed back the notebook. "There. Properly spelled."

"So what does this mean?"

"It's the name."

"No, I mean what's the significance of this particular shell?"

"Is it supposed to mean something? You're *Homo sapiens sapiens,* this is *Pisania maculosa.* That's just the way it is."

"This shell, is it rare?"

"Not at all. You can easily buy them over the Internet, from any number of dealers."

Which made the shell little more than useless as a way to track a killer. With a sigh, she put away her notebook.

"They're quite common in the Mediterranean," he said.

She looked up. "The Mediterranean?"

"And the Azores."

"I'm sorry. I'm not really clear exactly where the Azores are."

He gave her a sour look of disbelief. Then he waved her over to one of the cases, where dozens of shells were displayed, along with a faded map of the Mediterranean. "There," he said, pointing. "It's these islands here, to the west of Spain. *Pisania maculosa* ranges throughout this area, from the Azores to the Mediterranean."

"And nowhere else? The Americas?"

"I've just told you its range. Those shells I brought out to show you—they were all collected in Italy."

She was silent a moment, her gaze still on the case. She could not remember the last time she'd really studied a map of the Mediterranean. Her world, after all, was Boston; crossing the state line was the equivalent of a foreign trip. Why a seashell? Why *this* particular seashell?

Her eyes then focused on the eastern corner of the Mediterranean. On the island of Cyprus.

Red ocher. Seashells. What is the killer trying to tell us?

"Oh," said Von Schiller. "I didn't know anyone else was here."

Jane had not heard any footsteps, even on the creaking wood floors. She turned to see a young man looming right behind her. Most likely a graduate student, judging by his rumpled shirt and blue jeans. He certainly looked like a scholar, with heavy black-framed glasses, his face washed out to a wintry pallor. He stood so silent that Jane wondered if the man could speak.

Then the words came out, his stuttering so tortured that it was painful to hear. "P-p-professor Von Schiller. It's t-t-time to c-c-close."

"We're just finishing up here, Malcolm. I wanted to show Detective Rizzoli some examples of *Pisania*." Von Schiller placed the shells back in their box. "I'll lock up."

"B-b-but it's my—"

"I know, I know. Just because I've gotten on in years, no one trusts me to turn one stupid key anymore. Look, I've still got papers on my desk that I need to sort through. Why don't you show the detective out? I promise I'll lock the door when I leave."

The young man hesitated, as though trying to come up with the words to protest. Then he simply sighed and nodded.

Jane slipped the evidence bag containing the shell back into her pocket. "Thank you for your help, Dr. Von Schiller," she said. But the old man was already shuffling away to return the box of shells to its drawer.

The young man said nothing as he led Jane through the gloomy exhibit halls, past animals trapped behind glass, his sneakers setting off barely a creak on the wood floors. This was hardly the place a young man should be spending a Sunday evening, she thought. Keeping company with fossils and pierced butterflies.

Outside, through the gloom of early evening, Jane trudged back toward the parking lot, her shoes crunching across gritty snow. Halfway there she slowed, stopped. Turning, she scanned the darkened buildings, the pools of light cast by streetlamps. No one, nothing, moved.

On the night she died, did Eve Kassovitz see her killer coming?

She quickened her pace, her keys already in hand, and crossed to her car, which now sat alone in the lot. Only after she'd slid inside and locked the door did she let down her guard. *This case is freaking me out,* she thought. *I can't even walk across a parking lot without feeling like the Devil's at my back.*

And closing in.

NINETEEN

August 1. Phase of the moon: Full.

*Last night my mother spoke to me in my dreams.
A scolding. A reminder that I have been undisciplined. "I have taught you all the ancient rituals,
and for what?" she asked. "So that you will ignore
them? Remember who you are. You are the chosen
one."*

*I have not forgotten. How could I? Since my earliest years, she has recited the tales of our ancestors,
about whom Manetho of Sebennytos, in the age of
Ptolemy the Second, wrote, "They set our towns on
fire. They caused the people to suffer every brutality.
They waged war, desiring to exterminate the race."*

In my veins runs the sacred blood of hunters.

*These are secrets that even my distracted and
oblivious father did not know. Between my parents,
the ties were merely practical. But between my
mother and me, the bonds reach across time, across
continents, into my very dreams. She is displeased
with me.*

And so tonight, I lead a goat into the woods.

*It comes willingly, because it has never felt the
sting of human cruelty. The moon is so bright I need*

no flashlight to show me the way. Behind me I hear the confused bleating of the other goats that I've just released from the farmer's barn, but they don't follow me. Their calls recede as I walk deeper into the woods, and now all I hear is the sound of my footfalls and the goat's hooves on the forest floor.

When we have walked far enough, I tie the goat to a tree. The animal senses what is to come and gives an anxious bleat as I take off my clothes, stripping down to naked skin. I kneel on the moss. The night is cool, but my shivering is from anticipation. I raise the knife, and the ritual words flow from my lips as easily as they always have before. Praise to our lord Seth, to the god of my ancestors. The god of death and destruction. Through countless millennia, he has guided our hands, has led us from the Levant to the lands of Phoenicia and Rome, to every corner of the earth. We are everywhere.

The blood spurts in a hot fountain.

When it is over, I walk naked, except for my shoes, to the lake. Under the moon's glow I wade into the water and wash away the goat's blood. I emerge cleansed and exhilarated. Only as I pull on my clothes does my heartbeat finally slow, and exhaustion suddenly drapes its heavy arm around my shoulders. I could almost fall asleep on the grass, but I don't dare lie down; I am so tired, I might not awaken until daylight.

I trudge back toward the house. As I reach the top of the hill, I see her. Lily stands on the edge of the lawn, a slender silhouette with hair gleaming in the moonlight. She is looking at me.

"Where have you been?" she asks.

"I went for a swim."

"In the dark?"

"It's the best time." Slowly I walk toward her. She stands perfectly still, even as I move close enough to touch her. *"The water's warm. No one can see you swimming naked."* My hand is cool from the lake, and she shivers as I caress her cheek. Is it from fear or fascination? I don't know. What I do know is that she has been watching me these past weeks, just as I've been watching her, and something is happening between us. They say that Hell calls to Hell. Somewhere inside her, the darkness has heard my call and is stirring to life.

I move even closer. Though she's older than I am, I'm taller, and my arm slips easily around her waist as I lean in. As our hips meet.

Her slap sends me reeling backward.

"Don't you ever touch me again," she says. She turns and walks to the house.

My face is still stinging. I linger in the darkness, waiting for the imprint of her blow to fade from my cheek. She has no idea who I really am, who she has just humiliated. No idea what the consequences will be.

I do not sleep that night.

Instead I lie awake, thinking of all the lessons my mother taught me about patience and about biding one's time. *"The most satisfying prize,"* she said, *"is the one you're forced to wait for."* When the sun rises the next morning, I am still in bed, thinking about my mother's words. I am thinking, too, about *that humiliating slap. About all the ways that Lily and her friends have shown me disrespect.*

Downstairs, Aunt Amy is in the kitchen cooking breakfast. I smell coffee brewing and bacon crisping in a frying pan. And I hear her call out, "Peter? Have you seen my boning knife?"

TWENTY

AS USUAL on a hot summer's day, the Piazza di Spagna was a sea of sweating tourists. They milled elbow to elbow, expensive cameras dangling from their necks, flushed faces shaded from the sun beneath floppy hats and baseball caps. From her perch above, on the Spanish Steps, Lily surveyed the crowd's movements, noting the eddies that swirled around the vendors' carts, the crosscurrents of competing tour groups. Wary of pickpockets, she started down the steps, waving away the inevitable trinket hawkers who hovered like flies. She noticed several men glance her way, but their interest was merely momentary. A look, a flicker of a lascivious thought, and then their eyes were on to the next passing female. Lily scarcely gave them a thought as she descended toward the piazza, threading past a couple embracing on the steps, past a studious young man hunched over a book. She waded into the throng. In crowds she felt safe, anonymous, and insulated. It was merely an illusion, of course; there was no truly safe place. As she crossed the piazza, tacking past camera-snapping tourists and children slurping at gelato, she knew that she was all too easy to spot. Crowds provided cover for both prey and predator.

She reached the far end of the piazza and walked past a shop selling designer shoes and purses that she would never, in this lifetime, be able to afford. Beyond it was a bank with an ATM and three people waiting to use it. She joined the line. By the time it was her turn, she'd already taken a good look at everyone standing nearby and spotted no thieves ready to swoop in. Now was the time to make a large withdrawal. She'd been in Rome for four weeks, and had not yet landed any work. Despite her fluent Italian, not a single coffee stand, not a single souvenir shop, had a job for her, and she was down to her last five Euros.

She inserted her bank card, requested three hundred Euros, and waited for the cash to appear. Her card slid back out, along with a printed receipt. But no cash. She stared down at the receipt, her stomach suddenly dropping. She needed no translation to understand what was printed there.

Insufficient funds.

Okay, she thought, *maybe I just asked for too much at once. Calm down.* She inserted her card again, punched in the code, requested two hundred Euros.

Insufficient funds.

By now, the woman standing behind her in line was making *hurry up already!* sighs. For the third time, Lily slid in her card. Requested one hundred Euros.

Insufficient funds.

"Hey, are you going to be finished sometime

soon? Like, maybe, *today?*" the woman behind her asked.

Lily turned to face her. Just that one look, molten with rage, made the woman step back in alarm. Lily shoved past her and headed back to the piazza, moving blindly, for once not caring who was watching her, tracking her. By the time she reached the Spanish Steps, all the strength had gone out of her legs. She sank onto the stairs and dropped her head in her hands.

Her money was gone. She'd known her account was getting low, that eventually it would run out, but she'd thought there was enough to last at least another month. She had enough cash for maybe two more meals, and that was it. No hotel tonight, no bed. But hey, these stairs were comfortable enough, and she couldn't beat the view. When she got hungry, she could always go diving in the trash can for some tourist's leftover sandwich.

Who am I kidding? I've got to get some money.

She lifted her head, looked around the piazza, and saw plenty of single men. *Hello, guys, anyone willing to pay for an afternoon with a hot and desperate chick?* Then she spotted three policemen strolling the periphery and decided that this was not a good place to troll for prospects. Getting arrested would be inconvenient; it might also prove fatal.

She unzipped her backpack and feverishly dug around inside. Maybe there was a wad of cash she'd forgotten about, or a few loose coins rattling around on the bottom. Fat chance. As if she didn't keep track of every single penny. She found a roll of mints, a ballpoint pen. No money.

But she did find a business card, printed with the name FILIPPO CAVALLI. At once his face came back to her. The truck driver with the leering eyes. "If you have no place to stay," he'd said, "I have an apartment in the city."

Well, guess what? I have no place to stay.

She sat on the steps, mindlessly rubbing the card between her fingers, until it was pinched and bent. Thinking about Filippo Cavalli and his mean eyes, his unshaven face. How awful could it be? She'd done worse things in her life. Far worse.

And I'm still paying for it.

She zipped up the backpack and looked around for a telephone. Mean eyes or not, she thought, a girl's gotta eat.

She stood in the hallway outside apartment 4-G, nervously straightening her blouse, smoothing down her hair. Then she wondered why the hell she should even bother, considering how slovenly the man had looked the last time she'd seen him. *Lord, at least make his breath not be foul*, she thought. She could deal with fat men and ugly men. She could just close her eyes and not look. But a man with stinking breath . . .

The door swung open. "Come in!" Filippo said.

At her first glimpse of him, she wanted to turn and run. He was exactly as she'd remembered, his chin prickly with stubble, his hungry gaze already devouring her face. He had not even bothered to dress in nice clothes for her visit, but was wearing a sleeveless T-shirt and baggy trousers. Why should he bother to clean up? Surely he knew what had brought her here, and it wasn't his sculpted body or his scintillating wit.

She stepped into the apartment, where the smells of garlic and cigarette smoke battled for dominance. Aside from that, it was not too horrible a place. She saw a couch and chairs, a neat pile of newspapers, a coffee table. The balcony window faced another apartment building. Through the walls, she could hear a neighbor's TV blaring.

"Some wine, Carol?" he asked.

Carol. She'd almost forgotten which name she'd given him. "Yes, please," she answered. "And . . . would you happen to have something to eat?"

"Food? Of course." He smiled, but his eyes never stopped leering. He knew these were just the pleasantries before the transaction. He brought out bread and cheese and a little dish of marinated mushrooms. Hardly a feast; more like a snack. So this was what she was worth. The wine was cheap, sharp, and astringent, but she drank two glasses anyway as she ate. Better to be drunk than sober for what came next. He sat across the kitchen table watching her as he sipped his own glass of wine. How many other women had come to this apartment, had sat at this kitchen table, steeling themselves for the bedroom? Surely none of them came willingly. Like Lily, they probably needed a drink or two or three before getting down to business.

He reached across the table. She went stock-still as he opened the top two buttons of her blouse. Then he sat back, grinning at the view of her cleavage.

She tried to ignore him and reached for another

chunk of bread, then drained her glass of wine and poured herself another.

He stood up and came around behind her. He finished unbuttoning her blouse and slipped it off her shoulders, then unfastened her bra.

She stuffed a piece of cheese into her mouth, chewed, and swallowed. Almost coughed it up again as his hands closed over her breasts. She sat rigid, fists clenched, suppressing the instinct to twist around and slug him. Instead she let him reach around in front of her and unzip her jeans. Then he gave her a tug, and obediently she rose to her feet, so he could peel off the rest of her clothes. When she finally stood naked in his kitchen, he stepped back to enjoy the view, his arousal obvious. He did not even bother to remove his own clothes, but just backed her up against the kitchen counter, opened his trousers, and took her standing up. Took her so vigorously that the cabinets rattled and silverware clattered in the drawers.

Hurry. Finish, goddamn it.

But he was just getting started. He twisted her around, pushed her to her knees, and took her on the tiled floor. Then it was into the living room, in full view of the balcony window, as though he wanted the world to see that he, Filippo, could fuck a woman in every position, in every room. She closed her eyes and concentrated on the sounds from the TV next door. Thumping game show music, an excitable Italian host. She focused on the TV because she did not want to listen to Filippo's panting and grunting as he pounded against her. As he climaxed.

He collapsed on top of her, a flabby deadweight

that threatened to suffocate her. She squeezed out from beneath him and lay on her back, her body slick with their mingled sweat.

A moment later, he was snoring.

She left him there, on the living room floor, and went into his bathroom to take a shower. Spent a good twenty minutes under the water, washing away every trace of him. Hair dripping, she returned to the living room to make sure he was still asleep. He was. Quietly, she slipped into his bedroom and went through his dresser drawers. Beneath a mound of socks, she found a bundle of cash—at least six hundred Euros. *He won't miss a hundred,* she thought, counting out the bills. Anyway, she'd earned it.

She got dressed and was just picking up her backpack when she heard his footsteps behind her.

"You are leaving so soon?" he asked. "How can you be satisfied with just once?"

Slowly she turned to look at him and forced a smile. "Just once with you, Filippo, is like ten times with any other man."

He grinned. "That's what women tell me."

Then they're all lying.

"Stay. I'll cook you dinner." He came toward her and played with a strand of her hair. "Stay, and maybe—"

She gave it about two seconds' thought. While this would be a place to spend the night, it required too high a price. "I have to go," she said, turning away.

"Please stay." He paused, then added, with a note of desperation, "I'll pay you."

She stopped and looked back at him.

"That's it, isn't it?" he said softly. His smile faded,

his face slowly drooping into a weary mask. Not the strutting lover anymore, but a sad, middle-aged man with a big gut and no woman in his life. Once, she had thought his eyes looked mean; now those eyes looked merely tired, defeated. "I know it's true." He sighed. "You did not come because of me. It's money you want."

For the first time, it did not disgust her to look at him. Also for the first time, she decided to be honest with him.

"Yes," she admitted. "I need money. I'm broke, and I can't find a job in Rome."

"But you're American. You can just go home."

"I can't go home."

"Why not?"

She looked away. "I just can't. There's nothing there for me anyway."

He considered her words for a moment and came to a reasonable conclusion. "The police are looking for you?"

"No. Not the police—"

"Then who are you running from?"

I'm running from the Devil himself was what she thought. But she could not say that, or he'd think her crazy. She answered, simply, "A man. Someone who scares me."

An abusive boyfriend was probably what he thought. He gave a nod of sympathy. "So you need money. Come, then. I can give you some." He turned and started toward his bedroom.

"Wait. Filippo." Feeling guilty now, she reached into her pocket and took out the hundred Euros she'd taken from his sock drawer. How could she steal from a man who was so desperately hungry for companionship? "I'm sorry," she said. "This is yours. I really needed it, but I shouldn't have taken it." She reached for his hand and pressed the cash into his palm, barely able to look him in the eye. "I'll manage on my own." She turned to leave.

"Carol. Is that your real name?"

She paused, her hand on the knob. "It's as good a name as any."

"You say you need a job. What can you do?"

She looked at him. "I'll do anything. I can clean homes, wait on tables. But I have to be paid in cash."

"Your Italian is very good." He looked her over, thinking. "I have a cousin, here in the city," he finally said. "She organizes tours."

"What kind of tours?"

"To the Forum, the basilica." He shrugged. "You know, all the usual places tourists go in Rome. Sometimes she needs guides who speak English. But they must have an education."

"I do! I have a college degree in classical studies." Fresh hope made her heart suddenly thud faster. "I know a great deal about history, actually. About the ancient world."

"But do you know about Rome?"

Lily gave a sudden laugh and set down her backpack. "As a matter of fact," she said, "I do."

TWENTY-ONE

MAURA STOOD on the ice-glazed sidewalk, gazing up at the Beacon Hill residence where the windows were invitingly aglow. Firelight flickered in the front parlor, just as it had on the night she'd first stepped through the door, lured by the dancing flames, by the promise of a cup of coffee. Tonight what drew her up the steps was curiosity, about a man who both intrigued her and, she had to admit, frightened her a little. She rang the bell and heard it chime inside, echoing through rooms she had yet to see. She expected the manservant to answer the bell and was startled when Anthony Sansone himself opened the door.

"I wasn't sure you'd actually come," he said as she stepped inside.

"Neither was I," she admitted.

"The others will be arriving later. I thought it'd be nice for the two of us to talk first, alone." He helped her off with her coat and pushed open the secret panel to reveal the closet. In this man's house, the walls themselves hid surprises. "So why did you decide to come after all?"

"You said we had common interests. I want to know what you mean by that."

He hung up her coat and turned, a looming figure dressed in black, his face burnished in gold from the firelight. "Evil," he said. "That's what we have in common. We've both seen it up close. We've looked into its face, smelled its breath. And felt it staring back at us."

"A lot of people have seen it."

"But you've known it on a deeply personal level."

"You're talking about my mother again."

"Joyce tells me that no one's yet been able to tally all of Amalthea's victims."

"I haven't followed that investigation. I've stayed out of it. The last time I saw Amalthea was in July, and I have no plans to ever visit her again."

"Ignoring evil doesn't make it go away. It's still there, still part of your life—"

"Not part of mine."

"—right down to your DNA."

"An accident of birth. We're not our parents."

"But on some level, Maura, your mother's crimes must weigh down on you. They must make you wonder."

"Whether I'm a monster, too?"

"*Do* you wonder that?"

She paused, acutely aware of how intently he was watching her. "I'm nothing like my mother. If anything, I'm her polar opposite. Look at the career I've chosen, the work I do."

"A form of atonement?"

"I have nothing to atone for."

"Yet you've chosen to work on behalf of victims. And justice. Not everyone makes that choice, or does it as well and as fiercely as you do. That's why I invited you tonight." He opened the door to the next room. "That's why I want to show you something."

She followed him into a wood-paneled dining room, where the massive table was already set for dinner. Five place settings, she noted, surveying the crystal stemware and gleaming china edged in cobalt and gold. Here was another fireplace, with flames dancing in the hearth, but the cavernous room with its twelve-foot ceiling was on the chilly side, and she was glad she'd kept on her cashmere sweater.

"First, a glass of wine?" he asked, holding up a bottle of Cabernet.

"Yes. Thank you."

He poured and handed her the glass, but she scarcely glanced at it; she was focused instead on the portraits hanging on the walls. A gallery of faces, both men and women, gazed through the patina of centuries.

"These are only a few," he said. "The portraits my family managed to procure over the years. Some are modern copies, some are mere representations of what we think they looked like. But a few of these portraits are original. As these people must have appeared in life." He crossed the room to stand before one portrait in particular. It was of a young woman with luminous dark eyes, her black hair gently gathered at the nape of her neck. Her face was a pale oval, and in that dim and firelit room, her skin seemed translucent and so alive that Maura could almost imagine the throb of a pulse in that white neck. The young woman was partly turned toward the artist, her burgundy gown glinting with gold threads, her gaze direct and unafraid.

"Her name was Isabella," said Sansone. "This was painted a month before her marriage. The portrait required quite a bit of restoration. There were scorch marks on the canvas. It was lucky to survive the fire that destroyed her home."

"She's beautiful."

"Yes, she was. To her great misfortune."

Maura frowned at him. "Why?"

"She was married to Nicolo Contini, a Venetian nobleman. By all accounts it was a very happy marriage, until"—he paused—"until Antonino Sansone destroyed their lives."

She looked at him in surprise. "That's the man in the portrait? In the other room?"

He nodded. "My distinguished ancestor. Oh, he was able to justify all his actions in the name of rooting out the Devil. The church sanctioned it all—the torture, the bloodletting, the burnings at the stake. The Venetians in particular were quite expert at torture and creative at devising ever more brutal instruments to extract confessions. No matter how outlandish the accusations, a few hours in the dungeon with Monsignore Sansone would make almost anyone plead guilty to his charges. Whether the accusation was practicing witchcraft, or casting spells against your neighbors, or consorting with the Devil, confessing to any and all of it was the only way to make the pain stop, to be granted the mercy of death. Which, in itself, was not so merciful, since most of them were burned alive." He gazed around the room, at the portraits. The faces of the dead. "All these people you see here suffered at his hand. Men, women, children—he made no distinction. It's said he awakened each day, eager for the task, that he cheerfully fortified himself with a hearty morning meal of bread and meat. Then he'd don his blood-splattered robes and go to work, rooting out heretics. On the street outside, even through thick stone walls, passersby could hear the screams."

Maura's gaze circled the room, taking in the faces of the doomed, and she imagined these same faces bruised and contorted in pain. How long had they resisted? How long had they clung to the hope of escape, a chance to live?

"Antonino defeated them all," he said. "Except for one." His gaze was back on the woman with the luminous eyes.

"Isabella survived?"

"Oh, no. No one survived his attentions. Like all the others, she died. But she was never conquered."

"She refused to confess?"

"Or submit. She had only to implicate her husband. Renounce him, accuse him of sorcery, and she might have lived. Because what Antonino really wanted wasn't her confession. He wanted Isabella herself."

Her beauty was her misfortune. That's what he'd meant.

"A year and a month," he said. "That's how long she survived in a cell without heat, without light. Every day, another session with her torturer." He looked at Maura. "I've seen the instruments from those times. I can't imagine any version of Hell that could be worse."

"And he never defeated her?"

"She resisted until the end. Even when they took

away her newborn baby. Even when they crushed her hands, scourged the skin from her back, wrenched apart her joints. Every brutality was meticulously recorded in Antonino's personal journals."

"You've actually seen those journals?"

"Yes. They've been passed down through our family. They're stored in a vault now, with other unpleasant heirlooms from that era."

"What a horrible legacy."

"That's what I meant when I told you we had common interests, common concerns. We both inherited poisoned blood."

Her gaze was back on Isabella's face, and suddenly she registered something that he had said only moments ago. *They took away her newborn baby.*

She looked at him. "You said she had a baby in prison."

"Yes. A son."

"What happened to him?"

"He was placed in the care of a local convent, where he was raised."

"But he was the son of a heretic. Why was he allowed to live?"

"Because of who his father was."

She looked at him with stunned comprehension. "Antonino Sansone?"

He nodded. "The boy was born eleven months into his mother's imprisonment."

A child of rape, she thought. *So this is the Sansone bloodline. It goes back to the child of a doomed woman.*

And a monster.

She gazed around the room at the other portraits. "I don't think I'd want these portraits hanging in my home."

"You think it's morbid."

"Every day, I'd be reminded. I'd be haunted by how they died."

"So you'd hide them in a closet? Avoid even looking at them, the way you avoid thinking about your mother?"

She stiffened. "I have no reason to think about her. She has no part in my life."

"But she does. And you *do* think about her, don't you? You can't avoid it."

"I sure as hell don't hang her portrait in my living room." She set down her wineglass on the table. "This is a bizarre form of ancestor worship you're practicing. Displaying the family torturer in the front parlor, like some kind of icon, someone you're proud of. And here in the dining room, you keep a gallery of his victims. All these faces staring at you, like a trophy collection. It's the kind of thing a—"

A hunter would display.

She paused, staring down at her empty glass, aware of the silence in the house. Five place settings were on the table, yet she was the only guest who'd arrived, perhaps the only guest who'd actually been invited.

She flinched as he brushed her arm and reached for her empty glass. He turned to refill it, and she stared at his back, at the outline of muscles beneath the black turtleneck shirt. Then he turned to face her, wineglass held out. She took it, but did not sip, though her throat had suddenly gone dry.

"Do you know why these portraits are here?" he asked quietly.

"I just find it . . . strange."

"I grew up with them. They hung in my father's house, and in *his* father's house. So did the portrait of Antonino, but always in a separate room. Always in a place of prominence."

"Like an altar."

"In a way."

"You honor that man? The torturer?"

"We keep his memory alive. We never allow ourselves to forget who—and what—he was."

"Why?"

"Because this is our responsibility. A sacred duty the Sansones accepted generations ago, starting with Isabella's son."

"The child born in prison."

He nodded. "By the time Vittorio reached adulthood, Monsignore Sansone was dead. But his reputation as a monster had spread, and the Sansone name was no longer an advantage, but rather a curse. Vittorio could have fled from his own name, denied his own bloodline. Instead he did quite the opposite. He embraced the Sansone name, as well as the burden."

"You talked about a sacred duty. What sort of duty?"

"Vittorio took a vow to atone for what his father did. If you look at our family crest, you'll see the words: *Sed libera nos a malo*."

Latin. She frowned at him. "Deliver us from evil."

"That's right."

"And what, exactly, are Sansones expected to do?"

"Hunt the Devil, Dr. Isles. That's what we do."

For a moment she didn't respond. *He can't possibly be serious,* she thought, but his gaze was absolutely steady.

"You mean figuratively, of course," she finally said.

"I know you don't believe he actually exists."

"Satan?" She couldn't help but laugh.

"People have no trouble believing that God exists," he said.

"That's why it's called *faith.* It requires no proof, because there is none."

"If one believes in the light, one has to believe in the darkness as well."

"But you're talking about a supernatural being."

"I'm talking about evil, distilled to its purest form. Manifested in the shape of real flesh-and-blood creatures, walking among us. This isn't about the impulsive kill, the jealous husband who's gone over the edge, or the scared soldier who mows down an unarmed enemy. I'm talking about something entirely different. People who *look* human, but are the farthest thing from it."

"Demons?"

"If you want to call them that."

"And you really believe they exist, these monsters or demons or whatever you call them?"

"I know they do," he said quietly.

The ringing of the doorbell startled her. She glanced toward the front parlor, but Sansone made no move to answer the bell. She heard footsteps, and then the butler's voice speaking in the foyer.

"Good evening, Mrs. Felway. May I take your coat?"

"I'm a little bit late, Jeremy. Sorry."

"Mr. Stark and Dr. O'Donnell haven't arrived yet, either."

"Not yet? Well, I feel better then."

"Mr. Sansone and Dr. Isles are in the dining room, if you'd like to join them."

"God, I could really use a drink."

The woman who swept into the room was as tall as a man and looked just as formidable, her square shoulders emphasized by a tweed blazer with leather epaulets. Although her hair was streaked with silver, she moved with the vigor of youth and the assurance of authority. She didn't hesitate, but crossed straight to Maura.

"You must be Dr. Isles," she said, and gave Maura a matter-of-fact handshake. "Edwina Felway."

Sansone handed the woman a glass of wine. "How're the roads out there, Winnie?"

"Treacherous." She took a sip. "I'm surprised Ollie isn't here already."

"It's just eight o'clock now. He's coming with Joyce."

Edwina's gaze was on Maura. Her eyes were direct, even intrusive. "Has there been any progress on the case?"

"We haven't talked about that," said Sansone.

"Really? But it's the one thing on all our minds."

"I can't discuss it," said Maura. "I'm sure you understand why."

Edwina looked at Sansone. "You mean she hasn't agreed yet?"

"Agreed to what?" asked Maura.

"To join our group, Dr. Isles."

"Winnie, you're a bit premature. I haven't fully explained—"

"The Mephisto Foundation?" said Maura. "Is that what you're talking about?"

There was a silence. In the other room, a phone began to ring.

Edwina suddenly laughed. "She's one step ahead of you, Anthony."

"How did you know about the foundation?" he asked, looking at Maura. Then he gave a knowing sigh. "Detective Rizzoli, of course. I hear she's been asking questions."

"She's paid to ask questions," said Maura.

"Is she finally satisfied that we're not suspects?"

"It's just that she doesn't like mysteries. And your group is very mysterious."

"And that's why you accepted my invitation tonight. To find out who we are."

"I think I have found out," said Maura. "And I think I've heard enough to make a decision." She set down her glass. "Metaphysics doesn't interest me. I know there's evil in the world, and there always has been. But you don't need to believe in Satan or demons to explain it. Human beings are perfectly capable of evil all by themselves."

"You aren't in the least bit interested in joining the foundation?" asked Edwina.

"I wouldn't belong here. And I think I should

leave now." She turned to find Jeremy standing in the doorway.

"Mr. Sansone?" The manservant was holding a portable phone. "Mr. Stark just called. He's quite concerned."

"About what?"

"Dr. O'Donnell was supposed to pick him up, but she hasn't appeared yet."

"When was she supposed to be at his house?"

"Forty-five minutes ago. He's been calling, but she doesn't answer either her home phone or her cell."

"Let me try her number." Sansone took the phone and dialed, drumming the table as he waited. He disconnected, dialed again, his fingers tapping faster. No one in the room spoke; they were all watching him, listening to the accelerating rhythm of his fingers. The night Eve Kassovitz died, these people had sat in this very room, not realizing that Death was right outside. That it had found its way into their garden, and had left its strange symbols on their door. This house had been marked.

Perhaps the people inside it were marked as well.

Sansone hung up.

"Shouldn't you call the police?" asked Maura.

"Oh, Joyce may simply have forgotten," said Edwina. "It seems a little premature to ask the police to rush in."

Jeremy said, "Would you like me to drive over and check Dr. O'Donnell's house?"

Sansone stared for a moment at the phone. "No," he finally said. "I'll go. I'd rather you stayed here, just in case Joyce calls."

Maura followed him into the parlor, where he grabbed his overcoat from the closet. She, too, pulled on her coat.

"Please stay and have dinner," he said, reaching for his car keys. "There's no need for you to rush home."

"I'm not going home," she said. "I'm coming with you."

TWENTY-TWO

JOYCE O'DONNELL'S porch light was on, but no one answered the door.

Sansone tried the knob. "It's locked," he said, and took out his cell phone. "Let me try calling her one more time."

As he dialed, Maura backed away from the porch and stood on the walkway, gazing up at O'Donnell's house, at a second-floor window that cast its cheery glow into the night. Faintly, she heard a phone ringing inside. Then, once again, silence.

Sansone disconnected. "Her answering machine picked up."

"I think it's time to call Rizzoli."

"Not yet." He produced a flashlight and headed along the shoveled walkway toward the side of the house.

"Where are you going?"

He continued toward the driveway, black coat melting into the shadows. The beam of his light skimmed across flagstones and disappeared around the corner.

She stood alone in the front yard, listening to the rattle of dead leaves in the branches above her. "Sansone?" she called out. He didn't answer. She heard only the pounding of her own heart. She followed him around the corner of the house. There she halted in the deserted driveway, the shadow of the garage looming before her. She started to call his name again, but something silenced her: the creeping awareness of another presence watching her, tracking her. She turned and quickly scanned the street. She saw a scrap of windblown paper tumble down the road like a fluttering wraith.

A hand closed around her arm.

Gasping, she stumbled away. She found herself staring at Sansone, who had silently materialized right behind her.

"Her car's still in the garage," he said.

"Then where is she?"

"I'm going around to the back."

This time she did not let him leave her sight, but followed right at his heels as he moved through the side yard, tramping through deep and unbroken snow alongside the garage. By the time they emerged in the backyard, her trousers were soaked, and melted snow had seeped into her shoes, chilling her feet. His flashlight beam skittered across shrubs and deck chairs, all covered in a velvety blanket of white. No footprints, no disturbed snow. A vine-covered wall enclosed the yard, a private space completely hidden from the neighbors. And she was here alone, with a man she scarcely knew.

But he was not focused on her. His attention was on the kitchen door, which he could not get open. For a moment he stared at it, debating his next move. Then he looked at Maura.

"You know Detective Rizzoli's number?" he asked. "Call her."

She pulled out her cell phone and moved toward the kitchen window for more light. She was about to dial when her gaze suddenly focused on the kitchen sink, just inside the window.

"Sansone," she whispered.

"What?"

"There's blood—near the drain."

He took one glance, and his next move shocked her. He grabbed one of the deck chairs and hurled it against the window. Glass shattered, shards exploding into the kitchen. He scrambled inside, and seconds later the door swung open.

"There's blood down here on the floor, too," he said.

She looked down at smears of red on the cream tiles. He ran out of the kitchen, his black coat flapping behind him like a cape, moving so fast that when she reached the foot of the stairs, he was already on the second-floor landing. She stared down at more blood, swipes of it on the oak steps, along the baseboard, as though a battered limb had scraped against the wall as the body was dragged upstairs.

"*Maura!*" yelled Sansone.

She sprinted up the stairs, reached the second-floor landing, and saw more blood, like glistening ski marks down the hallway. And she heard the sound, like water gurgling in a snorkel. Even before she stepped into the bedroom, she knew what she was about to confront: not a dead victim, but one desperately fighting to live.

Joyce O'Donnell lay on her back on the floor, eyes wide open in mortal panic, a gout of red spurting from her neck. She wheezed in air, blood rattling in her lungs, and coughed. Bright red spray exploded from her throat, spattering Sansone's face as he crouched over her.

"I'll take over! Call nine-one-one!" Maura ordered as she dropped to her knees and pressed bare fingers to the slash wound. She was used to the touch of dead flesh, not living, and the blood that dribbled onto her hands was shockingly warm. *ABC,* she thought. Those were the first rules of life support: airway, breathing, circulation. But with one brutal slash across the throat, the attacker had compromised all three. *I'm a doctor, but there's so little I can do to save her.*

Sansone finished his call. "The ambulance is on its way. What can I do?"

"Get me some towels. I need to stop the bleeding!"

O'Donnell's hand suddenly closed around Maura's wrist, clenching it with the force of panic. The skin was so slick, Maura's fingers slipped off the wound, releasing a fresh spurt. Another wheeze, another cough, sent spray from the incised trachea. O'Donnell was drowning. With every breath, she inhaled her own blood. It gurgled in her airway, frothed in her alveoli. Maura had examined the incised lungs of other victims whose throats had been cut; she knew the mechanism of death.

Now I am watching it happen, and I can't do a thing to stop it.

Sansone dashed back into the bedroom carrying

towels, and Maura pressed a wadded washcloth to the neck. The white terry cloth magically turned red. O'Donnell's hand gripped her wrist even tighter. Her lips moved, but she could produce no words, only the rattle of air bubbling through blood.

"It's okay, it's okay," said Maura. "The ambulance is almost here."

O'Donnell began to tremble, limbs quaking as though in seizures. But her eyes were aware and fixed on Maura. *Does she see it in my eyes? That I know she's dying?*

Maura glanced up at the distant wail of a siren.

"There it is," said Sansone.

"The front door's locked!"

"I'll go down and meet them." He scrambled to his feet and she heard him pounding down the stairs to the first floor.

O'Donnell's eyes were still awake, staring. Her lips moved faster now, and her fingers tightened to a claw. Outside, the siren's wail drew closer, but in this room, the only sounds were the gurgling breaths of the dying woman.

"Stay with me, Joyce!" urged Maura. "I know you can hold on!"

O'Donnell tugged at Maura's wrist, panicked jerks that threatened to wrench Maura's hand from the wound. With each gasp, bright droplets sprayed from her throat in explosive bursts. Her eyes widened, as though glimpsing the darkness yawning before her. *No*, she mouthed. *No*.

At that instant, Maura realized the woman was no longer looking at her, but at something *behind* her. Only then did she hear the creak of the floorboard.

Her attacker never left the house. He's still here. In this room.

She turned just as the blow rushed toward her. She saw darkness swoop at her like bat's wings, and then she went sprawling. Her face slammed to the floor and she lay stunned, her vision black. But she could feel, transmitted through the boards, the thud of escaping footsteps, like the heartbeat of the house itself, pulsing against her cheek. Pain throbbed its way into her head and grew to a steady hammering that seemed to pound nails into her skull.

She did not hear Joyce O'Donnell take her last breath.

A hand grasped her shoulder. In sudden panic she flailed, fighting for her life, swinging blindly at her attacker.

"Maura, stop. Maura!"

Her hands now trapped in his, she managed only a few weak struggles. Then her vision cleared and she saw Sansone staring at her. She heard other voices and glimpsed the metallic sheen of a stretcher. Turning, she focused on two paramedics who were crouched over Joyce O'Donnell's body.

"I'm not getting a pulse. No respirations."

"This IV's wide open."

"Jesus, look at all the blood."

"How's the other lady doing?" The paramedic looked at Maura.

Sansone said, "She seems okay. I think she just fainted."

"No," whispered Maura. She grabbed his arm. "He was here."

"What?"

"He was still *here*. In the room!"

Suddenly he realized what she was saying, and he reared back with a look of shock and scrambled to his feet.

"No—wait for the police!"

But Sansone was already out the door.

She struggled to sit up and swayed, her vision watery and threatening to go gray. When at last the room brightened, she saw two paramedics kneeling in Joyce O'Donnell's blood, their equipment and discarded packaging splayed out around them. An EKG traced across the oscilloscope.

It was a flat line.

Jane slid into the backseat of the cruiser beside Maura and pulled the door shut. That one brief *whoosh* of cold air swept all the heat from the vehicle and Maura began to shake again.

"You sure you're feeling okay?" said Jane. "Maybe we should take you to the ER."

"I want to go home," said Maura. "Can't I go home now?"

"Is there anything else you remember? Any other details that are coming back to you?"

"I told you, I didn't see a face."

"Just his black clothes."

"Black *something*."

"Something? Are we talking man or beast here?"

"It all happened so fast."

"Anthony Sansone's wearing black."

"It wasn't him. He left the room. He went down to meet the ambulance."

"Yeah, that's what he says, too."

Jane's face was silhouetted against the lights of the cruisers parked across the street. The usual convoy of official vehicles had arrived, and crime-scene tape now fluttered between stakes planted in the front yard. Maura had sat in this vehicle for so long, the blood on her coat had dried, turning the fabric stiff as parchment. She would have to throw out this coat; she never wanted to wear it again.

She looked at the house, where all the lights were now blazing. "The doors were locked when we got here. How did he get in?"

"There's no sign of forced entry. Just that broken kitchen window."

"We had to break it. We saw blood in the sink."

"And Sansone was with you the whole time?"

"We were together all evening, Jane."

"Except when he gave chase. He claims he didn't see anyone outside. And he churned up the snow pretty good when he went searching around outside the house. Screwed up any shoe prints we might have been able to use."

"He's not a suspect in this."

"I'm not saying he is."

Maura paused, suddenly thinking of something Jane had just told her. *No sign of forced entry.* "Joyce O'Donnell let him in." She looked at Jane. "She let the killer into her own house."

"Or she forgot to lock the door."

"Of course she'd lock her door. She wasn't stupid."

"She didn't exactly play it safe, either. When you work with monsters, you never know which one will follow you home. These killings have always been about her, Doc. With the very first kill, he draws her attention by calling her. The second kill is right outside the home where she's having dinner. It was all leading up to this. To the main event."

"Why would she let him into her home?"

"Maybe because she thought she could control him. Think about how many prisons she's walked into, how many people like Warren Hoyt and Amalthea Lank she's interviewed. She gets up close and personal with them all."

At the mention of her mother, Maura flinched but said nothing.

"She's like one of those circus lion tamers. You work with the animals every day, and you start to think you're the one in control. You expect that every time you crack the whip, they'll jump like good little kitties. Maybe you even think they love you. Then one day you turn your back, and they're sinking their teeth in your neck."

"I know you never liked her," said Maura. "But if you'd been there—if you'd watched her die"—she looked at Jane—"she was terrified."

"Just because she's dead, I'm not going to start liking her. She's a victim now, so I owe her my best effort. But I can't help feeling that she brought this on herself."

There was a rap on the glass and Jane rolled down the window. A cop peered in at them and said, "Mr. Sansone wants to know if you're done questioning him."

"No, we're not. Tell him to wait."

"And the ME's packing up. You got any last questions?"

"I'll call him if I do."

Through the window, Maura saw her colleague, Dr. Abe Bristol, emerge from the house. Abe would be doing O'Donnell's autopsy. If what he'd just seen inside had upset him, he did not show it. He paused on the porch, calmly buttoning his coat and pulling on warm gloves as he chatted with a cop. *Abe didn't have to watch her die,* thought Maura. *He isn't wearing her blood on his coat.*

Jane pushed open the car door, and a fresh blast of cold air whooshed in. "C'mon, Doc," she said, climbing out. "We'll get you home."

"My car's still parked on Beacon Hill."

"You can worry about your car later. I've got you a ride." Jane turned and called out, "Father Brophy, She's ready to leave."

Only then did Maura notice him, standing in the shadows across the street. He walked toward them, a tall silhouette whose face took on flickering features only as he moved into the cruisers' dancing lights. "Are you sure you're feeling well enough?" he asked as he helped her out of the car. "You don't want to go to the hospital?"

"Please, just drive me home."

Although he offered his arm for support, she didn't take it, but kept her hands in her pockets as they walked to his car. She could feel the gazes of police officers watching them. There go Dr. Isles and that priest, together again. Was there anyone who hadn't noticed, hadn't wondered about them?

There's not a damn thing worth wondering about. She slid into his front seat and stared straight ahead as he started the engine. "Thank you," she said.

"You know I'd do this for you in a heartbeat."

"Did Jane call you?"

"I'm glad she did. You need a friend to drive you home tonight. Not some cop you hardly know." He pulled away from the curb and the garish lights of emergency vehicles faded behind them. "You came too close tonight," he said softly.

"Believe me, I wasn't trying to."

"You shouldn't have gone into that house. You should have called the police."

"Can we not talk about it?"

"Is there *anything* we can still talk about, Maura? Or is this how it's going to be from now on? You won't visit me, you won't answer my calls?"

She finally looked at him. "I'm not getting younger, Daniel. I'm forty-one, my only marriage was a spectacular disaster, and I have a knack for getting into hopeless affairs. I *want* to be married. I *want* to be happy. I can't afford to waste time on re- lationships that go nowhere."

"Even if the friendship, the feelings, are real?"

"Friendships are broken all the time. So are hearts."

"Yes," he said, and sighed. "That's true." They drove for a moment in silence. Then he said, "I never meant to break your heart."

"You haven't."

"But I have hurt you. I know that."

"We've hurt each other. We had to." She paused, and said bitterly, "It's what your almighty God demands, isn't it?" Her words were meant to wound, and by his sudden silence she knew they had found their mark. He said nothing as they approached her neighborhood, as he pulled into her driveway and shut off the engine. He sat for a moment, then turned to her.

"You're right," he said. "My God demands too damn much." And he pulled her toward him.

She should have resisted; she should have pushed him away and stepped out of his car. But she didn't, because for too long she had wanted this embrace, this kiss. And more, much more. This was crazy; this could never turn out right. But neither common sense, nor his God, stood between them now.

Lead us not into temptation. They kissed their way from the car to her front door. *Deliver us from evil.* Futile words, a mere sand castle standing against the relentless tide. They stepped into the house. She did not turn on the light, and as they stood in the shadowy foyer, the darkness seemed to magnify the harsh sound of their breathing, the rustle of wool. She shed the bloodstained coat and it fell to the floor in a puddle of black. Only the faint glow from the windows lit the hallway. There were no lights to illuminate their sin, no other eyes to witness their fall from grace.

She led the way to the bedroom. To her bed.

For a year they had been circling in this dance, every step inching them to this moment. She knew this man's heart, and he knew hers, but his flesh was a stranger's never before touched, never tasted. Her fingers brushed across warm skin and traced down the curve of his spine, all of it new territory that she was hungry to explore.

The last of their clothes slithered off; the last chance to turn back slipped away. "Maura," he whispered as he pressed kisses to her neck, her breasts. "My Maura." His words were soft as a prayer, not to his Lord, but to her. She felt no guilt at all as she welcomed him into her arms. It was not her vow that was broken, not her conscience that would suffer. *Tonight, God, for this moment, he's mine,* she thought, reveling in her victory as Daniel groaned against her, as she wrapped her legs around him, tormented him, urged him on. *I have what you, God, can never give him. I take him from you. I claim him. Go ahead and call in all your demons; I don't give a damn.*

Tonight, neither did Daniel.

When at last their bodies found release, he collapsed into her arms. For a long time they lay silent. By the light through her windows she could see the faint gleam of his eyes, staring at the darkness. Not asleep, but thinking. Perhaps regretting. As the moments passed, she could stand the silence no longer.

"Are you sorry?" she finally asked.

"No," he whispered. His fingers slid along her arm.

"Why am I not convinced?"

"Do you need to be?"

"I want you to be glad. What we did is natural. It's *human.*" She paused and said with a sigh, "But maybe that's just a poor excuse for sin."

"That's not what I'm thinking about at all."

"What are you thinking?"

He pressed a kiss to her forehead, his breath warming her hair. "I'm thinking about what happens next."

"What do you want to happen?"

"I don't want to lose you."

"You don't have to. It's your choice."

"My choice," he said softly. "It's like having to choose between breathing in and breathing out." He rolled onto his back. For a moment, he was silent. "I think I told you, once," he said, "how I came to take my vows."

"You said your sister was dying. Leukemia."

"And I made a bargain. A deal with God. He delivered, and Sophie's alive now. I kept my side of the bargain as well."

"You were only fourteen. That's too young to promise away the rest of your life."

"But I did make that promise. And I can do so much good in His name, Maura. I've been happy, keeping that promise."

"And then you met me."

He sighed. "And then I met you."

"You do have to choose, Daniel."

"Or you'll walk out of my life. I know."

"I don't want to."

He looked at her. "Then don't, Maura! Please. These past few months without you, I've been lost in the wilderness. I felt so guilty, wanting you. But you were all I thought about."

"So where does this leave me, if I stay in your life? You get to keep your church, but what do I get to have?" She stared up at the darkness. "Nothing has really changed, has it?"

"Everything has changed." He reached for her hand. "I love you."

But not enough. Not as much as you love your God.

Yet she let him pull her into his arms again. She met his kisses with her own. This time their love-making was not a tender joining; this coupling was fierce, bodies colliding. Not love, but punishment. Tonight they'd use each other. If she couldn't have love, then lust it would be. Give him something to remember that would haunt him on those nights when God was not enough. *This is what you'll give up when you leave me. This is the Heaven you'll walk away from.*

Before dawn, he did walk away. She felt him stir awake beside her, then slowly sit up on the side of the bed and begin to dress. But of course; it was Sunday morning, and the flock must be tended to.

He bent to kiss her hair. "I have to leave," he whispered.

"I know."

"I love you, Maura. I never thought I'd say that to a woman. But I'm saying it now." He stroked her face and she turned away, so he wouldn't see the tears welling in her eyes.

"Let me make you coffee," she said, starting to sit up.

"No, you stay warm in bed. I'll find my own way out." Another kiss, and he rose to his feet. She heard him walk down the hall, and the front door closed.

So it had finally happened. She'd become just another cliché. Eve with her apple. The temptress luring a holy man to sin. This time, the snake that seduced them was not Satan, but their own lonely hearts. *You want to find the Devil, Mr. Sansone. Just take a look at me.*

Take a look at any one of us.

Outside the sky slowly lightened to a cold, bright dawn. She pushed aside sheets, and the scent of their lovemaking rose from the warm linen: the heady scent of sin. She did not shower it off, but simply pulled on a robe, stepped into slippers, and went into the kitchen to make coffee. Standing at the sink, filling the carafe, she gazed out at clematis vines crystallized in ice, at rhododendrons huddling with leaves crumpled, and did not need to look at a thermometer to know that today the cold would be brutal. She imagined Daniel's parishioners hugging their coats as they stepped from their cars and walked toward the church of Our Lady of Divine Light, braving this Sunday chill for the uplifting words of Father Brophy. And what would he say to them this morning? Would he confess to his flock that even he, their shepherd, had lost his way?

She started the coffeemaker and went to the front door for her newspaper. Stepping outside, she was stunned by the cold. It burned her throat, stung her nostrils. She wasted no time retrieving the newspaper, which had landed on the front walkway, then turned and scurried back up the porch steps. She was just reaching for the doorknob when she suddenly froze, her gaze fixed on the door.

On the words, the symbols, scrawled there.

She spun around, frantically scanning the street. She saw sunshine glinting off icy pavement, heard only the silence of a Sunday morning.

She scrambled into the house, slammed the door shut, and rammed the dead bolt home. Then she ran for the phone and called Jane Rizzoli.

TWENTY-THREE

"ARE YOU SURE you didn't hear anything last night? No footsteps on the porch, nothing out of the ordinary?" asked Jane.

Maura sat on the couch, shivering despite her sweater and wool slacks. She had not eaten breakfast, had not even poured herself a cup of coffee, but she felt not the faintest stirring of hunger. During the half hour before Jane and Frost had arrived, Maura had remained at her living room window, watching the street, attuned to every noise, tracking every car that passed. *The killer knows where I live. He knows what happened last night, in my bedroom.*

"Doc?"

Maura looked up. "I didn't hear anything. The writing was just there, on my door, when I woke up. When I went outside to get my . . ." She flinched, her heart suddenly thudding.

Her phone was ringing.

Frost picked up the receiver. "Isles residence. This is Detective Frost. I'm sorry, Mr. Sansone, but we're dealing with a situation here right now, and this isn't a convenient time for you to talk to her. I'll let her know you called."

Jane's gaze returned to Maura. "Are you sure that writing wasn't already on your door when you got home last night?"

"I didn't see it then."

"You used the front door to enter the house?"

"Yes. Normally, I'd come in the garage. But my car's still on Beacon Hill."

"Did Father Brophy walk you to the door?"

"It was dark, Jane. We wouldn't have seen the writing." *We were only focused on each other. All we had on our minds was getting to my bedroom.*

Frost said, "I think I'll check around outside. See if there are any footprints." He went out the front door. Though he was now tramping right outside the house, the sound of his footsteps did not penetrate the double-pane windows. Last night a trespasser could have walked right past her bedroom, and she wouldn't have heard a thing.

"Do you think he followed you home last night?" Jane asked. "From O'Donnell's house?"

"I don't know. He could have. But I've been present at all three death scenes. Lori-Ann Tucker's. Eve Kassovitz's. On any one of those nights, he might have seen me."

"And followed you home."

She hugged herself, trying to suppress her shaking. "I never noticed. I never realized I was being watched."

"You have an alarm system. Did you use it last night?"

"No."

"Why not?"

"I—I simply forgot to arm it." *I had other things on my mind.*

Jane sat down in the chair across from her. "Why would he draw those symbols on your door? What do you think they mean?"

"How would I know?"

"And the message he left—it's the same one that he left in Lori-Ann Tucker's bedroom. Only this time, he didn't bother to write it in Latin. This time he made sure we'd understand exactly what he meant. *I have sinned.*" Jane paused. "Why direct those particular words at you?"

Maura said nothing.

"Do you think they were meant for you?" Jane's gaze was suddenly alert, probing.

She knows me too well, thought Maura. *She can see I'm not telling her the whole story. Or maybe she's caught the whiff of lust on my skin. I should have showered before they got here; I should have washed away Daniel's scent.*

Abruptly, Maura stood up. "I can't concentrate," she said. "I need a cup of coffee." She turned and headed toward the kitchen. There she busied herself, pouring coffee into mugs, reaching into the refrigerator for cream. Jane had followed her into the kitchen, but Maura avoided looking at her. She slid a steaming mug in front of Jane and then turned to the window as she sipped, delaying, as long as she could, the revelation of her shame.

"Is there something you want to tell me?" said Jane.

"I've told you everything. I woke up this morning

and found that writing on my door. I don't know what else to say."

"After you left O'Donnell's house, did Father Brophy drive you straight home?"

"Yes."

"And you didn't see any cars tailing you?"

"No."

"Well, maybe Father Brophy noticed something. I'll see what he remembers."

Maura cut in. "You don't need to talk to him. I mean, if he'd noticed anything last night, he would have told me."

"I still have to ask him."

Maura turned to face Jane. "It's Sunday, you know."

"I know what day it is."

"He has services."

Jane's gaze had narrowed, and Maura felt her cheeks flame with heat.

"What happened last night?" Jane asked.

"I told you. I came straight home from O'Donnell's house."

"And you stayed inside for the rest of the night?"

"I didn't leave the house."

"Did Father Brophy?"

The question, asked so matter-of-factly, startled Maura into silence. After a moment, she sank into a chair at the kitchen table but said nothing, just stared down at her coffee.

"How long did he stay?" asked Jane. Still no emotion in her voice, still the cop, although Maura knew there was disapproval behind that question, and guilt tightened its fist around her throat.

"He stayed most of the night."

"Till what time?"

"I don't know. It was still dark when he left."

"And what did you two do while he was here?"

"This isn't relevant."

"You know it is. We're talking about what the killer might have seen through your windows. What might have inspired him to write those words on your door. Were your living room lights on the whole night? Were you and Brophy sitting there, talking?"

Maura heaved out a breath. "No. The lights . . . they were off."

"The house was dark."

"Yes."

"And someone standing outside, watching your windows, would have to assume—"

"You know what the hell they'd assume."

"Would they be right?"

Maura met her gaze. "I was freaked out last night, Jane! Daniel was there for me. He's always been there for me. We didn't plan for this to happen. It's the only time—the one time—" Her voice faded. "I didn't want to be alone."

Jane sat down at the kitchen table as well. "You know, those words take on new meaning. *I have sinned.*"

"We've all sinned," shot back Maura. "Each and every damn one of us."

"I'm not criticizing you, okay?"

"Yes you are. You think I can't hear it in your voice?"

"If you're feeling guilty, Doc, it's not because of anything I said."

Maura stared back at Jane's unrelenting gaze and thought, *She's right, of course. My guilt is all my own.*

"We will have to talk to Father Brophy about this, you know. About what happened last night."

Maura gave a resigned sigh. "Please, when you do talk to him, just keep it discreet."

"I'm not exactly bringing in the TV cameras, okay?"

"Detective Frost doesn't have to know about this."

"Of course he has to know. He's my partner."

Maura dropped her head in her hands. "Oh, God."

"This is relevant to the case, and you know it. If I didn't tell Frost, he'd have every right to cry foul."

So I won't be able to look at Frost again without seeing a reflection of my own guilt, thought Maura, cringing at the thought of Frost's reaction. One's reputation was such a fragile thing; one tiny crack and it disintegrates. For two years, they had regarded her as the queen of the dead, the unflappable medical examiner who could gaze without flinching at sights that turned the stomachs of even the most seasoned investigators. Now they'd look at her and see the weaknesses, the flaws of a lonely woman.

Footsteps thumped on the front porch. It was Frost, coming back into the house. She did not want to be present when he learned the tawdry truth. Uptight, upright Barry Frost would be shocked to hear who'd been sleeping in her bed.

But he was not the only person who'd just stepped into the house. Maura heard voices talking, and she looked up in sudden recognition as Anthony Sansone swept into the kitchen, followed by Frost.

"Are you all right?" Sansone asked her.

Jane said, "This really isn't a good time for a visit, Mr. Sansone. Would you mind stepping outside?"

He ignored Jane; his gaze stayed on Maura. He was not dressed in black today, but in shades of gray. A tweed jacket, an ash-colored shirt. So different from Daniel, she thought; this man I cannot read, and he makes me uncomfortable.

"I just saw the markings on your door," he said. "When did that happen?"

"I don't know," she said. "Sometime last night."

"I should have driven you home myself."

Jane cut in. "I really think you should leave now."

"Wait," said Frost. "You need to hear what he says, about what's on the door. What it might mean."

"*I have sinned*? I think the meaning is pretty obvious."

"Not the words," said Sansone. "The symbols beneath them."

"We've already heard about the all-seeing eye. Your friend Oliver Stark explained it."

"He may have been mistaken."

"You don't agree that it's the eye of Horus?"

"I think it may represent something else entirely." He looked at Maura. "Come outside and I'll explain it to you."

Maura had no wish to once again confront those accusing words on her door, but his sense of urgency forced her to follow him. Stepping outside onto the porch, she paused, blinking against the sun's glare. It was such a beautiful Sunday morning, a morning to linger over coffee and the newspaper. Instead she was afraid to sit in her own house, afraid to look at her own front door.

She took a breath and turned to confront what had been drawn in ocher that was the color of dried blood. The words *I have sinned* screamed at her, an accusation that made her want to shrink, to hide her guilty face.

But it was not the words that Sansone focused on. He pointed to the two symbols drawn below them. The larger one they had seen before, on his garden door.

"That looks exactly like the all-seeing eye to me," said Jane.

"But look at this other symbol," said Sansone, pointing to a figure near the bottom of the door. It was so small, it almost seemed like an afterthought. "Drawn in ocher, as at the other crime scenes."

Jane said, "How did you know about the ocher?"

"My colleagues need to see this. To confirm what I think it represents." He took out his cell phone.

"Wait," said Jane. "This isn't some public showing."

"Do *you* know how to interpret this, Detective? Do you have any idea where to start? If you want to find this killer, you'd better understand his thinking. His symbols." He began to dial. Jane did not stop him.

Maura dropped to a crouch so that she could study the bottom sketch. She stared at arching horns, a triangular head, and slitted eyes. "It looks like a goat," she said. "But what does it mean?" She gazed up at Sansone. Backlit by the morning glare, he was a towering figure, black and faceless.

"It represents Azazel," he said. "It's a symbol of the Watchers."

*   *   *

"Azazel was the chief of the Se'irim," said Oliver Stark. "They were goat demons who haunted the ancient deserts before Moses, before the pharaohs. All the way back in the age of Lilith."

"Who's Lilith?" asked Frost.

Edwina Felway looked at Frost in surprise. "You don't know about her?"

Frost gave an embarrassed shrug. "I have to admit, I'm not all that well-versed in the Bible."

"Oh, you won't find Lilith in the Bible," said Edwina. "She's long been banished from accepted Christian doctrine, although she does have a place in Hebrew legend. She was Adam's first wife."

"Adam had another wife?"

"Yes, before Eve." Edwina smiled at his startled face. "What, you think the Bible tells the whole story?"

They were sitting in Maura's living room, gathered around the coffee table, where Oliver's sketchpad lay among the empty cups and saucers. Within half an hour of Sansone's call, both Edwina and Oliver had arrived to examine the symbols on the door. They'd conferred on the porch for only a few minutes before the cold drove them all into the house for hot coffee and theories. Theories that now struck Maura as cold-bloodedly intellectual. Her home had been marked by a killer, and these people calmly sat in her living room, discussing their bizarre theology. She glanced at Jane, who wore an undisguised expression of *these people are kooks.* But Frost was clearly fascinated.

"I never heard that Adam had a first wife," he said.

"There's a whole history that never appears in the Bible, Detective," said Edwina, "a secret history you can only find in Canaanite or Hebrew legends. They talk about the marriage between Adam and a free-spirited woman, a cunning temptress who refused to obey her husband, or to lie beneath him as a docile wife should. Instead she demanded wild sex in every position and taunted him when he couldn't satisfy her. She was the world's first truly liberated female, and she wasn't afraid to seek the pleasures of the flesh."

"She sounds like a lot more fun than Eve," said Frost.

"But in the eyes of the church, Lilith was an abomination, a woman who was beyond the control of men, a creature so sexually insatiable that she finally abandoned her boring old husband, Adam, and ran off to have orgies with demons." Edwina paused. "And as a result, she gave birth to the most powerful demon of all, the one who's plagued mankind ever since."

"You don't mean the Devil?"

Sansone said, "It's a belief that was commonly held in the Middle Ages: Lilith was the mother of Lucifer."

Edwina gave a snort. "So you see how history treats an assertive woman? If you refuse to be subservient, if you enjoy sex a little too much, then the church turns you into a monster. You're known as the Devil's mother."

"Or you disappear from history entirely," said Frost. "Because this is the first I've ever heard of Lilith. Or that goat person."

"Azazel," said Oliver. He tore off his latest sketch

and placed it on the coffee table so that everyone could see it. It was a more detailed version of the face that had been drawn on Maura's door: a horned goat with slitted eyes and a single flame burning atop its head. "The goat demons are mentioned in Leviticus and Isaiah. They were hairy creatures who cavorted with wild beings like Lilith. The name Azazel goes back to the Canaanites, probably a derivation of one of their ancient gods' names."

"And that's who the symbol on the door refers to?" asked Frost.

"That would be my guess."

Jane laughed, unable to contain her skepticism. "A guess? Oh, we're really nailing down the facts here, aren't we?"

Edwina said, "You think this discussion is a waste of time?"

"I think a symbol is whatever you want to make of it. You people think it's a goat demon. But to the weirdo who drew it, it may mean something entirely different. Remember all that stuff you and Oliver spouted about the eye of Horus? The fractions, the quarter moon? So all of that is suddenly a bunch of hooey?"

"I did explain to you that the eye can represent a number of different things," said Oliver. "The Egyptian god. The all-seeing eye of Lucifer. Or the Masonic symbol for illumination, for wisdom."

"Those are pretty opposite meanings," said Frost. "The Devil versus wisdom?"

"They're not opposite at all. You have to remember what the word *Lucifer* means. Translated, the name is 'Bringer of Light.'"

"That doesn't sound so evil."

"Some would claim that Lucifer *isn't* evil," said Edwina, "that he represents the questioning mind, the independent thinker, the very things that once threatened the church."

Jane snorted. "So now Lucifer isn't such a bad guy? He just asked too many questions?"

"Who you call the Devil depends on your perspective," said Edwina. "My late husband was an anthropologist. I've lived all over the world, collected images of demons that look like jackals or cats or snakes. Or beautiful women. Every culture has its own idea of what the Devil looks like. There's only one thing that almost all cultures, dating back to the most primitive tribes, agree on: the Devil actually *exists*."

Maura thought of that faceless swirl of black that she had glimpsed in O'Donnell's bedroom last night, and a chill prickled the back of her neck. She didn't believe in Satan. But she did believe in evil. *And last night, I was surely in its presence.* Her gaze fell on Oliver's sketch of the horned goat. "This thing—this Azazel—is he also a symbol of the Devil?"

"No," said Oliver. "Azazel is often used as a symbol for the Watchers."

"Who are these *watchers* you keep talking about?" asked Frost.

Edwina looked at Maura. "Do you have a Bible, Dr. Isles?"

Maura frowned at her. "Yes."

"Could you get it for us?"

Maura crossed to the bookcase and scanned the top shelf for the familiar worn cover. It had been her father's Bible, and Maura had not opened it in years.

She took it down and handed it to Edwina, who riffled through the pages, setting off a puff of dust.

"Here it is. Genesis, chapter six. Verses one and two: 'And it came to pass, when men began to multiply on the face of the earth, and daughters were born unto them, that the sons of God saw the daughters of men that they were fair; and they took them wives of all which they chose.' "

"The sons of God?" asked Frost.

"That passage almost certainly refers to angels," explained Edwina. "It says that angels lusted after earthly women, so they married them. A marriage between the divine and the mortal." She looked down at the Bible again. "And here's verse four: 'There were giants on the earth in these days; and also after that, when the sons of God came in unto the daughters of men, and they bore children to them, the same became mighty men which were of old, men of renown.' " Edwina closed the book.

"What does all that mean?" asked Frost.

"It says that they had children," said Edwina. "That's the one place in the Bible where these children are mentioned. These offspring resulted from matings between humans and angels. They were a mixed race of demons called the Nephilim."

"Also known as the Watchers," said Sansone.

"You'll find references to them in other sources that predate the Bible. In the Book of Enoch. In the Book of Jubilees. They're described as monsters, spawned by fallen angels who had intercourse with human women. The result was a secret race of hybrids that supposedly still walks among us. These creatures are said to have unusual charm and talent, unusual beauty. Often very tall, very charismatic. But they're demons nonetheless, and they serve the darkness."

"You people actually believe this?" asked Jane.

"I'm just telling you what's in holy writings, Detective. The ancients believed mankind was not alone on this earth, that others came before us and that some people today still carry the bloodline of those monsters."

"But you called them the children of angels."

"Fallen angels. Flawed and evil."

"So these things, these Watchers, are like mutants," said Frost, "hybrids."

Edwina looked at him. "A subspecies. Violent and predatory. The rest of us are merely prey."

"It's written that when Armageddon arrives," said Oliver, "when the world as we know it ends, the Antichrist himself will be one of the Nephilim. A Watcher."

And their mark is on my door. Maura stared at the sketch of the goat's head. Was that symbol intended as a warning?

Or an invitation?

"Well," said Jane, and she looked pointedly at her watch. "This has been a really *valuable* use of our time."

"You still don't see the significance, do you?" said Sansone.

"It makes for a great story around the campfire, but it doesn't get me any closer to our killer."

"It gets you into his head. It tells us what *he* believes."

"Angels and goat demons. Right. Or maybe our perp just likes to play head games with cops. So he makes us waste our time chasing after ocher and seashells." Jane rose to her feet. "The crime-scene unit should be here any minute. Maybe you people could all go home now, so we can do our jobs."

"Wait," Sansone cut in. "What was that you just said about seashells?"

Jane ignored him and looked at Frost. "Can you call CSU and find out what's taking them so long?"

"Detective Rizzoli," said Sansone, "tell us about the seashells."

"You seem to have your own sources. Why don't you ask them?"

"This could be very important. Why don't you just save us the effort and tell us?"

"First, you tell me. What's the significance of a seashell?"

"What kind of shell? A bivalve, a cone?"

"Does it make a difference?"

"Yes."

Jane paused. "It's sort of a spiral. A cone, I guess."

"It was left at a death scene?"

"You might say that."

"Describe the shell."

"Look, there's nothing special about it. The guy I spoke to says it's a common species found all over the Mediterranean." She paused as her cell phone rang. "Excuse me," she said, and walked out of the room. For a moment no one said anything. The three members of the Mephisto Foundation looked at one another.

"Well," Edwina said softly, "I'd say this just about clinches it."

"Clinches what?" said Frost.

"The seashell," said Oliver, "is on Anthony's family crest."

Sansone rose from his chair and crossed to the window. There he stood gazing out at the street, his broad back framed in black by the window. "The symbols were drawn in red ocher, mined from Cyprus," he said. "Do you know the significance of that, Detective Frost?"

"We have no idea," Frost admitted.

"This killer isn't playing games with the police. He's playing games with *me*. With the Mephisto Foundation." He turned to face them, but the morning glare made his expression impossible to read. "On Christmas Eve, he kills a woman and leaves satanic symbols at the scene—the candles, the ocher circle. But the single most significant thing he does that night is place a phone call to Joyce O'Donnell, a member of our foundation. That was the tug on our sleeve. It was meant to get our attention."

"Your attention? It seems to me this has always been about O'Donnell."

"Then Eve Kassovitz was killed in my garden. On a night we were meeting."

"It's also the night O'Donnell was your dinner guest. *She* was the one he stalked, the one he had his eye on."

"I would have agreed with you last night. All the signs, up till then, pointed to Joyce as the target. But these symbols on Maura's door tell us the killer hasn't completed his work. He's still hunting."

"He knows about us, Anthony," said Edwina. "He's cutting down our circle. Joyce was the first. The question is, who's next?"

Sansone looked at Maura. "I'm afraid he thinks you're one of us."

"But I'm not," she said. "I don't want anything to do with your group delusion."

"Doc?" said Jane. Maura had not heard her come back into the room. Jane was standing in the doorway, holding her cell phone. "Can you come into the kitchen? We need to talk in private."

Maura rose and followed her up the hallway. "What is it?" she asked as they stepped into the kitchen.

"Could you arrange to take the day off tomorrow? Because you and I need to go out of town tonight. I'm going home to pack an overnight bag. I'll be back to pick you up around noon."

"Are you telling me I should run and hide? Just because someone's written on my door?"

"This has nothing to do with your door. I just got a call from a cop out in upstate New York. Last night they found a woman's body. It's clearly a homicide."

"Why should a murder in New York concern us?"

"She's missing her left hand."

TWENTY-FOUR

AUGUST 8. Phase of the moon: Last Quarter.

Every day, Teddy goes down to the lake.

In the morning, I hear the squeal and slap of the screen door, and then I hear his shoes thump down the porch steps. From my window, I watch him walk from the house and head down toward the water, fishing pole propped on his thin shoulder, tackle box in hand. It is a strange ritual, and useless, I think, because he never brings back any fruits of his labor. Every afternoon, he returns empty-handed but cheerful.

Today, I follow him.

He does not see me as he rambles through the woods toward the water. I stay far enough behind him so that he can't hear my footsteps. He is singing anyway, in his high and childish voice, an off-key version of the "Kookaburra" song, and is oblivious to the fact he is being watched. He reaches the water's edge, baits his hook, and throws in his line. As the minutes pass, he settles onto the grassy bank and gazes across water so calm that not even a whisper of wind ruffles the mirrored surface.

The fishing pole gives a twitch.

I move closer as Teddy reels in his catch. It is a brownish fish and it writhes on the line, every muscle twitching in mortal terror. I wait for the fatal blow, for that sacred instant in time when the divine spark flickers out. But to my surprise, Teddy grasps his catch, pulls the hook from its mouth, and gently lowers the fish back into the water. He crouches close, murmuring to it, as though in apology for having inconvenienced its morning.

"Why didn't you keep it?" I ask.

Teddy jerks straight, startled by my voice. "Oh," he says. "It's you."

"You let it go."

"I don't like to kill them. It's only a bass, anyway."

"So you throw them all back?"

"Uh-huh." Teddy baits his hook again and casts it into the water.

"What's the point of catching them, then?"

"It's fun. It's like a game between us. Me and the fish."

I sit down beside him on the bank. Gnats buzz around our heads and Teddy waves them away. He has just turned eleven years old, but he still has a child's perfectly smooth skin, and the golden baby fuzz on his face catches the sun's glint. I am close enough to hear his breathing, to see the pulse throb in his slender neck. He does not seem bothered by my presence; in fact, he gives me a shy smile, as though this is a special treat, sharing the lazy morning with his older cousin.

"You want to try?" he says, offering me the pole.

I take it. But my attention remains on Teddy, on the fine sheen of perspiration on his forehead, on the shadows cast by his eyelashes.

The pole gives a tug.

"You've got one!"

I begin to reel it in, and the fish's struggles make my hands sweat in anticipation. I can feel its thrashings, its desperation to live, transmitted through the pole. At last it breaks the water, its tail flapping as I swing it over the bank. I grab hold of slimy scales.

"Now take out the hook," says Teddy. "But be careful not to hurt him."

I look into the open tackle box and see a knife.

"He can't breathe out of water. Hurry." Teddy urges me.

I think about reaching for the knife, about holding the wriggling fish down against the grass and piercing it behind the gills. About slitting it open, all the way down the belly. I want to feel the fish give a last twitch, want to feel its life force leap directly into me in a bracing jolt—the same jolt I felt when I was ten years old and took the oath of Herem. When my mother at last brought me into the circle and handed me the knife. "You have reached the age," she said. "It's time to be one of us." I think of the sacrificial goat's final shudder, and I remember the pride in my mother's eyes and the murmurs of approval from the circle of robed men. I want to feel that thrill again.

A fish will not do.

I remove the hook and drop the wriggling bass

back into the lake. It gives a splash of its tail and darts away. The whisper of a breeze ruffles the water and dragonflies tremble on the reeds. I turn to Teddy.

And he says, "Why are you looking at me like that?"

TWENTY-FIVE

FORTY-TWO EUROS in tips—not a bad haul for a chilly Sunday in December. As Lily waved good-bye to the tour group whom she'd just shepherded through the Roman Forum, she felt an icy raindrop fleck her face. She looked up at dark clouds hanging ominously low and she shivered. Tomorrow she'd certainly need a raincoat.

With that fresh roll of cash in her pocket, she headed for the favorite shopping venue of every penny-pinching student in Rome: the Porta Portese flea market in Trastevere. It was already one P.M., and the dealers would be closing down their stalls, but she might have time to pick up a bargain. By the time she reached the market, a fine drizzle was falling. The Piazza di Porta Portese echoed with the clatter of crates being packed up. She wasted no time snatching up a used wool sweater for only three Euros. It reeked of cigarette smoke, but a good washing would remedy that. She paid another two Euros for a hooded slicker that was marred only by a single streak of black grease. Now dressed warmly in her new purchases, and with money still in her pocket, she indulged in the luxury of browsing.

She wandered down the narrow passage between stalls, pausing to pick through buckets of costume jewelry and fake Roman coins, and continued toward Piazza Ippolito Nievo and the antiques stalls. Every Sunday, it seemed, she always ended up in this section of the market, because it was the old things, the ancient things, that truly interested her. A scrap of medieval tapestry or a mere chip of bronze could make her heart pound faster. By the time she reached the antiques area, most of the dealers were already carting away their merchandise, and she saw only a few stands still open, their wares exposed to the drizzle. She wandered past the meager offerings, past weary, glum-faced sellers, and was about to leave the piazza when her gaze fell on a small wooden box. She halted, staring.

Three reverse crosses were carved into the top.

Her mist-dampened face suddenly felt encased in ice. Then she noticed that the hinge was facing toward her, and with a sheepish laugh, she rotated the box to its proper orientation. The crosses turned right-side up. When you looked too hard for evil, you saw it everywhere. *Even when it's not there.*

"You are looking for religious items?" the dealer asked in Italian.

She glanced up to see the man's wrinkled face, his eyes almost lost in folds of skin. "I'm just browsing, thank you."

"Here. There's more." He slid a box in front of her, and she saw tangled rosary beads and a wooden carving of the Madonna and old books, their pages curling in the dampness. "Look, look! Take your time."

At first glance, she saw nothing in that box that interested her. Then she focused on the spine of one of the books. The title was stamped on the leather in gold: *The Book of Enoch*.

She picked it up and opened it to the copyright page. It was the English translation by R. H. Charles, a 1912 edition printed by Oxford University Press. Two years ago, in a Paris museum, she had viewed a centuries-old scrap of the Ethiopic version. *The Book of Enoch* was an ancient text, part of the apocryphal literature.

"It is very old," said the dealer.

"Yes," she murmured, "it is."

"It says 1912."

And these words are even older, she thought, as she ran her fingers across the yellowed pages. This text predated the birth of Christ by two hundred years. These were stories from an era before Noah and his ark, before Methusaleh. She flipped through the pages and paused at one passage that had been underlined in ink.

Evil spirits have proceeded from their bodies, because they are born from men, and from the holy Watchers is their beginning and primal origin; they shall be evil spirits on earth, and evil spirits shall they be called.

"I have many more of his things," said the dealer.

She looked up. "Whose?"

"The man who owned that book. This is all his." He waved at the boxes. "He died last month, and now everything must be sold. If you are interested in such items, I have another one just like it." He bent down to dig through another box and came up with a slim leather-bound book, its cover battered and stained. "The same author," he said. "R. H. Charles."

Not the same author, she thought, but the same translator. It was a 1913 edition of *The Book of Jubilees,* yet another holy text that predated the Christian era. Although she was familiar with the title *Jubilees,* she had never read this particular book. She lifted the cover, and the pages fell open to chapter ten, verse five, a passage that was also underlined in ink:

And thou knowest how thy Watchers, the fathers of these spirits, acted in my day: and as for these spirits which are living, imprison them and hold them fast in the place of condemnation, and let them not bring destruction on the sons of thy servant, my God; for these are malignant, and created in order to destroy.

In the margin, scrawled in the same ink, were the words: *The sons of Seth. The daughters of Cain.*

Lily closed the book and suddenly noticed the brown stains on the leather cover. *Blood?*

"Would you like to buy it?"

She looked up. "What happened to this man? The one who owned these books?"

"I told you. He died."

"How?"

A shrug. "He lived alone. He was very old, very strange. They found him locked inside his apartment, with all these books piled up against the door. So he couldn't even get out. Crazy, eh?"

Or terrified, she thought, *of what might get in.*

"I'll give you a good price. Do you want it?"

She stared at the second book, thinking of its owner, lying dead and barricaded in his cluttered apartment, and she could almost smell the scent of decaying flesh wafting up from the pages. Repulsed though she was by the stains on the leather, she wanted this book. She wanted to know why the owner had scrawled those words in the margins and whether he had written anything else.

"Five Euros," the dealer said.

For once, she did not dicker, but simply paid the asking price and walked away with the book.

It was raining hard by the time she climbed the dank stairwell to her flat. All afternoon it rained as she sat reading by the gray and watery light through her window. She read about Seth. The third son of Adam, Seth begat Enos, who begat Kenan. It was the same lofty bloodline from which later sprang the patriarchs Jared and Enoch, Methuselah and Noah. But from this very bloodline also sprang corrupted sons, wicked sons, who mated with the daughters of a murderous ancestor.

The daughters of Cain.

Lily stopped at another underlined passage, the words long ago marked by the man whose ghostly presence now seemed to hover at her shoulder, anxious to share his secrets, to whisper his warnings.

And lawlessness increased on the earth and all flesh corrupted its way, alike men and cattle and beasts and birds and everything that walks on the earth, all of them corrupted their ways and their orders, and they began to devour each other, and lawlessness increased on the earth and every imagination of the thoughts of all men was thus evil continually.

Daylight was fading. She had been sitting for so

long, she'd lost all feeling in her limbs. Outside, rain continued to tap at the window, and on the streets of Rome, traffic rumbled and honked. But here, in her room, she sat in numb silence. A century before Christ, before the Apostles, these words were already old, written about a terror so ancient that today mankind no longer remembered it, no longer marked its presence.

She looked down, once again, at *The Book of Jubilees,* at the ominous words of Noah, spoken to his sons:

For I see, and behold the demons have begun their seductions against you and against your children and now I fear on your behalf, that after my death ye will shed the blood of men upon the earth and that ye, too, will be destroyed from the face of the earth.

The demons are still among us, she thought. *And the bloodshed has already begun.*

TWENTY-SIX

JANE AND MAURA drove west on the Massachusetts Turnpike, Jane at the wheel as they hurtled through a stark landscape of snow and bare trees. Even on this Sunday afternoon, they shared the highway with a convoy of monster trucks that dwarfed Jane's Subaru as she sped around them like a daredevil gnat. It was better not to watch. Maura focused instead on Jane's notes. The handwriting was a hurried scrawl, but it was no less legible than the scrawls of physicians, which Maura had long ago learned to decipher.

Sarah Parmley, 28 years old. Last seen 12/23 checking out of the Oakmont Motel.

"She vanished two weeks ago," said Maura. "And they only just discovered her body?"

"She was found in a vacant house. Apparently, it's somewhat isolated. The caretaker noticed her car parked outside. He also found that the house's front door was unlocked, so he went in to investigate. He's the one who discovered the body."

"What was the victim doing in a vacant house?"

"No one knows. Sarah arrived in town on December twentieth to attend her aunt's funeral. Everyone assumed that she'd returned home to California right after the service. But then her employer in San Diego started calling, looking for her. Even then, no one in town considered the possibility that Sarah had never left."

"Look at the map, Jane. From upstate New York to Boston—the crime scenes are three hundred miles apart. Why would the killer transport her hand that far? Maybe it's not hers."

"It is her hand. I *know* it is. I tell you, the x-rays are going to fit together like a jigsaw puzzle."

"How can you be so sure?"

"Check out the name of the town where Sarah's body was found."

"Purity, New York. It's a quaint name, but it doesn't mean a thing to me."

"Sarah Parmley grew up in Purity. She graduated from high school there."

"So?"

"So guess where Lori-Ann Tucker went to high school?"

Maura looked at her in surprise. "She's from the same town?"

"You got it. And Lori-Ann Tucker was twenty-eight years old, too. Eleven years ago, they would have graduated from the same high school class."

"Two victims who grew up in the same town, went to the same high school. They would have known each other."

"And maybe that's where this perp met them. This is how he chose them. Maybe he was obsessed with them since high school. Maybe they snubbed him, and he's spent the last eleven years thinking about ways to get back at them. Then suddenly, Sarah shows up in Purity for her aunt's funeral, and he sees her. Gets all pissed off again. Kills her and cuts off her hand as a souvenir. Has so much fun doing it that he decides to do it again."

"So he drives all the way to Boston to kill Lori-Ann? It's a long way to go for a thrill."

"But not for good old-fashioned revenge."

Maura stared at the road, thinking. "If it was all about revenge, why did he call Joyce O'Donnell that night? Why did he turn his rage on her?"

"Only she knew the answer to that. And she refused to share the secret with us."

"And why write on my door? What's the message there?"

"You mean, *I have sinned*?"

Maura flushed. Closing the folder, she sat with clenched hands pressing against the file. So it was back to that again. The one subject she had no wish to talk about.

"I told Frost about it," said Jane.

Maura said nothing, just kept her gaze focused straight ahead.

"He needed to know. He's already spoken to Father Brophy."

"You should have let me talk to Daniel first."

"Why?"

"So he wouldn't be completely taken by surprise."

"That we know about you two?"

"Don't sound so damn judgmental."

"I wasn't aware that I did."

"I can hear it in your voice. I don't need this."

"Then it's a good thing you didn't hear what Frost had to say about it."

"You think this doesn't happen all the time? People fall in love, Jane. They make mistakes."

"But not *you*!" Jane sounded almost angry, betrayed. "I always thought you were smarter than this."

"No one's that smart."

"This can't go anywhere and you know it. If you ever expect him to marry you—"

"I've already tried marriage, remember? That was a rousing success."

"And what do you think you're going to get out of this?"

"I don't know."

"Well, I do. First there'll be all the whispers. Your neighbors wondering why that priest's car is always parked outside your house. Then you'll have to sneak out of town just to spend time with each other. But eventually, someone's going to see you two together. And then the gossip starts. It'll just get more and more awkward. Embarrassing. How long are you going to be able to keep that up? How long before he's forced to make a choice?"

"I don't want to talk about this."

"You think he'll choose *you*?"

"Cut it out, Jane."

"Well, do you?" The question was unnecessarily brutal, and for a moment Maura considered getting out at the next town, calling for a rental car, and driving home by herself.

"I'm old enough to make my own choices," she said.

"But what's *his* choice going to be?"

Maura turned her head to stare out the window at snowy fields, at toppling fence posts half-buried in drifts. *If he doesn't choose me, will I really be all that surprised? He can tell me again and again how much he loves me. But will he ever leave his church for me?*

Jane sighed. "I'm sorry."

"It's my life, not yours."

"Yeah, you're right. It's your life." Jane shook her head and laughed. "Man, the whole world's gone totally bonkers. I can't count on anything anymore. Not a single goddamn thing." She drove for a moment in silence, squinting at the setting sun. "I didn't tell you about my own wonderful news."

"What news?"

"My parents have split up."

At last Maura looked at her. "When did this happen?"

"Right after Christmas. Thirty-seven years of marriage, and my dad suddenly goes sniffing after some blondie from work."

"I'm so sorry."

"Then this thing with you and Brophy—it's like everyone's gone sex crazy. You. My idiot dad. Even my mom." She paused. "Vince Korsak asked her out on a date. *That's* how weird everything's gotten." Suddenly Jane gave a groan. "Oh, Christ. I just thought about it. Do you realize that he could end up being my *stepdad*?"

"The world hasn't gone that crazy."

"It could happen." Jane shuddered. "It gives me the creeps just thinking about the two of them."

"Then don't think about it."

Jane gritted her teeth. "I'm trying not to."

And I'll try not to think of Daniel.

But as they continued driving west toward the setting sun, through the city of Springfield and into the rolling Berkshire Hills, all she could think about was him. She breathed in and could still smell his scent, crossed her arms and could still feel his touch, as though the memories were engraved on her skin. And she wondered: *Is it the same for you, Daniel? When you stood before your congregation. this morning and looked around at the faces watching you, waiting for your words, was it my face you sought, my face you thought about?*

By the time they crossed the state line into New York, night had fallen. Her cell phone rang, and in the dark car it took her a moment to find it among the jumbled contents of her purse. "Dr. Isles," she answered.

"Maura, it's me."

At the sound of Daniel's voice, she felt her cheeks flame and was glad that darkness masked her face from Jane's gaze.

"Detective Frost came to see me," he said.

"I had to tell them."

"Of course you had to. But I wish you'd called me about it. You should have told me."

"I'm sorry. It must have been so embarrassing, to hear it from him first."

"No, I mean about the writing on your door. I had

no idea. I would have been there for you in an instant. You shouldn't have had to face that alone."

She paused, acutely aware that Jane was listening to every word. And would no doubt express her disapproval the instant the call ended.

"I went by your house a little while ago," he said. "I was hoping to find you at home."

"I'm going to be away tonight."

"Where are you?"

"I'm in the car with Jane. We just passed through Albany a while ago."

"You're in New York? Why?"

"They've found another victim. We think . . ." Jane's hand suddenly closed around Maura's arm, an unmistakable warning that the less revealed, the better. Jane didn't trust him anymore, now that he'd proven himself to be all too human. "I can't talk about it," she said.

There was a silence on the line. Then, a quiet "I understand."

"There are details we have to keep confidential."

"You don't need to explain. I know how it works."

"Can I call you back later?" *When there isn't another pair of ears listening.*

"You don't have to, Maura."

"I want to." *I need to.*

She hung up and stared at a night pierced only by the beams of their headlights. They had left the turnpike behind them, and their route now took them southwest, on a road that cut through snow-covered fields. Here, the only lights they saw came from the occasional passing car or the glow of a distant farm-house.

"You're not going to talk to him about the case, are you?" asked Jane.

"Even if I did, he's perfectly discreet. I've always trusted him."

"Well, so did I."

"Meaning you don't anymore?"

"You're in lust, Doc. That's not the best time to trust your judgment."

"We both know this man."

"And I never thought—"

"What, that he'd sleep with me?"

"I'm just saying, you may think you know some-one. And then they surprise you. They do something you never expected, and you realize you're in the dark about everyone. *Everyone.* If you told me a few months ago that my dad would leave my mom for some bimbo, I'd have said you were nuts. I'm telling you, people are a goddamn mystery. Even the people we love."

"And now you don't trust Daniel."

"Not when it comes to that vow of chastity."

"I'm not talking about that. I'm talking about this investigation. About telling him details that concern both of us."

"He's not a cop. He doesn't have to hear a thing."

"He was with me last night. The writing on my door was directed at him, too."

"You mean, *I have sinned*?"

Heat flooded Maura's face. "Yes," she said.

For a moment they drove without speaking. The

only sounds were the tires on the road, the hiss of the car heater.

"I respected Brophy, okay?" said Jane. "He's been good to Boston PD. When we need a priest on the scene, he comes right over, any time of night. I liked him."

"Then why have you turned against him?"

Jane looked at her. "Because I happen to like you, too."

"You certainly don't give me that impression."

"Yeah? Well, when you do something unexpected like this, something so self-destructive, it makes me wonder."

"What?"

"If I really know you, either."

It was after eight when they finally pulled into the parking lot of Lourdes Hospital in Binghamton. Maura was not inclined to make small talk as she stepped out of the car, her muscles stiff from the long journey. They had stopped only briefly for a silent dinner at a rest stop McDonald's, and her stomach was unsettled by Jane's driving, by the hastily devoured meal, but most of all by the tension between them, now spun so tight that one more twist could snap it. *She has no right to judge me,* Maura thought as they trudged past drifts of plowed snow. Jane was married and happy and so fucking morally superior. What did she know about Maura's life, about the nights she spent alone watching old movies or playing the piano to an empty house? The gap between their lives yawned too wide to be bridged by real friendship. *And what do I have in common, anyway, with this blunt and uncompromising bitch? Not a thing.*

They walked in through the ER entrance, cold wind sweeping in with them as the automatic doors slid shut. Jane crossed straight to the triage window and called out, "Hello? Can I get some information out here?"

"Are you Detective Rizzoli?" said a voice behind them.

They had not seen him sitting alone in the patient waiting area. Now he rose to his feet, a wan-faced man wearing a tweed jacket over a hunter-green sweater. Not a cop, guessed Maura, noting his shaggy head of hair, and he quickly confirmed her impression.

"I'm Dr. Kibbie," he said. "Thought I'd wait for you out here, so you wouldn't have to find your own way down to the morgue."

"Thanks for meeting us tonight," said Jane. "This is Dr. Isles, from our ME's office."

Maura shook his hand. "You've already done the autopsy?"

"Oh, no. I'm not a pathologist, just a humble internist. There are four of us who rotate as Chenango County coroners. I do the preliminary death investigation and decide if a postmortem is called for. The autopsy itself will probably be done tomorrow afternoon, assuming the Onondaga County ME can make it down here from Syracuse."

"You must have your own pathologist in this county."

"Yes, but in this particular case . . ." Kibbie shook

his head. "Unfortunately, we know this murder's going to generate publicity. A lot of interest. Plus, it could end up in a splashy criminal trial someday, and our pathologist wanted to bring in another ME on the case as well. Just so there'll be no question about their conclusions. Safety in numbers, you know." He picked up his overcoat from the chair. "The elevator's that way."

"Where's Detective Jurevich?" asked Jane. "I thought he was going to meet us here."

"Unfortunately, Joe got called away just a while ago, so he won't be seeing you tonight. He said he'd meet you in the morning, over at the house. Just give him a call tomorrow." Kibbie took a breath. "So, are you ready for this?"

"That bad, huh?"

"Let's put it this way: I hope I never see anything like this again."

They started up the hall to the elevator, and he pressed the Down button.

"After two weeks, I guess she's in pretty bad shape," said Jane.

"Actually, there's been minimal decomposition. The house was vacant. No heat, no power. It's probably about thirty degrees inside. Like storing meat in a freezer."

"How did she end up there?"

"We have no idea. There were no signs of forced entry, so she must have had a key. Or the killer did."

The elevator door opened and they stepped in, Kibbie flanked by the two women. A buffer between Maura and Jane, who still had not said a word to each other since they'd left the car.

"Who owns that vacant house?" asked Jane.

"A woman who lives out of state now. She inherited it from her parents, and she's been trying to sell it for years. We haven't been able to contact her. Even the Realtor doesn't know where she is." They stepped out of the elevator on the basement level. Kibbie led the way down the hall and pushed through a door, into the morgue anteroom.

"There you are, Dr. Kibbie." A young blond woman in hospital scrubs set down the paperback romance she'd been reading and stood to greet them. "I was wondering if you were still coming down."

"Thanks for waiting, Lindsey. These are the two ladies I told you about, from Boston. "Detective Rizzoli and Dr. Isles."

"You drove all that way to see our gal, huh? Well, let me roll her out for you." She stepped through double doors into the autopsy lab and flipped the wall switch. Fluorescent lights glared down on the empty table. "Dr. Kibbie, I've really got to leave soon. Could you roll her back into the cooler and lock up for me when you're done? Just pull the hallway door shut when you go."

"You going to try and catch the rest of the game?" asked Kibbie.

"If I don't show up, Ian's never going to talk to me again."

"Does Ian actually talk?"

Lindsey rolled her eyes. "Dr. Kibbie. *Please*."

"I keep telling you, you should give my nephew a call. He's premed at Cornell. Some other girl's going to snap him right up if you aren't quick."

She laughed as she pulled open the refrigerator door. "Yeah, like I'd ever want to marry a doctor."

"I'm truly hurt by that."

"I mean, I want a guy who'll be home for dinner." She tugged on a gurney, wheeling it out of the refrigerator. "You want her on the table?"

"The gurney's fine. We're not going to cut."

"Let me just double-check that I've pulled the right one." She glanced at the attached tag, then reached for the zipper. She betrayed no hesitation, no squeamishness, as she unzipped the bag to expose the corpse's face. "Yep, this is it," she said, and straightened, flipping back her blond hair, her face pink with the bloom of youth. A startling contrast to the lifeless face and desiccated eyes that stared up from the opening in the shroud.

"We can take it from here, Lindsey," said Dr. Kibbie.

The girl gave a wave. "Remember to pull the door shut all the way," she said cheerfully and walked out, leaving behind an incongruous trace of perfume.

Maura pulled latex gloves from a box on the countertop. Then she crossed to the gurney and unzipped the bag all the way open. As the plastic parted, no one said a word. What lay on that gurney silenced them all.

At four degrees Centigrade, bacterial growth is arrested, decay halted. Despite the passage of at least two weeks, the freezing temperatures of the vacant house had preserved the corpse's soft tissues, and there was no need for menthol ointment to mask any overwhelming odors. The harsh lights revealed far worse horrors than mere putrefaction. The throat lay open and exposed by a single deep slash that had transected the trachea, slicing all the way to the cervical spine. But that fatal stroke of the blade was not what captured Maura's gaze; she stared, instead, at the naked torso. At the multitude of crosses that had been carved on the breasts, on the abdomen. Holy symbols cut into the parchment of human skin. Blood encrusted the carvings, and countless rivulets had seeped from shallow incisions and dried in brick-red lines running down the sides of the torso.

Her gaze moved to the right arm, lying at the corpse's side. She saw the ring of bruises, like a cruel bracelet marking the wrist. She looked up and met Jane's gaze. For that one moment, all anger between the two women was forgotten, swept aside by the vision of Sarah Parmley's final moments.

"This was done while she was still alive," said Maura.

"All these cuts." Jane swallowed. "It could have taken hours."

Kibbie said, "When we found her, there was nylon cord around the remaining wrist and both ankles. The knots were nailed to the floor, so she couldn't move."

"He didn't do this to Lori-Ann Tucker," Maura said.

"That's the victim in Boston?"

"She was dismembered. But she wasn't tortured." Maura circled to the corpse's left side and stared down at the wrist stump. The incised flesh had dried to a leathery brown, and the soft tissues had contracted to expose the surface of cut bone.

"Maybe he wanted something from this woman," said Jane. "Maybe there was a reason to torture her."

"An interrogation?" said Kibbie.

"Or punishment," said Maura, focusing on the victim's face. She thought of the words that had been scratched on her own door. On Lori-Ann's bedroom wall. *I have sinned.*

Is this the reward?

"These aren't just random cuts," said Jane. "These are crosses. Religious symbols."

"He drew them on the walls, too," said Kibbie.

Maura looked up at him. "Was there anything else on the walls? Other symbols?"

"Yeah. Lots of weird stuff. I tell you, it gave me the willies just to step in that front door. Joe Jurevich will show you when you go to the house." He gazed at the body. "This is all there is to see here, really. Enough to tell you we're dealing with a very sick puppy."

Maura closed the body bag, zipping the plastic over sunken eyes, over corneas clouded by death. She would not be performing this autopsy, but she did not need a scalpel and probe to tell her how this victim had died; she had seen the answer engraved on the woman's flesh.

They wheeled the gurney back into the refrigerator and stripped off their gloves. Standing at the sink, washing his hands, Kibbie said, "Ten years ago, when I moved to Chenango County, I thought this was God's country. Fresh air, rolling hills. Folks who'd wave hello, feed me pie when I made a house call." He sighed, shut off the faucet. "You can't get away from it, can you? Big city or small town, husbands still shoot their wives, kids still smash and grab. But I never thought I'd see this kind of sick stuff." He yanked out a paper towel and dried his hands. "Certainly not in a village like Purity. You'll see what I mean when you get there."

"How far is it?"

"Another hour and a half, maybe two hours. Depending on whether you want to risk your lives speeding on back roads."

"Then we'd better get going," said Jane, "if we want to find a motel there."

"A motel?" Kibbie laughed. "If I were you, I'd stop in the town of Norwich instead. You're not going to find much in Purity."

"It's that small?"

He tossed the paper towel into the trash can. "It's that small."

TWENTY-SEVEN

THE MOTEL WALLS were paper-thin. Lying in bed, Maura could hear Jane talking on the phone in the next room. *How nice it must be,* she thought, *to call your husband and laugh out loud together. To share a public kiss, a hug, without first having to glance around, looking for anyone who might know you, and disapprove.* Her own call to Daniel had been brief and furtive. There'd been other people talking in the background, others in the room listening to him, which was why he'd sounded so reserved. Was this how it would always be? Their private lives cut off from their public lives, and never an intersection between them? Here were the real wages of sin. Not hellfire and damnation, but heartbreak.

In the next room, Jane ended her call. A moment later, the TV came on, and then Maura heard the sound of running water in the shower. Only a wall separated them, but the barrier between them was far more formidable than wood and plaster. They'd said hardly a word since Binghamton, and now, just the sound of Jane's TV was an escalating annoyance. Maura pulled a pillow over her head to shut out the noise, but it could not muffle the whispers of doubt in her mind. Even when Jane's room finally fell silent, Maura lay awake and aware of the minutes, then the hours, ticking by.

It was not yet seven the next morning when she finally climbed out of bed, exhausted from her restless night, and looked out the window. The sky was a claustrophobic gray. Snow had fallen overnight, and the cars in the parking lot were blanketed in white. She wanted to go home. To hell with the bastard who wrote on her door. She wanted the comfort of her own bed, her own kitchen. But a long day still stretched ahead of her, another day of resentful silences and disapproving jibes from Jane. *Just grit your teeth and get through it.*

It took two cups of coffee before she felt ready to face the day. Fueled by a stale cheese Danish, compliments of the motel's continental breakfast, she carried her overnight bag to the parking lot, where Jane already had the engine running.

"Jurevich will meet us at the house," said Jane.

"You know how to find it?"

"He gave me directions." Jane frowned at Maura. "Man, you look wiped out."

"I didn't sleep well."

"Mattress was pretty bad, huh?"

"Among other things." Maura tossed her bag onto the backseat and pulled her door shut. They sat without speaking for a moment, the heater blowing at their knees.

"You're still pissed at me," said Jane.

"I'm not feeling really chatty right now."

"I'm just trying to be a friend, okay? If I see a

friend's life going off the rails, I think it's my duty to say something about it."

"And I heard you." Maura snapped on her seat belt. "Can we get going now?"

They left the town of Norwich and headed northwest, along roads slippery with newly fallen snow. Thick clouds threatened yet more snow today, and the view that Maura saw from her window was smudged in shades of gray. The cheese Danish sat like a lump of concrete in her stomach, and she leaned back, eyes closed against the nausea.

She startled awake what seemed like only moments later, to find that they were now struggling along an unplowed road, Jane's tires churning through snow. Dense woods pressed in on both sides, and the clouds had darkened since Maura had fallen asleep.

"How much farther to Purity?" she asked.

"We already passed through the village. You didn't miss anything."

"You sure this is the right road?"

"These were his directions."

"Jane, we're going to get stuck."

"I've got all-wheel drive, okay? And we can always call a tow truck."

Maura took out her cell phone. "No signal. Good luck."

"Here. This has got to be the turnoff," said Jane, pointing to a realty sign that was half-buried in snow. "The house is for sale, remember?" She gunned the engine and the Subaru fishtailed, then the tires found purchase and they surged up the road, which now began to climb. The trees parted, giving way to a view of the house that stood on the knoll.

Jane pulled into the driveway and gazed up at a three-story Victorian towering above them. "Wow," she murmured. "This is a pretty big place."

Crime-scene tape fluttered on the railings of a broad covered porch. Although the clapboards were badly in need of paint, the signs of neglect could not disguise the fact that this was once a handsome home, with a view to match. They climbed out of the car and flying snow stung their faces as they mounted the steps to the porch. Peering through a window, Maura could see ghostly shapes of sheet-covered furniture but little else in the shadowy interior.

"Door's locked," said Jane.

"What time's he supposed to meet us?"

"Fifteen minutes ago."

Maura huffed out a cloudy breath. "This wind is freezing. How long are we supposed to wait?"

"Let me see if I can get a signal." Jane frowned at her cell phone. "One bar. That might do it."

"I'm going to sit in the car." Maura went down the steps and was just about to open the door when she heard Jane say, "There he is now."

Turning, Maura saw a red Jeep Cherokee driving up the road. Following right behind it was a black Mercedes. The Cherokee parked next to Jane's Subaru and a man with crew-cut hair stepped out, dressed for the weather in a voluminous down jacket and heavy boots. He held out a gloved hand to Maura, and she saw a humorless face, chilly gray eyes.

"Detective Rizzoli?" he asked.

"No, I'm Dr. Isles. You must be Detective Jurevich."

He nodded as they shook hands. "I'm with the Chenango County Sheriff's Office." He glanced at Jane, who was coming down the porch steps to meet him. "You're Rizzoli?"

"Yeah. We just got here a few minutes . . ." Jane stopped, her gaze suddenly freezing on the black Mercedes, on the man who had just stepped out of it. "What the hell is *he* doing here?"

"He predicted you'd react that way," said Jurevich.

Anthony Sansone strode toward them, black coat flapping in the wind. He nodded to Jane, a curt greeting that acknowledged the obvious: that she did not welcome him. Then his gaze fixed on Maura. "You've already seen the body?"

She nodded. "Last night."

"Do you think we're dealing with the same killer?"

"What's with this word *we*?" Jane cut in. "I wasn't aware you worked in law enforcement, Mr. Sansone."

Unruffled, he turned to face her. "I won't get in your way."

"This is a crime scene. You shouldn't even be here."

"I don't believe Chenango County is in your jurisdiction. This is up to Detective Jurevich."

Jane looked at Jurevich. "You're giving him access?"

Jurevich gave a shrug. "Our crime-scene unit's already processed this house. There's no reason he can't walk through it with us."

"So now it's a public tour."

"This has been cleared through the sheriff's office, by special request."

"Whose request?"

Jurevich glanced at Sansone, whose face revealed nothing.

"We're wasting time out here," said Sansone. "I'm sure we'd all like to get out of this wind."

"Detective?" pressed Jane.

"If you have any objections," said Jurevich, clearly unhappy at being caught in the middle, "you can take it up with the Department of Justice. Now, why don't we get inside before we all freeze?" He climbed the steps to the porch, with Sansone right behind him.

Jane stared after them and said softly, "What's his pull, anyway?"

"Maybe you should just ask him," said Maura, and she started up the steps. Jurevich had already unlocked the front door, and she followed the men into the house. Inside, she found it scarcely warmer, but at least they were now sheltered from the wind. Jane came in behind her and closed the door. After the glare of the snow, it took a moment for Maura's eyes to adjust to the interior gloom. Looking through a doorway into the front parlor, she saw sheet-draped furniture and the dull gleam of wood floors. Pale winter light shone in through the windows, casting the room in shades of gray.

Jurevich pointed to the bottom of the stairs. "You can't see them, but Luminol turned up lots of bloody smears on these steps and in this foyer. Looks like he wiped up after himself as he left the house, so any footwear evidence is pretty indistinct."

"You went over the whole house with Luminol?" asked Jane.

"Luminol, UV, alternate light source. We checked every room. There's a kitchen and dining room through that doorway. And a study beyond the parlor. Except for the shoe prints here in the foyer, nothing very interesting turned up on the first floor." He faced the stairway. "All the action took place upstairs."

"You said this house was vacant," said Sansone. "How did the killer get in? Was there any sign of forced entry?"

"No, sir. Windows were shut tight. And the Realtor swears she always locks the front door when she leaves."

"Who has a key?"

"Well, she does. And she says it never leaves her office."

"How old is the lock?"

"Ah, geez, I don't know. It's probably twenty years old."

"I assume the owner has a key, too."

"She hasn't been back to Purity in years. I hear she's living somewhere in Europe. We haven't been able to reach her." Jurevich nodded at the sheet-draped furniture. "There's a thick layer of dust on everything. You can see no one's lived here for a while. Damn shame, too. A house this solidly built was meant to last a century, and this one just sits here empty. The caretaker comes up once a month to check on it. That's how he found the body. He saw Sarah Parmley's rental car parked out front, and then he found the front door unlocked."

"Have you checked out the caretaker?" asked Jane.

"He's not a suspect."

"Why not?"

"Well, to start off with, he's seventy-one years old. And he just got out of the hospital three weeks ago. Prostate surgery." Jurevich looked at Sansone. "See what men have to look forward to?"

"So we've got a number of unanswered questions," said Sansone. "Who unlocked the front door? Why did the victim drive up here in the first place?"

"The house is for sale," said Maura. "Maybe she saw the realty sign. Maybe she drove up out of curiosity."

"Look, it's all speculation," said Jurevich. "We've talked and talked about this, and we just don't know why she came up here."

"Tell us more about Sarah Parmley," said Sansone.

"She grew up in Purity. Graduated from the local high school. But like too many other kids, she couldn't find anything to keep her here, so she moved out to California and stayed. The only reason she came back to town was because her aunt died."

"From what?" asked Sansone.

"Oh, it was an accident. Took a tumble down the stairs and broke her neck. So Sarah flew back for the memorial service. She stayed at a motel near town and checked out the day after the funeral. And that's the last time anyone saw her. Until Saturday, when the caretaker found her car here." He looked up at the stairs. "I'll show you the room."

Jurevich led the way. Halfway up the stairs, he halted and pointed to the wall. "This is the first one we noticed," he said. "This cross, here. It's the same symbol he cut all over her body. Looks like it's drawn in some kind of red chalk."

Maura stared at the symbol and her fingers went numb inside her gloves. "This cross is upside down."

"There are more of them upstairs," said Jurevich. "A lot more." As they continued toward the second-floor landing, other crosses appeared on the wall. At first it was just a sparse scattering of them. Then, in the gloomy upstairs hallway, the crosses multiplied like an angry infestation massing along the corridor, swarming toward a doorway.

"In here, it gets bad," said Jurevich.

His warning made Maura hesitate outside the room. Even after the others had walked through, she paused on the threshold, bracing herself for whatever awaited her on the other side of the doorway.

She stepped through, into a chamber of horrors.

It was not the dried lake of blood on the floor that captured her gaze; it was the handprints covering every wall, as though a multitude of lost souls had left their bloody testament as they'd passed through this room.

"These prints were all made with the same hand," said Jurevich. "Identical palm prints and ridge lines. I don't think our killer was stupid enough to leave his own." He looked at Jane. "I'm willing to bet these were all made with Sarah Parmley's severed hand. The one that turned up at your crime scene."

"Jesus," murmured Jane. "He used her hand like some kind of rubber stamp."

With blood as his ink, thought Maura, her gaze traveling the walls. How many hours did he spend in this room, dipping the hand in that pool of blood, pressing it to the wall like a child with a stamp kit? Then her gaze focused on the nearest wall, on writing that had been obscured by the overlying handprints. She moved closer, staring at the words that tracked across the wall. It was Latin, and the same three words were repeated again and again. She followed the text as it circled the room in an unbroken line, continuing through corners, like a serpent coiling ever more tightly around them.

Abyssus abyssum invocat abyssus abyssum invocat abyssus abyssum invocat . . .

Their meaning suddenly dawned on her and she took a step back, chilled to the marrow.

"*Hell calls to Hell,*" Sansone murmured. She had not noticed that he'd moved right beside her.

"Is that what it means?" asked Jane.

"That's the literal meaning. It also has another."

"*Hell calls to Hell* sounds ominous enough."

"*Abyssus abyssum invocat* is a saying that dates back at least a thousand years. It means, '*One evil deed leads to another.*' "

Maura stared at the words. "He's telling us this is only the beginning. He's just getting started."

"And these crosses"—Sansone pointed to a hornet's nest of them, clustered on one wall, as though massing for attack—"they're all upside down. It's a mockery of Christianity, a rejection of the church."

"Yeah. We've been told it's a satanic symbol," said Jurevich.

"These words and crosses were written here first," said Maura, her gaze on the rivulets of blood that had trickled down the wall, partly obscuring the stream of Latin. She read the splatters, saw the arcing droplets left by arterial spray. "Before he killed her, before he slashed her neck, he took the time to decorate these walls."

"The question is," said Jurevich, "did he write these words while she was lying here, waiting to die? Or was the room already prepared as a killing place before the victim even arrived?"

"And then he lured her here?"

"There's clearly evidence of preparation." Jurevich pointed to the wooden floor, where blood had dried in a frozen pool. "You see the nails there? He came equipped with a hammer and nylon cord. That's how he immobilized her. He tied the cord around her wrists and ankles. Nailed the knots to the floor. Once she was restrained, he could have taken his time."

Maura thought of what had been carved into Sarah Parmley's flesh. Then she looked up at the same symbols drawn on the walls in red ocher. A crucifix, turned upside down. Lucifer's cross.

Sansone said, "But how would he lure her up here? What could possibly have drawn her to this house?"

"We know that a call came in, to her motel room," said Jurevich. "It was the day she checked out. The motel desk clerk transferred it to her room."

"You didn't mention that," said Jane.

"Because we're not sure it's significant. I mean, Sarah Parmley grew up in this town. She probably knew a lot of people here, people who'd call her after her aunt's funeral."

"Was it a local call?"

"Gas station pay phone, in Binghamton."

"That's a few hours away."

"Right. Which is one reason we discount it as coming from the killer."

"Is there another reason?"

"Yes. The caller was a woman."

"The motel clerk's sure about that? It was two weeks ago."

"She doesn't budge. We've asked her several times."

Sansone said, "Evil has no gender."

"And what are the chances that a woman did this?" said Jane, pointing to the wall, to the bloody handprints.

"I wouldn't automatically reject the possibility it's a woman," said Sansone. "We have no usable footprints here."

"I don't reject anything. I'm just going with the odds."

"That's all they are. Odds."

"How many killers have *you* tracked down?" shot back Jane.

He regarded her with an unflinching stare. "I think the answer would surprise you, Detective."

Maura turned to Jurevich. "The killer must have

spent hours here, in this house. He must have left hair, fibers."

"Our crime-scene unit went over all these rooms with ALS."

"They couldn't have come up empty."

"Oh, they came up with plenty. This is an old house, and it's been occupied on and off for the last seventy years. We turned up hairs and fibers all over these rooms. Found something that surprised us. Let me show you the rest of the house."

They went back into the hallway, and Jurevich pointed through a doorway. "Another bedroom in there. Lot of dust, plus a few cat hairs, but otherwise nothing that caught our interest." He continued down the hall, past another bedroom, past a bathroom with black-and-white tiles, giving the rooms only dismissive waves. They came to the last doorway. "Here," he said. "This turned out to be a very interesting room."

Maura heard the ominous note in his voice, but when she stepped into the bedroom, she saw nothing at all alarming, just a space devoid of all furniture, with blank walls. The wood floor here was in far better shape than in the rest of the house, its boards recently refinished. Two bare windows looked out over the knoll's wooded slope, which swept down to the frozen lake below.

"So what makes this room interesting?" asked Jane.

"It's what we found on the floor."

"I don't see anything."

"It showed up when we sprayed it with Luminol. The crime-scene unit surveyed the whole house, to

see where our killer might have tracked blood.
Whether he left traces that we couldn't see in other
rooms. We found his footprints in the hallway, on
the stairs, and in the foyer, all of them invisible to
the naked eye. So we know he did try to clean up as
he exited the house. But you can't really hide blood.
Spray it with Luminol, and it'll light right up." Jurevich looked down at the floor. "It sure as hell lit up
in here."

"More shoe prints?" asked Jane.

"Not just shoe prints. It was like a wave of blood
had washed through this room, splashed on the wall.
You could see it in the cracks between the floorboards, where it seeped into the molding. That wall
there, there were big swipes of it, where someone
tried to wash it away. But they couldn't erase it. Even
though you can't see it now, it was all over the place.
We stood here, looking at this whole damn room
glowing, and it freaked the hell out of us, I can tell
you. Because when we turned on our lights, it
looked just the way it does now. Nothing. Not a
trace of blood visible to the naked eye."

Sansone stared at the walls, as though trying to see
those shocking echoes of death. He looked down at
the floor, its boards sanded smooth. "This can't be
fresh blood," he murmured. "Something else happened in this house."

Maura remembered the FOR SALE sign, half-
buried in snow, posted at the bottom of the knoll.
She thought of the weathered clapboards, the peel-
ing paint. Why was such a handsome home abandoned to years of neglect? "That's why no one will
buy it," she said.

Jurevich nodded. "It happened about twelve years ago, just before I moved to this area. I only found out about it when the Realtor told me. It's not something she likes to advertise, since the house is on the market, but it's a matter of disclosure. A little detail that every potential buyer would want to know. And it pretty much sends them running in the other direction."

Maura looked down at the floor, at seams and cracks harboring blood that she could not see. "Who died in here?"

"In this room, it was a suicide. But when you think about everything else that happened in this house, it's like the whole damn building is bad luck."

"There were other deaths?"

Jurevich nodded. "There was a family living here at the time. A doctor and his wife, a son and daughter. Plus a nephew staying with them for the summer. From what everyone says, the Sauls were good people. Close family, lots of friends."

Nothing is exactly what it seems, thought Maura. *Nothing ever is.*

"Their eleven-year-old son died first. It was a heartbreaking accident. Kid headed down to the lake to go fishing, and he didn't come home. They figure he must have fallen into the water and panicked. They found his body the next day. From there, it just got worse for the family. A week later, the mother takes a tumble down the stairs and snaps her neck. She'd been taking some sedatives, and they figure she just lost her balance."

"That's an interesting coincidence," said Sansone.

"What?"

"Isn't that how Sarah Parmley's aunt died? A fall down the stairs? A broken neck?"

Jurevich paused. "Yeah. I hadn't thought about it. That is a coincidence, isn't it?"

Jane said, "You haven't told us about the suicide."

Jurevich nodded. "It was the husband. Think about it—what he'd just suffered through. First his son drowns. Then his wife falls down the stairs. So two days later, he takes out his gun, sits here in his bedroom, and blows off his own head." Jurevich looked at the floor. "It's his blood on the floor. Think about it. A whole family, practically wiped out within a few weeks."

"What happened to the daughter?" asked Jane.

"She moved in with friends. Graduated from high school a year later, and left town."

"She's the one who owns this house?"

"Yeah. It's still in her name. She's been trying to unload it all these years. Realtor says there've been a few lookers, but then they hear what happened, and they walk away. Would you live in this house? You couldn't pay me enough. It's a bad-luck place. You can almost feel it when you walk in that front door."

Maura looked around at the walls and gave a shudder. "If there's such a thing as a haunted house, this would be it."

"*Abyssus abyssum invocat,*" said Sansone quietly. "It takes on a different meaning, now."

They all looked at him. "What?" said Jurevich.

"That's why he chose this for his killing place. He knew the history of this house. He knew what happened here, and he was attracted to it. You can call it a doorway to another dimension. Or a vortex. But there are dark places in this world, foul places that can only be called cursed."

Jane gave an uneasy laugh. "You really believe that?"

"What I believe doesn't matter. But if our killer believes it, then he chose this house because it called to him. *Hell calls to Hell.*"

"Oh man," said Jurevich, "you're giving me goose bumps." He looked around at the blank walls and shuddered, as though feeling a chill wind. "You know what I think? They should just burn this place. Burn it right down to the ground. No one in his right mind will ever buy it."

"You said it was a doctor's family living here," said Jane.

"That's right. The Sauls."

"And they had a nephew staying with them that summer."

Jurevich nodded. "Fifteen-year-old kid."

"What happened to that boy? After the tragedies?"

"The Realtor says the kid left Purity a short time later. His mother came and got him."

"Do you know anything else about him?"

"Remember, it was twelve years ago. No one knew him very well. And he was only here for that summer." Jurevich paused. "I know what you're thinking. The kid would be twenty-seven right now. And he'd know all about what happened here."

"He might also have a key to the front door," said Jane. "How can we find out more about him?"

"His cousin, I assume. The woman who owns this house, Lily Saul."

"But you don't know how to find her, either."

"The Realtor's been trying."

Jane said, "I'd like to see the police reports on the Saul family. I assume the deaths were all investigated."

"I'll call my office, have the files copied for you. You can pick them up on your way out of town. Are you driving back to Boston tonight?"

"We planned to, right after lunch."

"Then I'll try to have them ready by then. You might want to head over to Roxanne's Café. Great turkey club sandwiches. And it's right across the street from our office."

"Will that give you enough time to copy everything?"

"There's not much to the files beyond the autopsies and sheriff's reports. In all three cases, the manner and cause of death were pretty apparent."

Sansone had been standing at the window, gazing outside. Now he turned to Jurevich. "What's the name of your local newspaper here?"

"All of Chenango County's pretty much covered by the *Evening Sun*. Their office is in Norwich." Jurevich looked at his watch. "There's really nothing else to show you here."

Back outside, they stood in the biting wind as Jurevich locked the front door and gave it a hard rattle to make sure it was secure. "If we make any headway on our end," he said to Jane, "I'll give you a call. But I think this killer's going to be your catch." He zipped up his jacket and pulled on his gloves. "He's playing in your neighborhood, now."

TWENTY-EIGHT

"HE SHOWS UP in his fancy car and gets invited right into the crime scene," said Jane, shaking a French fry at Maura. "What's that all about? Who does Sansone know in Justice? Even Gabriel couldn't find out."

"They must have a reason to trust him."

"Oh, yeah." Jane popped the French fry into her mouth and snatched up another, agitation fueling her appetite. In a matter of minutes, she'd reduced an enormous club sandwich to a few crumbs of toast and bacon, and now she was dragging the last of her fries through a pool of ketchup. "Trust some millionaire with a crime-fighting hobby?"

"Multimillionaire."

"Who does he think he is, Bruce Wayne? Or the guy on that old TV show. The rich man who's a cop. My mom used to watch it."

"I think you're talking about *Burke's Law*."

"Yeah. How many rich cops do *you* know?"

Maura sighed and picked up her teacup. "Not a one."

"Exactly. It's a fantasy. Some bored guy with

money thinks it'd be a kick to play Dirty Harry, except he doesn't want to actually get down and dirty. He doesn't want to walk a beat or write up incident reports. He just wants to drive up in his Mercedes and tell us idiots how it should be done. You think I haven't dealt with people like him before? Everyone thinks they're smarter than the police."

"I don't think he's merely an amateur, Jane. I think he's worth listening to."

"Right. A former history professor." Jane drained her coffee cup and craned her neck around the booth, scanning the busy café for the waitress. "Hey, miss? Could I have a refill over . . ." She paused. She said to Maura, "Look who just walked in."

"Who?"

"Your friend and mine."

Maura turned toward the door, gazing past the dining counter where men in billed caps sat huddled over their coffee and burgers. She spotted Sansone at the same instant he saw her. As he crossed the room, a dozen heads swiveled, gazes fixed on the striking figure with silver hair as he strode past tables and headed toward Maura's booth.

"I'm glad you're still in town," he said. "May I join you?"

"We're about to leave," said Jane, reaching pointedly for her wallet, the coffee refill conveniently forgotten.

"This will only take a minute. Or would you rather I mail this to you, Detective?"

Maura looked at the sheaf of papers he was carrying. "What's all that?"

"From the *Evening Sun* archives." He placed the papers on the table in front of her.

She slid sideways across the bench, making room for him in the tight booth as he sat down beside her. She felt trapped in the corner by this man, whose mere presence seemed to dominate and overwhelm the small space.

"Their digital archives go back only five years," he said. "These are photocopies from the bound archives, so the reproduction isn't as good as I'd like. But it tells the story."

Maura looked down at the first page. It was from the front page of the *Evening Sun,* dated August 11, twelve years earlier. Her gaze at once fixed on the article near the top.

BOY'S BODY RECOVERED FROM PAYSON POND

The accompanying photo showed a grinning imp of a boy, cradling a tiger-striped cat in his arms. The caption read: *Teddy Saul had just turned eleven.*

"His sister Lily was the last known person who saw him alive," said Sansone. "She was also the one who spotted him floating in the pond a day later. What surprised everyone, according to the article, was the fact the boy was a very good swimmer. And there was one other interesting detail."

Maura looked up. "What?"

"He supposedly went down to the lake to fish. But his tackle box and pole were found a good twenty yards from the water's edge."

Maura handed the photocopy to Jane and looked at the next article, printed August 18. A week after little Teddy's body was found, tragedy again struck the Saul family.

GRIEVING MOTHER'S DEATH MOST LIKELY ACCIDENTAL

Accompanying the article was another photo, another heartbreaking caption. Amy Saul was pictured in happier times, beaming at the camera as she held a baby in her lap. The same child, Teddy, whom she'd lose eleven years later to the waters of Payson Pond.

"She was found at the bottom of the stairs," said Maura. She looked up at Jane. "By her daughter, Lily."

"Again? The daughter found both of them?" Jane reached for the photocopied article. "This is starting to sound like too much bad luck."

"And remember that call made to Sarah Parmley's motel room two weeks ago. It was a woman's voice."

"Before you go jumping to conclusions," said Sansone, "it wasn't Lily Saul who found her father's body. Her cousin did. It's the first and only time Dominic Saul's name appears in any of these articles."

Maura turned to the third photocopy and stared at a photo of a smiling Dr. Peter Saul. Beneath it was the caption: *Despondent over death of wife and son*. She looked up. "Is there any photo of Dominic?"

"No. But he's mentioned in that article as the one who found his uncle's body. He's also the one who called the police."

"And the girl?" asked Jane. "Where was Lily when this happened?"

"It doesn't say."

"I assume the police checked her alibi."

"You would assume so."

"I wouldn't assume anything."

"Let's hope that information's in the police files," said Sansone, "because you're not going to get it from the investigator himself."

"Why not?"

"He died last year of a heart attack. I found his obituary in the newspaper archives. So all we have to go on is what's in the files. But think about the situation. You're a local cop, dealing with a sixteen-year-old girl who's just lost her brother, her mother, and now her father. She's probably in shock. Maybe she's hysterical. Are you going to harass her with questions about where she was when her father died when it clearly looked like a suicide?"

"It's my job to ask," said Jane. "I would have."

Yes, she would have, thought Maura, looking at Jane's unyielding expression and remembering the relentless questions that had been asked of her yesterday morning. No mercy, no holding back. God help you if Jane Rizzoli decides you're guilty of something. Maura looked down at the photo of Peter Saul. "There's no picture of Lily. We don't know what she looks like, either."

"Actually, there is a photo," said Sansone. "And

you'll find it very interesting." He flipped to the next photocopied page and pointed to the article.

DOCTOR'S FUNERAL DRAWS MOURNERS
FROM ACROSS COUNTY

Friends, co-workers, even strangers gathered at Ashland Cemetery on a beautiful August afternoon to mourn Dr. Peter Saul, who died last Sunday of a self-inflicted gunshot wound. It was the third tragedy to befall the Saul family in the past two weeks.

"There she is," said Sansone, pointing to the accompanying photo. "That's Lily Saul."

It was an indistinct image, the girl's face partly obscured by two other mourners flanking her. All Maura could see was the profile of her bowed head, veiled by long dark hair.

"That doesn't show us much," said Jane.

"It's not the photo I wanted you to see," said Sansone. "It's the caption. Look at the names of the girls standing beside Lily."

Only then did Maura understand why Sansone had been so insistent on sharing these pages. The caption beneath the photo of a grief-stricken Lily Saul included two startlingly familiar names.

Lily Saul is comforted by friends Lori-Ann Tucker and Sarah Parmley.

"There's the link that wraps it all up," said Sansone. "Three friends. Two of them are now dead.

Only Lily Saul is still alive." He paused. "And we can't even be sure of *her* status."

Jane plucked up the page and stared at it. "Maybe because she doesn't want us to know."

"She's the one we have to find," said Sansone. "She'll know the answers."

"Or she could *be* the answer. We know next to nothing about this girl Lily. Whether she got along with her family. Whether she walked away with a nice inheritance."

"You can't be serious," said Maura.

"I have to admit, Mr. Sansone here said it earlier. Evil has no gender."

"But to kill her own family, Jane."

"We kill the ones we love. You know that." Jane regarded the photo of the three girls. "And maybe these girls knew it, too. Twelve years is a long time to keep a secret." She glanced at her watch. "I need to ask around town, see what else I can learn about Lily. Someone must know how to find her."

"While you're asking questions," said Sansone, "you might want to ask about this, too." He slid yet another photocopy to Jane. The headline read: *South Plymouth Boy Takes Top 4-H Honors.*

"Uh . . . I'm supposed to ask about prizewinning bulls?" asked Jane.

"No, it's the item under the *Police Beat*," said Sansone. "I almost missed it myself. In fact, I wouldn't have seen it at all, except for the fact it was on the same page, below the story about Teddy Saul's drowning."

"You mean this one? *Barn Vandalized, Goat Missing*?"

"Look at the story."

Jane read the article aloud. " 'Police received a complaint from Eben Bongers of Purity that vandals broke into his barn last Saturday night. Four goats escaped and three were recaptured, but one remains missing. The barn was also defaced with carvings of' "—Jane paused and looked up at Maura— " 'crosses.' "

"Keep reading," said Sansone.

Jane swallowed and looked back down at the article. " 'Similar carvings have been found on other buildings in the area. Anyone with information is asked to contact the Chenango County Sheriff's Office.' "

"The killer was here," said Sansone. "Twelve years ago, he was living right in this county. And no one realized what was walking among them. No one knew what was living in their midst."

He talks as though this killer isn't human, thought Maura. *He doesn't say who, but what. Not a some-one, but a* something.

"Then two weeks ago," said Sansone, "this killer returns to the house where the Sauls once lived. Draws the same symbols on the walls, pounds nails in the floor. All in preparation for his victim. For what he's going to do to Sarah Parmley." Sansone leaned forward, his gaze focused on Jane. "I don't think Sarah Parmley was his first kill. There were others before her. You saw how elaborate Sarah's death scene was, how much planning, how much ceremony was involved. This was a mature crime, by someone who's had months, even years, to refine his rituals."

"We requested a VICAP search. We looked for earlier kills."

"Your search parameters?"

"Dismemberment. Satanic symbols. Yes, a few cases showed up from other states, but nothing that matched to our satisfaction."

"Then widen the search."

"Any wider, and it becomes useless. It's too general, too big a net."

"I'm talking internationally."

"That's a pretty big net."

"There's no net too big for this killer. Look at all the clues he's left. Latin inscriptions. Drawings made with red ocher from Cyprus. A Mediterranean seashell. He's practically announced to you that he's lived abroad. And probably killed abroad. I guarantee you, if you search the Interpol database, you'll find more of his victims."

"How can you be so . . ." Jane paused, and her gaze suddenly narrowed. "You already know. You've checked."

"I took the liberty. This killer has left distinctive tracks everywhere. He's not afraid of the police. He's utterly confident in his own ability to stay invisible." He pointed to the photocopies. "Twelve years ago, the killer was living here. Already having his fantasies, already drawing those crosses."

Jane looked at Maura. "I'm going to stay here at least another night. There are other people I need to talk to."

"But I need to get home," said Maura. "I can't stay away that long."

"Dr. Bristol can cover for you, can't he?"

"I have other things I need to attend to." Maura did not like the look Jane suddenly shot her. *Other things being Daniel Brophy?*

"I'm driving back to Boston tonight," said Sansone. "You can ride with me."

TWENTY-NINE

"DETECTIVE RIZZOLI didn't look too happy when you took me up on my offer," Sansone said.

"She's unhappy about a lot of things these days," said Maura, staring out at fields covered in a snowy white skin. Although the last light of day had faded, the moon was rising, and its reflection was bright as a lantern on the snow. "Me included."

"I noticed the tension between you two."

"It's that obvious?"

"She doesn't try to hide much, does she?" He shot her a glance in the dark car. "You two couldn't be more different."

"I'm finding that out more and more."

"You've known each other long?"

"About two years. Since I took the job in Boston."

"Has it always been this edgy between you?"

"No. It's only because . . ." She fell silent. *Because she disapproves of me. Because she's on her moral high horse, and I'm not allowed to be human. I'm not allowed to fall in love.* "This has been a stressful few weeks" was how she finished the sentence.

"I'm glad we have this chance to talk in private,"

he said. "Because what I'm about to tell you is going to sound absurd. And she'd dismiss it without a second thought." Again he glanced at her. "I'm hoping you'll be more willing to listen."

"Because you think I'm less of a skeptic than she is? Don't bet on it."

"What did you think about the death scene today? What did it tell you about the killer?"

"I saw evidence of a severely disturbed mind."

"That's one possibility."

"What's your interpretation?"

"That there's real intelligence behind this. Not just some nutcase getting his jollies by torturing women. This is someone with a focused and logical motive."

"Your mythical demons, again."

"I know you don't accept their existence. But you saw that news article, about the barn that was defaced twelve years ago. Did anything else in that report stand out for you?"

"You mean, aside from the crosses carved in the barn?"

"The missing goat. There were four goats released from the barn, and the farmer recovered only three of them. What happened to the fourth?"

"Maybe it escaped. Maybe it got lost in the woods."

"In Leviticus, chapter sixteen, another name for Azazel is 'the scapegoat.' He who assumes all the sins, all the evils, of mankind. By tradition, the chosen animal is led into the wilderness, taking humanity's sins with it. And there it's released."

"We're back to your symbol of Azazel again."

"A drawing of his head appeared on your door. You can't have forgotten that."

No, I haven't. How could I forget that my door bears the mark of a killer?

"I know you're skeptical," he said. "I know you think this will turn out to be like so many other investigations. That it will lead to some rather ordinary, even pitiful character who lives quietly alone. Another Jeffrey Dahmer, or another Son of Sam. Maybe this killer hears voices. Maybe he's read Anton LaVey's *Satanic Bible* a few too many times and taken it to heart. But consider another possibility, something far more frightening." He looked at her. "That Nephilim—the Watchers—really exist. That they've always existed, and they still live among us."

"The children of fallen angels?"

"That's merely the biblical interpretation."

"This is all biblical. And you know I don't believe."

"The Old Testament is not the only place where these creatures are mentioned. They appear in the myths of earlier cultures."

"Every civilization has its mythical evil spirits."

"I'm not talking about spirits, but flesh and blood, with human faces. A parallel species of predators who've evolved right alongside us. Interbred with us."

"Wouldn't we know of their existence by now?"

"We know them by the evil they commit. But we don't recognize them for what they really are. We call them sociopaths or tyrants. Or Vlad the Impaler. They charm and seduce their way into positions of power and authority. They thrive on war, on revolution, on disorder. And we never realize they're different from the rest of us. Different in a fundamental way that goes right to our genetic codes. They're born predators, and the whole world is their hunting ground."

"Is this what the Mephisto Foundation is all about? A search for these mythical creatures?" She laughed. "You might as well hunt for unicorns."

"There are many of us who believe."

"And what will you do when you actually find one? Shoot him and mount his head as a trophy?"

"We're purely a research group. Our role is to identify and study. And advise."

"Advise whom?"

"Law enforcement. We provide them with information and analysis. And they use what we give them."

"Law enforcement agencies actually care what you have to say?" she asked, with an unmistakable note of disbelief.

"Yes. We are listened to" was all he said. The calm statement of a man so sure of his claims, he saw no need to defend them.

She considered how easily he had accessed confidential details of the investigation. Thought of how Jane's inquiries about Sansone had met with silence from the FBI and Interpol and the Department of Justice. *They are all protecting him.*

"Our work has not gone unnoticed," he said, and added softly, "unfortunately."

"I thought that was the point. To have your work noticed."

"Not by the wrong people. Somehow, they've discovered us. They know who we are, and what we do." He paused. "And they think you're one of us."

"I don't even believe *they* exist."

"They've marked your door. They've identified you."

She gazed out at moonlit snow, its whiteness startling in the night. It was almost as bright as day. No cover, no darkness. A prey's every movement would be seen in that merciless landscape. "I'm not a member of your club," she said.

"You might as well be. You've been seen at my home. You've been seen with me."

"I've also visited all three crime scenes. I've only been doing my job. The killer could have spotted me on any one of those nights."

"That's what I thought at first. That you just happened to cross his line of vision, as incidental prey. It's what I thought about Eve Kassovitz as well— that maybe he spotted her at the first crime scene on Christmas Eve, and she attracted his interest."

"You no longer think that's what happened?"

"No, I don't."

"Why not?"

"The seashell. If I'd known about it earlier, we all would have taken precautions. And Joyce might still be alive."

"You think that seashell was a message meant for you?"

"For centuries, Sansone men have marched into battle under the banner of the seashell. This was a taunt, a challenge aimed at the foundation. A warning of what's to come."

"What would that be?"

"Our extermination." He said it quietly, as though just speaking those two words aloud would bring the sword down on his neck. But she heard no fear in his voice, only resignation that this was the fate he'd been dealt. She could think of nothing to say in response. This conversation had strayed into alien territory, and she could not find her bearings. His universe was such a bleak landscape of nightmares that just sitting with him, in his car, altered her view of the world. Changed it to an unfamiliar country where monsters walked. *Daniel*, she thought, *I need you now. I need your touch and your hope and your faith in the world. This man is all darkness, and you are the light.*

"Do you know how my father died?" he asked.

She frowned at him, startled by the question. "I'm sorry?"

"Believe me, it's relevant. My whole family history is relevant. I tried to walk away from it. I spent thirteen years teaching at Boston College, thinking I could live a normal life like everyone else, convinced that my father was just a cranky eccentric, like *his* father, that all the bizarre stories he told me when I was growing up were quaint family lore." He glanced at her. "I believed it about as much as you do right now, which is to say, not at all."

He sounds so rational. Yet he isn't. He can't be.

"I taught history, so I'm familiar with the ancient myths," he said. "But you'll never convince me that there were once satyrs or mermaids or flying horses. Why should I believe my father's stories about Nephilim?"

"What changed your mind?"

"Oh, I knew *some* of what he told me was true. The death of Isabella, for instance. In Venice, I was able to find the record of her imprisonment and death in church documents. She *was* burned alive. She *did* give birth to a son, just prior to her execution. Not everything that was passed down in Sansone family lore was fantasy."

"And the part about your ancestors being demon hunters?"

"My father believed it."

"Do you?"

"I believe there are hostile forces who would bring down the Mephisto Foundation. And now they've found us. The way they found my father."

She stared at him, waiting for him to explain.

"Eight years ago," said Sansone, "he flew out to Naples. He was going to meet an old friend, a man he'd known since his college days in New Haven. Both of them were widowers. Both of them shared a passion for ancient history. They planned to visit the National Archaeological Museum there and catch up on each other's lives. My father was quite excited about the visit. It was the first time I'd heard any animation in his voice since my mother died. But when he got to Naples, his friend wasn't there at the airport. Or at the hotel. He called me, told me that something was terribly wrong, and he planned to return home the next day. I could hear he was upset, but he wouldn't say much more about it. I think he believed our conversation was being monitored."

"He actually thought the phone was tapped?"

"You see? You have the same reaction I did. That it was just dear eccentric old Dad imagining his goblins again. The last thing he said to me was, 'They've found me, Anthony. They know who I am.' "

"They?"

"I knew exactly what he was talking about. It was the same nonsense I'd been hearing since I was a kid. Sinister forces in government. A worldwide conspiracy of Nephilim, helping one another into positions of power. And once they assume political control, they're able to hunt to their hearts' content, without any fear of punishment. The way they hunted in Kosovo. And Cambodia. And Rwanda. They thrive on war and disorder and bloodshed. They feed off it. That's what Armageddon means to them: a hunter's paradise. It's why they can't wait to make it happen, why they look forward to it."

"That sounds like the ultimate paranoid delusion."

"It's also a way to explain the unexplainable: how people can do such terrible things to one another."

"Your father believed all that?"

"He wanted *me* to believe it. But it took his death to convince me."

"What happened to your father?"

"It could easily have been taken for a simple robbery gone wrong. Naples is a gritty place, and tourists do have to be careful there. But my father was on Via Partenope, alongside the Gulf of Naples, a street almost always crowded with tourists. Even so, it happened so quickly, he had no time to call for help. He simply collapsed. No one saw his assailant. No one saw what happened. But there was my father, bleeding to death on the street. The blade entered just beneath his sternum, sliced through the pericardium, and pierced the right ventricle."

"The way Eve Kassovitz died," she said softly. A brutally efficient killing.

"The worst part for me," he said, "is that he died thinking I'd never believe him. After our last phone call, I hung up and said to one of my colleagues, 'The old man's finally ready for Thorazine.'"

"But you believe him now."

"Even after I got to Naples, a few days later, I still thought it was a random act of violence. An unlucky tourist, in the wrong place at the wrong time. But while I was at the police station, waiting for a copy of their report, an older gentleman stepped into the room and introduced himself. I'd heard my father mention his name before. I never knew that Gott-fried Baum worked for Interpol."

"Why do I know that name?"

"He was one of my dinner guests the night that Eve Kassovitz was killed."

"The man who left for the airport?"

"He had a flight to catch that night. To Brussels."

"He's a member of Mephisto?"

Sansone nodded. "He's the one who made me lis-ten, made me believe. All the stories my father told me, all his crazy theories about the Nephilim—Baum repeated every one."

"*Folie à deux,*" said Maura. "A shared delusion."

"I wish it was a delusion. I wish I could shrug it off the way you do. But you haven't seen and heard the things I have, what Gottfried and others have. Mephisto is fighting for its life. After four centuries, we're the last ones." He paused. "And I'm the last of Isabella's line."

"The last demon hunter," she said.

"I haven't made an inch of headway with you, have I?"

"Here's what I don't understand. It's not that hard to kill someone. If you're the target, why don't they just eliminate you? You're not in hiding. All it takes is a gunshot through your window, a bomb in your car. Why play stupid games with seashells? What's the point of warning you that you're in their sights?"

"I don't know."

"You can see that it's not logical."

"Yes."

"Yet you still think these murders revolve around Mephisto."

He gave a sigh. "I won't even try to convince you. I just want you to *consider* the possibility that what I've told you is true."

"That there's a worldwide brotherhood of Nephilim? That the Mephisto Foundation, and no one else, is even aware of this vast conspiracy?"

"Our voice is starting to be heard."

"What are you going to do to protect yourselves? Load silver bullets in your gun?"

"I'm going to find Lily Saul."

She frowned at him. "The daughter?"

"Don't you find it strange that no one knows where she is? That no one can locate her?" He looked at Maura. "Lily knows something."

"Why do you think that?"

"Because she doesn't want to be found."

"I think I should go inside with you," he said, "just to be sure everything's all right."

They were parked outside her house, and through the living room curtains Maura could see lights shining, the lamps turned on by her automatic timer. Before she'd left yesterday, she had scrubbed off the markings on her door. Staring through the gloom, she wondered if there were new ones scrawled there that she couldn't see, new threats concealed in the shadows.

"I think I'd feel better if you came in with me, too," she admitted.

He reached into his glove compartment for a flashlight, and they both stepped out of the car. Neither of them spoke; they were focused instead on their surroundings: the dark street, the distant hiss of traffic. Sansone paused there on the sidewalk, as though trying to catch the scent of something he could not yet see. They climbed to the porch, and he turned on the flashlight to examine her door.

It was clean.

Inside her house, the phone was ringing. *Daniel?* She unlocked the front door and stepped inside. It took her only seconds to punch her code on the keypad and disarm the security system, but by the time she reached the telephone, it had fallen silent. Pressing the call history button, she recognized his cell phone number on caller ID, and she itched to pick up the receiver and call him back. But Sansone was now standing right beside her in the living room.

"Does everything seem all right to you?"

She gave a tight nod. "Everything's fine."

"Why don't you have a look around first before I leave?"

"Of course," she said, and headed up the hallway.

As he followed her, she could feel his gaze on her back. Did he see it in her face? Did he recognize the look of a lovesick woman? She went from room to room, checking windows, rattling doors. Everything was secure. As a simple matter of hospitality, she should have offered him a cup of coffee and invited him to stay for a few minutes, after he'd been kind enough to drive her home. But she was not in a hospitable mood.

To her relief, he didn't linger, but turned to leave. "I'll check in with you in the morning," he said.

"I'll be fine."

"You need to be careful, Maura. We all do."

But I'm not one of you, she thought. *I never wanted to be.*

The doorbell rang. They looked at each other.

He said, quietly, "Why don't you see who it is?"

She took a breath and stepped into the foyer. She took one glance through the window and immediately opened the door. Even the blast of cold air could not drive the flush of heat from her cheeks as Daniel stepped inside, his arms already reaching for her. Then he saw the other man in the hallway, and he froze in place.

Sansone smoothly stepped into the silence. "You must be Father Brophy," he said, extending his hand. "I'm Anthony Sansone. I saw you at Dr. O'Donnell's house the other night, when you came to pick up Maura."

Daniel nodded. "I've heard about you."

The two men shook hands, a stiff and wary greeting. Then Sansone had the good sense to make a quick exit. "Arm your security system," he reminded Maura.

"I will."

Before he stepped out the front door, he shot one last speculative look at Brophy. Sansone was neither blind nor stupid; he could probably guess what this priest was doing in her house. "Good night," he said, and walked out.

She locked the door. "I missed you," she said, and stepped into Daniel's arms.

"It felt like such a long day," he murmured.

"All I could think of was coming home. Being with you."

"That's all I could think of, too. I'm sorry to just show up and take you by surprise. But I had to stop by."

"It's the kind of surprise I like."

"I thought you'd be home much earlier."

"We stopped on the road, for dinner."

"It worried me, you know. That you were driving home with him."

"You had absolutely nothing to worry about." She stepped back, smiling. "Let me take your coat."

But he made no move to remove it. "What have you learned about him, since you've spent the whole day together?"

"I think he's just an eccentric man with a lot of money. And a very strange hobby."

"Seeking all things satanic? That goes a little beyond what I think of as *strange*."

"The truly strange part is that he's managed to

gather a circle of friends who all believe the same thing."

"Doesn't it worry you? That he's so completely focused on the dark side? That he's actually *searching* for the Devil? You know the saying. 'When you look long into the abyss . . .'"

"'The abyss also looks into you.' Yes, I know the quote."

"It's worth remembering, Maura. How easily darkness can draw us in."

She laughed. "This sounds like something from one of your Sunday sermons."

"I'm serious. You don't know enough about this man."

I know he worries you. I know he's making you jealous.

She touched his face. "Let's stop talking about him. He doesn't matter. Come on, let me take your coat."

He made no move to unbutton it. Only then did she understand.

"You're not staying tonight," she said.

He sighed. "I can't. I'm sorry."

"Then why did you come here?"

"I told you, I was worried. I wanted to make sure he got you home safely."

"You can't stay, even for a few hours?"

"I wish I could. But at the last minute, they asked me to attend a conference in Providence. I have to drive down there tonight."

They. She had no claim to him. The church, of course, directed his life. *They* owned him.

He wrapped his arms around her, his breath

warming her hair. "Let's go away sometime," he murmured. "Somewhere out of town."

Where no one knows us.

As he walked to his car, she stood with her door wide open, the cold streaming around her, into the house. Even after he drove away, she remained in the doorway, heedless of the cruel sting of the wind. It was her just punishment for wanting him. This was what his church demanded of them. Separate beds, separate lives. Could the Devil Himself be any crueler?

If I could sell my soul to Satan for your love, I think I would.

THIRTY

MRS. CORA BONGERS leaned her considerable weight against the barn door and it slid open with a tortured creak. From the dark interior came the nervous bleating of goats, and Jane smelled the gamey scent of damp straw and crowded animals.

"I'm not sure how much you'll be able to see right now," said Mrs. Bongers, aiming her flashlight into the barn. "Sorry I didn't get your message earlier, when we would've had daylight."

Jane flicked on her own flashlight. "This should be fine. I just want to see the marks, if they're still there."

"Oh, they're still here. Used to irritate the heck outta my husband every time he came in here and saw them. I kept telling him to paint over 'em, just so he'd stop complaining about it. He said that'd just make him madder, if he had to paint the inside of a barn. Like he was doing up *House Beautiful* for the goats." Mrs. Bongers stepped inside, her heavy boots tramping across the straw-covered dirt floor. Just the short walk from the house had winded her and she paused, wheezing loudly, and aimed her flashlight at a wooden pen, where a dozen goats massed in an uneasy huddle. "They still miss him, you know. Oh, Eben complained all the time about how much work it was, milking them every morning. But he loved these girls. He's been gone six months now, and they're still not used to anyone else milking them." She unlatched the pen and glanced at Jane, who was hanging back. "You're not scared of goats, are you?"

"Do we have to go in there?"

"Aw, they won't hurt you. Just watch your coat. They like to nibble."

Now you be nice goats, thought Jane as she stepped into the pen and latched the door shut behind her. *Don't chew the cop.* She picked her way across the straw, trying to avoid soiling her shoes. The animals watched her with cold and soulless stares. The last time she'd been this close to a goat had been on a second-grade school trip to a petting zoo. She had looked at the goat, the goat had looked at her, and the next thing she knew, she was flat on her back and her classmates were laughing. She did not trust the beasts, and clearly they did not trust her; they kept their distance as she crossed the pen.

"Here," said Mrs. Bongers, her flashlight focused on the wall. "This is some of it."

Jane moved closer, her gaze riveted on the symbols cut deeply into the wooden planks. The three crosses of Golgotha. But this was a perverted version, the crosses flipped upside down.

"Some more up there, too," said Mrs. Bongers, and she pointed the beam upward, to show more crosses, cut higher in the wall. "He had to climb onto some straw bales to carve those. All that effort. You'd think those darn kids would have better things to do."

"Why do you think it was kids who did this?"

"Who else would it be? Summertime, and they're all bored. Nothing better to do than run around carving up walls. Hanging those weird charms on trees."

Jane looked at her. "What charms?"

"Twig dolls and stuff. Creepy little things. The sheriff's office just laughed it off, but I didn't like seeing them dangling from the branches." She paused at one of the symbols. "There, like that one."

It was a stick figure of a man, with what appeared to be a sword projecting from one hand. Carved beneath it was: *RXX–VII.*

"Whatever that means," said Mrs. Bongers.

Jane turned to face her. "I read in the *Police Beat* that one of your goats went missing that night. Did you ever get it back?"

"We never found her."

"There was no trace of her at all?"

"Well, there are packs of wild dogs running around here, you know. They'd pretty much clean up every scrap."

But no dog did this, thought Jane, her gaze back on the carvings. Her cell phone suddenly rang, and the goats rushed to the opposite side of the pen in a panicked, bleating scramble. "Sorry," said Jane. She pulled the phone out of her pocket, surprised that she'd even gotten a signal out here. "Rizzoli."

Frost said, "I did my best."

"Why does that sound like the beginning of an excuse?"

" 'Cause I'm not having much luck finding Lily

Saul. She seems to move around quite a bit. We know she's been in Italy at least eight months. We've got a record of ATM withdrawals during that period from banks in Rome, Florence, and Sorrento. But she doesn't use her credit card very much."

"Eight months as a tourist? How does she afford that?"

"She travels on the cheap. And I do mean cheap. Fourth-class hotels all the way. Plus, she may be working there illegally. I know she had a brief job in Florence, assisting a museum curator."

"She has the training for that?"

"She has a college degree in classical studies. And when she was still a student, she worked at this excavation site in Italy. Some place called Paestum."

"Why the hell can't we find her?"

"It looks to me like she doesn't want to be found."

"Okay. What about her cousin, Dominic Saul?"

"Oh. That one's a real problem."

"You're not going to give me any good news tonight, are you?"

"I've got a copy of his academic record from the Putnam Academy. It's a boarding school in Connecticut. He was enrolled there for about six months, while he was in the tenth grade."

"So he would have been—what, fifteen, sixteen?"

"Fifteen. He finished up that year and was expected to come back the following fall. But he never did."

"That's the summer he stayed with the Saul family. In Purity."

"Right. The boy's father had just died, so Dr. Saul took him in for the summer. When the boy didn't return to school in September, the Putnam Academy tried to locate him. They finally got a letter back from his mother, withdrawing him from the school."

"So which school did he attend instead?"

"We don't know. Putnam Academy says they never got a request to forward the boy's transcripts. That's the last record of him anywhere that I can find."

"What about his mother? Where is she?"

"I have no idea. I can't find a damn thing about the woman. No one at the school ever met her. All they have is a letter, signed by a Margaret Saul."

"It's like all these people are ghosts. His cousin. His mother."

"I do have Dominic's school photo. I don't know if it does us much good now, since he was only fifteen at the time."

"What does he look like?"

"Really good-looking kid. Blond, blue eyes. And the school says he tested in the genius range. Obviously he was a smart boy. But there's a note in the file, says the kid didn't seem to have any friends."

Jane watched as Mrs. Bongers soothed the goats. She was huddled close to them, cooing to them in the same shadowy barn where, twelve years ago, someone had carved strange symbols on the wall, someone who could very well have moved on to carving women.

"Okay, here's the interesting part," said Frost. "I'm looking at the boy's school admission forms right now."

"Yeah?"

"There's this section his father filled out, about any special concerns he might have. And the dad writes that this is Dominic's first experience at an American school. Because he'd lived abroad most of his life."

"Abroad?" She felt her pulse suddenly kick into a faster tempo. "Where?"

"Egypt and Turkey." Frost paused, and added, significantly, "And Cyprus."

Her gaze turned back to the barn wall, to what had been carved there: *RXX–VII.* "Where are you right now?" she asked.

"I'm at home."

"You got a Bible there?"

"Why?"

"I want you to look up something for me."

"Let me ask Alice where it is." She heard him call out to his wife, then heard footsteps, and then Frost said, "Is the King James version okay?"

"If that's what you've got. Now look at the contents. Tell me which sections start with the letter *R.*"

"Old or New Testament?"

"Both."

Over the phone, she heard pages flipping. "There's the Book of Ruth. Romans. And there's Revelation."

"For each of the books, read me the passages for chapter twenty, verse seven."

"Okay, let's see. Book of Ruth doesn't have a chapter twenty. It only goes to four."

"Romans?"

"Romans ends at chapter sixteen."

"What about Revelation?"

"Hold on." More pages rustling. "Here it is. Revelation, chapter twenty, verse seven. 'And when the thousand years are expired, Satan' "—Frost paused. His voice softened to a hush. —" 'Satan shall be loosed out of his prison.' "

Jane could feel the pounding of her own heart. She stared at the barn wall, at the carving of the stick figure wielding the sword. It's not a sword. *It's a scythe.*

"Rizzoli?" said Frost.

She said, "I think we know our killer's name."

THIRTY-ONE

BENEATH THE Basilica di San Clemente, the sound of rushing water echoed from the blackness. Lily shone her flashlight through the iron grate that barred the way into the tunnel, her beam revealing ancient brick walls and the faint glimmer of moving water far below.

"There's a subterranean lake under this basilica," she said. "And you can see the underground river here, which never stops flowing. Beneath Rome is another world, a vast underworld of tunnels and catacombs." She gazed at the rapt faces staring at her through the gloom. "When you return to the surface, when you walk the streets, think about that, about all the dark and secret places that lie right beneath your feet."

"Can I get a closer look at the river?" one of the women asked.

"Yes, of course. Here, I'll hold the light while you each get a peek through the grate."

One by one, the people in her tour group took turns squeezing in beside Lily to peer into the tunnel. There was nothing much to see, really. But when you travel all the way to Rome, for perhaps your once-in-a-lifetime visit, it's a tourist's duty to look. Today, Lily had only six on the tour, two Americans, two Brits, and a pair of Germans. Not such a good haul; she wouldn't be taking home much in the way of tips. But what could one expect on a chilly Thursday in January? The tourists in Lily's group were the only visitors in the labyrinth at the moment, and she allowed them to take their time as they each pressed against the metal grate, their crackling raincoats brushing against her. Damp air whooshed up from the tunnel, musty with the smell of mold and wet stone: the scent of ages long past.

"What were these walls, originally?" asked the German man. Lily had pegged him as a businessman. In his sixties, he spoke excellent English and wore an expensive Burberry coat. But his wife, Lily suspected, was not so fluent in English, as the woman had said scarcely a word all morning.

"These are the foundations of homes that were here in Nero's time," said Lily. "The great fire of A.D. 64 reduced this neighborhood to charred rubble."

"Is that the fire when Nero fiddled while Rome burned?" the American man asked.

Lily smiled, for she'd heard that question dozens of times before and could almost always predict who in the group would ask it. "Actually, Nero didn't fiddle. The violin wasn't invented yet. While Rome burned, he was said to have played the lyre and sung."

"And then he blamed the fire on the Christians," the man's wife added.

Lily shut off the flashlight. "Come, let's move on. There's a lot more to see."

She led the way into the shadowy labyrinth. Aboveground, traffic was roaring on busy streets, and vendors were selling postcards and trinkets to tourists wandering the ruins of the Colosseum. But here, beneath the basilica, there was only the sound of the eternally rushing water and the rustle of their coats as they moved down the gloomy tunnel.

"This type of construction is called *opus reticulatum*," said Lily, pointing to the walls. "It's masonry work that alternates bricks with tufa."

"Two-fer?" It was the American man again. The stupid questions were always his. "Is that, like, stronger than *one-fer*?" Only his wife laughed, a high, annoying whinny.

"Tufa," said the Englishman, "is actually compacted volcanic ash."

"Yes, that's exactly what it is," said Lily. "It was used quite often as a building block in Roman homes."

"How come we never heard of this tufa stuff before?" the American woman asked her husband, implying that, since they did not know about it, it could not possibly exist.

Even in the gloom, Lily could see the Englishman's eyes roll upward. She responded with an amused shrug.

"You're American, right?" the woman asked Lily. "Miss?"

Lily paused. She did not like this personal question. "Actually," she lied, "I'm Canadian."

"Did *you* know what tufa was before you became a guide? Or is that, like, just a European word?"

"Many Americans aren't familiar with the word," Lily said.

"Well okay, then. It's just a European thing," the woman said, satisfied. If Americans didn't know it, it couldn't possibly be important.

"What you're seeing here," said Lily, quickly moving on with the tour, "is what's left of the villa of Titus Flavius Clemens. In the first century A.D., this was a secret meeting place for Christians, before they were openly accepted. It was still an early cult then, just gaining popularity among the wives of noblemen." She turned on her flashlight again, using the beam to direct their attention. "Now, we're moving into the most interesting section of these ruins. This part was uncovered only in 1870. Here we'll see a secret temple for pagan rituals."

They crossed the passageway, and Corinthian columns loomed ahead in the shadows. It was the temple antechamber, lined with stone benches, decorated with ancient frescoes and stucco. They wandered deeper into the sanctuary, past two shadowy niches, the site of initiation rites. In the world above, the passing centuries had altered streets and skylines, but in this ancient grotto, time had frozen. Here, still, was the carving of the god Mithras slaying the bull. Here, still, the gentle rush of water whispered from the shadows.

"When Christ was born," said Lily, "the cult of Mithras was already ancient; he was worshipped for centuries by the Persians. Now, let's consider the life story of Mithras, what the Persians believed about him. He was God's messenger of truth. He was born in a cave at the winter solstice. His mother, Anahita, was a virgin, and his birth was attended by shepherds bearing gifts. He had twelve disciples who accompanied him as he traveled. He was buried in a tomb, and later rose from the dead. And every year, his rising is celebrated as a rebirth." She paused for dramatic effect, looking around at their faces. "Does any of this sound familiar?"

"That's Christian gospel," said the American woman.

"Yet centuries before Christ, this was already part of Persian lore."

"I've never heard of this." The tourist looked at her husband. "Have you?"

"Nope."

"Then perhaps you should visit the temples at Ostia," said the Englishman. "Or the Louvre. Or the Frankfurt Archaeological Museum. You *might* find it educational."

The American woman turned to him. "You don't need to be patronizing."

"Trust me, madam. Nothing our delightful guide here has told us is either shocking or untrue."

"Now you know as well as I do that Christ was *not* some Persian guy in a funny hat who kills bulls."

Lily said, "I only wanted to point out the interesting parallels in the iconography."

"What?"

"Look, it's not that important, really," said Lily, hoping, desperately, that the woman would just let it go, realizing, too, that any hope she had of a generous tip from the American couple had long since vanished. "It's just mythology."

"The Bible isn't mythology."

"I didn't mean it that way."

"What does anyone really know about the Persians, anyway? I mean, where's *their* holy book?" The other tourists said nothing, just stood around looking uncomfortable.

Let it go. It's not worth an argument.

But the woman wasn't finished yet. Since stepping aboard the tour van that morning, she had complained about everything to do with Italy and Italians. Rome traffic was chaotic, not like in America. The hotels were too expensive, not like in America. The bathrooms were so small, not like in America. And now, this final irritation. She had walked into the Basilica di San Clemente to view one of the earliest Christian meeting places, and instead was getting an earful of pagan propaganda.

"How do we know what the Mithrans really believed?" she asked. "Where are they now?"

"Exterminated," said the Englishman. "Their temples were destroyed long ago. What do you think happened after the church claimed that Mithras was the spawn of Satan?"

"That sounds like rewritten history to me."

"Who do you suppose did all the rewriting?"

Lily cut in. "This is where our tour ends. Thank you all very much for your attention. Feel free to linger here if you'd like. The driver will be waiting for you in the van when you're ready to leave. He'll take you all back to your hotels. If you have any other questions, I'd be happy to answer them."

"I think you should let tourists know ahead of time," the American woman said.

"Ahead of time?"

"This tour was called 'The Dawn of Christianity.' But it's not history. It's pure mythology."

"Actually," sighed Lily, "it *is* history. But history isn't always what we've been told."

"And you're an expert?"

"I have a degree in"—Lily paused. *Careful*—"I've studied history."

"And that's it?"

"I've also worked in museums around the world," Lily answered, too annoyed now to be cautious. "In Florence. Paris."

"And now you're a tour guide."

Even in that chilly subterranean room, Lily felt her face go hot. "Yes," she said, after a long silence. "I'm just a tour guide. Nothing else. Now, if you'll excuse me, I'll go check on our driver." She turned and headed back into the labyrinth of tunnels. She certainly would not be getting any tips today, so they could damn well find their own way back upstairs.

She climbed from the Mithraeum, with each step moving forward in time, ascending to the Byzantine foundations. Here, beneath the current Basilica di San Clemente, were the abandoned hallways of a fourth-century church that had lain hidden for eight centuries, buried beneath the medieval church that later replaced it. She heard voices approaching, speaking French. It was another tour group, on their descent to the Mithraeum. They came through the narrow corridor, and Lily moved aside to let the three tourists and their guide pass. As their voices faded, she paused beneath crumbling frescoes, suddenly feeling guilty that she had abandoned her own

group. Why had she let the comments of one igno-
rant tourist so upset her? What was she thinking?

She turned, and froze as she confronted the silhouette of a man standing at the far end of the corridor.

"I hope she did not upset you too much," he said.
She recognized the voice of the German tourist and
released a breath, all her tension instantly gone.

"Oh, it's all right. I've had worse things said to
me."

"You did not deserve it. You were only explaining
the history."

"Some people prefer their own version of history."

"If they don't like to be challenged, then they
should not come to Rome."

She smiled, a smile he probably could not see from
the far end of the murky tunnel. "Yes, Rome has a
way of challenging us all."

He moved toward her, stepping slowly, as though
approaching a skittish deer. "May I offer a suggestion?"

Her heart sank. So he had his criticisms, too. And
what would his be? Couldn't she satisfy anyone today?

"An idea," he said, "for a different sort of tour,
something that would almost certainly draw a different group of visitors."

"What would the theme be?"

"You are familiar with biblical history."

"I'm not an expert, but I have studied it."

"Every travel agency offers tours of the holy sites,
for tourists like our American friends, people who
wish to walk in the footsteps of the saints. But some
of us aren't interested in saints or holy sites." He

had moved close beside her in the tunnel, so close that she could smell the scent of pipe tobacco on his clothes. "Some of us," he said softly, "seek the unholy."

She went absolutely still.

"You have read the Book of Revelation?"

"Yes," she whispered.

"You know of the Beast."

She swallowed. *Yes.*

"And who is the Beast?" he asked.

Slowly she backed away. "Not a he, but an *it.* It's . . . a representation of Rome."

"Ah. You know the scholarly interpretation."

"The Beast was the Roman Empire," she said, still backing away. "The number 666 was a symbol for the emperor Nero."

"Do you really believe that?"

She glanced over her shoulder, toward the exit, and saw no one barring her escape.

"Or do you believe he's real?" he pressed. "Flesh and blood? Some say the Beast lies here, in this city. That he's biding his time, waiting. Watching."

"That—that's for philosophers to decide."

"You tell me, Lily Saul. What do you believe?"

He knows my name.

She spun around to flee. But someone else had magically materialized in the tunnel behind her. It was the nun who had admitted Lily's group into the underground passage. The woman stood very still, watching her. Blocking her way.

His demons have found me.

Lily made her choice in an instant. She lowered her head and slammed straight into the woman, sending her sprawling backward in a swoop of black fabric. The nun's hand clawed at her ankle as Lily stumbled forward, kicking free.

Get to the street!

She was at least three decades younger than the German. Once outside, she could outrun him. Lose him in the crowds milling near the Colosseum. She scrambled up the steps, bursting through a door into the stunning brightness of the upper basilica, and ran toward the nave. Toward the exit. She managed only a few steps across the brilliant mosaic floor when, in horror, she slid to a halt.

From behind marble columns, three men emerged. They said nothing as they closed in, drawing the trap shut. She heard a door slam behind her and footsteps approach: the German and the nun.

Why are there no other tourists? No one around to hear me scream?

"Lily Saul," said the German.

She turned to face him. Even as she did so, she knew the other three men were moving in even more tightly behind her. *So this is where it ends,* she thought. *In this holy place, beneath the gaze of Christ on the cross.* She did not ever imagine it would happen in a church. She'd thought it would be in a dark alley, perhaps, or in a dreary hotel room. But not here, where so many had looked up to the light.

"We've finally found you," he said.

She straightened, her chin lifting. If she had to face the Devil, she'd damn well do it with her head high.

"So where is he?" the German asked.

"Who?"

"Dominic."

She stared at him. This question she had not expected.

"Where is your cousin?" he said.

She shook her head in bewilderment. "Isn't he the one who sent you?" she asked. "To kill me?"

Now the German looked startled. He gave a nod to one of the men standing behind Lily. She flinched in surprise as her arms were yanked behind her, as handcuffs snapped shut over her wrists.

"You will come with us," the German said.

"Where?"

"A safe place."

"You mean . . . you're not going to—"

"Kill you? No." He crossed toward the altar and opened a hidden panel. Beyond was a tunnel that she had never known existed. "But someone else very well may."

THIRTY-TWO

LILY STARED through the limousine's tinted windows as the Tuscan countryside glided past. Five months ago, she had traveled south down this very road, but under different circumstances, in a rattling truck driven by an unshaven man whose only goal had been to get inside her pants. That night she had been hungry and exhausted, her feet sore from trudging half the night. Now she was on the same road, but heading north, back toward Florence, not a weary hitchhiker this time, but traveling in style. Everywhere she looked, in the backseat of the limo, she saw luxury. The upholstery was black leather, supple as human skin. The seat pocket in front of her held a surprising range of newspapers: today's issues of the *International Herald Tribune,* the London *Times, Le Figaro,* and *Corriere della Sera.* Warm air whispered from heating vents, and in a refreshment rack were bottles of sparkling water and wine and a selection of fresh fruits, cheese and crackers. But comfortable though it was, it was still a prison, for she could not unlock the door. Shatterproof glass separated her from the driver and his companion in the front seat. For the past two hours, neither man had bothered to glance back at her. She couldn't even be sure they were human. Maybe they were just robots. All she'd seen was the backs of their heads.

She turned and looked through the rear window at the Mercedes following them. She saw the German man stare back at her through his windshield. She was being escorted north by three men in two very expensive cars. These people had resources, and they knew what they were doing. What chance did she have against them?

I don't even know who they are.

But they knew who she was. As careful as she'd been all these months, somehow these people had managed to track her down.

The limo took a turn off the highway. So they were not going all the way to Florence. Instead they were headed into the countryside, climbing the gentle hills of Tuscany. Daylight was almost gone, and in the thickening dusk she saw bare grapevines huddled on windswept slopes and crumbling stone houses, long abandoned. Why take this road? There was nothing out here except farms gone fallow.

Maybe that was the point. Here there'd be no witnesses.

She had wanted to believe the German when he'd said he was taking her to a safe place, had wanted it so badly that she had let herself be temporarily lulled by a little luxury, a comfortable ride. Now, as the limo slowed down and turned onto a private dirt road, she felt her heart battering against her ribs, felt her hands turn so slick she had to wipe them on her jeans. It was dark enough now. They'd take her on a short walk into the fields and put a bullet in her brain. With three men, it would be quick work, digging the grave, rolling in the body.

In January, the soil would be cold.

The limo climbed, winding through trees, the headlights flashing across gnarled undergrowth. She saw the brief red reflection from a rabbit's eyes. Then the trees opened up, and they were stopped at an iron gate. A security camera glowed above an intercom. The driver rolled down his window and said, in Italian, "We have the package."

Blinding floodlights came on, and there was a pause as the camera panned the occupants of the car. Then the gate whined open.

They drove through, followed by the Mercedes that had tailed them all the way from Rome. Only then, as Lily's vision readjusted back to the darkness, did she see the silhouettes of statuary and clipped hedges lining the drive. And ahead, looming at the end of the gravel road, was a villa with lights blazing. She leaned forward in astonishment, staring at stone terraces and enormous urns and tall cypresses, like a row of dark spears pointing at the stars. The limo pulled up beside a marble fountain, now dry and silent for the winter. The Mercedes parked behind them, and the German stepped out and opened her door.

"Ms. Saul, shall we go into the house?"

She looked up at the two men flanking him. These people were taking no chances that she might escape. She had no choice but to go with them. She stepped out, her legs stiff from the ride, and followed the German up stone steps to the terrace. A cold wind swept leaves across her path, scattering them like ashes. Even before they'd reached the entrance, the door swung open and an elderly man stood waiting to greet them. He gave Lily only a cursory glance, then turned his attention to the German.

"The room is ready for her," he said in Italian-accented English.

"I'll be staying as well, if that's all right. He'll arrive tomorrow?"

The elderly man nodded. "A night flight."

Who was coming tomorrow? Lily wondered. They climbed a magnificent balustrade to the second floor. As their party swept past, hanging tapestries stirred, trembling against stone walls. She had no time to ogle the artwork. They hurried her up a long hallway now, past portraits with eyes that watched her every step.

The elderly man unlocked a heavy oak door and gestured for her to enter. She stepped into a bedroom that was ponderously furnished with dark wood and thick velvets.

"This is only for tonight," said the German.

She turned, suddenly realizing that no one had followed her into the room. "What happens tomorrow?" she said.

The door swung shut, and she heard the key turn, locking her in.

Why will no one answer a single damn question?

Alone now, she quickly crossed to the heavy drapes and yanked them aside, revealing a window secured with bars. She strained to pry them apart, pulled and pulled until her arms were exhausted, but the bars were cast iron, welded into place, and she was nothing more than flesh and bone. In frustration, she turned and stared at her velvet prison. She saw an enormous bed of carved oak, covered with a wine-red canopy. Her gaze lifted to the dark wood moldings, to carvings of cherubs and grapevines that laced across the tall ceiling. *It may be a prison,* she thought, *but it's also the nicest damn bedroom I'll ever sleep in. A room fit for a Medici.*

On an exquisitely inlaid table were a covered silver tray, a wineglass, and a bottle of Chianti, already uncorked. She lifted the lid and saw cold sliced meats, a salad of tomatoes and mozzarella, and unsalted Tuscan bread. She poured a glass of wine, then paused as she brought it to her lips.

Why would they poison me when it's just as easy to fire a bullet into my head?

She drank the entire glass of wine and poured another. Then she sat down at the table and attacked the tray of food, ripping apart the bread, stuffing chunks into her mouth and washing them down with Chianti. The beef was so tender and sliced so thin, it was like cutting into butter. She devoured every sliver and drank almost the entire bottle of wine. By the time she rose from the chair, she was so clumsy she could barely stumble her way to the bed. *Not poisoned,* she thought. *Just plain old drunk.* And beyond caring what happened tomorrow. She did not even bother to undress but collapsed, fully clothed, onto the damask cover.

A voice awakened her, a man's voice, deep and unfamiliar, calling her name. She opened one aching eye and squinted at light glaring in through the barred window. Promptly she closed her eye again. Who the hell had opened the drapes? When had the sun come up?

"Ms. Saul, wake up."

"Later," she mumbled.

"I didn't fly all night just to watch you sleep. We need to talk."

She groaned and turned over. "I don't talk to men who won't tell me their names."

"My name is Anthony Sansone."

"Am I supposed to know you?"

"This is my house."

That made her open her eyes. She blinked away sleep and turned to see a man with silver hair gazing down at her. Even in her hungover state, she registered the fact that this was one damn good-looking guy, despite the obvious fatigue shadowing his eyes. He said he'd flown all night and she didn't doubt it, looking at his wrinkled shirt and the dark stubble on his jaw. Sansone had not come into the room alone; the German man was there as well, standing near the door.

She sat up in bed and clutched her throbbing temples. "You really own this villa?"

"It's been in my family for generations."

"Lucky you." She paused. "You sound like an American."

"I am."

"And that guy over there?" She lifted her head and squinted at the German. "He works for you?"

"No. Mr. Baum is a friend. He works for Interpol."

She went very still. She dropped her gaze back to the bed, so they could not see her face.

"Ms. Saul," he said quietly, "why do I get the feeling you're afraid of the police?"

"I'm not."

"I think you're lying."

"And I think you're not a very good host. Locking me up in your house. Barging in here without knocking."

"We did knock. You didn't wake up."

"If you're going to arrest me, you want to tell me why?" she asked. Because now she realized what this was all about. Somehow, they'd found out what she'd done twelve years ago, and they'd tracked her down. Of all the endings she'd imagined, this was not one of them. A cold unmarked grave, yes—but the police? She felt like laughing. *Oh right, arrest me. I've faced far worse terrors than the threat of prison.*

"Is there a reason why we should arrest you?" asked Mr. Baum.

What did he expect, that she was going to blurt out a confession right here and now? They'd have to work a little harder than that.

"Lily," said Sansone, and he sat down on the bed, an invasion of her personal space that instantly made her wary. "Are you aware of what happened in Boston a few weeks ago?"

"Boston? I don't know what you're talking about."

"Does the name Lori-Ann Tucker mean anything to you?"

Lily paused, startled by the question. Did Lori-Ann talk to the police? Is that how they found out? *You promised me, Lori-Ann. You told me you'd keep it a secret.*

"She was your friend, correct?" he asked.

"Yes," Lily admitted.

"And Sarah Parmley? She was also a friend?"

Suddenly she registered the fact that he'd used the word *was*. Not *is*. Her throat went dry. This was starting to sound very bad.

"You knew both of these women?" he pressed her.

"We—we grew up together. The three of us. Why are you asking about them?"

"Then you haven't heard."

"I've been out of touch. I haven't talked to anyone in the States for months."

"And no one's called you?"

"No." *How could they? I've done my damnedest to stay out of sight.*

He looked at Baum, then back at her. "I'm so sorry to have to tell you this. But your friends—both of them—are dead."

She shook her head. "I don't understand. Was it an accident? How could both of them . . . ?"

"Not an accident. They were murdered."

"Together?"

"Separately. It happened around Christmas. Lori-Ann was killed in Boston. And Sarah was killed in Purity, New York. Sarah's body was found in your parents' house, the house you've been trying to sell. That's why the police have been looking for you."

"Excuse me," she whispered. "I think I'm going to be sick." She scrambled off the bed and bolted into the adjoining bathroom. She slammed the door shut and dropped to her knees over the toilet bowl. The wine she'd drunk the night before came up, scorching like acid as it burned its way up her throat. She clung to the toilet, retching until her stomach was empty, until she had nothing left to throw up. She flushed the toilet and staggered to the sink, where she splashed water in her mouth, on her face. Staring at her own dripping reflection, she scarcely recognized the woman she saw there. How long had it been since she'd looked, really looked, into a mirror? When had she transformed into that feral creature? The running had taken its toll. *Run too long, and eventually you'll leave behind your soul.*

She dried her face on a thick cotton towel, used her fingers to comb back her hair, and retied the ponytail. Mr. Good-Looking-and-Rich was waiting to interrogate her, and she needed to stay on her toes. *Tell him just enough to keep him happy. If he doesn't know what I did, then I sure as hell won't tell him.*

The color was returning to her face. She lifted her chin and saw the old warrior's glint in her eyes. Both her friends were dead. She was the only one left. *Help me, girls. Help me survive this.* She took a deep breath and stepped out of the bathroom.

The men looked at her with expressions of concern. "I'm sorry to have sprung that news on you so abruptly," said Sansone.

"Tell me the details," Lily said bluntly. "What did the police find?"

He seemed taken aback by her coolheaded directness. "The details aren't pleasant."

"I didn't expect they would be." She sat down on the bed. "I just need to know," she said softly. "I need to know how they died."

"First, may I ask you something?" said the Ger-

man man, Mr. Baum. He moved closer. Now both
men were standing above her, watching her face.
"Do you know the significance of the reverse cross?"

For a few seconds, she stopped breathing. Then
she found her voice again. "The upside-down cross
is . . . it's a symbol that's meant to mock Christianity. Some would consider it satanic."

She saw Baum and Sansone exchange surprised
glances.

"And what about this symbol?" Baum reached
into his jacket pocket and took out a pen and a scrap
of paper. Quickly he made a sketch, which he
showed to her. "It's sometimes called the all-seeing
eye. Do you know its significance?"

"This is Udjat," she said, "the eye of Lucifer."

Again, a look passed between Baum and Sansone.

"And if I were to draw a picture of a goat's head,
with horns?" said Baum. "Would it mean anything
to you?"

She met his mild-mannered gaze. "I assume you're
referring to the symbol for Baphomet? Or Azazel?"

"You're familiar with all these symbols."

"Yes."

"Why? Are you a Satanist, Ms. Saul?"

She felt like laughing. "Hardly. I just happen to
know about them. It's my own peculiar interest."

"Is your cousin Dominic a Satanist?"

Lily went absolutely still, her hands flash-frozen in
her lap.

"Ms. Saul?"

"You'd have to ask him," she whispered.

"We'd like to," said Sansone. "Where can we find
him?"

She looked down at her hands, clenched tightly in her lap. "I don't know."

He sighed. "We devoted a lot of manpower to tracking your whereabouts. It's taken us ten days to find you."

Only ten days? God, I've gotten careless.

"So if you could just tell us where Dominic is, you'd save us a great deal of trouble."

"I told you, I don't know."

"Why are you protecting him?" asked Sansone.

That made her chin jerk up. "Why the hell would I protect him?"

"He's your only living blood relative. And you don't know where he is?"

"I haven't seen him in twelve years," she shot back.

Sansone's gaze narrowed. "You remember exactly how long it's been?"

She swallowed. *That was a mistake. I've got to be more careful.*

"The things that were done to Lori-Ann and Sarah—that was Dominic's work, Lily."

"How do you know that?"

"Would you like to hear what he did to Sarah? How many hours she must have screamed as he carved crosses into her skin? And guess what he drew on the wall in Lori-Ann's bedroom, the same room where he dismembered her body. Upside-down crosses. The same symbol he carved on that barn when he was fifteen years old, when he was living with you that summer, in Purity." Sansone moved closer to her, his nearness suddenly threatening. "Is he the one you've been running from? Your own cousin, Dominic?"

She said nothing.

"You're obviously running from *something*. Since you left Paris, you haven't lived anywhere longer than six months. And you haven't been back to Purity in years. What happened that summer, Lily, the summer you lost your family?"

She wrapped her arms around herself, coiling into a tight ball. Suddenly she was shaking, at a moment when she needed, more than ever, to hold herself together.

"First your brother Teddy drowns. Then your mother tumbles down the stairs. Then your father shoots himself. All within a few weeks. That's a lot of tragedy for a sixteen-year-old girl."

She hugged herself even tighter, afraid that if she didn't, she would shake apart, shatter to pieces.

"*Was* it just bad luck, Lily?"

"What else would it be?" she whispered.

"Or was something else going on that summer, something between you and Dominic?"

Her head snapped up. "What are you implying?"

"You're refusing to help us find him. All I can conclude is that you're protecting him."

"You—you think we had a *relationship*?" Her voice rose to a hysterical pitch. "You think I *wanted* my family to die? My brother was only eleven years old!" She stopped, then repeated in a whisper, "He was only eleven years old."

"Maybe you didn't realize how dangerous it all was," said Sansone. "Maybe you just joined him in a few incantations, a few harmless rituals. A lot of kids do, you know, out of curiosity. Maybe to show they're different from everyone else, unique. Maybe to shock their parents. Were your parents shocked?"

"They didn't understand him," she whispered. "They didn't realize . . ."

"And the other girls. Your friends Lori-Ann and Sarah. Did they join in his rituals? When did the game get scary? When did you realize there are powers you don't ever want to awaken? That's what happened, isn't it? Dominic lured you in."

"No, that's not what happened at all."

"And then you got scared. You tried to pull away, but it was too late, because their eyes were on you. And on your family. Once you've invited the darkness into your life, it's not so easy to get rid of it. It burrows in, becomes part of you. Just as you become part of *it*."

"I didn't." She looked at him. "I wanted no part of it!"

"Then why do you continue to seek it out?"

"What do you mean?"

Sansone glanced at Baum, who opened his briefcase and removed a sheaf of papers. "These are reports we compiled on your whereabouts these past years," said Baum. "Interviews with people you've worked with. Museum curators in Florence and Paris. The tour group company in Rome. An antiques dealer in Naples. It seems you impressed them all, Ms. Saul, with your rather arcane expertise. In demonology." He dropped the interview transcripts on the table. "You know a great deal about the subject."

"I've taught myself," she said.

"Why?" asked Sansone.

"I wanted to understand him."

"Dominic?"

"Yes."

"And do you now?"

"No. I realize I never will." She met his gaze. "How can we understand something that's not even human?"

He said, quietly, "We can't, Lily. But we can try our best to defeat him. So help us."

"You're his cousin," said Baum. "You lived with him that summer. You may know him better than anyone else does."

"It's been twelve years."

"And he hasn't forgotten you," said Sansone. "That's why your friends were killed. He was using them to find *you*."

"Then he killed them for nothing," she said. "They didn't know where I was. They couldn't have revealed a thing."

"And that may be the only reason you're still alive," said Baum.

"Help us find him," said Sansone. "Come back to Boston with me."

For a long time she sat on the bed, under the gazes of the two men. *I have no choice in this. I have to play along.*

She took a deep breath and looked at Sansone. "When do we leave?"

THIRTY-THREE

LILY SAUL looked like some young druggie who'd been plucked straight off the street. Her eyes were bloodshot and her greasy dark hair was pulled back in a sloppy ponytail. Her blouse had clearly been slept in, and the blue jeans were frayed to within a few washings of disintegration. Or was that just the style with kids these days? Then Jane remembered that this was no kid she was looking at. Lily Saul was twenty-eight years old, certainly a woman, but at the moment she looked far younger and more vulnerable. Sitting in Anthony Sansone's ornate dining room, her thin frame dwarfed by the massive chair, Lily was painfully out of place and she knew it. Her gaze flicked nervously between Jane and Sansone, as though trying to guess from which direction the assault would come.

Jane opened a folder and removed the enlarged print copied from the Putnam Academy yearbook. "Can you confirm that this is your cousin, Dominic Saul?" she asked.

Lily's gaze dropped to the photo and remained there. It was, in truth, an arresting portrait that stared back at her: a sculpted face with golden hair and blue eyes, a Raphaelite angel.

"Yes," said Lily. "That's my cousin."

"This photo is over twelve years old. We don't have any more recent ones. Do you know where we can find one?"

"No."

"You sound pretty definite."

"I've had no contact with Dominic. I haven't seen him in years."

"And the last time was?"

"That summer. He left the week after my father's funeral. I was staying over at Sarah's house, and he didn't even bother to come tell me good-bye. He just wrote me a note and left. Said that his mother had come to pick him up, and they were leaving town immediately."

"And you haven't seen or heard from him since?"

Lily hesitated. It was just a few beats of a pause, but it made Jane lean forward, suddenly alert. "You have, haven't you?"

"I'm not sure."

"What does that mean?"

"Last year, when I was living in Paris, I got a letter from Sarah. She'd received a postcard in the mail that upset her. She forwarded it to me."

"Who was the postcard from?"

"It had no return address, no signature. The postcard was of a painting from the Royal Museum in Brussels. A portrait by Antoine Wiertz. *The Angel of Evil.*"

"Was there a message?"

"No words. Just symbols. Symbols that Sarah and I recognized because we'd seen him cut them into trees that summer."

Jane slid a pen and notebook to Lily. "Draw them for me."

Lily picked up the pen. She paused for a moment, as though loath to reproduce what she had seen. At last she pressed the pen to paper. What she drew sent a sliver of ice through Jane: three upside-down crosses, and the notation: *R17:16.*

"Does that refer to a biblical quotation?" asked Jane.

"It's from Revelation."

Jane glanced at Sansone. "Can you look it up?"

"I can recite the quote," said Lily softly. " 'And the ten horns which thou sawest upon the beast, these shall hate the whore, and shall make her desolate and naked. And shall eat her flesh, and burn her with fire.' "

"You know it by heart."

"Yes."

Jane turned to a fresh page and slid the notebook back to Lily. "Could you write it for me?"

For a moment Lily just stared at the blank page. Then, reluctantly, she began to write. Slowly, as though each word was painful. When at last she handed it to Jane, it was with a relieved sigh.

Jane looked down at the words, and again felt that sliver of cold pierce her spine.

And shall eat her flesh, and shall burn her with fire.

"It looks to me like a warning, a threat," said Jane.

"It is. I'm sure it was meant for me."

"Then why did Sarah get it?"

"Because I was too hard to find. I'd moved so many times, to so many cities."

"So he sent it to Sarah. And she knew how to find you." Jane paused. "It was from him, wasn't it?"

Lily shook her head. "I don't know."

"Come on, Lily. Who else would it be but Dominic? That's almost exactly what he carved in that barn twelve years ago. Why is he searching for you? Why's he threatening you?"

Lily's head drooped. She said, softly, "Because I know what he did that summer."

"To your family?"

Lily looked up, her eyes bright with tears. "I couldn't prove it. But I knew."

"How?"

"My father *never* would have killed himself! He knew how much I needed him. But no one would listen to me. No one listens to a sixteen-year-old girl!"

"What happened to that postcard? With the symbols?"

Her chin lifted. "I burned it. And I left Paris."

"Why?"

"What would you do if you received a death threat? Sit tight and wait?"

"You could have called the police. Why didn't you?"

"And tell them what? That someone sent me a biblical quotation?"

"You didn't even think of reporting it? You knew in your heart that your cousin was a murderer. But you never called the authorities? That's what I don't get, Lily. He threatened you. He scared you enough to make you leave Paris. But you didn't ask for help. You just ran."

Lily dropped her gaze. A long silence passed. In another room, a clock ticked loudly.

Jane glanced at Sansone. He appeared to be just as baffled. She focused again on Lily, who steadfastly refused to meet her gaze. "Okay," said Jane, "what are you not telling us?"

Lily didn't respond.

Jane was out of patience. "Why the hell won't you help us catch him?"

"You can't catch him," said Lily.

"Why not?"

"Because he's not human."

In the long silence that followed, Jane heard the chiming of the clock echo through the rooms. That sliver of a chill that Jane had felt was suddenly an icy blast up her spine.

Not human. *And the horns, which thou sawest upon the beast . . .*

Sansone leaned close and asked, softly, "Then what is he, Lily?"

The young woman gave a shudder and wrapped her arms around herself. "I can't outrun him. He always finds me. He'll find me here, too."

"Okay," said Jane, her nerves snapping back under control. This interview had swerved so far off the tracks that it made her doubt everything the woman had said earlier. Lily Saul was either lying or delusional, and Sansone was not only lapping up every weird detail, he was actually feeding her delusions with his own. "Enough woo-woo," said Jane.

"I'm not looking for the Devil. I'm looking for a man."

"Then you'll never catch him. And I can't help you." Lily looked at Sansone. "I need to use the restroom."

"You can't help us?" said Jane. "Or you won't?"

"Look, I'm tired," Lily snapped. "I just got off the plane, I'm jet-lagged, and I haven't taken a shower in two days. I'm not answering any more questions." She walked out of the room.

"She didn't tell us a single useful thing," said Jane.

Sansone stared at the doorway that Lily had just walked through. "You're wrong," he said. "I think she did."

"She's hiding something." Jane paused. Her cell phone was ringing. "Excuse me," she muttered, and dug it out of her purse.

Vince Korsak didn't bother with a preamble. "You gotta get over here right now," he snapped. Over the phone, she heard music in the background and noisy conversation. *Oh God,* she thought, *I forgot all about his stupid party.*

"Look, I'm really sorry," she said. "I'm not going to be able to make it tonight. I'm in the middle of an interview."

"But you're the only one who can handle this!"

"Vince, I have to go."

"They're *your* parents. What the hell am I supposed to do with them?"

Jane paused. "What?"

"They're screaming at each other over here." He paused. "Uh-oh. They've just gone into the kitchen. I gotta go hide the friggin' knives."

"My *dad's* at your party?"

"He just showed up. I didn't invite him! He got here right after your mom did, and they've been going at it for twenty minutes now. Are you coming? 'Cause if they don't calm down, I'm gonna have to call nine-one-one."

"No! Jesus, don't do that!" *My mom and dad carted off in handcuffs? I'll never live it down.* "Okay, I'll be right there." She hung up and looked at Sansone. "I have to leave."

He followed her into the front parlor, where she pulled on her coat. "Will you be back tonight?"

"Right now, she's not being too cooperative. I'll try again tomorrow."

He nodded. "I'll keep her safe till then."

"Safe?" She gave a snort. "How about you just keep her from running?"

Outside, the night was cold and clear. Jane crossed the street to her Subaru and was just unlocking it when she heard a car door slam shut. She looked up the street to see Maura walking toward her.

"What're you doing in the neighborhood?" Jane asked.

"I heard he found Lily Saul."

"For what it's worth."

"You've already interviewed her?"

"And she's not giving away anything. This doesn't bring us one step closer." Jane glanced down the street as Oliver Stark's van pulled into a parking place. "What's going on here tonight?"

"We're all here to see Lily Saul."

"*We?* Don't tell me you've actually joined these freaks?"

"I haven't joined anything. But my house was marked, Jane, and I want to know why. I want to hear what this woman has to say." Maura turned and headed toward Sansone's house.

"Hey, Doc?" Jane called out.

"Yes?"

"Watch yourself around Lily Saul."

"Why?"

"She's either crazy, or she's hiding something." Jane paused. "Or both."

Even through Korsak's closed apartment door, Jane could hear the thump of disco music, like a heartbeat throbbing in the walls. The man was fifty-five years old, he'd had a heart attack, and "Staying Alive" was probably a good choice for his theme song. She knocked, dreading the thought of Korsak in a leisure suit.

He opened the door, and she stared at his shimmering silk shirt, the armpits damp with circles of sweat. The collar was unbuttoned, the neckline open far enough to reveal a gorilla's thatch of chest hair. The only thing missing was a gold chain around his fat neck.

"Thank *God*," he sighed.

"Where are they?"

"Still in the kitchen."

"And still alive, I assume."

"They've been yelling loud enough. Geez, I can't believe the language outta your ma's mouth!"

Jane stepped through the doorway, into the psychedelic light show of a spinning disco ball. In the gloom, she could see about a dozen listless partygoers standing around nursing drinks or slouched on a sofa as they mechanically dredged potato chips through dip. This was the first time Jane had ever been inside Korsak's new bachelor apartment and she had to pause, stupefied by the spectacle. She saw a smoked-glass-and-chrome coffee table and a white shag carpet, plus a big-screen TV and stereo speakers so huge you could nail a roof on one of them and call it home. And she saw black leather—lots and lots of black leather. She could almost imagine the testosterone oozing from the walls.

Then she heard, over the bouncy beat of "Staying Alive," two voices yelling in the kitchen.

"You are *not* staying here, looking like that. What the hell? Do you think you're seventeen again?"

"You have no right to tell me what to do, Frank."

Jane walked into the kitchen, but her parents didn't even notice her, their attention was so completely focused on each other. *What did Mom do to herself?* Jane wondered, staring at Angela's tight red dress. When did she discover spike heels and green eye shadow?

"You're a grandmother, for God's sake," said Frank. "How can you go out wearing a getup like that? Look at you!"

"At least *someone's* looking at me. You never did."

"Got your boobs practically hanging outta that dress."

"I say, if you got it, flaunt it."

"What are you trying to prove? Are you and that Detective Korsak—"

"Vince treats me very well, thank you."

"Mom," said Jane. "Dad?"

"Vince? So now you call him Vince?"

"*Hey,*" said Jane.

Her parents looked at her.

"Oh Janie," said Angela. "You made it after all!"

"You knew about this?" said Frank, glaring at his daughter. "You *knew* your mom was running around?"

"Ha!" Angela laughed. "Look who's talking."

"You let your mom go out dressed like *that*?"

"She's fifty-seven years old," said Jane. "Like I'm supposed to measure her hemline?"

"This is—this is *inappropriate*!"

"I'll tell you what inappropriate is," said Angela. "It's *you,* robbing me of my youth and beauty and tossing me on the garbage heap. It's *you,* sticking your dick in some stray ass that just happens to wiggle by."

Did my mom just say that?

"It's *you* having the gall to tell *me* what's inappropriate! Go on, go back to her. I'm staying right here. For the first time in my life, I'm going to enjoy myself. I'm going to par-*tee!*" Angela turned and clacked on spike heels out of the kitchen.

"Angela! You come right back here!"

"Dad." Jane grabbed Frank's arm. "Don't."

"Someone's gotta stop her before she humiliates herself!"

"Humiliates *you,* you mean."

Frank shook off his daughter's hand. "She's your mother. You should talk some sense into her."

"She's at a party, so what? It's not like she's committing a crime."

"That dress is a crime. I'm glad I got here before she did something she'd regret."

"What *are* you doing here, anyway? How'd you even know she'd be here?"

"She told me."

"*Mom* did?"

"Calls to tell me she's forgiven me. Says I should go ahead and have my fun, 'cause she's having fun, too. Going out to a party tonight. Says my leaving was the best thing ever happened to her. I mean, what the *hell* is going on in her head?"

What's going on, thought Jane, *is that Mom is having the ultimate revenge. She's showing him she doesn't give a damn that he's gone.*

"And this Korsak guy," said Frank, "he's a younger man!"

"Only by a few years."

"You taking her side now?"

"I'm not taking any sides. I think you two need a time-out. Stay away from each other. Just leave, okay?"

"I don't want to leave. Not till I have this out with her."

"You really don't have the right to tell her anything. You know that."

"She's my wife."

"What's your girlfriend gonna say about that, huh?"

"Don't call her that."

"What should I call her? The bimbo?"

"You don't understand."

"I understand that Mom's finally having some fun. She doesn't get enough."

He waved in the direction of the music. "You call that just fun? That orgy out there?"

"What do you call what *you're* having?"

Frank gave a heavy sigh and sank into a kitchen chair. He dropped his head into his hands. "What a mess. What a big, fucking mistake."

She stared at him, more shocked by his use of the *F* word than by his admission of regret.

"I don't know what to do," he said.

"What do you want to do, Dad?"

He raised his head and looked at her with tormented eyes. "I can't decide."

"Yeah. That's going to make Mom feel great, hearing that."

"I don't know her anymore! She's like some alien with her boobs pushed up. All those guys are probably staring down her dress." Abruptly he stood. "That's it. I'm gonna put my foot down."

"No, you're not. You're gonna leave. Right now."

"Not while she's still here."

"You'll only make things worse." Jane took his arm and guided him out of the kitchen. "Just *go*, Dad."

As they crossed the living room, he looked at Angela, standing with a drink in her hand, the disco ball casting multicolored sequins of light across her dress. "I want you home by eleven!" he yelled to his wife. Then he walked out of the apartment, slamming the door shut behind him.

"Ha," said Angela. "Fat chance."

Jane sat at her kitchen table, papers spread out in front of her, her gaze on the wall clock as the minute hand ticked past 10:45 P.M.

"You can't just go dragging her home," said Gabriel. "She's an adult. If she wants to spend the whole night there, she has every right to."

"Don't. Even. *Mention* that possibility." Jane clutched her temples, trying to block out the thought of her mother sleeping over at Korsak's place. But Gabriel had already thrown open the gates, and the images came stampeding in. "I should go back there right now, before something happens. Before—"

"What? She has too good a time?"

He came around behind her and placed his hands on her shoulders, massaging her taut muscles. "Come on, sweetheart, lighten up. What are you going to do, give your mom a curfew?"

"I'm thinking about it."

In the nursery, Regina gave a sudden wail.

"None of the women in my life are happy tonight." Gabriel sighed and walked out of the kitchen.

Jane glanced up at the clock again. Eleven P.M. Korsak had promised to put Angela safely in a cab. Maybe he already had. *Maybe I should call and find out if she's left yet.*

Instead she forced her attention back to the papers on the table. It was her file on the elusive Dominic Saul. Here were the few fading clues to a young man who, twelve years ago, had simply walked into the mists and vanished. Once again, she studied the boy's school photo, gazing at a face that was almost angelic in its beauty. Golden hair, intense blue eyes, an aquiline nose. *A fallen angel.*

She turned to the handwritten letter from the

boy's mother, Margaret, withdrawing her son from the Putnam Academy.

Dominic will not be returning for the fall semester. I will be taking him back with me to Cairo . . .

Where they had simply disappeared. Interpol had found no record of their arrival, no documentation that Margaret or Dominic Saul had ever returned to Egypt.

She rubbed her eyes, suddenly too tired to focus on the page, and began gathering up the papers and returning them to the folder. Reaching for her notebook, she suddenly paused, staring at the page in front of her. She saw the quote from Revelation that Lily Saul had written:

And the ten horns which thou sawest upon the beast, these shall hate the whore and make her desolate and naked. And shall eat her flesh. And burn her with fire.

But it was not the words themselves that made Jane's heart suddenly start to pound. It was the handwriting.

She riffled through the folder and once again pulled out Margaret Saul's letter withdrawing her son from the Putnam Academy. She laid the letter next to her notebook. She looked back and forth, between the biblical quote and Margaret Saul's letter.

She jumped to her feet and called out. "Gabriel? I've got to leave."

He came back out of the baby's room, holding Regina. "She's not going to appreciate it, you know. Why don't you give her another hour at the party?"

"This isn't about my mom." Jane went into the living room. He watched, frowning, as she unlocked a drawer, took out her holster, and buckled it on. "It's about Lily Saul."

"What about her?"

"She lied. She knows exactly where her cousin is hiding."

THIRTY-FOUR

"I'VE TOLD YOU everything I know," said Lily.

Jane stood in Sansone's dining room, where the dessert dishes had not yet been cleared from the table. Jeremy quietly placed a cup of coffee in front of Jane, but she didn't touch it. Nor did she look at any of the other guests seated around the table. Her gaze remained on Lily.

"Why don't we go into the other room, Lily, where we can talk in private?"

"I have nothing else to tell you."

"I think you have a great deal to tell me."

Edwina Felway said, "Then ask your questions right here, Detective. We'd all like to hear them."

Jane looked around the table at Sansone and his guests. The so-called Mephisto Club. Even though Maura claimed not to be part of it, there she was, seated in their circle. These people might think they understood evil, but they couldn't recognize it, even when it was sitting right here at the same table. Jane's gaze returned, once again, to Lily Saul, who sat stubbornly in place, refusing to move from her chair. *Okay,* thought Jane. *This is the way you want to play the game? That's how we'll play it, with an audience watching.*

Jane opened the file folder she'd brought into the house and slapped the page down in front of Lily, setting off the musical clatter of wineglasses and china. Lily looked at the handwritten letter.

"Dominic's mother didn't write that," said Jane.

"What is it?" asked Edwina.

"It's a letter withdrawing fifteen-year-old Dominic from the Putnam Academy boarding school in Connecticut. It was supposedly written by his mother, Margaret Saul."

"Supposedly?"

"Margaret Saul didn't write that letter." Jane looked at Lily. "You did."

Lily gave a laugh. "Do I look old enough to be his mother?"

Jane placed the notebook on the table now, open to the page with the quote from Revelation. "You wrote that passage for me tonight, Lily. We know it's your handwriting." She pointed back to the letter. "So is that."

Silence. Lily's mouth had tightened to two thin lines.

"That summer, when you were sixteen, your cousin Dominic wanted to vanish," said Jane. "After the things he did in Purity, maybe he *needed* to vanish." Her eyes narrowed on Lily. "And you helped him. You told everyone a convenient cover story: that his mother suddenly came to town to fetch him. That they left the country. But it was a lie, wasn't it? Margaret Saul never came to get her son. She never showed up at all. Isn't that right?"

"I don't need to answer you," said Lily. "I know my rights."

"Where is he? Where is Dominic?"

"When you find him, let me know." Lily shoved back her chair and stood up.

"What went on between you two that summer?"

"I'm going to bed." Lily turned and started out of the dining room.

"Did he do all your dirty work for you? Is that why you're protecting him?"

Lily stopped. Slowly, she turned, and her eyes were as dangerous as radium.

"When your parents died, you came into a nice little inheritance," said Jane.

"I inherited a house that no one will ever buy. And a bank account that paid for my college education, but not much more."

"Did you get on with your parents, Lily? Did you have arguments?"

"If you think I'd ever—"

"All teenagers do. But maybe your fights went a little further. Maybe you couldn't wait to get out of that dead little town and get on with your life. Then your cousin moves in for the summer and he gives you ideas, ways to make your escape happen a little easier, a little quicker."

"You have no idea what happened!"

"Then tell me. Tell me why *you* were the one to find Teddy's body in the lake, why *you* were the one who found your mother at the bottom of the stairs."

"I'd never hurt them. If I'd known—"

"Were you lovers? You and Dominic?"

Lily's face went white with rage. For one knife-edged moment, Jane thought the woman might actually lunge at her.

A loud ringing suddenly cut through the silence. Everyone glanced at Sansone.

"It's our intruder alert," he said, and rose to his feet. He crossed to a control panel on the wall. "There's a breach in the garden window."

"Someone's in the house?" asked Jane.

Lily said softly, "It's him."

Jeremy came into the dining room. "I just checked, Mr. Sansone. The window's locked."

"Then maybe it's just a malfunction." Sansone looked at the others. "I think it'd be best if you all stayed right here for the moment, while I check the system."

"No," said Lily, her gaze darting from doorway to doorway, as though expecting an attacker to suddenly burst through. "I'm not staying. Not in this house."

"You'll be perfectly safe. We'll protect you."

"And who's going to protect *you*?" She looked around the room at Maura, Edwina, and Oliver. "Any of you? You don't even know what you're dealing with!"

"Look, everyone just sit tight, okay?" said Jane. "I'll go outside and take a look around."

Sansone said, "I'll come with you."

Jane paused, on the verge of refusing his offer. Then she thought of Eve Kassovitz, dragged bleeding across the icy walkway, her weapon still strapped to her waist. "All right," she said to him. "Let's go."

They pulled on their coats and stepped outside.

Beneath streetlamps, pools of light glistened with ice. It was a frozen world, every surface polished and gleaming like glass. Even if an intruder had walked this way, they'd see no footprints tonight. Her Maglite beam skimmed across pavement hard as diamonds. She and Sansone circled around to the iron gate and stepped through, into the narrow side yard. This was where the killer had brought down Eve Kassovitz. Along this path, he'd dragged her body, the blood from her torn scalp smearing across the granite pavers, freezing in streaks of red.

Jane's weapon was already out of her holster, the gun an extension of her own body, magically materializing in her grasp. She moved toward the back garden, her light slashing the shadows, the soles of her shoes skating on ice. Her beam swept across winter-shriveled wisps of ivy. She knew Sansone was right behind her, but he moved so silently she had to pause and glance over her shoulder, just to confirm that he was really there, that he was watching her back.

She edged toward the corner of the building and swept her Maglite across the enclosed garden, across the courtyard where, only a few weeks ago, Eve had lain, her muscles stiffening, her blood freezing on the cold stones. Jane saw no movement, no hulking shadows, no demon in a black cape.

"That's the window?" she asked. She aimed her beam and saw light bounce back in the glass. "The one your system says was breached?"

"Yes."

She crossed the courtyard for a closer look. "No screen?"

"Jeremy takes them down for the winter."

"And it's always kept latched on the inside?"

"Always. Security is of paramount concern to us."

She ran the light along the sill and spotted the telltale gouge in the wood. *Fresh.*

"We've got a problem here," she said softly. "Someone tried to force this."

He stared at the sill. "That wouldn't have set off the alarm. The only way to do that is to actually open the window."

"But your butler says it's locked on the inside."

"That means . . ." Sansone stopped. "Jesus."

"What?"

"He got in and relatched it. He's already *inside* the house!" Sansone turned and ran back along the side yard, moving so fast his shoes skidded across the walkway. He almost fell but caught himself and kept running. By the time Jane came through the front door, he was already in the dining room, urging everyone to their feet.

"Please get your coats," he said. "I need you all to leave the house. Jeremy, I'll help Oliver down the steps, if you could bring the wheelchair."

"What on earth is going on?" asked Edwina.

"Just do it, okay?" ordered Jane. "Grab your coats and go out the front door."

It was Jane's weapon that caught their attention, the fact it was out of her holster and in her hands, a detail that screamed: *This isn't a game; this is serious.*

Lily was the first to bolt. She darted from the room, leading the rush into the parlor, the scramble for coats. As everyone spilled out the front door and into the cold, Jane was right behind them, already on her phone and calling for backup. She might be armed, but she wasn't foolhardy; she had no intention of searching that entire house by herself.

Moments later, the first cruiser appeared, its lights flashing but the siren silent. It skidded to a stop and two patrolmen stepped out.

"I need a perimeter," ordered Jane. "No one gets out of that building."

"Who's inside?"

"We're about to find out." She looked up as the headlights of a second cruiser approached. Two more cops arrived on the scene. "You," she said, and pointed to one of the younger patrolmen. Tonight she wanted fast reflexes and a sharp eye. "Come with me."

Jane entered the house first, the patrolman right behind her, his weapon drawn. He gave a quick double take as they stepped into the parlor, as he surveyed the elegant furniture, the oil painting above the hearth. She knew exactly what he was thinking: *This is a rich man's house.*

She slid open the hidden panel and gave the closet a quick glance just to confirm it was empty. Then they moved on, through the dining room, through the kitchen, and into a massive library. No time to ogle the floor-to-ceiling bookshelves. They were on a monster hunt.

They moved up the staircase, along a curved banister. Eyes gazed down at them from oil portraits. They passed beneath a brooding man, a doe-eyed woman, beneath two cherub-faced girls seated at a harpsichord. At the top of the stairs, they stared down a carpeted hall, past a series of doorways. Jane did not know the layout of this house or what to expect. Even with the patrolman backing her up, even with three other officers stationed right outside the house, her hands were sweating and her heart was pounding its way into her throat. Room by room they moved, sliding open closets, edging through doorways. Four bedrooms, three baths.

They reached a narrow stairway.

Jane halted, staring up at an attic door. *Oh man,* she thought. *I don't want to go up there.*

She grasped the banister and ascended the first step. She heard it creak beneath her weight and knew that anyone upstairs would also hear it, and know she was coming. Behind her, she could hear the patrolman's breathing accelerate.

He feels it, too. The malevolence.

She climbed up the creaking steps to the door. Her hand was slick against the knob. She glanced at her backup and saw him give a quick, tense nod.

She flung open the door and scrambled through, her flashlight beam sweeping an arc through the darkness, skittering across shadowy forms. She saw the gleam of reflected brass, saw hulking shapes poised to attack.

Then, behind her, the cop finally found the light switch and he flicked it on. Jane blinked in the sudden glare. In an instant, crouching attackers transformed to furniture and lamps and rolled-up carpets. Here was a treasure trove of stored antiques. Sansone was so damn rich, even his cast-off furniture was probably worth a fortune. She moved through the attic, her pulse slowing, her fears melting into relief. No monsters up here.

She holstered her gun and stood in the midst of all those treasures, feeling sheepish. The intruder alert must have been a false alarm. *Then what gouged the wood in that windowsill?*

The cop's radio suddenly came to life. "Graffam, what's your status?"

"Looks like we're all clear in here."

"Rizzoli there?"

"Yeah, she's right here."

"We got a situation down here."

Jane shot a questioning look at the cop.

"What's going on?" he said into the radio.

"Dr. Isles wants her out here ASAP."

"On our way."

Jane gave a last glance around the attic, then headed back down the steps, back down the hallway, past bedrooms they had already searched, past the same portraits that had stared at them moments before. Once again her heart was drumming as she stepped out the front door, into a night awash with flashing lights. Two more cruisers had since arrived, and she halted, temporarily blinded by the kaleidoscopic glare.

"Jane, she ran."

She focused on Maura, who stood backlit by the cruisers' rack lights. "What?"

"Lily Saul. We were standing over there, on the sidewalk. And when we turned, she was gone."

"Shit." Jane scanned the street, her gaze sweeping across the shadowy forms of cops, across curious onlookers who'd spilled out of their houses into the cold to watch the excitement.

"It was only a few minutes ago," said Maura. "She can't have gone far."

THIRTY-FIVE

LILY SAUL darted down one side street, and then another, weaving ever deeper into the maze of an unfamiliar neighborhood. She did not know Boston, and she had no idea where she was going. She could hear the sirens of cruisers, circling like sharks. The flash of headlights sent her scrambling into an alley. There she crouched behind garbage cans as a patrol car slowly crept up the street. The instant it disappeared around the corner, she was back on her feet and moving in the other direction. She was going downhill now, slipping on cobblestones slick with ice, her backpack slapping against her shoulder blades. She was not dressed for this bitter weather, and already her feet stung from the cold, and her ungloved hands were numb. Her tennis shoes suddenly skated out from beneath her and she landed on her rump. The impact sent a spear of pain straight up her spine. She sat stunned for a few seconds, her skull ringing. When her vision finally cleared, she saw she was at the bottom of the hill. Across the street was a park, ringed with shrubs, bare trees casting their spindly gloom over ice-glazed snow. A glowing symbol caught her eye.

It was a sign for the subway station.

She'd just jump on a train and in minutes she could be on her way anywhere in the city. And she'd be warm.

She clambered to her feet, her tailbone aching from the fall, her scraped palms stinging. She limped across the street, took a few steps along the sidewalk, and halted.

A police cruiser had just rounded the corner.

She dashed into the park and ducked behind the bushes. There she waited, her heart banging in her throat, but the cruiser did not pass. Peering through the branches, she saw that it was parked and idling outside the subway station. Damn. Time to change plans.

She glanced around and spotted the glowing sign of yet another T station on the other side of the park. She rose to her feet and started across the common, moving beneath the shadow of trees. Ice crusted the snow, and every footstep gave a noisy crack as her shoe broke through the glaze into deep snow beneath. She struggled forward, almost losing a shoe, her lungs heaving now with the effort to make headway. Then, through the roar of her own breathing, she heard another sound behind her, a crunch, a creak. She stopped and turned, and felt her heart freeze.

The figure stood beneath a tree—faceless, featureless, a black form that seemed more shadow than substance. *It's him.*

With a sob, Lily fled, stumbling through the snow, shoes smashing through the icy crust. Her own breathing, the slamming of her own heart, drowned out any sound of pursuit, but she knew he was right behind her. He'd always been right behind her, every minute, every breath, dogging her steps, whispering her doom. But not this close, never this close! She didn't look back, didn't want to see the creature of her nightmares moving in. She just plunged ahead, her shoe lost now, her sock soaked with frigid water.

Then, all at once, she stumbled out of a drift, onto the sidewalk. The T entrance was straight ahead. She went flying down the steps, almost expecting to hear the swoop of wings and feel the bite of claws in her back. Instead, she felt the warm breath of the subway tunnel on her face and saw commuters filing out toward the stairs.

No time to fool with money. Jump the turnstile!

She scrambled over it, and her wet sock slapped down onto the pavement. Two steps, and she skidded to a stop.

Jane Rizzoli was standing right in front of her.

Lily spun around, back toward the turnstile she'd just jumped. A cop stood barring her escape.

Frantically she gazed around the station, looking for the creature that had pursued her, but she saw only startled commuters staring back at her.

A handcuff closed over her wrist.

She sat in Jane Rizzoli's parked car, too exhausted to think of trying to escape. The wet sock felt like a block of ice encasing her foot, and even with the heater running, she could not get warm, could not stop shaking.

"Okay, Lily," said Jane. "Now you're going to tell me the truth."

"You won't believe the truth."

"Try me."

Lily sat motionless, tangled hair spilling across her face. It didn't matter anymore. She was so tired of running. *I give up*.

"Where is Dominic?" asked Jane.

"He's dead," said Lily.

A moment passed as the detective processed that information, as she reached her own conclusions. Through the closed window came the wail of a passing fire truck, but inside this car, there was only the hiss of the heater.

Jane said, "You killed him?"

Lily swallowed. "Yes."

"So his mother never came for him, did she? She never took him abroad. That's why you wrote that letter to the school."

Lily's head drooped lower. There was no point in denying anything. This woman had already put it all together. "The school called. They kept calling, wanting to know if he was coming back. I had to write the letter so they'd stop asking me where he was."

"How did you kill him?"

Lily took in a shuddering breath. "It was the week after my father's funeral. Dominic was in our garage looking at my mother's car. He said she wouldn't need it anymore, so maybe he could have it." Lily's voice dropped to a tight whisper. "That's when I told him I knew. I knew he killed them."

"How did you know?"

"Because I found his notebook. He kept it under his mattress."

"What was in the notebook?"

"It was all about us. Pages and pages about the boring Saul family. What we did every day, the things we said to each other. He had notes about which path Teddy always took to the lake. About which pills we kept in the bathroom cabinet. What we ate for breakfast, how we said good night." She paused. Swallowed. "And he knew where my father kept the key to his gun cabinet." She looked at Jane. "He was like a scientist, studying us. And we were nothing but lab rats."

"Did he actually write in his notebook that he'd killed your family?"

She hesitated. "No. His last entry was August eighth, the day that Teddy . . ." She stopped. "He knew better than to actually write about it."

"Where is that notebook now? Do you still have it?"

"I burned it. Along with all his other books. I couldn't stand the sight of them."

Lily could read the look in Jane's eyes. *You destroyed the evidence. Why should I believe you?*

"Okay," said Jane. "You said you found Dominic in the garage, that you confronted him there."

"I was so upset, I didn't think about what would happen next."

"What did happen?"

"When I told him I knew what he'd done, he just stared right back at me. No fear, no guilt. 'You can't prove it,' " he said. She took a breath and slowly released it. "Even if I could have proved it, he was only fifteen. He wouldn't have gone to jail. In a few years, he would have been free. But my family would still be dead."

"Then what happened?"

"I asked him why. Why he'd do something so terrible. And you know what he said?"

"What?"

" 'You should have been nicer to me.' That was his answer. That's all he said. Then he smiled and walked out of the barn, as if he didn't have a care in the world." She paused. "That's when I did it."

"How?"

"I picked up a shovel. It was leaning up against the wall. I don't even remember reaching for it. I didn't even feel the weight of it. It was like—like my arms were someone else's. He fell, but he was still conscious, and he started to crawl away." She released a deep sigh and said softly, "So I hit him again."

Outside the night had fallen quiet. The bitter weather had driven pedestrians off the street, and only an occasional car glided past.

"And then?" asked Jane.

"All I could think of was how to get rid of the body. I got him into my mother's car. I thought, maybe I could make it look like an accident. It was nighttime, so no one would see anything. I drove the car over to this quarry a few miles out of town. I rolled it over the edge, into the water. I assumed that someone would eventually spot it. Someone would report that a car was down there." Lily gave a disbelieving laugh. "But nobody did. Can you imagine that?" She looked at Jane. "Nobody ever found it."

"So then you went on with your life."

"I graduated from high school. And I left town, for good. I didn't want to be there if they ever found his body."

They stared at each other for a moment. Jane said, "You realize you've just confessed to murdering Dominic Saul. I'll have to place you under arrest."

Lily didn't flinch. "I'd do it again. He deserved it."

"Who knew about this? Who knew you killed him?"

Lily paused. Outside, a couple walked past, heads bent against the wind, shoulders hunched inside winter coats.

"Did Sarah and Lori-Ann know?"

"They were my best friends. I had to tell them. They understood why I did it. They swore to keep it secret."

"And now your friends are dead."

"Yes." Lily shuddered and hugged herself. "It's my fault."

"Who else knows?"

"I never told anyone else. I thought it was over with." She took a breath. "Then Sarah received that postcard."

"With the reference to Revelation?"

"Yes."

"Someone else must know what you did. Someone who saw you that night, or heard about it. Someone who's now having fun tormenting you."

Lily shook her head. "Only Dominic would have sent that postcard."

"But he's dead. How could he?"

Lily fell silent for a moment, knowing that what she was about to say would surely sound absurd to this coldly logical woman. "Do you believe in an afterlife, Detective?" she asked.

As Lily could have predicted, Jane gave a snort. "I

believe we get one shot at life. So you can't afford to screw it up."

"The ancient Egyptians believed in an afterlife. They believed that everyone has a Ba, which they depicted as a bird with a human face. The Ba is your soul. After you die, it's released, and can fly back to the world of the living."

"What's this Egyptian stuff have to do with your cousin?"

"Egypt is where he was born. He had books and books from his mother, some of them quite old, with incantations from Egyptian coffin texts, magical spells to shepherd the Ba back to life. I think he found a way."

"Are you talking about resurrection?"

"No. Possession."

The silence lasted for what seemed like forever.

"You mean demonic possession?" Jane finally asked.

"Yes," said Lily softly. "The Ba finds another home."

"It takes over some other guy's body? Makes him do the killing?"

"The soul has no physical form. It needs to command real flesh and blood. The concept of demonic possession isn't new. The Catholic Church has always known about it, and they have documented cases. They have rites of exorcism."

"You're saying that your cousin's Ba has hijacked a body, and that's how he's managed to come after you, how he's managed to kill your two friends?"

Lily heard the skepticism in Jane's voice, and she

sighed. "There's no point in talking about this. You don't believe any of it."

"Do you? I mean, really?"

"Twelve years ago, I didn't," said Lily softly. She looked at Jane. "But I do now."

Twelve years underwater, thought Jane. She stood shivering at the edge of the quarry as engines rumbled and the cable groaned taut, tugging against the weight of the long-submerged car. What happens to flesh that's been steeped in water through the algal blooms of twelve summers, through the freeze and thaw of twelve winters? The other people standing beside her were grimly silent, no doubt dreading, as she did, their first glimpse of Dominic Saul's body. The county medical examiner, Dr. Kibbie, lifted his collar and pulled his scarf over his face, as though he wanted to disappear into his coat, wanted to be anywhere else but here. In the trees above, a trio of crows cawed, as though eager for a glimpse, a taste, of carrion. *Let there not be any flesh left,* thought Jane. Clean bones she could deal with. Skeletons were merely Halloween decorations, like clattering plastic. Not human at all.

She glanced at Lily, who stood beside her. *It must be even worse for you. You knew him. You killed him.* But Lily did not turn away; she remained at Jane's side, her gaze fixed on the quarry below.

The cable strained, lifting its burden from the black waters, where chunks of fractured ice bobbed. Already a diver had been down to confirm the car was there, but the water had been too murky, the swirling sediment too thick to clearly view the interior. Now the water seemed to boil, and the vehicle surfaced. The air in the tires had caused it to flip upside down when it had fallen in, and the underside emerged first, water streaming off rusted metal. Like a whale breaching, the rear bumper broke the surface, the license plate obscured by a decade's worth of algae and sediment. The crane's engine revved harder, the piercing whine of machinery drilling straight into Jane's skull. She felt Lily cringe against her and thought that the young woman would now surely turn and retreat to Jane's car. But Lily managed to hold her ground as the crane swung its burden away from the quarry and gently lowered it onto the snow.

A workman released the cable. Another rev of the engines, a nudge from the crane, and the car rolled right side up. Water streamed from the vehicle, staining the snow a dirty brown.

For a moment, no one approached it. They let it sit there, draining water. Then Dr. Kibbie pulled on gloves and trudged across the now-muddy snow to the driver's door. He gave it a tug, but it would not open. He circled to the passenger side and yanked on the handle. He jumped back as the door swung open, releasing a sudden rush of water that drenched his boots and trousers.

He glanced at the others, then focused again on the open door, which continued to drip. He took a breath, steeling himself against the view, and leaned inside the car. For a long moment he held that pose, his body bent at the waist, his rump poking out of the vehicle. Abruptly he straightened and turned to the others.

"There's nothing in here," he said.

"What?" asked Jane.

"It's empty."

"You don't see *any* remains?"

Dr. Kibbie shook his head. "There's no body in this car."

"The divers came up with nothing, Lily. No body, no skeleton. No evidence at all that your cousin was ever in that water."

They sat in Jane's parked car as flakes of falling snow gently settled on the windshield in an ever-thickening veil of lace.

"I didn't dream it," Lily said. "I know it happened." She looked at Jane with haunted eyes. "Why would I make it up? Why would I confess to killing him if it wasn't true?"

"We have confirmed it's your mother's car. The registration hasn't been renewed in twelve years. The keys are still in the ignition."

"I told you they would be. I told you exactly where you'd find the car."

"Yes, everything you said has checked out, except for that one small detail. There's no body."

"It could have rotted away."

"There should still be a skeleton. But there's nothing. No clothing, no bones." Jane paused. "You know what that means."

Lily swallowed and stared at the windshield, now blanketed in snow. "He's alive."

"You haven't been running from a ghost or an evil spirit. He's still living flesh and blood, and I'd guess he's pretty damn pissed at you for trying to kill him. That's what this is all about, Lily. Revenge. Twelve years ago, he was only a kid. But now he's a man, and he can finally get his payback. Last August, he lost your trail in Italy and had no idea how to find you. So he went after Sarah and Lori-Ann for information. But they didn't know where you were, either; they were useless to him. He had to figure out another way to locate you."

"The Mephisto Foundation," Lily murmured.

"If Mephisto's as well regarded as Sansone claims, then its reputation has probably spread beyond law enforcement. Clearly, Dominic's heard about them, too. He certainly knew how to entice them. That phone call to Joyce O'Donnell. The Latin words, the seashell, the satanic symbols—it made Mephisto think they were finally tracking Satan. But I think they were being played."

"Dominic used them to find me."

"And they did a good job, didn't they? In just ten days, Mephisto found you."

Lily thought about this for a moment. She said, "There's no body. You can't charge me with any crime now. You can't hold me any longer."

Jane stared into eyes glittering with fear and thought: *She wants to run.*

"I'm free to go, right?"

"Free?" Jane laughed. "You call it freedom, to live like a scared rabbit?"

"I've survived, haven't I?"

"And when are you going to fight back? When are

you going to take a stand? This isn't the Devil we're talking about, this is a man. He can be brought down."

"Easy for you to say. You're not the one he's hunting!"

"No, but I'm hunting *him,* and I need your help. Work with me, Lily. You know him better than anyone."

"That's why he can't afford to let me live."

"I promise, you'll be safe."

"You can't keep that promise. You think he doesn't already know where I am? You don't know how meticulous he is. He misses no detail, no opportunity. He may be alive and breathing. But you'll never convince me he's *human.*"

Jane's cell phone rang, startling them both. As she answered the call, she could feel Lily's gaze, tense and questioning. *She assumes the worst.*

It was Barry Frost on the phone. "Where are you right now?"

"We're still in Norwich. It's late, so we'll probably check into a motel tonight and get back to the city tomorrow."

"I think it'd be better if you don't bring her back here."

"Why not?"

"Because we have a big problem. Oliver Stark is dead."

"What?"

"Someone used Stark's phone to call nine-one-one, then left the receiver off the hook. That's how we found out about it. I'm in his house right now. Christ, it's a bloody mess in here. He's still tied to his wheelchair, but you can't even recognize him. The poor kid never had a chance." There was a silence as he waited for her to speak. "Rizzoli?"

"We have to warn the others. Sansone and Mrs. Felway."

"I've already called them, and Dr. Isles as well. Mephisto also has members in Europe, and they're all taking precautions."

Jane thought of what Lily had just said. *You'll never convince me he's human.* What precautions could anyone take against a killer who seemed able to walk through walls?

She said, "He's hunting them all down."

"That's what it looks like. This has grown way bigger than we thought. It's not just about Lily Saul. It's about the whole foundation."

"Why the hell is he doing this? Why's he going after all of them?"

"You know what Sansone called it?" said Frost. "An extermination. Maybe we're wrong about Lily Saul. Maybe she's not the real target."

"Either way, I can't bring her back now."

"Lieutenant Marquette thinks she'll be safer outside Boston, and I agree. We're working on a long-term arrangement, but it'll take a day or two."

"Until then, what do I do with her?"

"Sansone suggested New Hampshire. A house up in the White Mountains. He says it's secure."

"Whose house is it?"

"It belongs to a friend of Mrs. Felway's."

"And we're going to trust Sansone's judgment on this?"

"Marquette okayed it. He says the brass doesn't have any doubts about him."

Then they know more about Sansone than I do.

"Okay," she said. "How do I find this house?"

"Mrs. Felway will call you with directions."

"What about Sansone and Maura? What are they going to do?"

"They're all heading to the same place. They'll meet you there."

THIRTY-SIX

IT WAS ONE in the afternoon when they crossed the Massachusetts state line, into New Hampshire. Lily had hardly said a word since they'd checked out of the motel that morning in Oneonta. Now, as they drove north into the White Mountains, the only sound was the squeak of the wipers scraping snowflakes off the windshield. *She's too nervous for chitchat,* thought Jane, glancing at her silent companion. Last night, in their shared motel room, Jane had heard all the tossing and turning in the next bed, and today Lily's eyes were sunken, her face gaunt enough almost to reveal the whiteness of bones through that pale skin. With a few extra pounds on her, Lily Saul might be pretty. But now, when Jane looked at her, what she saw was a walking corpse.

That may be exactly what she is.

"Are you going to stay with me tonight?" The question was so soft, it was almost lost in the sweep of the wipers.

"I'm going to check out the situation," said Jane. "See what I think about it."

"So you might not stay."

"You won't be alone up there."

"I suppose you want to go home, don't you?" Lily sighed. "Do you have a husband?"

"Yeah, I'm married."

"And kids?"

Jane hesitated. "I have a daughter."

"You don't want to tell me about yourself. You don't really trust me."

"I don't know you well enough."

Lily looked out the window. "Everyone who really knew me is dead"—she paused—"except Dominic."

Outside, the falling snow was a thickening veil of white. They climbed through a dense forest of pine, and for the first time Jane felt uneasy about whether her Subaru could handle the road if this snowfall continued.

"Why should you trust me?" said Lily with a bitter laugh. "I mean, all you know about me is that I tried to kill my cousin. And screwed it up."

"That message on Lori-Ann's wall," Jane said. "It was meant for you, wasn't it? *I have sinned.*"

"Because I have," murmured Lily. "And I'll never stop paying for it."

"And the four place settings on her dining table. That was meant to represent the Saul family, wasn't it? A family of four."

Lily wiped a hand across her eyes and looked out the window. "And I'm the last one. The fourth place setting."

"You know what?" Jane said. "I would have killed the son of a bitch, too."

"You would have done a better job."

The road grew steeper. The Subaru struggled up the mountain, tires churning through ever-deepening fresh powder. Jane glanced at her cell phone and saw zero bars. They had not passed a house in at least five miles. *Maybe we should turn around,* she thought. *I'm supposed to keep this woman alive, not strand her in the mountains where she'll freeze to death.*

Was this the right road?

She squinted through the windshield, trying to see the top of the hill. That's when she spotted the lodge, perched like an eagle's nest on the cliff's peak. There were no other homes nearby, and only this one access road led up the mountain. At the top there would surely be a sweeping view over the valley. They passed through a gate, left open to admit them.

Jane said, "This looks about as secure as you can get. Once that gate's locked, this place is unapproachable. Unless he has wings, he can't reach you up here."

Lily stared up at the cliff. "And we can't escape," she said softly.

Two vehicles were parked in front of the lodge. Jane pulled up behind Sansone's Mercedes and they climbed out of the car. Pausing in the driveway, Jane stared up at rough-hewn logs, at a peaked roof soaring into the snow-swirled sky. She went around to the trunk for their bags and had just slammed the trunk shut when she heard a growl right behind her.

The two Dobermans had emerged like black wraiths from the woods, moving so silently that she hadn't heard their approach. The dogs closed in with teeth bared as both women froze in place.

"Don't run," Jane whispered to Lily. "Don't even move." She drew her weapon.

"Balan! Bakou! Back off!"

The dogs halted and looked at their mistress, who had just emerged from the lodge and was standing on the porch.

"I'm so sorry if they scared you," said Edwina Felway. "I had to let them out for a run."

Jane did not holster her weapon. She didn't trust these animals, and clearly they didn't trust her. They remained planted in front of her, watching with eyes black as a snake's.

"They're very territorial, but they're quick to figure out who's friend and who's foe. You should be fine now. Just put away the gun and walk toward me. But not too fast."

Reluctantly, Jane holstered her weapon. She and Lily eased past the dogs and climbed up to the porch, the Dobermans watching them every step of the way. Edwina led them inside, into a cavernous great room that smelled of wood smoke. Huge beams arched overhead, and on the walls of knotty pine hung the mounted heads of moose and deer. In a stone fireplace, flames crackled at birch logs.

Maura rose from the couch to greet them.

"At last you made it," Maura said. "With this storm blowing in, we were beginning to worry."

"The road coming up here was pretty bad," said Jane. "When did you get here?"

"We drove up last night, right after Frost called us."

Jane crossed to a window that looked out across

the valley. Through the heavy curtain of falling snow, she caught glimpses of distant peaks. "You've got plenty of food?" she asked. "Fuel?"

"There's enough for weeks," said Edwina. "My friend keeps it well stocked. Right down to the wine cellar. We have plenty of firewood. And a generator, if the power goes out."

"And I'm armed," said Sansone.

Jane had not heard him walk into the room. She turned and was startled to see how grim he looked. The last twenty-four hours had transformed him. He and his friends were now under siege, and it showed in his haggard face.

"I'm glad you'll be staying with us," he said.

"Actually"—Jane glanced at her watch—"I think the situation looks pretty secure."

"You're not thinking of leaving tonight," said Maura.

"I was hoping to."

"It'll be dark in an hour. The roads won't be plowed again till morning."

Sansone said, "You really should stay. The roads will be bad."

Jane looked out, once again, at the falling snow. She thought about skidding tires and lonely mountain roads. "I guess it makes sense," she said.

"So the gang's all here for the night?" asked Edwina. "Then I'll go lock the gate."

"We need to drink a toast," said Edwina, "in memory of Oliver."

They were all sitting in the great room, gathered

around the huge stone fireplace. Sansone dropped a birch log into the flames, and papery bark hissed and sparked. Outside, darkness had fallen. The wind whined, windows rattled, and a sudden downdraft blew a puff of smoke from the chimney into the room. *Like Lucifer announcing his entrance,* thought Jane. The two Dobermans, who were lying beside Edwina's chair, suddenly lifted their heads as if scenting an intruder.

Lily rose from the couch and moved closer to the hearth. Despite the roaring fire, the room was chilly, and she clutched a blanket around her shoulders as she stared into the flames, their orange glow reflected in her face. They were all trapped there, but Lily was the real prisoner. The one person around whom the darkness swirled. All evening, Lily had said almost nothing. She had scarcely touched her dinner, and did not reach for her glass of wine as everyone else drank the toast.

"To Oliver," Sansone murmured.

They raised the glasses in a sad and silent tribute. Jane took only a sip. Craving a beer instead, she slid her glass to Maura.

Edwina said, "We need fresh blood, Anthony. I've been thinking of candidates."

"I can't ask anyone to join us. Not now." He looked at Maura. "I'm just sorry you got pulled into this. You never wanted to be part of it."

"I know a man in London," said Edwina. "I'm sure he'd be willing. I've already suggested his name to Gottfried."

"This isn't the time, Winnie."

"Then when? This man worked with my husband years ago. He's an Egyptologist, and he can probably interpret anything that Oliver—"

"*No one can replace Oliver.*"

Sansone's curt response seemed to take Edwina aback. "Of course not," she finally said. "I didn't mean it that way."

"He was your student at Boston College?" asked Jane.

Sansone nodded. "He was only sixteen, the youngest freshman on campus. I knew he was gifted from the first day he wheeled into my class. He asked more questions than anyone else. The fact he was a math major turned out to be one of the reasons he was so good at what he did. He'd take a look at some obscure ancient code and immediately see the patterns." Sansone set down his wineglass. "I've never known anyone like him. From the moment you met him, you just knew he was brilliant."

"Unlike the rest of us," said Edwina with a wry laugh. "I'm one of the unbrilliant members who had to be recommended by someone first." She looked at Maura. "I guess you know that you were Joyce O'Donnell's suggestion?"

"Maura has mixed feelings about that," said Sansone.

"You didn't like Joyce very much, did you?"

Maura finished off Jane's wine. "I prefer not to speak ill of the dead."

"I don't mind being up front about it," said Jane. "Any club that would have Joyce O'Donnell as a member isn't one that I'd want to join."

"I don't think you'd join us anyway," said Edwina

as she opened a new bottle, "since you don't be-lieve."

"In Satan?" Jane laughed. "No such guy."

"You can say that even after all the horrors you've seen in your job, Detective?" said Sansone.

"Committed by regular old human beings. And no, I don't believe in satanic possession, either."

Sansone leaned toward her, his face catching the glow of the flames. "Are you familiar with the case of the Teacup Poisoner?"

"No."

"He was an English boy named Graham Young. At fourteen, he began to poison members of his own family. His mother, father, sister. He finally went to jail for the murder of his mother. After he was re-leased years later, he went right back to poisoning people. When they asked him why, he said it was all for fun. And fame. He was not a regular human be-ing."

"More like a sociopath," said Jane.

"That's a nice, comforting word to use. Just give it a psychiatric diagnosis, and it explains the unexplain-able. But there are some acts so terrible you can't ex-plain them. You can't even conceive of them." He paused. "Graham Young inspired another young killer. A sixteen-year-old Japanese girl, whom I inter-viewed last year. She'd read Graham Young's pub-lished diary and was so inspired by his crimes, she decided to emulate him. First she killed animals. Cut them up and played with their body parts. She kept an electronic log, describing in meticulous detail what it was like to plunge a knife into living flesh. The warmth of the blood, the shudder of the dying creature. Then she advanced to killing humans. She poisoned her mother with thallium and recorded in her diary every painful symptom her mother suffered." He leaned back, but his gaze was still on Jane. "You'd call her merely a sociopath?"

"And you'd call her a demon?"

"There's no other word for what she is. Or for what a man like Dominic Saul is. We know they exist." He turned and stared into the fire. "The problem is," he said quietly, "they seem to know *we* exist, too."

"Have you ever heard of *The Book of Enoch,* Detective?" asked Edwina, refilling wineglasses.

"You've mentioned it before."

"It was found among the Dead Sea Scrolls. It's an ancient text, pre-Christian. Part of the apocryphal literature. It foresees the destruction of the world. It tells us that the earth is plagued by another race called the Watchers, who first taught us to make swords and knives and shields. They gave us the instruments of our own destruction. Even in ancient times, people clearly knew about these creatures and recognized that they were different from us."

"The sons of Seth," said Lily softly. "The descendants of Adam's third son."

Edwina looked at her. "You know about them?"

"I know they have many names."

"I never heard that Adam had a third son," said Jane.

"He actually appears in Genesis, but the Bible conveniently glosses over so many things," said Edwina. "There's so much history that's been censored and suppressed. Only now, nearly two thousand years later, are we able to read the Gospel of Judas."

"And these descendants of Seth—these are the Watchers?"

"They've been called so many different names through the centuries. The Elohim, the Nephilim. In Egypt, the Shemsu Hor. All we know is, their bloodline is ancient, its origins in the Levant."

"Where?"

"The Holy Land. *The Book of Enoch* tells us that ultimately we will have to fight them for our own survival. And we'll suffer terrible miseries while they slaughter and oppress and destroy." Edwina paused to refill Jane's glass. "Then, in the end, it will all be decided. There'll be the final battle. The Apocalypse." She looked at Jane. "Whether you believe it or not, the storm is coming."

The flames seemed to blur before Jane's tired eyes. And just for a moment she imagined a sea of fire, consuming everything. *So this is the world you people inhabit,* she thought. *A world I don't recognize.*

She looked at Maura. "Please don't tell me you believe this, Doc."

But Maura simply finished her glass of wine and stood up. "I'm exhausted," she said. "I'm going to bed."

THIRTY-SEVEN

SOMEONE WAS tapping at the edge of Lily's consciousness, asking to be admitted into the secret landscape of her dreams. She came awake in darkness and felt a moment's panic when nothing seemed familiar. Then she saw the glow of moonlight and remembered where she was. Through the window, she gazed out at startlingly bright snow. The storm had blown past, and the moon now shone down on a pure white world, silent and magical. For the first time in months, she felt safe. *I'm not alone anymore,* she thought. I'm with people who understand my fears, people who'll protect me.

She heard a *click-click* move past the room and fade away down the hallway. It was just one of the Dobermans, she thought. Bakou and Balan. What hideous names. She lay in bed, listening for the claws to tap their way past the door again, but the dog did not return.

Good. Because she needed to use the bathroom and didn't want to face either one of those animals in the hallway.

She climbed out of bed and crossed to the door. Poking her head into the hallway, she looked around for the dogs but saw no sign of them, heard no tapping of claws. Light glowed faintly from the stairway, enough to help her navigate up the hall to the bathroom. Just as she reached the threshold, her bare foot touched something wet. She looked down, saw the faint gleam of a puddle, and pulled her foot back in disgust. The dogs, of course. What other accidents had they left on the floor? She didn't want to step in anything worse.

She felt for the wall switch, flipped it on, and scanned the floor. She saw more puddles, but realized that these had not been left by dogs; they were melted snow, in the form of shoe prints. Someone had been walking outside and had tracked snow into the house. Her gaze lifted to the mirror, where she stared into her own pinched and sleepy eyes. And she saw something else, something that lifted every hair on the back of her neck, a reflection of what had been drawn in red on the wall behind her.

Three upside-down crosses.

Gasping, she stumbled backward and fled from the bathroom. Panic sent her tearing down the hall, bare feet skidding across the wet floor as she sprinted toward the nearest door. It was Maura's bedroom.

"Wake up!" she whispered. "You have to wake up!" She shook the sleeping woman so hard that the headboard rattled, the springs protested. Maura merely sighed, but did not stir.

What's wrong with you? Why can't I wake you?

Something creaked in the hallway. Lily's head snapped around toward the door. She felt her heart thudding hard enough to crack ribs as she crossed back to the doorway. There she stood listening, trying to hear through the banging of her own heart.

Nothing.

She eased her head around the doorjamb and peered into the hall. It was empty.

Wake the others. They have to know he's in the house!

She slipped into the hall and scurried barefoot toward the room she thought must be Jane's. She reached for the knob and gave a soft sob of frustration when she found it was locked. *Should I pound on the door to wake her? Do I dare make any noise?* Then she heard the whine of a dog, the faint tapping of claws moving across the great room downstairs. She eased toward the stairway. Gazing over the banister, she almost laughed in relief.

Downstairs, a fire was burning in the hearth. Seated on the couch, facing the flames, was Edwina Felway.

As Lily scurried down the steps, the two Dobermans glanced up, and one of them gave a warning growl. Lily froze at the bottom of the stairs.

"There, there, Balan," said Edwina. "What's got you upset now?"

"Edwina!" Lily whispered.

Edwina turned to look at her. "Oh. You're awake. I was just about to add some more logs."

Lily glanced at the fire, which was already roaring, the flames leaping, consuming a precariously tall pile of wood. "Listen to me," whispered Lily, moving a step forward, halting again as one of the dogs rose to its feet, fangs bared. "He's inside the house! We have to wake everyone!"

Edwina calmly picked up two logs and tossed them onto the already raging fire, stoking the inferno. "I noticed that you hardly touched your wine tonight, Lily."

"Dominic's *here*!"

"You could have slept through the whole thing, along with everyone else. But this works out so much better. Having you awake."

"*What?*"

The dog gave another growl, and Lily stared down at teeth gleaming orange in the flame's glow. *The dogs,* she thought suddenly. They hadn't barked, not once tonight. An intruder had slipped into the house. He'd tracked wet shoe prints across the floor. And the dogs gave no warning.

Because they know him.

As Edwina turned to face her, Lily darted forward and snatched the poker from the hearth. "You led him here," she said as she backed away, poker brandished in defense. "You told him."

"Oh, I didn't have to. He was already here on the mountain, waiting for us."

"Where is he?"

"Dominic will come out in his own good time."

"Goddamn you," Lily cried as her grip tightened around the poker. "*Where is he hiding?*"

She saw the attack too late. She heard the growl, the clatter of claws across wood, and she glanced sideways as twin streaks of black flew at her. The impact sent her crashing to the floor and the poker fell from her hands with a loud thud. Jaws closed around her arm. She screamed as teeth ripped into flesh.

"Balan! Bakou! Release."

It was not Edwina's voice that issued the command, but another: the voice of Lily's nightmares. The dogs released her and backed away, leaving her stunned and bleeding. She tried to push herself up, but her left hand was floppy and useless, the tendons torn by powerful jaws. With a groan, she rolled onto her side and saw her own blood pooling on the floor. And beyond that pool of blood, she saw the shoes of a man walking toward her. Her breathing now coming in sobs, she pushed herself up to a sitting position. He halted by the fireplace and stood backlit by the flames, like a dark figure emerging from the inferno. He gazed down at her.

"Somehow, you always manage to do it, Lily," he said. "You're always the one causing me trouble."

She scrabbled backward in retreat, but her shoulders bumped up against a chair and she could move no farther. Frozen in place, she stared up at Dominic, at the man he had become. He still had the same golden hair, the same striking blue eyes. But he had grown taller, his shoulders broader, and the once-angelic face had acquired sharp, cruel angles.

"Twelve years ago," he said, "you killed me. Now I'm going to return the favor."

"You have to watch her," said Edwina. "She's quick."

"Didn't I tell you that, Mother?"

Lily's gaze snapped to Edwina, then back to Dominic. *The same height. The same eyes.*

Dominic saw her look of shock and said, "Who else would a fifteen-year-old boy turn to when he's in trouble? When he's climbed out of a flooded car with nothing but the clothes on his back? I had to stay dead and out of sight, or you would have turned the police on me. You took away all my options, Lily. Except one."

His mother.

"It was months before my letter reached her. Didn't I always say she'd come for me? And your parents never believed it."

Edwina reached out to caress her son's face. "But you knew I would."

He smiled. "You always keep your promises."

"I kept this one, too, didn't I? I delivered her. You just needed to be patient and finish your training."

Lily stared at Edwina. "But you're with the Mephisto Foundation."

"And I knew how to use them," said Edwina. "I knew just how to entice them into the game. You think this is all about you, Lily, but it's really about *them*. About the damage they've done to us over the years. We're going to bring them down." She looked at the fire. "We'll need more wood. I'll go out and get some."

"I don't think it's necessary," said Dominic. "This building's as dry as a tinderbox. All it takes is a spark to set it off."

Lily shook her head. "You're killing them all . . ."

"That's always been the idea," said Edwina. "They'll sleep right through it."

"Not nearly as much fun as killing Joyce O'Donnell," said Dominic. "But at least you're awake to enjoy it, Lily." He picked up the poker and shoved the tip deep into the flames. "Convenient thing about fire. How completely it consumes flesh, leaving nothing but charred bone. No one will ever know what your death was really like, because they'll never see the cuts. The sear marks. They'll think you simply perished like the others, in your sleep. An unlucky accident, which only my mother will manage to survive. They'll never know that you screamed for hours before you died." He pulled the poker from the fire.

Lily stumbled to her feet, blood streaming down her hand. She lunged toward the door, but before she could reach it, the two Dobermans darted in front of her. She froze, staring at their bared teeth.

Hands closed around her arms as Edwina dragged Lily backward, toward the fireplace. Shrieking, Lily whirled around and flailed out blindly. She felt the satisfaction of her fist thudding into Edwina's cheek.

It was the dogs that again brought her down, both of them hurling themselves at her back, sending her sprawling.

"Release!" Dominic ordered.

The dogs backed off. Edwina, clutching her bruised face, aimed a punishing kick at Lily's ribs, and Lily rolled away, in too much agony even to draw a breath. Through a haze of pain, she saw Dominic's shoes move closer. She felt Edwina grasp her wrists and pin them against the floor. She looked up, into Dominic's face, into eyes that reflected the fire's glow like burning coals.

"Welcome to Hell," he said. In his hand was the hot poker.

Lily twisted, screaming, as she tried to wrench free, but Edwina's grasp was too powerful. As Dominic lowered the poker, she turned away, cheek pressed to the floor, eyes closed against the pain to come.

The explosion sprayed warmth across her face. She heard Edwina give a gasp, heard the poker thud to the floor. And suddenly Lily's hands were free.

She opened her eyes to see the two Dobermans sprinting across the room toward Jane Rizzoli. Jane raised her weapon and fired again. One of the dogs dropped, but the other was already in the air, flying like a black rocket. Jane got off one last shot, just as the dog slammed into her. Her gun tumbled and slid away as they both went down, Jane grappling at the wounded Doberman.

"No," Edwina moaned. She was on her knees beside her fallen son, cradling his face, stroking back his hair. "You can't die! You're the *chosen*."

Lily struggled to sit up, and the room tilted around her. By the glow of the ravenous flames, she saw Edwina rise like an avenging angel to her feet. She saw the woman reach down and pick up Jane's fallen gun.

The room spun even more crazily as Lily staggered to her feet. The whirl of images refused to remain still. The flames. Edwina. The spreading pool of Dominic's blood, glistening in the firelight.

And the poker.

The dog gave a last convulsive twitch and Jane shoved it aside. The carcass, tongue lolling, flopped onto the floor. Only then did Jane focus on Edwina standing over her, on the weapon gleaming in Edwina's hands.

"It all ends here. Tonight," said Edwina. "You. And Mephisto." Edwina raised the gun, the muscles of her arm pulling taut as she squeezed the grip. Her attention was fixed so completely on Jane that she did not see her own death hurtling toward her head.

The poker slammed into Edwina's skull, and Lily felt the crack of crushing bone, transmitted straight to her hand through wrought iron. Edwina dropped to the floor without uttering a sound. Lily lost her grip, and the falling poker clanged as it hit wood. She stared down at what she had just done. At Edwina's head, the skull caved in. At the blood, flowing like a black river. And suddenly the room darkened, and her legs wobbled out from beneath her. She slid to the floor, landing on her rump. She dropped her head in her lap and could feel nothing: no pain, no sensation at all in her limbs. She was floating disembodied on the edge of blackness.

"Lily." Jane touched her shoulder. "Lily, you're bleeding. Let me see your arm."

She gasped in a breath. The room brightened. Slowly she raised her head and focused on Jane's face. "I killed her," she murmured.

"Just don't look at her, okay? Come on, let's move you to the couch." Jane reached down to help Lily to her feet. She froze, her fingers suddenly taut around Lily's arm.

Lily heard the whispers, too, and her blood turned to ice in her veins. She stared at Dominic and saw that his eyes were open and aware. His lips moved, the words so soft she could barely hear what he was saying.

"Not . . . not . . ."

Jane bent over him to listen. Lily did not dare move any closer, fearful that Dominic would suddenly spring up at her, like a cobra. They could kill him again and again, but he'd always come back. He'd never die.

Evil never does.

The fire glowed in the reflecting pool of spreading blood, as though the flames themselves were seeping across the floor, an expanding inferno with Dominic at its source.

Again his lips moved. "We're not . . ."

"Say it," said Jane. "Tell me."

"We are not . . . the only . . . ones."

"What?" Jane knelt down, grabbed Dominic by the shoulders, and shook him hard. "Who else is there?"

A last breath rushed out of Dominic's lungs. Slowly his jaw sagged open, and the lines of his face smoothed like melting wax. Jane released the body and straightened. Then she looked at Lily. "What did he mean by that?"

Lily stared at Dominic's unfocused eyes, at a face now slack and lifeless. "He just told us," she said, "that it's not over yet."

THIRTY-EIGHT

A SNOWPLOW scraped its way up the mountain
road, the rumble of its engine echoing up from the
valley. Standing on the lodge's snow-covered deck,
Jane looked down over the railing to catch a view of
the road below. She watched the plow's steady
progress as it wound its way toward them, scraping
a path through fresh-fallen powder. Inhaling a
breath of cold and cleansing air, she lifted her face to
the sun, trying to clear the last wisps of fog from her
brain. Once the road was clear, a whole host of official vehicles would be arriving on the mountain: the
state police, the medical examiner, the crime-scene
unit. She had to be fully alert and ready for their
questions.

Even though she didn't have all the answers.

She stomped the snow off her boots, slid open the
glass door, and stepped back into the lodge.

The other survivors were seated around the
kitchen table. Although it was warmer in the great
room where the fire was burning, none of them
wanted to move from the kitchen. None of them
wanted to be in the same room with the corpses.

Maura finished rebandaging Lily's arm. "There's

damage to your flexor tendons. I think you're going to need surgery. At the very least, antibiotics." She looked at Jane. "When the road's clear, the first thing we need to do is get her to a hospital."

"It won't be too much longer," said Jane. "The plow's halfway up the mountain." She sat down and looked at Lily. "You realize the police will have questions for you. A lot of them."

Maura said, "It can wait until after she gets medical attention."

"Yes, of course. But Lily, you know you're going to get asked about what happened here last night."

"Can't you back up everything she says?" said Maura.

"I didn't see it all," said Jane. "I slept through half of it."

"Thank God you didn't finish your wine. Or we'd all be ashes today."

"I blame myself," said Sansone. "I shouldn't have fallen asleep at all. That was my mistake, letting Edwina pour me a glass."

Jane frowned at Sansone. "You were planning to stay up all night?"

"I thought someone should be awake. Just in case."

"Then you already suspected Edwina?"

"No, I'm embarrassed to admit. You have to understand how careful we are when we bring in a new member. They come to us only through referrals, from people we know. And then we make inquiries, background checks. Edwina wasn't the one I had doubts about." He looked at Lily. "You were the one I didn't trust."

"Why Lily?" asked Jane.

"That night, when my garden window was forced open, you remember I told you that we always keep it locked?"

"Yes."

"Which means that someone unlatched it from the inside, someone who was in my house that night. I assumed it was Lily."

"I still don't understand," said Maura. "If you're that careful about who joins the foundation, how could you be so wrong about Edwina?"

"That's what Gottfried and I have to find out. How she infiltrated. How it was planned and executed. She didn't just show up one day on our doorstep; she had assistance, from someone within Mephisto, someone who scrubbed away anything suspicious in her background check."

"It's the last thing Dominic told us," said Lily. *"We're not the only ones."*

"I'm sure there are more." Sansone looked at Jane. "Whether you realize it or not, Detective, we're engaged in a war. It's been going on for centuries, and last night was just one of the battles. The worst is coming."

Jane gave a shake of the head, a tired laugh. "I see we're talking about those demons again."

"I believe in them," Lily declared, her jaw squared in certainty. "I know they're real."

They heard the scrape of the snowplow over pavement, the approaching rumble of a truck engine. At last the road was clear and they could leave this mountain; they could return to their lives. Maura, back to the arms of Daniel Brophy, who could bring her either heartbreak or hope. Jane, back to the job of peacemaker between her battling mother and father.

And I'm going home to Gabriel. He's waiting for me.

Jane rose and crossed to the window. Outside, sunshine sparkled on perfect snow. The skies were cloudless, and by now the road home would be plowed and sanded. It was a beautiful day to drive home. To hug her husband and kiss her baby. *I can't wait to see you both.*

"You still don't believe me, do you, Detective?" said Sansone. "You don't believe there's a war going on."

Jane looked up at the sky and she smiled. "Today," she said, "I choose not to."

THIRTY-NINE

DARK CLOUDS hung low, and Lily could smell the tang of impending snow in the air as she stared up at the house where she had grown up. She did not see it as it was today, a derelict shell, the porch sagging, the clapboards weathered to gray. No, she saw it as it once was in summertime, with clematis flowering on the lattice and pots of red geraniums hanging from the eaves. She saw her brother Teddy come out of the house, heard the squeal and the slap of the screen door swinging shut behind him as he ran grinning down the porch steps. She saw her mother in the window, waving, as she called out, "Teddy, don't be late for dinner!" And she saw her father, sunburned and whistling as he carried his hoe across the yard toward his beloved vegetable plot. She'd been happy here once. Those were the days she wanted to remember, the days she'd hold on to.

Everything else, everything that has happened since, I will consign to the ashes.

"Are you sure about this, Ms. Saul?" said the fire chief.

His crew stood fully garbed in firefighting gear, waiting for the order. Farther down the hill, a small crowd from town had gathered to watch. But it was Anthony Sansone and Gottfried Baum whom she focused on. She trusted them, and now they stood with her, to witness the exorcism of her demons.

She turned back to the house. The furniture had been removed and donated to local charities. Except for the straw bales that the firemen had stacked inside an upstairs bedroom, what stood there now was merely an empty husk.

"Ms. Saul?" said the fire chief.

"Burn it," she said.

He gave the signal, and his crew moved in with their hoses and their cans of kerosene mixed with diesel fuel. Not often was a house this substantial offered up in sacrifice for a training burn, and the men went at the task with gusto, eager to touch off the fire. For practice, they would douse it, then reset it again and again, until it was time to let the flames triumph.

As black smoke spiraled into the sky, Lily backed away, to stand between the two men whom she had come to regard as mentors, even fathers. Sansone and Baum said nothing, but Lily heard Baum's sharp intake of breath when the first flames appeared in an upstairs window, and she felt Sansone place a steadying hand on her shoulder. She needed no support; she stood with her back straight, her gaze fixed on the fire. Inside, the flames would be consuming floorboards still stained with the blood of Peter Saul, and licking up walls that had been defiled by unholy crosses. Such places should not be allowed to survive. Such evil can never be cleansed; it can only be destroyed.

Now the firemen retreated from the house to watch the final conflagration. Flames crackled across the roof and melting snow hissed into steam. Orange claws reached through windows and scrabbled up tinder-dry clapboards. Heat drove the firemen backward as the flames fed and grew, like a beast roaring its victory.

Lily gazed into the heart of that fire, now consuming the last remnants of her childhood, and she saw, framed in the glow, a single moment in time. A summer's evening. Her mother and father and Teddy standing on the porch, watching her scamper about on the grass, waving a net. And fireflies—so many fireflies, like a constellation of stars winking in the night. "Look, your sister's caught another one!" her mother says, and Teddy laughs, holding up a jar to receive the prize. They smile at her, from across the years, from a place that no flames could ever touch, because it was safe within her own heart.

Now the roof collapsed, and sparks flew into the sky, and Lily heard the gasps of people caught up in the primal thrill of a winter's fire. As the flames slowly died, the spectators from town began to drift down the hill, back to their cars, the excitement of their day now over. Lily and her two friends remained, watching as the last flames were extinguished and smoke curled from blackened ash. After this rubble was cleared, she would plant trees here. Flowering cherries and crab apples. *But there must never be another house on this hill.*

Something cold kissed her nose and she looked up

to see fat flakes fluttering from the sky. It was a final blessing of snow, sacred and purifying.

"Are you ready to go, Lily?" Baum asked.

"Yes." She smiled. "I'm ready." Then she turned to follow them, and the three demon hunters walked together down the hill.

AFTERWORD

As an anthropology major at Stanford University, I was fascinated by myths from the ancient world. I like to think that there's a nugget of truth to stories that have been passed down to us through the ages. The mists of time may have altered the details, but even the most improbable tale could well be based on real people and real events.

A few years ago, while browsing a bookstore in Oxford, England, I came across a copy of R. H. Charles's translation of *The Book of Enoch*, and could not resist purchasing it. *The Book of Enoch* is an ancient text, dating back to perhaps two centuries before the birth of Christ. Though it contains the history of an Old Testament patriarch, Enoch, the great-grandfather of Noah, the book was struck from Hebrew scripture and discredited as apocryphal by early Christian fathers. It vanished from history, and for centuries, the text was thought to be forever lost.

But it was not, in fact, lost. Hidden in various secret places, *The Book of Enoch* had survived. In the

1700s, intact copies of the text, translated from Greek, were discovered in Ethiopia. And in 1947, in a cave on the northwest shore of the Dead Sea, a Bedouin shepherd made a magnificent discovery: jars containing ancient scrolls. From that complex of caves emerged seven fragments of *The Book of Enoch,* written in Aramaic.

Within the pages of this long-lost text lies a mystery that continues to puzzle scholars. It is the story of The Watchers, fallen angels who had sexual congress with women, producing an unholy race that would forever plague mankind:

> *Evil spirits have proceeded from their bodies; because they are born from men and from the holy Watchers is their beginning and primal origin; they shall be evil spirits on earth, and evil spirits shall they be called.*

These mixed-race creatures, also known as Nephilim, appear in yet another ancient text, *The Book of Jubilees.* Here, also, they are described as evil and malignant. According to *Jubilees,* most Nephilim were destroyed during Noah's time, but God allowed one tenth of their number to survive as subjects of Satan. Through their line, evil would continue to afflict the earth.

Angels and women mating to produce hybrid monsters? This is a fantastical tale indeed, and some biblical scholars suggest quite reasonably that these matings were, in truth, simply forbidden marriages between different tribes. That the "angels" were men from the lofty line of Seth, and the women came from a much lowlier tribe, descended from Cain.

Still, as a novelist, I could not help thinking: What if the tale of The Watchers was not merely allegory but history? What if Nephilim were real, and their descendants are still among us, still wreaking havoc?

Throughout the history of mankind, certain people have committed acts of such appalling cruelty that one wonders if they are truly members of the human race, or if they are a violent subspecies, driven by different needs and instincts. If one believes what was written in *Enoch* and *Jubilees,* then the acts of real monsters such as mass slaughterers Pol Pot and Vlad the Impaler can be explained. Nephilim have simply co-existed alongside us, invisible predators among the prey. And when the opportunity arises, when society breaks down during wartime or civil chaos, when the force of laws cannot keep us safe, those predators come out to play.

Only then do we discover who they really are.

Evil has no easy explanation. Today, more than two thousand years after *The Book of Enoch* was written, we are no closer to understanding why evil exists. All we know is that it does.

Read on for an exciting look at

THE BONE GARDEN

by Tess Gerritsen

Coming soon from Ballantine Books

The Present

So THIS IS how a marriage ends, thought Julia Hamill as she rammed the shovel into the soil. Not with sweet whispers goodbye, not with the loving clasp of arthritic hands, not with children and grandchildren grieving around your hospital bed. She lifted a scoop of earth and flung it aside, sending rocks clattering onto the growing mound. It was all clay and stones, good for growing nothing except blackberry canes. Such barren soil, just like her marriage, out of which nothing long-lasting, nothing worth holding onto, had sprouted.

She stamped down on the shovel and heard a clang, felt the concussion slam up her spine as the blade hit a rock—a big one. She repositioned the blade, but even when she attacked the rock at different angles, she could not pry it loose. Demoralized and sweating in the heat, she stared down at the hole. She had been digging like a woman obsessed all morning, and beneath her leather gloves, blisters had peeled open. Her digging had stirred up a cloud of mosquitoes that whined around her face and infiltrated her hair.

There was no way around it; if she wanted to plant a garden in this spot, if she wanted to transform this weed-choked yard, she had to keep digging. And this rock was in her way.

Suddenly the task seemed hopeless, beyond her puny efforts. She dropped the shovel and slumped to the ground, her rump landing on the stony pile of dirt. Why did she ever think she could restore this garden, salvage this house? She looked up across the tangle of weeds and stared at the sagging porch, the weathered clapboards. JULIA'S FOLLY—that's what she should name the place. Bought at a time when she hadn't been thinking straight, a time when the rest of her life was collapsing. Why not add another bit of flotsam to the wreckage? This was supposed to be her consolation prize for surviving the divorce—a house in her own name, a house with a past, a soul. When she had first walked through those rooms with the realtor, and had gazed at the hand-hewn beams, had spied the bit of antique wallpaper peeking through a tear in the many layers that had since covered it, she'd known that this house was special. This house was calling to her, asking for help.

"The location's unbeatable," the realtor had said. "It comes with nearly an acre of land, something you seldom find anymore this close to Boston."

"Then why is it still for sale?" Julia had asked.

"You can see what bad shape it's in. When we first got the listing, there were boxes and boxes of books and old papers, stacked to the ceiling. It took a month for the heirs to haul it all away. Obviously it needs bottom-up renovations, right down to the foundation."

"But I like the fact it has an interesting past. It wouldn't put me off buying it."

The realtor hesitated. "There's another issue I should tell you about. Full disclosure."

"What issue?"

"The previous owner was a woman in her nineties, and—well, she died here. That makes some buyers a bit squeamish."

"In her nineties? Of natural causes, then?"

"That's the assumption."

Julia had frowned. "They don't know?"

"It was summertime. And it took almost two weeks before anyone noticed . . ." The realtor's voice trailed off. Suddenly she brightened. "But hey, the land alone is special. You could tear down this whole place. Get rid of it and start fresh!"

The way you get rid of old wives like me, Julia had thought. *This house and I both deserve better.*

That same afternoon, she had signed the purchase agreement.

Now, as she slumped on the mound of dirt, slapping at mosquitoes, she thought: What did I get myself into? If Richard ever saw this wreck, it would only confirm what he already thought of her. Gullible Julia, dumb putty in a realtor's hands. Proud owner of a junk heap.

She swiped a hand over her eyes, smearing sweat across her cheek. Then she looked down at the hole again. How could she get her life in order when she couldn't even summon the strength to move one stupid rock?

She picked up a trowel and, leaning into the hole, began to scrape away dirt. More of the rock emerged, like an iceberg whose size she could only guess at. Maybe big enough to sink the Titanic. She kept digging, deeper and deeper, heedless of the mosquitoes and the sun glaring on her bare head. Suddenly the rock symbolized every obstacle, every challenge that she'd ever wobbled away from.

I will not let you defeat me.

With the trowel, she hacked away at the soil beneath the rock, trying to free up enough space to pry the shovel underneath it. Her hair slid into her face, strands clinging to sweaty skin as she reached deeper into the hole, scraping, tunneling. *Before Richard sees this place, I'll turn it into a paradise.* She'd uproot these weeds, nourish the soil, put in roses. Richard told her that if she ever planted roses in their Brookline yard, they'd probably die on her. You need to know what you're doing, he'd said. It had been just a casual remark, but it had stung nevertheless, because she knew what he'd really meant.

You need to know what you're doing. And you don't.

She dropped onto her belly and hacked at what looked like soil, but her trowel collided with something solid. Oh god, not another rock. Shoving back her hair, she stared down at what her trowel had just hit. The metal tip had fractured the surface, and she saw cracks radiating from the impact point. She brushed away dirt and pebbles, exposing an unnaturally smooth dome. Lying belly-down on the ground, she felt her heart thudding against the earth and suddenly found it hard to take a breath. But she kept digging, with both hands now, gloved fingers scraping through stubborn clay. More of the dome emerged, curves knitted together by a jagged seam. Deeper and deeper she clawed, her pulse accelerating as she uncovered a small dirt-filled hollow. She pulled off her glove and prodded the caked earth with a bare finger. Suddenly the dirt fractured and crumbled away.

Julia jerked back onto her knees and stared down at what she had just revealed. The whine of mosquitoes suddenly seemed to build to a shriek, but she did not wave them away; she was too numb to feel their sting. A breeze feathered the grass and stirred the sweet-syrup smell of Queen Anne's Lace. Julia's gaze lifted to her weed-ridden property, a place she had once thought she would transform to a paradise. She'd imagined a garden of roses and peonies, an arbor twined with clematis. Now when she looked at this yard, she no longer saw a garden.

She saw a graveyard.